PRAISE FOR THE #1 BESTSELLING NYPD RED SERIES COAUTHORED BY MARSHALL KARP AND JAMES PATTERSON

"*NYPD Red 2*, like its forebear, stands out due to
Karp's unmistakable style. Karp, already one of my favorite
authors because of his wonderful Lomax and Biggs mysteries,
gets a chance in the mega-selling spotlight with this terrific series, and
he soars with the opportunity."
—SCOTT COFFMAN, *LOUISVILLE COURIER-JOURNAL*

"In the case of *NYPD Red*, there is simply
too much fun—in the form of inventive murder,
sex, chemistry, investigation, more murder, more sex,
and the like. Though the book is complete in itself,
there are plenty of interesting characters who could
carry this as a series for as long as Patterson
and Karp will want it to go."
—BOOKREPORTER.COM

"Patterson and Karp spare no plot twist in this page-
turning thriller…Love triangles, mafia ties, and political
entanglements abound, layering this character-driven
mystery in such a way that no dull moment ever arises."
—*HAMPTON SHEET MAGAZINE* ON *NYPD RED 2*

"Patterson and Karp once again prove that this is
one crime series that's not to be missed—the literary
equivalent of your favorite summer blockbuster movie."
—NIGHTSANDWEEKENDS.COM ON *NYPD RED 2*

PRAISE FOR MARSHALL KARP'S
SNOWSTORM IN AUGUST

PRAISE FOR MARSHALL KARP'S LOMAX AND BIGGS MYSTERIES

"The comedy never overshadows this smart,
many-layered thriller...Lomax, Biggs, and the FBI have
their work cut out for them in a clever plot that will keep
readers guessing to the very end. Enthusiastic readers
will anxiously await the return of detectives
Lomax and Biggs."
—PUBLISHERS WEEKLY (STARRED REVIEW) ON *THE RABBIT FACTORY*

"Karp offers multiple twists that will keep most
readers guessing until the end, and balances the grim plot with Biggs's
inexhaustible supply of genuinely humorous one-liners. Kinky Fried-
man and Carl Hiaasen fans
should latch onto this series."
—PUBLISHERS WEEKLY (STARRED REVIEW) ON *CUT, PASTE, KILL*

"Totally original, a sheer roller coaster ride, packed
with waves of humor and a dynamic duo in Lomax and Biggs. Karp
shows a master's touch in his debut."
—DAVID BALDACCI ON *THE RABBIT FACTORY*

"Read this book and you'll be grinning the whole way
through. Marshall Karp knows how to keep a story
running full speed, full time. This one's a blast."
—MICHAEL CONNELLY ON *FLIPPING OUT*

"Irrepressible and often poignant...Like the best
of Donald Westlake and Carl Hiaasen, *The Rabbit Factory*
is deftly plotted and deliciously askew."
—BOOKLIST (STARRED REVIEW)

"Probably the hottest crime caper this year. Lomax and Biggs are fun, fun, fun, page after page, and... the tension never flags for an instant."
—BOOK OF THE MONTH, GATEWAYMONTHLY.COM (UK), ON *THE RABBIT FACTORY*

"You're going to love meeting Mike Lomax and Terry Biggs, a pair of hip homicide detectives with the LAPD; unless, of course, you're the perp. Smart, funny and intuitive, Lomax and Biggs glide through the overlit shoals of Los Angeles like sharks through ginger ale. As up to the minute as they are intensely observant, the guys, this time, prowl the golden muck of the LA real estate bubble to fine effect; an exhilarating read."
—DONALD WESTLAKE ON *FLIPPING OUT*

"This outstanding fourth chapter in the canon of Detectives Lomax and Biggs provides further proof of the indisputable: Marshall Karp writes the funniest dialogue in the detective genre. If you have not yet read the Lomax and Biggs books, you simply must start."
—*LOUISVILLE COURIER-JOURNAL* ON *CUT, PASTE, KILL*

"Marshall Karp could well be the Carl Hiaasen of Los Angeles—only I think he's even funnier. *The Rabbit Factory* will touch your funny bone, and your heart."
—JAMES PATTERSON

"Brings to mind Robert B. Parker, Janet Evanovich, Dean Koontz, Stuart Woods, and a lot of other fast-paced authors."
—JANET MASLIN, *NEW YORK TIMES BOOK REVIEW*, ON *THE RABBIT FACTORY*

"Better than mostly anything on the market...
The Rabbit Factory is, quite simply, stunning...
Worth every single second it takes to fly through...
632 pages of unadulterated magic."
—CHRIS HIGH, *TANGLED WEB* AND *SHOTS MAGAZINE* (UK)

"This is a nigh-on flawless first novel—I thoroughly enjoyed
both the story and the writing style of the author
and I implore you to simply read it!"
**—DEBUT BOOK OF THE MONTH,
CRIMESQUAD.COM (UK), ON *THE RABBIT FACTORY***

"Just the right blend of belly laughs and suspense...
Karp's second offering is every bit as funny
and fast-paced as *The Rabbit Factory*."
—*BOOKLIST* (STARRED REVIEW) ON *BLOODTHIRSTY*

"Wickedly funny...this quirky, off-kilter novel also has
a really big heart...[and] an emotional core that will make
readers care about these tough but vulnerable crime
fighters and keep them hoping for a sequel."
—BOOKREPORTER.COM ON *THE RABBIT FACTORY*

"Blending the gritty realism of a Joseph Wambaugh
police procedural with the sardonic humor of
Janet Evanovich, Karp delivers a treat that's not only
laugh-out-loud funny but also remarkably suspenseful."
—*PUBLISHERS WEEKLY* ON *FLIPPING OUT*

"*The Rabbit Factory* was a joy to read...
[It] has been compared to the work of Carl Hiaasen,
but I'm happy to say it's much better."
—THEBOOKBAG.CO.UK

"The frenetic plotting and outrageous characterisation are in [Carl Hiassen]'s line... but the anti-establishment humour is reminiscent of another darkly humorous novelist, Joseph Heller."

—*PUBLISHING NEWS* (UK) ON *THE RABBIT FACTORY*

"I strongly suspect that Marshall Karp is the secret love child of Raymond Chandler and the Marx Brothers, with some Dorothy Parker around the edges. Karp should be considered a national treasure."

—CORNELIA READ, EDGAR NOMINEE FOR
BEST FIRST NOVEL, ON *BLOODTHIRSTY*

"Unplug the phone, pull up your favorite chair, and settle in for the best mystery novel this year. This strong debut is an often hilarious head-scratcher, and features a smartly drawn cast of characters...A page-turner."

—SCOTT COFFMAN, *LOUISVILLE COURIER-JOURNAL*,
ON *THE RABBIT FACTORY*

"Karp craftily engineers a statement on ethical values, both institutional and personal."

—*KIRKUS REVIEWS* ON *THE RABBIT FACTORY*

"Marshall Karp needs a blurb from me like Uma needs a facelift. This guy is the real deal, and *Bloodthirsty* is a first class, fast, funny, and fabulous read by a terrific writer. Great entertainment, highly recommended to one and all."

—JOHN LESCROART, *NEW YORK TIMES* BESTSELLING AUTHOR

"Laugh-out-loud funny, realistically portrayed, break-neck-paced, and powered by literally hundreds of hilarious one-liners...Karp has hit the jackpot with Lomax and Biggs. The most endearing and wildly entertaining protagonists to grace the pages of a mystery novel in years."
—PAUL GOAT ALLEN ON *BLOODTHIRSTY*

"With this fifth long-awaited book in the Lomax and Biggs series, we see Marshall Karp return in full force with his poignant trademark humour that never seems to leave the room, even under the direst of circumstances.
— DAVID BEN EFRAIM, *QUICK BOOK REVIEWS*, ON *TERMINAL*

"Blending edge of your seat mystery and laugh-out-loud humor in such a way that neither steps on the other's toes is not easy, yet once again Karp proves himself a master of that delicate operation in *Cut, Paste, Kill*. So what are you waiting for? Buy, Read, Enjoy!"
— ELIZABETH A. WHITE, *EDITING BY ELIZABETH*

"Marshall Karp is the Woody Allen of the murder mystery. He's up there with Carl Hiaasen and Donald Westlake and Janet Evanovich—smart, fast-paced, clever, and really, really funny."
—JOSEPH FINDER, *NEW YORK TIMES* BESTSELLING AUTHOR, ON *BLOODTHIRSTY*

"Nobody writes smart criminals and smarter cops better than Marshall Karp."
—NYPD DETECTIVE JOHN CORCORAN (RETIRED)

NYPD RED 7
THE MURDER SORORITY

ALSO BY MARSHALL KARP

DANNY CORCORAN AND THE BALTIC AVENUE GROUP

Snowstorm in August

THE LOMAX AND BIGGS MYSTERIES

Terminal
Cut, Paste, Kill
Flipping Out
Bloodthirsty
The Rabbit Factory

COAUTHORED WITH JAMES PATTERSON

NYPD Red 6
Red Alert (aka NYPD Red 5)
NYPD Red 4
NYPD Red 3
NYPD Red 2
NYPD Red
Kill Me If You Can

For details and sample chapters, please visit
www.KarpKills.com

THE MURDER SORORITY

MARSHALL KARP

**BLACK
STONE**
PUBLISHING

Printed in the United States of America

First edition: 2022
ISBN 979-8-200-71405-6
Fiction / Thrillers / Crime

Version 1

CIP data for this book is available
from the Library of Congress

Blackstone Publishing
31 Mistletoe Rd.
Ashland, OR 97520

www.BlackstonePublishing.com

For Pearl Ziffer Diamond,
my aunt, my friend, my confidante, my rock.
Love you, love you, love you.

CHAPTER 1

MY PHONE CHIRPED, and I looked down at the gray text bubble on my screen. It was from Selma Kaplan at the District Attorney's Office. The message was one I had seen or heard hundreds of times over the course of my career as a cop. Six words that I knew had the power to change people's lives. What I didn't know—what I could not even have possibly imagined—is that this time those words would change my life. Forever.

THE JURY HAS REACHED A VERDICT.

I looked up at my partner, Detective Kylie MacDonald, who had gotten the same text. "It's about goddamn time," she said. "How long have they been sequestered? A week? A month? A year?"

"Four and a half days," I said.

"It doesn't matter, Zach," she said. "You know how it goes. The longer the jury deliberates, the worse it is for our side. Convictions come fast. Acquittals take forever."

"Four and a half days isn't forever."

"It is this time. Our testimony was airtight. Selma's closing was brilliant. The case was a slam dunk. If they were going to find him guilty, they could have done it in four and a half hours."

"Ye of little faith," I said, grabbing a radio. "Let's go. Judge Hollander isn't going to wait for us."

"Twenty bucks says Hellman walks," Kylie said.

"You're betting *against* us?"

"I'm betting with my head, Zach, not my heart," she said as we headed down the stairs. "Warren Hellman is filthy rich and has the power to turn ordinary mortals into superstars. There were five women on the jury, and he was eyeball-fucking every one of them. Juror number seven barely looked at me when I testified. She just gawked at him. She probably went home every night, flipped on the TV, and masturbated to his reruns. If anybody turned the jury, it was her."

A minute later we were speeding toward the Manhattan Criminal Courthouse at 100 Centre Street. Normally we're too busy to drive downtown and sit through the proceedings just to hear the verdict read. We wait for a call from the DA's Office and win or lose, we move on without missing a beat.

But this was different. This time it was personal, and we both wanted to be there when Warren Hellman went down. He'd killed a cop.

The first time I met Jonas Belmont, I was working in the Three-Two up in Harlem. I was a rookie, and he was a legend—a detective first grade with more medals of honor than anyone in the history of the department.

That night, I brought a homeless guy into the station. The desk sergeant got one whiff of the man and asked me what the charges were.

"He was jaywalking, sir."

The sergeant exploded. "Are you fucking serious, Jordan? Give that bag of shit a summons and get him the hell out of here."

"I will, sir," I said, "but if I could just talk to a detective for two minutes."

"Get him out of here," the sergeant repeated. "Now."

I started to leave when a voice boomed out. "Hold it right there, Officer."

I turned around. A hulk of a man was walking toward me. Six six, ginger hair, muscled chest straining against his suit jacket, and steel-blue eyes that were lasered in on me and my homeless persona non grata.

"Detective Jonas Belmont," he said.

I knew who he was. Everybody knew who he was. "Jordan, sir. Zach Jordan."

"How much time do you have on the job, kid?" he said.

"Two years next month, sir."

"And how many foul-smelling, raggedy-ass jaywalkers have you arrested?"

"This is my first, sir."

"And I'm betting you're smart enough to know he doesn't have the means to pay for a summons even if you slapped him with one."

I felt a smile coming on, but I held it back. Belmont was on my wavelength. He knew what I was up to, and he was ready to inform the sergeant that he was about to join the party.

"You're going to have to hold your nose a little while longer, Hank," Belmont said, "This astute young officer and I are going to take this egregious jaywalker upstairs for questioning."

The sergeant gave him a sour stare. "You working traffic violations now, Detective Belmont?"

Jonas pointed at the derelict's feet. "The shoes, Sergeant. The shoes."

The man, a human dumpster from his head to his ankles, was wearing a brand-new pair of rich brown Ferragamo alligator leather oxfords. As soon as I saw him shuffling across Broadway against the red light, I figured they had to cost a thousand bucks. I was wrong. They were twelve thousand, and two days earlier they had been inside a suitcase that disappeared from a taxi rank outside the Pierre Hotel.

Belmont took it from there, and I watched in awe from the other side of the two-way mirror as he sweet-talked a confession out of the man and got him to give up the name of the pawnshop that was dealing in stolen luggage.

When he was done, he gave me his card. "Good job, kid. Keep in touch."

Did I ever, hanging around the squad room like a fanboy. Even after he retired, we stayed friends, and every couple of months I'd meet him for dinner and listen to him tell war stories and, of course, brag about his kids.

Evan, who had always wanted to be a cop like his dad, was now a detective working out of the Tenth Precinct in Manhattan. Vivian, who'd had the acting bug ever since she was a kid, had followed her dream to the High School of Performing Arts, then NYU, and was now out there occasionally landing a small part and waiting tables at a restaurant near Lincoln Center, hoping for her first big break.

And that's where she met Warren Hellman. It started with a simple "Here's my card. Call my office." Then came the audition. She was perfect to star in his upcoming series. But of course, other young women were also perfect. The way Hellman spun it, beauty and talent were just the cost of entry. If he was going to work with an actress week in, week out, for the next five years, he had to make sure they had chemistry.

Vivian knew what that meant. Fuck the producer; become a star. The classic show business *quid pro quo*. She didn't hesitate.

It was heady at first. Restaurants, clubs, paparazzi, a key to his suite at the Sherry-Netherland. She knew there was a price to pay. Sex with a man who repulsed her in every way. But she could do it. She was an actress, and his bedroom was just another stage. The alcohol and the cocaine helped.

The heroin came later. One night she was soaking in the tub, a glass of champagne at her side. The bathroom door opened. "I'm Jeff," the man said. "Warren had to go to London. He sent me."

"For what?"

"To keep you company till he gets back," he said, peeling off his clothes.

"Jeff, please . . . I think . . ."

"No," he said. "You don't think. Warren doesn't want you to think. That's not part of the deal."

He stood there naked except for the gold wedding band around his pudgy ring finger. "I'm an executive producer on the new show. The networks love the premise, love you, but they're screaming for script changes before they sign off. Fucking networks, right?"

He produced a glassine envelope and tapped some powder onto the edge of the tub. "Help yourself."

She put her finger to one nostril and snorted the white line with the other. Nothing. He licked his lips, waiting. And then it hit her. It was like nothing she'd ever felt before. Her body slipped back into the tub as the first wave of heroin bliss enveloped her. She felt his hand between her legs.

"Beats the piss out of cocaine, doesn't it, sugar?" he said, sliding into the tub with her.

She couldn't stop him. She didn't want to stop him. She never felt so good in her life.

Three months later, hooked on heroin, forcibly removed from the hotel suite, unable to face her friends and family, Vivian Jean Belmont went down into the Columbus Circle subway station and threw herself in front of a moving train. The last dozen calls on her cell phone were all to Hellman. He never picked up. He was three thousand miles away in Hollywood, no doubt exploiting the dreams of other young beautiful women.

A month later Kylie and I were called to a town house on East Seventy-First Street. An intruder had broken in, and the homeowner had shot him in self-defense. The shooter was Warren Hellman.

My knees buckled when I saw the body. The man sprawled on the rug with a bullet through his head was my friend, my mentor, my hero: Jonas Belmont.

CHAPTER 2

THERE ARE THREE CLASSES of people in New York City: the haves, the have-nots, and the most rarefied of them all, the have-lots. They are the superrich, the overprivileged few, the 1 percent of the 1 percent. Of course, there's a downside to having all that money. A lot of people want to get their hands on it.

One of those people was Stanley Spellman, our former mayor. Stanley came up with an ingenious plan for winning the love and financial support of his richest and most powerful constituents. He ordered the police commissioner to create a special squad dedicated to solving crimes committed against them.

And so NYPD Red was born. Mayor Spellman lost his bid for reelection, but by then the Red team had made its mark, and the new mayor wasn't about to deprive the city's movers and shakers of their elite task force.

On the night that he shot and killed Detective Jonas Belmont, Warren Hellman made two calls. One was to 911. The system identified Mr. Hellman as one of New York's platinum frequent flyers, and his case was routed to NYPD Red. When Kylie and I arrived at the house, Sonia Blakely, Hellman's lawyer, met us at the front door. She was the first call he had made, and phone records would verify that there was a ninety-two-minute gap between the time he called her and the time he reported the crime. A solid hour and a half for the two of them to concoct a believable story.

She led us to Hellman's office, where Chuck Dryden and his crime scene investigators were already at work. Kylie pulled Chuck aside while I knelt beside Jonas, whose ginger hair was now caked with dark-red blood, his blue eyes fixed in a death stare.

"His name is Jonas Belmont," I said to Blakely. "He was a police officer."

"I know who he is, Detective, and don't try to hide that man behind a badge," she said. "He's a deranged psychopath."

I knew her reputation. I'd seen her in court. She's a barracuda who attacks perfectly reliable witnesses, chews them up, and decimates their testimony. Her favorite defense tactic is to vilify the victim, and she wasted no time in creating the myth that my dead friend was a monster.

I stood up. "Counselor," I said, my jaw clenched, "Jonas Belmont was a decorated cop."

"Of course he was. That's the culture at NYPD. Kill someone, get a medal. So why stop just because he retired? Your *hero cop* came here to murder my client."

She was baiting me to do or say something I'd regret, and I might have if Kylie hadn't stepped in.

"Is your client okay?" she asked. "Does he need medical attention?"

Kylie almost never plays the good cop. It doesn't matter who she's up against. She doesn't kiss ass; she butts heads.

"We can have an officer drive him to a hospital," she said, gilding the lily.

"That won't be necessary," Blakely said. "He's in the living room trying to regain his composure."

"I'm sure he's in shock, and the last thing he wants to do is rehash what happened," Kylie said. "But as you know, the best time to talk to him is now while the details are still fresh in his mind."

"Right," Blakely said, leading the way. "But make it brief."

Warren Hellman was sitting in a wing chair, regaining his composure with the aid of a bottle of Johnnie Walker Blue.

"It was self-defense," he said as soon as we entered the room. "He came at me with a gun. He was going to kill me."

"Calm down, Warren," Blakely said. "Let the detectives ask the questions, and then you answer them to the best of your ability."

"Oh, yeah, right," he said, which I took to mean he'd already forgotten the ground rules she laid out for him earlier.

"Let's start with how you discovered the man was in your house," Kylie said.

Hellman gave her a vacant look. "I didn't discover him. He rang the doorbell, said he was a cop and he wanted to talk to me, so I let him in."

"Oh, I was confused," Kylie said, "because you told the 911 operator that he was an intruder. Now you're saying you invited him in."

"Stop right there, Detective," Blakely said. "The man rang the bell, flashed a badge, and my client did what any law-abiding citizen would do. He *granted* him entry. But he was a total stranger, not an invited guest. He used his police credentials the same way a burglar would use a crowbar. He *was* an intruder."

"I understand," Kylie said. "Did he say what he wanted?"

"Yes. He was here to serve me papers. He was suing me for the wrongful death of his daughter. I . . . I was dumbfounded. I said that's impossible. Who is your daughter? He told me her name—Vivian Belmont."

"Did you recognize the name?"

"I did. She was a wannabe actress. Not very good at all, but I didn't want to tell him that, so I said I never heard of her. That was my mistake. He went berserk and started screaming, 'You killed my daughter, and now you're going to deny even knowing her?' He pulled a gun from his waistband. He was standing between me and the door. I had nowhere to run. I was in fear for my life, but I knew I had a gun in my desk drawer."

"It's perfectly legal," Blakely said. "I can get you the permit."

Kylie ignored her. "Go on, Mr. Hellman."

"I backed away and sat down in my desk chair, sobbing, begging for my life. I said, 'You're a police officer. How can you do this?' He said,

'The best thing about being a cop is getting away with murder,' and he began to move toward me. I reached into the drawer, pulled out my gun, and I shot him."

"Which drawer was your gun in?" Kylie asked.

"Bottom right drawer of my desk."

"And you keep it loaded?"

"Yes."

"Thank God for that," Blakely said.

"So you backed away from the assailant, sat down in your chair, pleaded with the man not to shoot you, but he kept advancing toward you, so you opened that bottom right drawer, pulled out the gun, and shot him," Kylie said. "Is that basically it?"

"Yes," Hellman said. "That's exactly it."

"Detective, I think you got what you came for," Blakely said. "My client has cardiac issues. He's been through enough stress for one night."

"Absolutely," Kylie said. "Your client's well-being is our primary concern. If you give me your card, someone from the District Attorney's Office will want to speak to you tomorrow. I think it best if Mr. Hellman finds another place to spend the night. Our crime scene people will be here for several hours. Thank you so much for your help."

Blakely handed over a business card, and Kylie and I returned to Hellman's office.

"*Your client's well-being is our primary concern? Thank you so much for your help?*" I said. "What happened to the nasty-ass cop I used to work with?"

"Have no fear," Kylie said. "She's back, and she's going to nail that dirtbag's balls to the wall." She bared her teeth. "One at a time."

She wiggled a finger at Chuck Dryden, who has a not-so-secret crush on my blond, green-eyed partner, and he came right over, thrilled to be the man she wanted, even if it was strictly professional.

"Chuck, tell Zach what you told me," she said.

"Well, this is strictly preliminary. Nothing official," he said, giving his standard disclaimer. "The weapon that killed Detective Belmont is a Glock 9mm Model 43. The bullet penetrated his head, just above the left eyebrow at about a forty-five-degree downward angle. The autopsy will give us the exact trajectory."

"Which means that Hellman, who is at least eight inches shorter than Jonas, could not have been sitting in his chair pointing the gun up at him," Kylie said. "He was standing up, aiming down. My best guess is, Hellman pulled the gun, and Jonas bent down to retrieve his from his ankle holster."

"He never got to it," Dryden said. "Detective Belmont's weapon, a Smith & Wesson .38 special, is still in the holster."

"But Hellman said that Jonas pulled a gun from his waistband and came at him with it," I said.

"That would be the Taurus .357 Magnum Model 65 that was found next to the body. It hadn't been fired," Dryden said, "and I would be surprised if Detective Belmont had it in his waistband. It's a heavy gun, and he wasn't wearing a belt that would secure it."

The story that Warren Hellman and his attorney had slapped together was full of holes, and three days later the DA's Office decided they had a strong case against him, and he was charged with murder two.

He spent one night in jail and the next ten months confined to his home, an electronic monitor strapped to his ankle. The trial took three weeks, and the jury was out for almost another five days.

Nearly a year had passed since the deaths of Vivian and Jonas Belmont, and as Kylie pulled the car into an illegal space two blocks from the courthouse, I was more than ready for the verdict.

What I wasn't ready for was the shitstorm that would follow it.

CHAPTER 3

THE TRIAL HAD BLOSSOMED into a media circus. The private tragedy that had befallen the Belmont family had turned into a public spectacle. Centre Street was lined with satellite trucks, and Collect Pond Park, the tranquil urban green space that sits directly opposite the courthouse, had given up its serenity for as many as fifty camera crews, all jostling for position to get the best shot of the key players as they entered the building for their day of reckoning.

The first row of the gallery on the prosecutor's side was reserved for family and friends, and Kylie and I sat down next to Jonas's son and daughter-in-law, Evan and Trish. Next to them were five cops, all retired—Jonas's crew from back in the day.

Normally, fewer than half a dozen court officers are on hand. Today, I counted twenty-eight lining the walls, and there was another contingent in the hallway outside.

Every seat was filled. Noticeably absent was Warren Hellman's brother Curtis. Three years ago, Curtis was also responsible for the death of a young actress. According to TMZ, he picked up the woman at a party in LA and invited her to drive with him to his house near Joshua Tree National Park.

Starstruck and high on coke, she said yes. Two hours later, Curtis pulled over onto the side of a dark desert highway, yanked her out of the car, and sped off. Her body was found the next morning. Cause of death: snakebite.

The rest of the details were sketchy because he paid her family three million dollars for their silence, but the smart money says that he wanted sex, she said no, so he dumped her on the side of the road because nobody says no to the king.

It was Sonia Blakely's decision to keep Curtis out of the spotlight. During the trial, she had painted a grim picture of Jonas. He was a failed father whose daughter grew up to be a hopeless junkie—a gun-happy cop who would rather settle a dispute with a bullet than with a law book. The last thing Sonia needed in the courtroom was for Curtis to show up and remind the jury of the evil that coursed through the Hellman family bloodlines.

Instead, she made sure that the gallery was peppered with Hollywood's biggest and brightest. The entourage changed daily, and it had to have an effect on the jury. If these superstars support Warren Hellman, how bad can he be?

The bailiff announced, "All rise," and the assemblage stood as Judge Mark Hollander entered the room.

I liked Hollander. He was fair, impartial, and less of a hard-ass than most. He took the bench. "Please remember that this is a courtroom," he said. "I respect that emotions are high, but I will tolerate no outbursts from the gallery."

It was a standard speech at the close of any case as charged as this one. The crowd was divided. No matter what the outcome, a lot of people were going to be unhappy. Outbursts were inevitable, and I suspected Hollander would bang his gavel, but he would let the crowd have their moment.

The jury filed in, and finally, the moment of truth had arrived. "Will the forewoman please read the verdict?" Hollander said.

The woman, a fifty-year-old professor at Baruch College, stood up. "In the case of the People of the State of New York versus Warren Hellman," she said, her voice shaky, her pitch high, "we the jury find the defendant not guilty."

Bedlam. The zero-tolerance speech forgotten. The rapping of the judge's gavel echoed through the chamber.

Selma Kaplan, the prosecutor, who had done an outstanding job, buried her face in one hand and shook her head. I closed my eyes and felt that gut punch of emotions cops go through when they know the charge was good, but a person of wealth and power has beaten the system.

But Evan Belmont couldn't keep his outrage to himself. He jumped to his feet, waving his fist at the jury. "How could you!" he screamed. "My father dedicated thirty-five years to protecting this city. And this is the payback he gets?"

Hollander had had enough. "Officers," he yelled above the din, "remove Detective Belmont from my courtroom!"

Two officers approached. Evan held his arms up in surrender, turned, took his wife's hand, and walked down the aisle and out of the room. Kylie and I, along with the five retired cops, joined him in solidarity.

We followed him out of the courthouse into the bright summer sunshine. A podium and a phalanx of microphones had been set up, and a swarm of reporters who now knew the verdict began yelling questions, none of which were worth responding to.

Evan stepped up to the podium, and the noise died down.

"My father always left this courthouse knowing he did the best he could for the victims he was representing. But today that didn't happen for him," he said. "My father did not go to Warren Hellman's house that night to kill him. He went there to expose him, to tell him that my sister Vivian's tragic death was on his hands and that he would dedicate his life to finding every woman whose lives Hellman destroyed, and bankrupt him in civil court. Hellman's response was to shoot my father in cold blood."

"Why do you think the jury found him not guilty?" a reporter yelled out.

"Hellman is a Hollywood showman," Evan said. "He lied, and despite the prosecution's brilliant job of refuting those lies, the jury bought it. My family and I are heartbroken, and I'm sure that many New Yorkers who knew and respected the legend of Detective Jonas Belmont are equally devastated."

A barrage of questions, but Evan waved them off. He'd said his piece. Just as he finished, there was another roar from the crowd.

Warren Hellman and Sonia Blakely, flanked by a cadre of Hollywood royalty, exited the courthouse and walked toward the media frenzy.

Hellman, smiling, ebullient, took center stage. Two fingers of each hand were raised high in a *V*, and he stood there beaming, obnoxiously victorious, without a trace of humility or concern for the lives he had crushed.

"He got away with murder and he's proud of it," Kylie said to me.

He stepped up to the microphones. "This has been quite an ordeal for my family and me," he said. "But justice has prevailed. I'd like to thank my attorney, Sonia Blakely, and her outstanding team, and I'd especially like to express my gratitude to the twelve men and women—a jury of my peers—who believed in my innocence. Thank you for giving me my life back."

Bullets can travel faster than the speed of sound, so I saw the geyser of blood erupt from his neck a split second before I heard the gunshot.

Kylie and I instinctively hit the ground, drawing our pistols, scanning the surroundings for the shooter, and scrambling for cover before the next bullet ripped through the air. But there was no second shot.

"Thank you for giving me my life back" would be Warren Hellman's last words. His life was over even before his body crumpled to the ground. And while we didn't know it at the time, the assassin, wherever he was hiding, was already breaking down his weapon and following through with his exit strategy.

The crowd, conditioned by mass shootings over the years, ran for their lives. People in the courthouse evacuated out the back. Judges were secured in windowless offices. Within ten minutes, NYPD had locked everything down, and the area was secured.

There were no eyewitnesses who could help us pinpoint where the bullet came from, but half a dozen earwitnesses all agreed that it came from somewhere north of the courthouse.

A team of cops fanned out to canvass the area. Kylie and I zeroed in on the nine-story office complex on Centre Street between White and Walker. At least two dozen people were standing outside.

As soon as they saw the shields on our lapels, several of them pointed at the roof.

"The gunshot came from up there," one man said.

"What did you see?" I asked.

"Nothing. But I heard it loud and clear. I was in the waiting room at the dentist's office on the ninth floor. It definitely came from the roof."

"Did you go up there?"

"Hell, no. I raced down nine flights of stairs. I'm an accountant. Going up there is your job, man."

I nodded. I was going up there. But I sure as hell wasn't going alone.

CHAPTER 4

THERE WERE AT LEAST a hundred cops on the street. Kylie saw the one she was looking for. "Captain!" she yelled.

He turned and glowered at her. This man was not used to being barked at.

"Sir," she said, "Detectives MacDonald and Jordan from Red."

Red was the magic word. He walked toward us, the scowl fading rapidly.

"Sir, we believe the shot came from the roof of this building. Can we get some backup?"

"What do you need, Detective?"

"A team to cover the lobby. Nobody comes in. Anybody wants to leave, they get searched. A floor-by-floor canvass and another team to accompany us up to the roof."

Within seconds, dozens of uniformed police poured into the building. Six got in the elevator with us. We drew our guns, got off on the eighth floor, and took the stairs to the roof.

Kylie and I weren't wearing vests, so two of the uniforms took the lead.

The rooftop door was open. "The screamer's been disabled," one of the cops said, pointing at the wires dangling from the alarm.

Whoever killed Warren Hellman had silenced the security system, found his position on the roof, and taken the shot from here. Odds were, he didn't stick around for the cops to show up, but we weren't taking any chances.

My adrenaline kicked up a notch. I split the eight of us into four teams and hand-signaled the game plan to breach the roof. On my go, we charged through the door and fanned out in our assigned directions. The shooter was gone.

"Okay, guys, let's shut it down and wait for Crime Scene to get here," I said. I radioed Central to let them know that the roof was clear.

One by one, the cops went back into the building.

"Zach," Kylie called out. She was standing on the east side of the roof, looking out at the courthouse.

"What have you got?" I said.

"Look at this," she said. "There's a clean line of sight from this spot to the podium where Hellman was standing. Dryden can verify it with a laser, but the evidence is starting to mount up. There's no security, the building is easy to get in and out of, the rooftop alarm was cut, and the guy in the dentist's office one floor below heard the shot loud and clear. This has to be it. And our shooter was a pro—a long-distance sniper who was smart enough to take the shot, disassemble the weapon, and leave without a trace."

"Yo! Dee-tee. Dee-tee."

Hearing the street slang for "detective," we both looked around.

"Yo! Dee-tee. Up here. The Tombs."

Directly across the street from where we were standing was the Manhattan Detention Complex, better known as "the Tombs" because the original structure built in the nineteenth century was inspired by a picture of an Egyptian tomb.

Today it has been replaced by two towers that house close to a thousand male inmates, most of them awaiting trial at the courthouse. One of those men was desperately trying to get our attention. He was on the top floor of the jail, three barred windows in from the corner of White Street.

"I saw him take the shot," he hollered.

Kylie pointed to a spot on the parapet.

"No. Not there. Over more."

She started to her right.

"No. The other way."

She walked along the rooftop wall.

"Keep going."

She took a few more steps.

"Right there! You got it. Right there."

She bent down and studied the limestone slab on top of the parapet. "Looks like traces of gunpowder stippling," she said. She took a
deep breath. "I can smell the burnt powder."

She stood up.

"I told you! I told you!" the man yelled triumphantly. "I saw him.
Come over here and get me out. Tell the CO you want to talk to Elroy."

"Looks like we've got a witness," I said.

"But altruism doesn't permeate the halls of the Tombs," Kylie said.
"Elroy is going to be angling for a get-out-of-jail-free card in return for
his generous cooperation."

"If he gives us the guy who just put a bullet through Warren Hellman's neck," I said, "I'm pretty sure Selma Kaplan will escort him out
the front door herself."

My phone rang. It was our boss, Captain Cates. I put her on speaker.

"Jordan," she said, "where are you and MacDonald right now?"

"We're on a roof two blocks from the courthouse. It's where the shot
came from," I said. "Crime Scene is on the way, but we're running over
to the Tombs to talk to one of the inmates who witnessed the shooting."

"No, you're not," she said. "I'll send another team down there. I
need the two of you uptown forthwith."

"Captain," I said, "this has been our case since the day Warren
Hellman killed Jonas Belmont. We have an eyewitness to the shooting.
What's going on uptown that's more important than this?"

"A runner was stabbed to death on the West Side Highway jogging
path," she said.

"And you can't lay that off on someone else?" I said.

"No, I can't," Cates said. "And even if I could, you wouldn't want me
to. Your newest victim is your current victim's brother—Curtis Hellman."

CHAPTER 5

THE HUDSON RIVER GREENWAY is a thirteen-mile jogging path that runs from the tip of Manhattan to the top. To the west are expansive views of the water and the Jersey shoreline, to the east highway traffic that at rush hour can creep along slower than the joggers.

Curtis Hellman met his demise at 102nd Street. When we got there, the path had been cordoned off three hundred feet in either direction. Ordinarily, I'd expect to see eight to ten cops working the scene. But this was no ordinary victim. And on top of that, he was the city's second celebrity homicide in a few hours. So it came as no surprise that the place was crawling with uniforms, many of them white shirts. Brass. Including the borough chief, who let us know that he was counting on us, and whatever it takes, blah, blah, blah. The usual bullshit.

Olivia Dorsey-Jones was in charge of the crime scene unit. She's every bit as good as Chuck Dryden and a hell of a lot less socially awkward.

"Zach, Kylie," she said. "I spoke to Chuck. He thinks the downtown hit was a professional job. It looks like we've got the same thing here."

"Hey, Livvy," I said. "Lay it out for us."

"Start with the location. Look around. This running path is in full view of the parkway. Until you get here. This clump of trees, which is maybe eighty feet long, is so thick that it's nearly impossible for drivers to see the joggers even if they're sitting in bumper-to-bumper traffic." She held up a hand before we could comment. "Now, that doesn't mean the killer is a pro. Maybe he's just smart. Or he got lucky. Take a look at the body."

The dead man was wearing blue running shorts, a gray T-shirt, black Nikes on his feet, and a Garmin heart monitor on his wrist. A water bottle and a portable audio player were on the ground. There was blood everywhere.

Dorsey-Jones knelt beside the body. "I bagged his hands," she said. "They're manicured, pristine. He didn't put up a fight. He likely never saw the killer coming. Now, here's where it gets interesting."

She pointed to the dark-red line that started at Hellman's right ear. "Cause of death: an edged weapon sliced the trachea and slashed him to the jugular, nearly decapitating him. Most stab victims get knifed in the torso, but this has all the earmarks of someone who knew exactly where to plunge the blade so that he'd bleed out fast. One slice. One and done."

"You have a time of death?" I asked.

"Forty-five to seventy-five minutes ago."

"Shit," Kylie said.

"I know," Dorsey-Jones said. "That's just about when his brother was shot ten miles from here. Based on the timing and the method of execution, it looks like you're looking for two different killers, both of whom are virtuosos at their craft."

"You have a way with words, Livvy," I said.

"I only sound like that on the job. Ten years of working with Chuck Dryden will do that to a girl from a Hundred-and-Twenty-Eighth and Lenox."

"Detectives."

Kylie and I turned around.

"Detectives Buddy Henry and Alma Cardona from the Two-Four squad," the man said. "We were called to the scene before the case was kicked up to Red."

"What've you got?" I said.

"We just interviewed the people who made the 911 call. Two women, regulars, they take this path three, four times a week. They walked past this spot going north and turned around at a Hundred-and-Sixth Street. Ten minutes later when they got back, there he was. No one in sight. Just the body. One of them is a retired nurse, so she checked for signs of life. Otherwise, they didn't touch anything."

"What time did they call it in?" Kylie asked.

Cardona checked her notepad. "Eleven-oh-nine."

Kylie gave me a look. That put the time of death at about eleven a.m. We were definitely looking for two different killers.

"Witnesses?" I said.

Henry shook his head. "We're canvassing, but nothing yet. We'll hit up the local homeless, and we'll be back tomorrow morning handing out flyers to joggers. I wouldn't get my hopes up. This is a hot spot for muggings. Clump of trees, solo runner, mugger jumps out. Even if the vic doesn't have much money, they grab his phone, jewelry—whatever they can."

"Cameras?" Kylie asked.

"No, ma'am," Cardona said. "We sure could use them. But the city isn't paying for cameras."

"Has the family been notified?" I asked.

"We wouldn't do that without running it past you," Henry said.

"We'll take care of it," I said.

Cardona checked her notes again. "The victim's wife is Brooke Hellman."

"Thanks," I said. "We've met her."

"Oh, good," Cardona said. "It's always better to come from someone you know."

"Not in this case," Kylie said. "We've met Mrs. Hellman. And she's definitely not a fan."

CHAPTER 6

"NOT A FAN" was an understatement. The last words Brooke Hellman ever said to Kylie were "Get the fuck out of my house, or I'll call a real cop."

It was the day after we arrested Warren for the murder of Jonas Belmont. We had already interviewed Curtis, who had made his brother sound like a candidate for sainthood. Kylie figured we'd have a better shot at getting some straight answers by talking to Brooke.

"What do we know about her?" I asked.

"Not much. I've seen pictures. She's tall—even without heels, she's taller than her husband. She used to work in the restaurant business, which is where they met twenty years ago. He's fifty-nine, she's forty-one, and what else . . . oh, yeah, big boobs and eternally blond." Kylie mimed, picking up a telephone. "Hello, Central Casting, send me a trophy wife."

"What makes you think she'll give us anything we can use against her brother-in-law?"

"She supports a number of feminist causes, and coming from a business that caters to men like Warren Hellman, I'm sure she's fended off her fair share of creeps. I'm hoping if we tell her what he did to Vivian Belmont, she may open up."

It was a good idea but it backfired. Kylie had underestimated her.

Instead of sandbagging her meal ticket, Brooke saw right through the just-between-us-girls ruse and told Kylie to get the fuck out.

Now we were back. The apartment was on Riverside Drive, less than a mile from where Curtis got his throat slit. We didn't give our names to the doorman. We showed him our shields and told him to let Mrs. Hellman know that NYPD was on the way up.

We took the elevator to the penthouse and rang the doorbell.

"Oh, Christ," she said when she opened the door. "You two again? You didn't get to lock Warren up. Now he's dead. I hope you're happy."

"I'm sorry for your loss," I said.

"Spare me your bullshit," she said. "I've got nothing to say to you. If you're here for my husband, he's not home."

"Where is he?" I said.

"Curtis is out running."

"Whereabouts?"

"None of your fucking business. He doesn't take his phone with him, just his music, so he doesn't know about Warren yet. I don't want you tracking him down and telling him. I'll break the news. And I don't need you here when I do it. Show a little respect, for God's sake, and leave."

"I'm afraid we can't, Mrs. Hellman," I said. "Can we all sit down, please? We need to talk to you."

"Why?" she said, the tough-as-nails veneer fading from her face. "What's wrong?" She lowered her body to a sofa.

"I'm sorry, but we have some terrible news for you," I said. "We responded to a person injured on the Greenway this morning. It was your husband."

She bolted up. "Where is he? I want to see him."

"Unfortunately, he's deceased."

She let out a wail and dropped back to the sofa. "No, no. He was just here. I just spoke to him. It can't be Curtis. Are you sure it's him?"

"We'll need you to identify him, but yes. We're sure."

"What happened? Was it his heart? He's got type two diabetes, so he's a high risk for—"

"He was stabbed."

She looked at me as if I were speaking in tongues. "Stabbed? Who would stab Curtis?"

"We were hoping you could help us. Did your husband have any enemies?"

She shook her head. "Competitors in business, but enemies? No."

"Respectfully, ma'am, I know that in the past there was the incident with a woman in the desert."

She stood up again. "Oh, you vultures. He's not even cold, and you're digging skeletons out of the closet? We're done here. Where's my husband? I want to see him."

"Absolutely. But it will be a few hours," I said. "Ma'am, I don't want to alarm you, but your husband and your brother-in-law were both murdered. You may also be at risk. We can have a police officer stay with you and escort you to the morgue when the medical examiner is ready."

"The morgue? Curtis and I are driving to the Hamptons in a few hours. He can't be dead. It's like the whole world has gone crazy. I can understand Warren. He was . . . he was . . . He got off on humiliating and degrading women. But Curtis was an angel. He helped so many people launch their careers. Everybody loved him."

"Yes, ma'am," I said. "I'm sure everybody did."

Except for the guy who raked a knife across his neck.

CHAPTER 7

"THANK YOU," I said as soon as we were back in the car.

I'm pretty sure Kylie knew what I was talking about, but she gave me a vacant look. "For what?"

"For not getting in her face. You didn't say a single word the entire time."

"We were there to notify her that her husband was murdered, Zach. I know I can be aggressive, but getting in her face would be a new low even for me."

Kylie turned onto West End Avenue and headed south. "Do you believe her?" she asked.

"She was believable," I said. "We've seen a lot of people get hit with devastating news. Her reaction felt genuine. I mean, she took it hard. She seemed shocked."

"You're right," Kylie said, not taking her eyes off the road. "She *seemed* shocked."

"You think she had something to do with it?"

"I'm just playing out a scenario in my head."

"Pretend we're partners and play it out loud," I said.

"Warren Hellman isn't married."

"So?"

"Who do you think inherits his share of the company when he dies?"

"I don't know. Wild guess, I'd say his brother-slash-business part-ner, Curtis."

"And who gets it when Curtis dies?" Kylie said.

"So you think Brooke Hellman hired a couple of hit men to whack her husband and his brother?"

"It makes sense. If we're right and she does inherit the company, then she has a motive. And even though two hit men can be pricey, we know she has the means. So yeah. I underestimated her once. I'm not going to do it again. She's officially a suspect in my book."

My phone rang. "Hold that thought," I said. "It's Selma Kaplan." I took the call and put it on speaker. "Hey, Selma, you've got both of us. How are you doing?"

"I just lost a case that I should have won in my sleep, and I'm up to my ass in dead Hellmans. That's how I'm doing." Selma is not only the smartest ADA in New York County, she's also the most caustic. Which is probably why we like her so much.

"We feel your pain, but we're on it," I said. "The homicides were so close together that we're looking for two killers, most likely profession-als funded by one person. Top of our list is Curtis's widow."

"Oh, Jesus. Brooke Hellman is a champion of women's rights, and she puts her money where her mouth is. She was one of Mayor Sykes's biggest supporters. Don't even suggest to Her Honor that Brooke is a suspect unless you find her holding a receipt that says, 'Thank you for using our services. Please call again if there's anyone else you want dead.'"

"Thanks for the heads-up. Anything else?"

"Yes. Detective MacDonald has a friend at the Tombs. His name is Elroy Lafontant. He says he saw the shooter and he's happy to make a deal, but he wants the blond lady cop from the roof to be there."

"Where and when?" Kylie asked.

"He'll be in the seventh-floor conference room with his attorney in thirty minutes."

"Zach and I were pulled away from the crime scene at the court-house. We're going to make a quick stop there. Then we'll walk over to your office."

Selma hung up, and Kylie grinned at me. "I knew Elroy and I connected. I could feel the vibe. Do me a favor—don't tell Chuck Dryden. You know how jealous he can get."

Chuck's face lit up as soon as we arrived. "Detectives," he said, looking at only one of us. "I'm glad you're back."

"What have you got for us, Chuck?" Kylie said.

"The bullet was a .50-caliber BMG," Dryden said. "The gun was probably a Barrett sniper rifle."

Kylie gave him a warm smile. "So you're saying you don't think the shooter was an amateur."

Chuck laughed. "Oh, I'd say he was a pro, but even then, that would be selling him short. The distance from the perch you found on the rooftop to the point of impact is five hundred and twenty-seven yards. A trained professional could easily have shot the victim in the heart. The head would be even more challenging. But this hit him dead center in his neck. It severed his spine—practically took his head off. That's Olympic gold."

We thanked him and walked to the DA's Office at 80 Centre Street. As soon as we cleared security, Kylie stopped.

"Do I look okay?" she asked.

"What are you talking about?" I said.

"You heard Selma. Elroy didn't ask for you, Zach. He specifically asked for me. I just want to know how I look."

Kylie was still smarting from having to sit in silence while I questioned Brooke Hellman. She needed some balls to bust, and mine were handy.

"You look great," I said. "I'm sure you're the blond lady cop of Elroy's dreams."

"Thanks," she said, tossing her hair. "You know how giddy I get on the first date."

CHAPTER 8

CAPTAIN DELIA CATES IS the best boss I ever worked for. A street-smart kid from Harlem with a master's in criminal justice from John Jay College, she's a tough, insightful leader with a deft hands-on/hands-off approach. She's immersed in every case, but she doesn't micromanage. She trusts her detectives to do their jobs.

So both Kylie and I were a little surprised to see her sitting in the conference room with Selma Kaplan.

"Hey, boss," I said. "You just happen to be in the neighborhood?"

"Actually, I just happened to be heading to the Bronx when the PC called me and changed my plans. This Elroy Lafontant character is the best lead we have, and the commissioner wants me to be his eyes and ears so he doesn't miss a beat."

I nodded. "So what you're saying is, the mayor is breathing down the PC's neck, so he's breathing down yours."

"That's not what I said, Detective Jordan, but if that's what you heard, you may have a future in politics." She turned to Kaplan. "Selma, tell us about our star witness."

The ADA opened a file. "Elroy Lafontant is a predicate felon with a passion for guns," she said. "He's forty-four and he's been using the same tried-and-true formula for success ever since he was eighteen. He drives down to Virginia, gets a local to buy him a couple of dozen guns, drives them back up north, sells them to the gangbangers, and in pretty short order he gets himself caught, which may explain why he's spent thirteen of the last twenty-six years in prison.

"This time around, he made the mistake of selling a trunk load of Glock 9mms to an undercover cop, and he's looking at his third strike, which means he's looking at twenty years. I can knock it down to a lesser charge, but only if his information pans out."

"Let's see what he's got," Cates said. She stood up and went into the adjoining room to watch it unfold on a closed-circuit hookup. I wouldn't be surprised if several honchos from the DA's office were in there as well.

Five minutes later, Elroy Lafontant, his hands and legs shackled, clanked into the room. He was tall and dark, and by the look of his upper torso straining against his shirt, he must have spent every day of his prison years working out, because he was jailhouse jacked.

He gave us a big toothy smile. "Detective," he said, looking at Kylie. "It's excellent to see you again. I'm Elroy Lafontant. And what do I call you?"

"Detective MacDonald," she said. "This is my partner, Detective Jordan."

Elroy grinned. "Lucky you, Detective Jordan."

"And this is Assistant District Attorney Kaplan," Kylie added. "Have a seat."

Elroy sat, and his attorney, who had probably been roped into the relationship less than two hours ago, sat next to him. "Russell Shinbauer," he said.

Nobody cared. This was the Elroy show, and he knew it. He cleared his throat and went into his act. "Little did I realize when I heard that gunshot this morning that I was destined to become a key player in helping the police solve one of the most heinous murders this city has ever witnessed."

"Excuse me, Elroy," Kylie said.

"Yes, ma'am, Detective MacDonald."

"Do I look like a rookie?"

"No, ma'am. You look seasoned to a fare-thee-well."

"Then tone down the bullshit, give us the God's honest truth, and you shall be rewarded in kind. Now, take it from the top."

"Right," he said. "I was at the window sneaking a smoke. I heard the shot. Boom! Loud enough to wake the dead, if you know what I mean. Even before the smoke clears, he's breaking down the gun like a pro. Then he packs it up and beats it out of the roof door. Wham bam. One shot, and he's outta there."

"Describe the gun."

"It was a Barrett .50-caliber."

Kylie's expression didn't change, but she let her eyes drift toward mine. Chuck Dryden had said the bullet was a .50-caliber and the weapon was most likely a Barrett sniper rifle. Elroy might have been full of shit, but his facts were spot-on.

"A Barrett .50?" Kylie said. "Are you sure?"

He laughed hard. "Am I sure? You've seen my rap sheet. Guns are my passion."

"I know. But you sell Chevys. The Barrett .50 is a Ferrari."

"That don't mean I don't know a Ferrari when I see one. Or hear one. They got a range in Vegas where you can shoot any damn gun you can think of. I fired me a Barrett .50 once. Let me tell you, those babies got some kick. My shoulder was killing me for weeks. This guy—your shooter up on that roof—he was no deer hunter. That cannon's gotta cost a minimum ten grand legal. Sweet Jesus, if I had that kind of money, I could triple it on the street in no time."

His lawyer nudged him.

"Yeah, right," Elroy said, taking the not-too-subtle hint. "Not that I'd ever go back to selling guns again. My last stretch, I learned me some culinary skills. I get out this time, I'm gonna get me a job as a short-order cook. I got a friend who owns a diner in—"

"Describe the shooter," Kylie said.

"He was white, short—"

"How short?"

"I'm six-two, so a lot of people seem short, but . . . come to think of it, I remember when you was on the roof, your head came up to about the same level as him. How tall are you, Detective MacDonald?"

"I'm five-seven."

"I'm going with that. Your shooter, he's five-seven."

"What else can you tell me about him?" Kylie said. "Skinny? Fat?"

"Average."

"What else?"

"What else? You mean like what color was his eyes, and did he have any tattoos? Come on, Detective, I was half a football field away, and I'm looking through a steel mesh window that don't get cleaned regular."

"You're doing fine," Kylie said. "What was he wearing?"

Elroy gave her another big smile. "Well, now, that's the question I was hoping you would ask, because this is how you gonna catch this dude. You ready for this?"

Kylie smiled back. "I'm ready, Elroy."

Selma and I were ready, and I'll bet Cates and whoever else was watching the performance from the next room were just as ready.

"He's wearing one of them brown UPS uniforms," Elroy announced. "I mean, you know he's not a real delivery guy. That's his cover. This dude is smart. He knows you can walk in and out of any building dressed like that and nobody gives a shit. Them guys is, like, invisible. But not this one. Elroy Lafontant seen this one." He turned to Selma to make sure she knew where all this valuable information was coming from.

"Are you sure it was a UPS uniform?" Kylie asked.

"Sure I'm sure."

"You just told me you were half a football field away, looking through a dirty window," Kylie said. "You might be able to see brown pants and a brown shirt, but there's no way you could make out a UPS logo. They're too small."

He looked at Kylie as if she'd just betrayed him. He thought they were on the same side, and all of a sudden, she went all lady cop on him.

"I didn't say I seen a logo. I said he was pretending to be a UPS guy."

"Or just a guy dressed in brown."

"Yeah, well, this man—the one who's all dressed in brown—after he takes the shot, he breaks down the Barrett .50 and he puts it in a big, long box. I couldn't see no words on it, but you could make out that it was red and brown. Then he gets his ass off the roof, and me, I keep looking out my cell window, and sure enough, a couple minutes later, the guy in the *brown pants and brown shirt* comes out the front door. Only now he's got a dolly with a bunch of boxes, and I'll bet you a dinner at Sylvia's that that big-ass gun is in one of them. And then . . ."

A born showman, Elroy sat back, puffed up his prison-buff chest, and made sure he had total command of his audience. "And then he rolls his dolly to a big motherfucking brown truck with a big motherfucking *U, P, S* on the side, loads up, and drives away, slick as snail snot. You find that guy, you got your killer. And don't forget who helped you nail him."

Elroy's lawyer, a reluctant participant who had spent most of the interview in stony silence, suddenly saw a big *W* light up on the scoreboard. "Ms. Kaplan," he said, "I think my client has proven beyond a shadow of a doubt that he brings critical new evidence that will definitely benefit the police in solving this very public homicide. Are you ready to make a deal?"

"Yes," she said.

One final broad smile spread across Elroy Lafontant's face, and he turned to Kylie. "You and me, Detective MacDonald—we sure do make one hell of a team, don't we?"

CHAPTER 9

TWO DETECTIVES from the DA's office led Elroy back to his cell. His lawyer, energized by his newfound negotiating power, followed Selma to her office to hammer out a deal.

As soon as the room cleared, Cates reentered. "I have the commissioner," she said, holding up her phone.

"Kylie, Zach," the PC said. "Great job."

"Thank you, sir," we replied in unison.

"We have to find that UPS truck," he said.

"Kylie and I are all over it, sir."

"Anything I can do to help—I mean anything: manpower, overtime—just say the word," he said.

"Well, now that you mention it, there is one thing you can do, sir," Kylie said.

"Name it, Detective."

"You got a guy at UPS?"

He laughed hard. "You mean you don't want to shovel through six levels of corporate bullshit before you can talk to somebody who has the juice to get things done?"

"Couldn't have said it better myself, sir."

"I've got your man. Ted White. I'll call him as soon as I hang up."

"Thank you, boss," I said.

"Happy to help. Two more things."

I took out my notepad. It's not every day the PC is heavily invested in one of our cases.

"Brooke Hellman," he said. "I know you're taking a good look at her."

"Commissioner, the Hellman brothers were murdered by professionals," Kylie said. "Someone paid a lot to have them killed. Mrs. Hellman is about to inherit a small fortune as the result of their deaths. So yes sir, we are taking a long, hard look at her."

"As you should. And if she's behind it, you can lock her up, and I'll explain to Mayor Sykes that not all her political supporters are the stand-up citizens they pretend to be. But . . ." He paused. Maybe it was for effect. Or maybe it was to make sure he chose his words carefully. "There's enough friction between One-PP and Gracie Mansion as it is, so unless you have concrete evidence against Brooke Hellman, I need you to tread lightly."

"Understood, sir."

"Last but a long damn way from least," he said, "Warren Hellman's lawyer, Sonia Blakely, is raising hell in the media. She's saying that nobody had more of a motive to murder her client than Evan Belmont. That woman works the media the same way she works a jury. The first thing she did was turn Evan Belmont's words against him. He stood there with the cameras rolling, and he made it clear that he believed he didn't get justice in the courthouse. Blakely twisted that to imply that he dealt out his own brand of vigilante justice."

Cates jumped in. "She's just grandstanding, sir."

"You know that, and I know that, Delia, but the average New Yorker watching the five o'clock news doesn't. Blakely is on the warpath, and she doesn't have a judge to reel her in. She said NYPD should have Belmont at the very top of their list of suspects. They should treat him like someone who had a bitter grudge against Warren Hellman, and not sweep it under the rug because he has a badge."

"Sir," Cates said, "Red has treated this case like any other high-profile homicide. We always have been, and will continue to be, thorough and totally impartial."

"Seen and noted, Captain. And in the interest of thoroughness and impartiality, I want Red to interview Belmont."

"Yes sir. I'll assign a team immediately," Cates said.

"You already have the best team right there," the PC said. "I'm confident that Detectives Jordan and MacDonald would never let their personal relationships interfere with their professional responsibilities."

"Yes, sir, but they were sitting with Evan Belmont when the verdict was read. Blakely knows they're close friends with him. She'll accuse us of treating him with kid gloves."

"And if Ms. Blakely were the police commissioner, she could decide who interviews Belmont. But the last time I looked, I was still the boss."

"Absolutely, sir."

"Zach, Kylie," the PC said. "I know this is not what you want to do, but someone has to interview Evan Belmont."

"We're on it, sir," I said.

"Thank you. Keep me posted."

I was about to yes-sir him again, but he hung up.

Cates shook her head. "I agree with Commissioner Radcliffe on one thing. You are the best team we've got. Where we disagree is that I would rather you were out there looking for the killers than wasting your time interviewing Evan Belmont just to check a box that any rookie detective on the job could check. But like he said, he's the boss."

"It's not going to be pretty suggesting to Evan Belmont that he might be guilty of murder," Kylie said, "but it's got to be done. And better us than Internal Affairs. They're witch hunters. They'd crucify him."

My phone rang. I didn't recognize the number. "Detective Jordan," I answered.

"Hello, Detective. This is Ted White, head of security at UPS."

"Mr. White, thanks for getting back to us so fast."

"When Colin Radcliffe calls, I drop everything. How soon can we meet?"

"Immediately, sir. Where's your office?"

"Forget my office. I'll meet you on West Twenty-Seventh Street between Eleventh and Twelfth Avenues."

"What's there?"

"I found your truck."

CHAPTER 10

NYPD HAS SECRET SQUIRRELS all over the city. One of them is the Lower Manhattan Security Initiative. Shortly after the September 11 attacks, NYPD blanketed the Financial District and much of the southern tip of Manhattan with thousands of high-tech surveillance cameras. Over the years, the network has expanded, and today they can tap into any one of eighteen thousand cameras around the city.

As soon as Elroy told us that the shooter was driving a UPS truck, Cates called a detective at LMSI, who pulled screenshots from multiple cameras in the vicinity of 139 Centre Street, recorded the truck number, and quickly passed the information straight to the PC's office.

When Kylie asked the commissioner if he had a guy at UPS, she had no idea she was a lobbing a softball right over the plate. We found out later that Ted White wasn't just "a guy." He and the commissioner met at the Academy back in the '80s, became friends, partnered up for five years, and each went on to have stellar careers with the department. White, who had recently retired as a deputy chief, dropped everything as soon as his old buddy Colin Radcliffe called.

Theodore Francis White was a decorated cop who now headed up security for UPS's Northeast Region. I'm sure the job has some kind of lofty title attached to it, but when Cates, Kylie, and I arrived on West

Twenty-Seventh Street, he introduced himself with a simple "Hi, I'm Ted." He was tall, lanky, with a firm handshake and an equally firm grasp of police procedure.

"This is truck number one-zero-one-two-seven-zero," he said, pointing at the big brown box on wheels that fit in perfectly with the rest of the commercial vehicles parked along the street. "It was out of service this morning, so we didn't know it was missing till we got the call. That's the problem when you have a worldwide fleet of over a hundred thousand trucks. It's like trying to keep track of every damn crawly creature in an ant colony. It's easy for any one of them to slip through the cracks."

"How did this one disappear?" Kylie asked.

"I don't know yet, but my best guess is that someone in a brown uniform who knew a little bit about how we operate just walked into the garage and took it. The keys would have been in the ignition for their convenience. I know it sounds counterintuitive, but if the keys are always in the truck, they're never going to wind up on the D train to the Bronx in some driver's pocket."

"It's that easy to steal a truck?" Kylie said.

"An *empty* truck," White said. "We lose about a million dollars' worth of packages every day to porch pirates, grab-and-run drug addicts who wait for the driver to go into a store with a delivery, and sometimes by crazies who put a gun to the driver's head. We focus on the security of our customers' property and the safety of our people. An empty truck that was scheduled for routine maintenance wasn't on our radar this morning, but as soon as I get back, I will personally interview everyone who was in it, near it, or might have caught it out of the corner of their eye."

"What about GPS?" I asked. "Can you track it from the time it left the garage? LMSI tried to trace its route from the crime scene, but the driver drove to the garment center, got lost in a sea of identical trucks, and it'll take them a while to figure out how he got from there to here."

"Sorry," White said. The GPS units in these trucks aren't built in. They're portable, like police radios. The driver unplugged it as soon as he hit the road at eight twenty-seven this morning. He plugged it back in at eleven-oh-four, and the truck hasn't moved from this spot since."

"I'm sure you know you won't be getting it back for a while," Cates said. "CSU will be here to print, swab, and photograph the exterior; then they'll take it to their garage to do the interior. After that—"

"I know the drill, Captain," White said. "With a crime of this magnitude, NYPD will hold on to this truck for years. I've already drafted a memo in my head letting corporate know that old one-zero-one-two-seven-zero has delivered her last package."

"Our shooter may not be as smart as he thinks," Kylie said, pointing up at a lamppost thirty yards away. "That's an NYPD globe camera up there. Hopefully, it's angled right, and we can get a clean shot of him leaving the truck. And if that doesn't work, I can see two more cameras from here."

"There are six cameras on this street from Eleventh to Twelfth Avenue," White said. "I canvassed the block as soon as I got here. Old habits . . . anyway, more bad news. Every one of them has been disabled. Shot out."

"Shot?" Cates said. "The man had a Barrett .50-cal. We know he didn't use that, or he'd have vaporized half the lamppost."

White nodded. "The PC told me your killer was packing heavy artillery," he said. "But clearly, he had a game plan, and his backup weapon was a lot smaller."

"And a lot quieter," Cates added.

"Let's call LMSI and see if they've got a read on any of the cameras," Kylie said.

She called. Ted had been right. Every camera on the block had been shot out.

"And there's no way that I can make out the shooter," the LMSI detective said. "All I got is the flash from his muzzle. This guy is a total pro."

Kylie looked over at me and held up two fingers in the sign of a *V.* I know my partner. She wasn't talking about victory. She was silently correcting the LSMI detective and confirming something we pretty much knew.

If whoever shot Warren Hellman left his getaway vehicle on West

Twenty-Seventh Street at 11:04, and the murder of Curtis Hellman five miles uptown was called in at 11:09, we weren't up against just one total pro.

We had to find two.

CHAPTER 11

IF THIS WERE ANY other case, Kylie and I would have spent the next six to eight hours watching the crime scene techs painstakingly retrieving hair, fibers, and other virtually imperceptible evidence that might lead us to the killer. They love laboring over every speck of minutiae that goes with their job, but for us, it's the homicide detective equivalent of watching paint dry.

But this time we were off the hook. Cates would assign another team of detectives to stare at the UPS truck. We were on a priority mission for the PC—tell a good cop who lost his sister and his father, then got kicked in the balls by the justice system, that he was a person of interest in one, maybe two, homicides.

Evan Belmont lived in Staten Island. The drive from Lower Manhattan through the tunnel into Brooklyn, then over the Verrazzano Bridge to his quiet neighborhood in Dongan Hills took close to an hour. Kylie and I didn't talk much. I just sat there with the same feeling of dread that I get in the pit of my stomach when I'm on the way to notify a family that someone they love was murdered. However they deal with it, I know that their life—and how they feel about me—will never be the same.

"Shit," Kylie said as we pulled up to Evan's house. His driveway was lined with cars and pickups that spilled out onto the street for almost a block. The house would be packed with Evan's support group, who would be cursing out the jury and drinking to the health of the sniper who shot Warren Hellman.

"I thought we were just going to lose one friend today," I said. "Looks like we're going to piss off a lot more cops than we planned on."

The white clapboard house was a notch or two above the typical working-class Staten Island home. Three stories, a wide covered porch, and a two-car garage. It was above Evan's pay grade, but he'd inherited it when Jonas died, and I could just hear Sonia Blakely saying, "If he can afford to live in a magnificent house like this, he could easily afford to pay a hit man."

Four women were sitting on the front porch. I'd never seen any of them before, but based on their ages and the fact that they were drinking either Diet Cokes or water, I figured they were all cop wives—designated drivers who had no other interest in being there except to get their drunken husbands home safely.

"How you doing?" one of them said. "Evan is in the backyard."

"They're all back there," a second one said. "Commiserating."

The group laughed their approval.

Kylie and I walked around the side of the house. The backyard was spacious, more than enough to accommodate the twenty-five or thirty cops who were smoking, drinking, and talking loud enough for Kylie and me to know that the drinking had started hours before we arrived.

I scanned the group and recognized some cops from Evan's squad, plus the five retired detectives from Jonas's crew who had been sitting in the gallery with us that morning. Then I saw Evan, weaving his way toward us.

"Zach! Kylie!" he said, giving each of us a sloppy drunk hug. "Fuck, man, it means so much to me that you guys came all the way out here. Grab some food. There's a shit ton of it. The baked ziti is incredible, and the linguini with white clam sauce is so fucking good—"

"Evan, thanks, but we're not going to eat," I said.

"You don't know whatcha missing," he slurred. "But suit yourself. At least have a beer."

"Can't," I said. "We're here on business."

He looked at me, bleary-eyed. "Business? What are you talking about?"

One of the detectives from Jonas's old squad moved in and put a hand on Evan's shoulder. "They want to know if you were involved in Hellman's shooting."

"Bullshit," Evan said, shaking the man's hand off his shoulder. "You don't know these guys, Harry. Zach, tell him how far back we go."

"Evan," I said, "we do have to ask you a few questions. Preferably in private. It's procedure. It won't take long."

He backed away from us. "Are you fucking *serious*? Is that why you're here?"

"Come on, Evan. We're investigating Warren Hellman's homicide. You know the drill. We have to go by the book."

"You can shove the fucking book up your ass," Harry said. "And if Jonas were alive, he'd ram it up there for you."

"You cocksuckers have got a lot of fucking nerve." It was another retired detective. "After all this man has gone through, you come here to rip out what's left of his heart?"

"It was that bitch Sonia Blakely, wasn't it?" Evan said. "She fucking went on TV and said NYPD was behind killing Hellman. She was screaming, 'Blue Justice! Blue Justice!' And now you're pointing the finger at me? I thought you two were NY-fucking-PD Red, not Internal fucking Affairs."

"Evan, please." It was Kylie, her voice soft, calm. "You're a third-generation cop. You know how this works. We have to go through the motions. Just a few questions."

A voice boomed out. "Not now! And definitely not here!" A short, stocky man with thick black hair and a matching Tom Selleck mustache pushed his way toward us. "I'm Tony Sisto, the delegate from the Tenth, and this is bullshit. You show up here on the day that the scumbag who killed Officer Belmont's father is turned loose? The two of you have got some fucking balls. Now, get out. And if you or whoever's ass you're kissing wants to talk to Evan, put it in writing. I'll have the union attorney get back to you. We're done here."

"No, Tony, we're not done," Evan said. "Zach, Kylie, I swear on my father's and sister's souls that I had nothing to do with it. I was positive the jury would convict. Do you think I hired a sniper to sit on some rooftop on the off chance that Hellman would walk out of the courthouse a free man?"

I shook my head. Kylie did the same.

"You want to know the truth? Part of me is glad that scumbag is dead. But another part of me is in a lot of fucking pain, because . . ." He choked up, trying to hold back the sobs that were welling up in his throat. "Because with Hellman gone, I'll never know what really happened to my sister and my father, and that will haunt me till the day I die. Please, believe me. I didn't do it."

"We believe you," I said. "That's all we came for."

"Then get the fuck out," somebody said. I couldn't tell who, because by now every cop in the backyard had closed in around Evan.

"We're going," I said. "But first I think you should know that this case just exploded."

Evan shook his head. "What are you talking about?"

"This morning at around eleven a.m., Warren Hellman's brother Curtis was murdered."

The news was a gut punch. Nobody moved. Nobody said a word. Finally, Tony Sisto broke the silence. "Oh, wait . . . Curtis Hellman? I did that one. Blew his fucking brains out."

"He was stabbed," I said.

"In that case, I did it," someone yelled.

A third voice. "Bullshit! I did it."

Kylie and I turned around and started to leave. Most of them followed us.

We got into our car listening to a chorus of hooting shit-faced cops vying for our attention so they could confess to a murder they had just found out about.

My career has had its low points. But I can't remember a day more rock bottom than this one.

CHAPTER 12

AS WE PULLED AWAY from the house, I slouched in my seat so I could get comfortable while I mentally licked my wounds for five or ten minutes. But Kylie has this singular ability to joke her way through the worst of times.

"Well, that certainly sucked even more than I expected," she said. "Let me just check the rearview mirror and see if they're coming after us with torches and pitchforks."

She got half a laugh out of me.

"Come on, Zach, we knew it was going to be ugly. We just didn't expect that much rage and alcohol-infused testosterone to come at us at once. But hey, we did what the PC asked us to do. My only regret is that I didn't grab a plateful of that baked ziti before we left. I'm fucking famished."

I coughed up the other half of the laugh. "What's your take on Evan?" I asked.

"Sonia Blakely can point her fifteen-hundred-dollar-an-hour finger at him all she wants," Kylie said, "but as far as I'm concerned, he didn't do it."

"I agree," I said. "And it's not about anything he said. It's how he said it. You and I can smell a lie before it even comes out of the liar's mouth. Evan's denial was one hundred percent credible."

"We're in sync," she said. "Call it in."

I got Captain Cates on the phone. "Detective MacDonald and I interviewed Detective Evan Belmont, and we both concluded that he had nothing to do with killing either Warren or Curtis Hellman," I said.

"Thank you," she said. "I'll pass that on to the PC."

The call was over in less than fifteen seconds.

"I've been thinking," Kylie said as we crossed the bridge into Brooklyn. "Why don't we go over to Silvercup Studios tomorrow morning and ask Shelley Trager for some insider dirt on the Hellman brothers?"

"You think he knew them?" I said.

"Probably. Spence always used to say that everybody in the film business either knows, worked with, slept with, or fucked over everybody else in the film business."

She caught me by surprise. She hadn't mentioned Spence's name in months. Spence Harrington is Kylie's husband. Unless he's dead.

A year ago, he was a successful writer-producer, one of the bright young stars in the industry. And having a powerhouse like Shelley Trager as his mentor made his future even brighter. But that all started to crumble when Spence went back to his old love, cocaine. Six months ago, Spence checked out of his most recent rehab and vanished in the wind. Kylie almost never talks about him. She's moved on with her life.

My phone rang. "Oh, Christ," I said, looking at the caller ID. "Just when I thought the day couldn't get any worse. It's Megan Rollins."

"Don't take the call," Kylie said.

"That doesn't work with Megan. The last time I let her go to voice mail, she rattled some cages at One-PP, and I got a call from DCPI *strongly suggesting* that I get back to her forthwith."

"Give me the phone. I'll talk to her."

"Fantastic idea," I said. "She hates you. You hate her. What could possibly go wrong?"

"Fine. Put it on speaker. I won't say a word."

I took the call, but I kept my finger close to the mute button because Kylie is genetically incapable of keeping her mouth shut. "This is Detective Jordan."

"Zach." The voice was like warm honey—soft, smooth, and unabashedly sexy. "It's Megan Rollins. Can we meet up? I've got something for you."

Kylie silently flipped her the bird.

"Hold on a minute, Megan. Let me just put that through my bullshit translator app. Okay. It came out, 'Hi, Zach, I *want* something from you.'"

"Oh, Zach. Why don't you trust me?"

"You're a reporter."

"Investigative journalist, sweetheart. You really should watch the eleven o'clock news. Do you know how many people go to bed with me every night?"

Kylie stuck her finger down her throat and mimed a gag.

"Megan, I don't trust reporters, investigative journalists, politicians—it's a long list, but you get the picture. It's a cop thing, so don't take it personally."

"I'm serious, Zach. I have something that can help you and your partner, who I'm sure is listening, with this dual homicide."

"You're damn right I'm listening," Kylie said, grabbing the phone out of my hand. "If you've got something, call DCPI. If they tell us to talk to you, we will, but not without putting up a fight."

"Detective MacDonald," Megan said, "if I tell DCPI, they'll go straight to the commissioner, and then the two of you will wind up on the nasty end of a clusterfuck."

"Been there, not worried," Kylie said.

"Put Zach back on."

"I hate to disappoint you, Lois Lane, but you've got us both. Take it or leave it." Kylie looked at me with a self-satisfied expression that said, "*This* is how you deal with reporters."

"Okay," Megan said. "Full disclosure. I can't call DCPI."

"Why not?" I said.

"I've got information that can help you crack the Hellman case. But how I came by that information is not something I'm proud of."

"I'm sure it's not the first time," Kylie said. "Elaborate on this one."

"I know something, Kylie. It's big. If I take it to DCPI, they're going to want to know how I came by it, and if that gets out, my picture-perfect upstanding journalist image will be fucked. If I tell you and Zach, you'll protect your source. It's Quid Pro Quo 101, kids. Are you interested?"

Kylie handed me the phone. "Maybe," I said. "Give us a taste."

"Six months ago, Brooke Hellman tried to murder her husband, Curtis."

Kylie mouthed a silent F-bomb.

"Yeah," I said. "We're interested. Where can we meet?"

CHAPTER 13

MEGAN GAVE ME AN address on East Twenty-Eighth Street. It was a two-bedroom corporate apartment leased by the station, where its senior reporters could hold private meetings, crash for a few hours between news cycles, or, in the case of Megan Rollins, share a bottle of tequila and a bed with a cop who couldn't say no to a dark-haired, beautiful woman whose body was every bit as spectacular as I imagined it would be after watching her on camera.

I was off duty, not in a relationship at the time, and we never once talked about my work, so for me, it was pure sex. No remorse, no guilt, just another one-night stand. And while I'd like to think she found me irresistibly attractive and gave me at least four and a half stars for performance, I don't kid myself. Megan's speed dial is filled with men—and women—who take her calls because she is no longer just another anonymous face in a sea of reporters.

I haven't told a soul, especially Kylie. And while many would question Megan's professional integrity, as a willing victim I'm comforted that she still stands behind the journalistic credo of never revealing her sources.

The apartment was functional and uninspired, a cross between a Best Western and Office Max. Megan, on the other hand, was a cross between an intrepid reporter hell-bent on winning a Pulitzer, and Scarlett Johansson in any movie ever.

The three of us sat down at a round laminate-top table. There was no tequila, no foreplay. Megan just did what she does every night at eleven. She looked straight at us and started talking.

"Brooke Hellman is smarter than you think. She studied economics at Barnard. In her junior year, she got a part-time job as a coat-check girl in a big-ticket restaurant, and the customers—and by customers, I mean men—loved her. By the time she graduated, she realized she could make more money working in high-end restaurants than she could on Wall Street.

"She took to the business fast and worked her way up even faster. In a few years, she was managing one of those if-you-have-to-ask-how-much-it-costs-you-don't-belong-here steak houses downtown. She instinctively knew the value of schmoozing every night with CEOs, EVPs, and other captains of industry. The more they drank, the faster they parted with corporate secrets. Brooke, in turn, researched, analyzed, capitalized on the insider information, and put together a tidy little nest egg.

"And then she met the Hellman brothers. Bigger nest. A lot more eggs. Warren made it clear from the get-go that he wanted to fuck her, but he was too much of a pig and she was too much of a feminist, so it never happened. Curtis was another story. He had just as much money as his brother, and I think she genuinely liked him—at least in the beginning. There were other guys worth nine figures, but she liked the glam of the film business, so she married him. It worked for about twenty years, and then one day she realized that Warren's sexual escapades were costing the company a fortune in hush money."

"What about the woman who died in the desert?" Kylie said. "That was Curtis."

"Curtis was one and done. Two million dollars and he learned his lesson. Warren was a serial predator. Over the past ten years, it probably cost fifty million dollars to pay off the women he forced himself on. And it didn't come out of his pocket. The business paid for it. I checked—it's legal. All you need is a smart lawyer. Curtis could accept his brother's sex addiction, but Brooke did the math. Twenty-five million out of her pocket, and there were more lawsuits on the horizon. She wanted out. She begged Curtis to sell his half of the business to Warren while there was still something worth selling. But Curtis said no. That, Detectives, is what is known in the business as *motive.*"

A lot of the backstory on Brooke was new to us, and Megan knew it. She flashed a close-up camera-worthy smile and went on.

"Did you know that Curtis Hellman was a diabetic?"

"No," Kylie said.

"He's been injecting himself with insulin since he was eleven. But on January nineteenth of this year, he somehow wound up with a massive overdose. Brooke was conveniently out of the house when it happened, but luckily for Curtis, he was on the phone setting up a tennis date with a friend just before he passed out. The friend heard him fall, called 911, and for the next three days Curtis was touch and go in a diabetic coma at Columbia Presbyterian."

"And you think Brooke was responsible for the overdose," Kylie said.

"Somebody fucked with Curtis's insulin, and she was the only one who had access. She failed the first time, but she's not the type to give up. She's too smart to try the same thing twice, and she has more than enough money to hire a professional to do the job right. In fact, I'll bet she hired *two* professionals and had both Warren and Curtis whacked."

Brooke had been at the top of our suspect list, but the PC had directed us to tread lightly unless we had concrete evidence. Megan reinforced what we'd been thinking, and had just handed us a strong lead we could follow.

"This is a big help," I said. "I'm glad you called. Thanks."

"You're welcome. And all I want in return is first dibs when you break this case. Fair enough?"

"Fair enough," I said.

"One question," Kylie said. "If Curtis Hellman had this near-death experience, how come nobody ever reported on it—including you?"

"It was a closely guarded family secret, and at the time I couldn't get my hands on his hospital records to verify it. But now that you're investigating his murder, I'm sure you can."

"How did you even know about it?" Kylie said.

She gave us a seductive smile. "Let's just say a reliable source told me."

"Megan," Kylie said, "you're asking us for quid pro quo. There are God knows how many reporters in New York, all of whom want to be at the top of our list. You're going to have to give us a lot more than 'reliable source.'"

Megan weighed her options. "Fine," she said. "Warren told me."

"Just like that?" Kylie said. "Warren Hellman told you? Why?"

"It's that old devil quid pro quo, Detective. I slept with the fucker."

CHAPTER 14

"REFRESH MY MEMORY," KYLIE said as soon as we were back in the car. "When we interviewed Brooke Hellman earlier today, did she mention anything about trying to murder her husband back in January?"

"Let me check my notes," I said, flipping open an imaginary notepad. "Let's see . . . Curtis was an angel, he helped so many people, everybody loved him . . . Nothing about his loving wife trying to whack him."

"It could have slipped her mind. Get Selma Kaplan on the phone and ask her to find out if Brooke Hellman has been cutting checks to any contract killers lately."

"You know she's going to push back," I said, dialing Selma's mobile and putting the call on speaker.

"They all push back—the DA, the PC, the mayor. But isn't it comforting to know that if anything happens to you and me there are so many people in the system who can do our jobs better than we can?"

Selma picked up on the first ring.

"It's Zach and Kylie," I said. "We need you to do a deep dive on Brooke Hellman's financial records for us."

"I'll get right on it," she said. "As soon as I'm ready to cut my career short."

"Selma," Kylie said. "We know Brooke has got a hot line to Gracie

Mansion, but we have reliable information that says she may have financed both hits to gain control of the entire Hellman empire."

"How reliable?"

"Reliable enough that Zach and I are willing to put our asses on the line."

"Your asses are your business. I'm trying to protect mine," Selma said. "Have you met my boss? He's a professional politician. He gets real cranky when people don't vote for him, and guess who gets the brunt of it?"

"Tell your boss that on January nineteenth, Curtis Hellman had a near-death experience," Kylie said. "An overdose of insulin. A friend called 911, and they took him to Columbia Presbyterian. The details are sketchy, but it sounds more like attempted homicide than a self-inflicted wound."

"And you think Brooke was behind it?"

"She had a multimillion-dollar motive, and as far as we can tell, she's the only one who had the means."

Selma took a deep breath and exhaled audibly. "I have a court date at nine tomorrow morning," she said. "But my team can dig up a lot before then. How early can you meet me in my office?"

"Sunrise," Kylie said.

"Make it seven a.m.," Selma said.

We hung up.

"I think we've done enough for one shift," Kylie said. "Let's get some dinner."

"There's a great little pizza place on Twenty-First and Lex," I said.

"*Pizza?* After the day we just put in, we are not wrapping it up with a couple of slices, some garlic knots, and a Coke. We deserve a real dining experience."

"We also deserve a good night's sleep," I said, "and if we're meeting Selma at seven in the morning, we should get going on that."

"Sleep? Jesus, what happened to the Zach I used to know back in the day? Work, eat, drink, work some more—sleep was always an afterthought."

I smiled. *Back in the day.* Kylie and I were both starting out at the Academy. She had just dumped her drug addict boyfriend, and I caught her on the rebound. We went from zero to Mach one in a heartbeat, and I was positive that we'd be together for the rest of our lives. But twenty-eight days after it all began, Spence Harrington got out of rehab and begged her for one more chance. A year later, they were married.

Ten years after that, life took a strange turn. Kylie and I wound up as partners, Spence relapsed, and their marriage crashed and burned. At this point, our love affair was a fond but distant memory. But some things never changed—like the devilish look on Kylie's face when she was taking over my life.

"Here's the deal," she said. "There will be absolutely no pizza. There will be some sleep. But there will be plenty of good food and lots of laughs. We're having dinner at Shane's place."

Shane's place was Farm to Fork, a restaurant that had opened only a few weeks earlier but now had a thirty-day waiting list to get a table.

Unless, of course, you were dating the owner, Chef Shane Talbot.

Shane was the new man in Kylie's life. He'd recently moved from Houston, and his new restaurant was winning the hearts, minds, and palates of New York's most critical foodies. He was on the verge of becoming the city's next celebrity chef, but he didn't fit the mold. There were no reports of histrionics or other culinary artists' tantrums coming from his kitchen. Shane Talbot knew how to roll with the punches—an excellent quality for any man in a relationship with Kylie.

"I texted Shane an hour ago," she added, "and as booked up as they are, he promised that a table will magically open up when we get there."

"Okay, but I'm not going to sit there and watch you and Shane eye-fucking each other all night. I'm calling Cheryl and telling her to meet us."

"Don't bother. She's on the way. I already texted her."

"You texted? Y'know, I realize you barely have a passing regard for boundaries, but don't you think I should be the one to invite my own girlfriend to dinner?"

"Don't be so possessive. Cheryl may be your girlfriend, but she's also a friend of mine *and* a coworker, and she's Shane's cousin. Any one of us could've invited her."

"I get it, but you could have asked me."

"I would have," Kylie said, "but you were too busy eye-fucking Megan Rollins."

I turned toward the window and put my hand over my mouth to cover the grin that was spreading over my face.

That's two more things about Kylie that have never changed. She never gives up on an argument until she's had the last word. And she loves to plan other people's lives. Whether they ask for her help or not.

CHAPTER 15

THE RESTAURANT was on Bank Street in the West Village. It was a warm July evening, and patrons who were lucky enough to score a reservation spilled out onto the sidewalk, drinks in hand, chattering away as they waited for their names to be called.

We didn't have to wait. As soon as we approached the front door, Nico, the manager, spotted us. "Kylie! Zach!" he boomed. "Welcome back."

After chasing bad guys for more than twelve hours, we were dog-tired, rumpled, and as far from downtown chic as you can get. And yet, we appeared to be restaurant royalty. Shit like that drives the New York glitterati crazy. Nico added to our mystique with a double-clasp handshake for me and a cheek-to-cheek air kiss for Kylie. I could feel the undercurrent of *who the fuck are those two?* in the air.

Let them wonder.

"Is Cheryl here?" I asked.

"Not yet," Nico said.

"I'll wait for her out front," I said.

Nico escorted Kylie to a table, and I stepped out to the center of the road so I could get an unobstructed view of the billowy swaths of red, orange, and gold as the sun slowly splashed down on the Hudson.

A few minutes later, a cab pulled up to the restaurant, and Cheryl emerged. Men unabashedly turned to check her out, starting as they invariably do, from the neck down. Women were subtler but just as curious about this raven-haired, brown-eyed beauty with the flawless caramel skin. On the outside, Cheryl has the smoldering Latina looks of her Puerto Rican grandmother. But that's just a genetic anomaly. In truth, most of her DNA is pure Irish, with roots that go back to the auld sod.

She beamed when she saw me, and I felt the same rush I get every time I see her. How did I get this lucky?

"How's the case going?" she whispered in my ear as she leaned in to kiss me.

Most detectives can't share the details of their work with their girlfriend. But that's not an issue for us. Cheryl is a cop doc—Dr. Cheryl Robinson, a psychologist with the department. She works with Kylie and me.

"I think we just caught a break," I said. "I'll know more tomorrow."

"And how is my little project going?" she said.

Her little project. A month ago, Cheryl's aunt Janet called and begged a favor. Her son Shane was thirty-five years old, but he was too busy cooking for people to settle down and procreate. Aunt Janet's instructions were simple and to the point: "Find your cousin a nice girl. I want grandbabies."

Cheryl decided that the most Shane-worthy woman she knew was Kylie. It took a bit of coaxing because Kylie was still digging out of the rubble of her failed marriage, but eventually she agreed. As soon as she said yes, Cheryl backed off. As she put it, "I wasn't about to screw things up by telling her Aunt Janet would like to know where you stand on the reproductive process."

"Your project seems to be going well," I said. "Even if no progeny result from this alliance, at least we have a backstage pass to the hottest restaurant in town."

Nico ushered us to a quiet booth in the back, where Shane, still in his chef's whites, was sitting with Kylie. As soon as he saw us, he stood up. Unlike his cousin, Shane had the red hair, blue eyes, and fair skin of his Irish ancestry. He kissed Cheryl, gave me a bro hug, and signaled to his wait staff. "I didn't know what you were in the mood for," he said, "but Kylie said you guys were starved, so I told the kitchen to surprise us with some of everything and keep it coming till we beg for mercy."

Wine was poured, and the first of many little tasting plates arrived.

"I know you can't say much about the Hellman murders," Shane said as soon as we started eating, "but Curtis Hellman and his wife had dinner here last week."

"Wow," Kylie said. "Are you serious?"

"Yeah. Just the two of them. They sat over there," he said, pointing. "In Rebecca's station."

"Do you know how much he tipped her?" Kylie asked.

"No, but I can check the credit card records. Why do you ask?"

Kylie looked left, then right, and then edged closer to him, her face and body language all business. "Because," she said in a near whisper, "if the son of a bitch stiffed her, Rebecca is definitely a suspect."

She nailed us all. Me included.

"So I guess," Shane said when he stopped laughing, "you're not willing to discuss the case."

"Correct," Kylie said.

"Even though I bought you dinner."

"If you're trying to bribe me," Kylie said, flirting with him over a forkful of sautéed zucchini ribbons, "you're going to have to do a lot more than buy me dinner."

I didn't hear Shane's reply. I was too busy looking at Cheryl, who was clearly enjoying how well her little project was going.

Not only was Shane a brilliant chef, he knew how to orchestrate a tasting menu. Each little plate was better than the one before it, and by the time the two-bite lollipop lamb chops infused with rosemary and garlic arrived, I publicly thanked Kylie for saving me from ending another long day with pepperoni pizza.

Fifteen minutes later, my phone vibrated, and even before I looked at the caller ID, I instinctively knew that my long day was about to get longer.

"Sorry," I said, taking the call.

"Zach, it's Buddy Henry from the Two-Four."

Kylie looked at me and mouthed the words *who is it?*

"One of the detectives from the jogging path this morning." I went back to the call. "I'm still with my partner. What have you got?"

"We've got a possible witness to the stabbing. Cardona and I addressed the four-to-twelve roll call and asked them to touch base with their park regulars. Two of our uniforms just brought in a homeless guy who saw a man covered in blood run into a pedestrian tunnel and clean himself off."

"When?"

"He says it was about eleven o'clock this morning."

"Where is the tunnel?"

"A Hundredth Street. Two blocks from the crime scene."

"So far, that's right on the money. Where's your witness?"

"Right here at the precinct."

"Kylie and I will be there in twenty minutes. Till then, keep him happy: burgers, pizza, soft drinks, candy bars, cigarettes—whatever he wants."

"We already fed him. He's incredibly low maintenance. All he wanted was a couple of spring rolls, some beef with broccoli, and hot tea."

"He sounds promising," I said.

"Better than that," Henry said. "Cardona and I interviewed him. He didn't witness the stabbing, but he got a really good look at the man who was wiping off the bloodstains."

"Fantastic. See if you can line up a sketch artist so we can get a poster out there."

"Not necessary, Zach. After he finished his dinner, he asked for a pad and some pencils. This guy is an artist. He's working on a sketch of the perp as we speak."

CHAPTER 16

THE HOMELESS MAY BE the most misunderstood, most misjudged community in New York.

Yes, some of them have addiction problems, some of them have hygiene issues, and none of them have permanent addresses, but those are their circumstances, not who they are.

They're homeless, not worthless. Certainly not to the police. In a city filled with self-absorbed people racing through life, phones pressed to their ears, oblivious to the world around them, the homeless are our invisible watchdogs, quietly observing, processing, and sometimes even putting their lives on the line by rushing in to break up a mugging or a rape.

Our witness stood up as soon as Kylie and I entered the room. He was about sixty, tall, gangly, clean-shaven, with clothes that were worn but relatively clean. I'd seen millennials with Apple watches dressed far more shabbily.

"Good evening, Detectives," he said, his voice warm and amiable, with a distinct Jamaican lilt. "I am Izaak Weathers. My friends call me Ike."

We introduced ourselves, sat down, and asked him if there was anything he needed before we started.

"No, thank you, I'm fine. The other detectives bought me dinner.

A few months ago, I sold my computer; otherwise, I'd give this place a stellar review on Yelp." He laughed to make sure we knew he was joking.

But it was more than a joke. He wanted us to know that not too long ago he had a computer on his desk, a roof over his head—a life.

Not to be heartless about it, but Kylie and I didn't care. All we wanted from Izaak were the details of what he had seen. But if it turned out to be a solid lead, we'd need him again to identify a suspect, and maybe again to testify in court. We were on the verge of a possible long-term relationship with this man, and he'd feel better about going forward with it if we gave him his moment of dignity.

"I'm new at this homeless business," he said. "For the past eight years, I was working for a retired history professor, Lloyd Braithwaite. He had Parkinson's and couldn't manage on his own, so he hired me to live in. It was a little apartment on West Ninety-Fourth, but it's all we needed. At first, I just cooked and shopped and took him to medical appointments, but after a while, we became good friends. We'd have a beer, watch a ball game, play chess, talk into the wee hours . . . What do they call it these days? A bromance."

He sat back and sighed. "I'm sorry," he said. "That's not what you came to talk about."

"No, please, finish," Kylie said.

"Anyway, Lloyd passed in February. He didn't have a lot of money, but I was happy with room, board, and whatever he paid me. Problem is, when he died, I didn't have enough put away to get a place of my own, and with all due respect to Mayor Sykes, the city's men's shelters are not for me. So now I'm on my own, but I know in my heart that God has more information than I do, and there must be a reason why I'm out there on the streets. I'm hoping that maybe if I can help you find the person who killed Mr. Curtis Hellman, then I'll understand what the Good Lord was planning for me."

"Thank you," Kylie said. "Why don't you tell us what you saw."

"There's a pedestrian tunnel in the park near where the murder took place. I was about twenty feet away, lying down on the grass. It's one of the perks of my new lifestyle—stretch out whenever and wherever you can. I was looking up at the heavens when this man came into the tunnel. I heard him before I saw him, because his footsteps reverberated against the walls. And then he stopped. He didn't come out the other side. Now I'm curious, so I sit up and take a look, and I see that he's covered in blood."

"You're sure it was blood?" Kylie said.

"He's wearing a black shirt and shorts, so it's hard to spot it on his clothes, but he's a white dude, and his face, his arms, his legs are smeared with red. I figure it's either blood or my grandma Leola's raspberry preserves." He hesitated. "I'm sorry if I sound irreverent, but Lloyd and I always used to crack wise when things got real serious. It takes the edge off things."

Kylie rewarded him with a dazzling smile. "It's your story, Ike," she said. "You tell it your way."

"Thanks. Anyway, this fellow, he's shorter than me, maybe five-nine. He's got a backpack, and he takes this envelope out of it. It's black with a light-blue logo on it, which is too far away to read. He rips open the envelope and pulls out something I've never seen before. You know those disposable moist towelettes that come in little packages? You open them up, and they're saturated with some kind of cleaner. They give them to you in Chinese restaurants so you can wipe down your hands and face after you finish eating spare ribs."

"Wet Wipes," I said.

"Exactly. Only this isn't one of those little-bitty things. He unfolded it. It's big as a beach towel, and he starts wiping himself down. My first thought is, I want to ask him where I can get me some of those. It's not a hot shower, but it's doing a darn good job of getting him clean. My second thought is, it's not too bright to start asking questions of a stranger who's washing blood off himself."

"Was your third thought to call the police?" Kylie asked.

"And say what? 'I just saw a fellow in the park wiping blood off him'? It's not a crime. No, ma'am, I couldn't go to the cops, so I did the next best thing. I studied his face. I figured if he is a troublemaker, the cops will come looking for anyone who could describe him. And sure enough, they did."

"Detective Henry told us you're an artist and you were making a sketch of him for us," I said.

He laughed. "Van Gogh was an artist. Michelangelo was an artist. My countryman Albert Huie was an artist. I'm just a guy with a pad and some pencils who can cobble together a reasonable likeness of someone if I put my mind to it."

"Can we see what you've done?" Kylie asked.

His pad was on the table. He turned it over to reveal a portrait that was as detailed and nuanced as the best police sketch I'd ever seen. But it wasn't the artistry that blew me away. It was the suspect—deep wrinkles around his eyes and mouth, sagging jowls, a disappearing jawline, and a pronounced turkey neck.

"Ike," I said without taking my eyes off the drawing. "How *old* is this guy?"

"Late sixties," he said. "Pretty close to seventy."

"Are you sure he's *this* old?" I said.

"I know what you're thinking, Detective," Ike said. "He looks more like somebody's grandfather than a madman who stabs joggers in the park. But I saw this fellow up close. He can move like an athlete, but he can't hide the age of his face."

"This is excellent, Ike," Kylie said. "You certainly did put your mind to it."

"It's not exactly ready to hang in the Met, but this is your guy," he said. "I'm sure of it."

We thanked him and went back out to talk to Henry and Cardona.

"We've sealed off the tunnel, and our guys are spraying it with luminol," Cardona said. "If we find any blood, we'll see if we can get a match with the victim."

"How'd our witness do with the sketch?" Henry asked.

I handed it to him.

"Damn," he said. "Don't these hit men have a mandatory retirement age?"

"He looks a lot like Father Dominick at my church," Cardona said. "Or maybe Mr. Porzuczek from the butcher shop. He's really handy with a knife."

"At least, he looks like a real person," Henry said. "I've seen police sketches that look like they were drawn by a first-grader. All they need is a refrigerator magnet."

"I've never made a single arrest based on a sketch," Kylie said. "But this is a big help. We knew both of our killers were pros. Now we know that at least one of them is an *old* pro."

"Yeah, but it puts us in a real bind," Cardona said.

"What do you mean?" I asked.

"We better find this old codger in a big hurry," she said, flashing me a grin. "Before he dies of natural causes."

CHAPTER 17

IT WAS AFTER ELEVEN when I got to Cheryl's place. We have separate apartments, but more often than not we cohabit, and this was one of those nights I didn't want to go to bed alone. She was sitting on the sofa doing the *New York Times* crossword puzzle.

"What's a five-letter word for hardworking cop desirous of physical intimacy?" I said, leaning over and giving her a long, hungry kiss.

She waved her hand and pointed at the armchair—the universal sign for *you're not getting laid till we talk*.

I plopped down in the chair.

"How'd it go with your witness?" she asked.

"He was solid and gave us an amazingly detailed sketch."

"I had a long talk with Shane after you left," she said.

My first clue. We were going to be talking about her little project.

"How'd that go?" I said. "By now Shane must be getting used to Kylie walking out in the middle of a date."

"Oh, he's not only used to it. He thinks that bolting from the room to fight crime is just another fascinating layer of this high-octane hotheaded, gun-toting, up-for-anything mystery woman he's dating."

"Did he elaborate on *up-for-anything*?" I asked, leering salaciously.

She ignored my frat-boy humor. "Shane is smitten," she said. "There's only one problem."

"All relationships have problems," I said. "Take us, for instance. I put in a long hard day at work, I come home exhausted, and you don't even crack a smile at my up-for-anything joke."

She cracked a smile. It was genuine.

"That's better," I said. "Now, what's Shane's problem?"

"Spence."

"What about Spence?"

"In case you've forgotten, Kylie is still married to him."

"*Legally* married to him. There's a difference."

"Correct me if I'm wrong, Zach, but 'legally' is the very essence of the definition of the word 'marriage.'"

"And your point is . . .?"

"My point? Shane is falling hard for a married woman, and that's unnerving, to put it mildly. What happens to him if Spence decides to come back?"

"You can tell Shane that if Spence ever shows up again, Kylie will get a lawyer and pull the plug on the marriage."

"Are you sure? Because that hasn't been her MO in the past."

"Ouch," I said.

"I'm sorry, babe. That came out wrong."

"No, it came out right. Twelve years ago, Kylie and I were going at it hot and heavy. Spence suddenly showed up with his hat and his one-month clean-and-sober chip in hand, and bam—it's goodbye, Zachary; hello, Mrs. Spencer Harrington."

"That's where I was going with this," she said. "I don't want Shane to be the next stopgap boyfriend for Kylie while she's waiting for Spence to come home."

"Gosh, I never thought of myself as a *stopgap boyfriend*, but thank you for enlightening me, doctor. This session is really helping me deal with my low-self-esteem issues."

"Zach, I'm trying to have a serious conversation."

"Then start off by taking a serious look at your flawed analogy. How can you compare what's going on today with something that happened a lifetime ago? Back then Kylie and I were two young kids in the Academy.

We ignited in an instant, and as soon as the first love of her life reappeared, we crashed and burned like the *Hindenburg*. She's changed since the Dark Ages. She's a card-carrying adult now, and she's not going to buy Spence's bullshit if he comes back yet again and swears that this time he's changed for good."

She looked at me, her dark eyes intense. "Don't . . . be . . . so . . . sure," she said, her tone filled with purpose. "Do you have any idea how many cops I've talked to who keep going back to their same toxic relationships because they think that this time they can make it work?"

"No."

"Lots."

"Male cops or female cops?"

"Both, but it skews more toward women. They go back because they think this time they're going to get it right. Or they feel guilty because they've decided that they didn't try hard enough the last time around."

"And how many of these women have met a great guy like Shane and still go back anyway?"

"Kylie met you, and she went back to Spence."

"At the risk of repeating myself, ouch."

"I don't mean to open up an old wound, but did you ever stop to think that maybe Kylie went back to Spence because you *were* a great guy? I know it's difficult to understand, but some people actually get off on the pain and the instability of an unhealthy relationship. It's familiar. It's what they know."

I sat there in silence.

"I'm sorry," she said. "Professional hazard. I think like a shrink."

"Not always," I said. "You think like a shrink when you're dealing with your patients. But this time, you're thinking like the person who set Shane and Kylie up at the behest of your aunt Janet. I know how much she would like her world populated with lots of little Shanes, and if it happens, it happens. But until then, here's my *unprofessional* opinion. Tell Aunt Janet that her baby boy is a grown-ass man now. It's time for her to let him make his own damn life decisions. And as for you, you did your part. Stop second-guessing yourself, and let Kylie and Shane work this weird fucking relationship out on their own."

"Wow," she said. "Are we having a healthy discussion, or are we fighting?"

"I don't know what you call it, but I sure as hell hope it's a fight."

She smiled. "Are you serious? You *hope* it's a fight? Why?"

"Because, Dr. Robinson, healthy discussions don't end in hot, crazy, mind-blowing makeup sex."

She stood up. Even at this hour, with no makeup and wearing shorts and one of my old shirts, she was absolutely breathtaking to look at.

"In that case, Detective Jordan," she said, unbuttoning her shirt and walking toward the bedroom, "this session is officially over."

CHAPTER 18

AT SEVEN the next morning, Kylie and I were in Selma Kaplan's office. The two of us looked worn out but happy. For the same reason, I suspect. I didn't ask.

Selma got right to it.

"I woke up yesterday morning thinking I was going to send Warren Hellman to prison," she said. "A few hours later, justice takes it up the wazoo, there's a shooting outside my courthouse, and suddenly I'm dedicating my life to finding the people who killed a cop killer and his equally soulless brother who let an innocent young girl die on a godforsaken desert road.

"And then you two top off my evening by telling me that Brooke Hellman, the one person who my boss, your boss, and the entire city's boss wants us to tiptoe around, may have funded both murders. So if I seemed a little cranky when you called last night, that ought to explain it."

To some, that might have sounded like an apology. Kylie and I knew better. Selma Kaplan is the first to own her mistakes, but she has never once apologized for her born-and-bred-in-New-York approach.

"I don't know who your source is," Selma said, "but he, she, or it is someone you should cultivate. When you first said Curtis OD'd on insulin, I thought, hell, that shit happens all the time. There's no doctor, no nurse involved. The man administers his own shots. Nobody's fault but his own if there's too much insulin in the syringe. Turns out there's a lot more to it than that. Not only are there different brands of insulin from different pharmaceutical companies, but there are different strengths."

She brought up a Google Images page on her computer. It was filled with pictures of insulin vials.

"This is the U-100 dose," she said, tapping a finger on the screen. "U-100 is the go-to insulin for the majority of diabetics, and according to the report the ME got from Columbia Presbyterian, it's the one Curtis Hellman has been using all his life."

She pointed to a second vial and clicked on it. Another page came up. The headline said "U-500: Not For Ordinary Use."

"This is the U-500," she said. "It's five times more potent than what Curtis needed. It could have killed him, and yet he injected it into his own arm. So your first question is going to be, was he trying to kill himself, or was somebody trying to do it for him?"

"Hopefully, you have the answer," Kylie said.

"We got lucky," Selma said. "The paramedic who answered the 911 call grabbed the vial and the syringe that Curtis had used. The label said U-100, but when they sent the insulin to the lab it turned out to be U-500. The hospital immediately called the FDA, because if the drug company was putting the wrong label on a dose that would be deadly for most people, the feds can shut them down immediately."

"Clearly that didn't happen," Kylie said, "or it would have been front-page news."

"Exactly," Selma said. "The FDA determined that the bottle labeled U-100 was from one drug company, and the U-500 insulin that was inside was a proprietary formula from a different company."

"So our source was right," I said. "Somebody switched the insulin and tried to kill him."

"That's what it looks like," Selma said.

"Was it reported?" Kylie asked.

"No. The FDA contacted Curtis. They were trying to ascertain where along the chain from manufacturer to injection the compromise occurred, but he refused to cooperate, so they dropped it."

"Just like that? No investigation?"

"It's not their job. Once they determined that the drug companies were not at fault, Curtis's overdose was no longer their problem. I read their summation. The doctor who wrote it cautioned that it could have been an attempted homicide, but it also could have been attempted suicide, and it's possible that Hellman was too embarrassed to talk about it."

"Somebody should tell that doctor to stick to medicine, because he sucks at criminology," Kylie said. "If Curtis wanted to punch his own ticket, he'd have injected the superstrength shit into his body straight from the U-500 vial. He wouldn't go through the trouble of transferring it to a low-octane bottle."

"But somebody did," I said. "And if the paramedic hadn't brought that vial in to be analyzed, it would probably have gotten lost."

"More like Brooke would have destroyed it as soon as she got home," Kylie said.

"Slow down," Selma said. "Last night, you said Brooke was the only one who had the means."

"That's what our source told us."

"Oh, really? I can just hear Sonia Blakely now. 'Your source, Detective? Did you ask your source if the Hellmans have a maid? Does your source know how many days or weeks the insulin was sitting around the house? Did any guests drop by during that time? And who delivered it from the pharmacy? Did the doorman sign for it?' I'm sorry, guys, but unless I can prove that Brooke Hellman had *exclusive access* to that vial, we don't have a case."

"Let's talk about motive," I said. "Two dead brothers, a shit ton of money. Who gets it all?"

"The wills haven't been filed yet, so nothing is official, but I made a few calls," Selma said. "With Warren and Curtis both gone, the entire company, which is valued at a half billion or more, all goes to Brooke."

"Bingo," Kylie said.

"Not so fast. That may be a motive for *me* to kill somebody, but Brooke already has more money than she needs. She had a hefty stockpile when she met Curtis. Since they've been married, she's added to her own personal wealth, and looking at her credit card and checking transactions, she's pampered and well cared for. Her husband didn't deny her anything. If we try to convince a jury that she farmed out a double homicide for money, we will be laughed out of 100 Centre Street. Sonia Blakely beat us when we had all the answers. If we're going up against her a second time, we better have all our ducks in—"

Kylie's phone rang, cutting Selma off. It wasn't her standard ringtone. It was the one I knew she'd set up for Shane.

"Sorry," she said. "It's my . . ." She decided not to finish the sentence. "Sorry, Selma. I'll make it quick."

"Go ahead, take it," Selma said.

She stood up, turned away from Selma, and answered the call. "Hey, babe, I'm in the middle of a meeting, and I really can't—" She stopped. Her tone changed. "Yes, this is Kylie MacDonald."

She put her hand to her mouth. "Oh, my God. Is he okay?"

Selma and I could hear only one side of the conversation, and we were doing our best to fill in the blanks.

"I'm a detective with Red," Kylie said. "Don't sugarcoat it for me. I want to know what happened. Break it down for me."

Kylie lowered herself back into her chair as she listened, her body shaking. "Where is he now? Thank you, Detective Edlund. I'm on my way. I'll be there as soon as I can."

"What's going on?" I said as soon as she hung up.

She was trembling, fighting tears. "It's Shane. He's been shot. He's in surgery at Lincoln Hospital."

CHAPTER 19

"I'M DRIVING," I said as we sprinted to the car.

Kylie didn't argue. She tossed me the keys.

I got behind the wheel, and Kylie reached for the lights and sirens, which is justified only when a cop is racing to respond to an incident in progress. This was definitely not that.

"Fuck the rules," she said, flipping them on. "Boyfriend emergency."

"What do you know?" I asked, making a hard left onto White Street.

"Not a hell of a lot. Even though I told the guy I was a cop, you know the drill, Zach. He's not going to give up anything to me on the phone. All I know is, Shane was at the Hunts Point Market picking out vegetables. Somebody walked up to him and shot him. He took a bullet to the chest."

"Just him? Nobody else was shot?"

"No. Shane was the target."

"And the shooter?"

"Fled the scene. Got away," she said. "But we'll get him. We will absolutely track the fucker down and bring him in."

No, we wouldn't. Somebody would, but it wouldn't be us. Kylie knew that, but she's always been quick to break the rules when they get in her way.

Thirty minutes later, we rolled up to the busiest emergency room in the city. Lincoln Hospital in the Bronx. Two detectives were wait-ing for us.

"Steve Edlund from the Four-One. I spoke to you on the phone. This is my partner, Dave McDaniel."

"How is he?" Kylie asked.

"He was conscious and alert when they brought him in," Edlund said. "Unlocked his phone for us; told us to call you. And you know these docs here at Lincoln. Give 'em a gunshot, and they'll give you a miracle."

It was a bit of an overstatement, but it was just the kind of pep talk Kylie needed to give Edlund what he was looking for—her undivided attention.

She let out a sigh of relief. "Thanks," she said. "Whatever I can do to help. What went down?"

"Mr. Talbot was at the produce market at Hunts Point," Edlund said. "I'm sure you know the place—over a million square feet, and it's crawling with people at that ungodly hour of the morning. Greengro-cers, restaurateurs, buyers from the big chain stores."

"Did any of those people see the shooting?" Kylie asked.

"The 911 caller said it came out of nowhere. The shooter just walked up to Mr. Talbot, shot him point-blank, and took off," Edlund said.

"We have a dozen uniforms there now, trying to round up witnesses before they disappear," McDaniel said. "We came directly here to see if we could get a statement from the vic—sorry, Mr. Talbot."

"What'd he say?" Kylie asked.

"He couldn't really speak. He managed to get out 'Never saw him before in my life.'"

"That and 'Call Kylie,'" Edlund said. "What can you tell us?"

"Shane moved up here from Houston and opened a restaurant in the West Village," Kylie said. "A mutual friend thought we'd hit it off, and she was right. It's been pretty intense, so I may not know a lot about him, but I'll tell you everything I can."

"What do you know about his personal life?"

Kylie shrugged. "Never married. So no ex-wife, no kids."

"What about ex-girlfriends?" McDaniel said.

"Oh, God, I know these fucking questions, because I've asked them a thousand times," Kylie said. "In fact, they're the same questions I asked myself on the ride over."

"They suck," McDaniel said, "but we appreciate that you understand why we've got to ask."

"Shane is a sweet guy from a nice family. As far as I know, there are no acrimonious girlfriends, no jealous husbands, no disgruntled employees. The biggest drama in his life is when a soufflé falls."

"When did you last speak with him?" Edlund said.

"We spent the night together at my place. He was in a great mood. He got up at four thirty this morning and drove to the market."

"Is that his normal routine?"

"Not every day. Maybe three or four times a week. He loves that place. He could probably have one of his people do it for him, but it's his restaurant, his signature, so he handpicks all the produce that goes into his kitchen."

So far, Kylie hadn't given anything to go on, and the four of us knew it.

"Look, we're still trying to put the pieces together," Edlund said, "but the one thing we do know is that this wasn't random. Mr. Talbot was singled out. We've got to find the connection between him and the shooter."

"What about his business?" McDaniel said. "Opening a new restaurant in this city is a major crapshoot. Was he having any problems in that area?"

"Shane's biggest problem right now is that everybody loves what he puts on the table," Kylie said. "The place is booked. There's a waiting list to get a reservation. And it's not just the business that's doing well. People love the man. Shane is not one of those arrogant, narcissistic, micromanaging chef bullies. His staff loves working with him, he takes the time to circulate and chat with his customers, the critics rave about him—"

"But one man tried to kill him," Edlund said. "I'm sorry for your pain, Detective MacDonald, but we know who you are, and we will do everything we can to find the person who—"

"Steve," McDaniel said, gesturing to the black SUV that just pulled up onto the sidewalk. "Captain's here."

Kylie is not a big fan of authority. She turned to Edlund. "Do we like him?"

"Captain Graham?" Edlund said. "Everybody likes him. He was only thirty-two when they put him in charge of the detective squads in three precincts in the South Bronx. Couldn't ask for a better boss."

Graham looked like a young Kevin Bacon. He extended his hand and introduced himself by name. Tony Graham. No mention of rank.

"Sorry to meet you under these circumstances," he said. "But we'll be all over this case. I'm glad these guys caught it. They're my go-to team in the Four-One. I promise you, the two of them will crack this."

"The *four* of us will crack it," Kylie said.

Edlund and McDaniel were new to Kylie's in-your-face style, and I could sense them cringe imperceptibly.

"I appreciate the offer, Kylie," Graham said, "but I'm going to have to give you a hard no on that one."

"It wasn't an offer," Kylie said. "I want in."

"Listen, I know how you feel—"

"With all due respect, sir," Kylie snapped, her tone dripping with disrespect, "someone I care deeply about is on the operating table with a bullet in his chest. You have *no idea* what I'm feeling right now."

"Step over here, Detective," Graham said.

She followed him to a spot about forty feet away.

"I guess he *is* a decent guy," I said. "Most captains would tear her a new one in front of the entire squad."

"Oh, he's not going to dress her down," Edlund said. "Not even in private. He's going to tell her a little story, and she's going to apologize and back off."

I grinned. "You don't know my partner."

"You don't know the story. Three years ago, there was an armed robbery at a jewelry store on Burnside Avenue. The owner had been robbed twice before, and he was damned if he'd let it happen again. He pulled a gun from behind the counter. The perp had a semiautomatic, opened fire, grabbed what he could, and ran. When the dust settled, the owner was dead, and a young couple who had come in to buy an engagement ring were both wounded. The male died en route to the ER. The girl lived but she's in a wheelchair for the rest of her life."

I knew where this was going. "And there was a connection to Captain Graham?" I asked.

"She's his sister. Graham was hell-bent for justice—ready to hunt the motherfucker down. But his boss had the talk with him. Nothing hurts a prosecution more than a cop with an axe to grind. Those are the cases that get shredded at trial. Tony stepped aside, and two days later Dave and I collared the perp. He's having that same talk with your partner, and I guarantee you he'll promise her that this unit will treat her boyfriend like he's one of our own."

Kylie and Graham were out of earshot, but I watched their body language. I could see her face soften as the anger dissipated.

Finally, Graham put his hand out. Kylie took it, and then, totally out of character, her face somber, she wrapped her other arm around him and hugged him.

It wasn't hard to see why Tony Graham made captain at thirty-two.

CHAPTER 20

I CALLED CHERYL. Her first response was the same as ours. Who would want to kill Shane?

"I can be there in forty-five minutes," she said.

"We have enough people pacing the floor here as it is," I said. "Kylie and I will wait till he's out of surgery, but then we've got to get back to work. Why don't you hold off for a few hours."

"Okay. I have to tell Aunt Janet," she said, "but I'm not going to call her till you get back to me with some good news."

The good news came ninety minutes later. Edlund, McDaniel, Kylie, and I were all in the waiting room when the woman who operated on Shane entered.

Dr. June Lu was a short, good-natured, gray-haired woman of indeterminate age who had come to America from China as a teenager, gone to Harvard Medical School, and nearly half a century later was still saving lives every day. She was also the most joyful trauma surgeon I've ever met.

"Four cops for one bullet?" she said in mock surprise. "I'm happy Mr. Talbot made it. Otherwise, I'd be in big trouble." She flashed us one of her infectious smiles.

"Good to see you again, Doc," Edlund said. "Dave and I are handling the case. I guess you've met Kylie and Zach before."

Dr. Lu rolled her eyes. "Many times. Too many, I'm afraid, but you know what they say, four detectives are better than two."

"Two *detectives*," Edlund said, pointing to himself and McDaniel. Then he nodded at Kylie and me to make sure the cast of characters was properly identified. "Two *friends* of the victim."

Dr. Lu, never one to equivocate, grinned at Kylie. "New man in your life, Detective?"

Kylie shrugged and answered the question with a sly nod.

"Good for you," Dr. Lu said. "He's a good-looking fellow and very, very lucky. The bullet caught him square in the sternum." She tapped her chest. "A little bit to the left, a little bit to the right, and it could have ripped him up inside and killed him. But it didn't penetrate the chest cavity. It lodged in the chest wall. Made my job very, very easy. But the hospital doesn't care. Easy, hard—makes no difference. I still get credit for the win."

She pumped a fist in the air, and the four of us couldn't help but laugh. Anyone watching us from afar would never guess we were there to talk about an attempted homicide.

"You've got the round?" Edlund asked.

She held up a plastic specimen cup. Inside was a mushroomed bullet.

"Looks to me like a 9mm," Dr. Lu said, handing it over to Edlund. "But I could be wrong."

McDaniel glanced at me knowingly. Dr. Lu had never been wrong in the past.

"What's the prognosis?" Kylie said.

"A hundred percent chance he will recover and make you happy for the rest of your life."

"Slow down, June girl," Kylie said. "I hardly know him."

Dr. Lu peered over her rimless glasses and wagged a finger. "That's not what I saw in your eyes when I gave you the good news."

"Can we see him?" Kylie asked.

"Two minutes for friends. Five minutes for police. He needs rest. Also, I have him on a hydrocodone drip for the pain, so he may be a little loopy. Best to save the important questions for tomorrow. Good luck," she said, and scurried down the corridor to save more lives and spread her special brand of joy.

The four of us entered Shane's room. His face lit up when he saw Kylie. "Thanks for coming," he said. "Did you catch the guy?"

"Not yet," she said, leaning over and kissing him. "But we will."

Edlund cleared his throat.

"Sorry," Kylie said, stepping away from the bed. "*They* will." She turned back to Edlund. "Can I at least ask him what happened? You know, asking for a friend."

"I'll ask," Edlund said. "You can listen. Can you tell us what happened, Mr. Talbot?"

"I'm not sure," Shane said. "I was checking out a crate of eggplants. I lifted my head up to order some, and I saw this man standing eight, maybe ten feet away with a gun pointing straight at me."

"When you're up to it," Edlund said, "we'd like to get you together with a sketch artist."

"He was white, about my age, but beyond that, I don't think I'll be much help. All I could see was that gun. My brain, my body—everything froze. And then . . . bang!"

"Did he say anything before he pulled the trigger?" Kylie blurted out.

I could see the look of exasperation on both Edlund's and McDaniel's faces. Kylie was pushing the envelope, but they let it go.

Shane caught it too. He winked at the two cops, then turned to Kylie. "Yeah, babe. I'm pretty sure he said, 'Thirty dollars for a bowl of linguini with white clam sauce? You're gonna die, motherfucker.'"

Kylie flipped him the bird. Edlund, McDaniel, and I all cracked up. It's a rare moment to watch my partner get her comeuppance.

"Your two minutes are up, *friends*," McDaniel said. "Time to go."

"Wait. Hold on," Shane said. He buried his head in one hand and massaged his forehead with his thumb and forefinger. I had seen it before. Victims can sometimes be so overwhelmed by the trauma that they let the little details fade. But when you're a cop, there are no *little* details. We stood in silence as Shane tried to pull a critical memory from his drug-altered brain.

"Fuck!" he said, his head snapping up quickly. "He *did* say something. It made no sense, so I guess I didn't process it."

"What did he say?" Kylie asked.

"'Hell hath no fury.'"

"Hell hath no fury," Kylie repeated. "You mean 'hell hath no fury like a woman scorned'?"

"He didn't say 'like a woman scorned,'" Shane said. "If he did, it was after he pulled the trigger."

"Do you know what woman he could have been talking about?" Kylie asked.

"Kylie," Edlund said, shooting her a look. "I think he needs some time to recoup from the surgery." He turned to Shane. "And, Mr. Talbot, this is very encouraging. More details may come back to you. For now we just want you to rest."

Kylie knew she had pushed the other two cops to the limit. She walked back to the bed, whispered something in Shane's ear, and kissed him. Deeper, longer than she had when she first walked in. She held his hand and gazed into his eyes for another ten seconds, let it go, and left the room.

I don't know which was harder for her: to walk away from the man she was crazy about, or not to be knee-deep in the investigation.

Fortunately, we had two homicides to keep us busy.

CHAPTER 21

IT HAD BEEN FIVE hours since Kylie and I bolted out of Selma Kaplan's office and raced to the hospital. We had called Captain Cates immediately to tell her that Shane had been shot, but it was the wrong time to fill her in on what Selma dug up overnight.

Now we were back at the station, and Cates was wrestling with the bomb we'd just dropped. Someone had tried to murder Curtis Hellman six months ago, and our prime suspect was the untouchable Brooke Hellman.

Cates sat at her desk, her right elbow digging into the arm of her chair, her mouth and chin resting on the knuckles of her right hand. It's the familiar pose of Rodin's bronze sculpture *The Thinker*, and when the captain is in statue mode everyone else in the room knows to keep their mouth shut.

"It's all circumstantial," Cates said, breaking the silence. "I can think of a dozen reasons why Hellman got the wrong dose of insulin, any one of which would be all Sonia Blakely needs to convince a grand jury that the DA doesn't have a case."

"On the other hand," Kylie said, "the fact that Curtis Hellman's adoring wife didn't file a police report or call for an investigation means she has something to hide."

Cates already knew that. She also knew that if a serious probe into

Brooke Hellman's personal, professional, and financial life went belly-up, it could bring the wrath of Mayor Sykes down on the department, and she would be the first casualty. She was looking at a political Pandora's box.

But that had never stopped her before. Delia Cates was a decorated marine and a third-generation NYPD cop. Politics didn't dictate her life.

"Do it," she said. "Under the radar. Submarine. Run silent; run deep."

"Aye, aye, Captain," Kylie said.

"One more thing, MacDonald," Cates said. "I'm glad to hear your boyfriend is out of the woods."

"Yes, ma'am."

"You understand this is not a Red case."

"Understood," Kylie said.

"But since we have a vested interest in the outcome, I called Captain Graham at the Four-One, and he assured me that he's put his best team on it."

"He said that to me as well."

"He didn't tell me that the two of you had talked, but it doesn't surprise me," Cates said. "Let me guess. You volunteered to help."

Kylie shrugged. "You know me, Captain."

"All too well. Fill me in on the conversation."

"I offered to work with his team. He said I was too close to the victim. I told him I didn't agree with the department policy but that I would abide by the rules and stay out of it."

"Can I personally have your word on that as well?" Cates said.

"Yes, ma'am. You have my solemn promise. But as I said to Captain Graham, if those boys from the Four-One ever decide they need a fresh pair of eyes, I'll be glad to pitch in on my own time. It won't cost the department a dime."

"I'll keep it in mind," Cates said. "But for now why don't you focus on the double homicide that the department is paying you to solve."

"Clearly nobody trusts me," Kylie said once we were back in the car.

"It's terrible," I said, mustering up as much mock sympathy as I could. "I don't understand why everyone thinks you're an incorrigible chronic rule breaker willing to push the envelope whenever she feels justified. Oh, wait, I have a list right here in my pocket of transgressions you've committed over the past year."

"You are such a fucking Boy Scout," Kylie said. "But I'll bet if you check that list, every one of those transgressions wound up with us collaring someone."

"Possibly. But we've also made a lot of arrests just playing it by the book."

"I know, Zach," she said, flashing me a devilish grin, "but if you obey all the rules, you miss a lot of the fun."

We crossed the Ed Koch Queensboro Bridge into Long Island City and pulled into the parking lot at Silvercup Studios. We were there to talk to Shelley Trager. We had checked the IMDb website, and Shelley's company, Noo Yawk Films, had never done a joint venture with the Hellmans. But in a tight-knit community like the television and film business, where the gossip mill cranks out the latest scandal, rumors, and bullshit around the clock, we figured Shelley might have picked up some dirt on them.

It was a long shot, a total fishing expedition, but we've learned that if you ask enough people enough questions, sooner or later you're bound to get lucky and pick up that one little nugget of truth that helps you crack the case. And since he and Kylie were old friends, he wouldn't hesitate to tell us.

"The Hellmans?" Shelley said when we told him why we'd stopped by. "They were total assholes."

We were off to a good start.

"I mean, we're all assholes," Shelley said. "It's the nature of the business. It can bring out the worst in people. But those two fuckers, they didn't just screw someone out of money or backstab an old friend—they actually *murdered* people. I mean, I know what the courts said, but Curtis leaving that actress by the side of the road? Murder! And Warren shooting that cop in *self-defense*? Murder! But you hire a hotshot lawyer like Sonia Blakely, and she's going to bamboozle a jury into an acquittal. Hey, can I get you some coffee? I've got a dark roast from Guatemala. It's fantastic."

"No thanks," I said.

"So, I guess you caught the Hellman homicides," Shelley said. "Who do you want to play you in the movie?"

Kylie laughed. "What the hell are you talking about, old man?"

"Sweetheart, the way they died—it was pretty fucking cinematic. Warren gets shot by a sniper on live TV. Curtis gets shanked in broad daylight—no clues left behind. That's great cop drama. You two catch the people who killed them, and I guarantee you someone is going to want to turn it into a movie. Especially if the bad guys are as smart as I think they are."

"What do you mean?" Kylie said.

"The villains. They can't be bumbling idiots. Think about it. The Joker, Hannibal Lecter, Keyser Söze—they're not just evil; they're brilliant. The audience loves it when the cops are up against a worthy adversary."

"We prefer bumbling idiots," I said, "but in this case, these adversaries seem pretty damn worthy."

"You're looking for professionals, right?" Shelley said.

I nodded. "It looks that way."

Shelley put a hand to his chin, got lost in thought for about ten seconds, started to say something, and then changed his mind.

"What?" Kylie said. "Tell us what you're thinking. Don't hold back."

"It's nothing. You said you're looking for professionals. It reminds me of a pitch I took a few months back."

"What pitch?" Kylie asked.

"It was for a TV series. The heroes, if you want to call them that, were hit men. I've seen it before, but I did like the spin this writer took on it."

"What spin?" Kylie said.

"The hit men," Shelley said. "They were old. Pushing seventy. It was clever, but I passed on it. I want my protagonists to be more like you—young, attractive men and women who fight crime. Not a bunch of geezers who run around the globe whacking people for money."

Kylie and I looked at each other. *Geezers whacking people for money.* It sure felt like a nugget.

She turned to Shelley. "I think Zach and I will have some of that coffee after all," she said. "It looks like we just might be here for a while."

CHAPTER 22

"YOU'RE RIGHT," KYLIE SAID, taking a sip of Shelley's Guatemalan dark roast. "This is excellent coffee."

"Thanks, but that's not why you're sticking around," Shelley said. "I just said something that piqued your interest."

"Maybe yes, maybe no," she said. "We're curious about these aging hit men. I thought most guys who retire take up golf."

"Are you kidding?" Shelley said. "Contract killing is more popular with my generation than shuffleboard. I got my *How to Murder for Fun and Profit* pamphlet as soon as I signed up for AARP." He gave her a stone-cold stare. "Don't give me this 'maybe yes, maybe no' bullshit. I struck a nerve, didn't I? Your hit man is no spring chicken."

"You know we can't say anything," Kylie said. "But we need all the help we can get."

Shelley nodded. He was happy to help. He just didn't like being played.

"Remember Travis Wilkins?" he said. "He was one of our writer-producers on *K-Mac.*"

Kylie winced. *K-Mac* was a TV series created by Kylie's husband, Spence. It was about a female detective who solves the toughest cases but doesn't always go by the book. Spence had given his fictional cop,

Katie MacDougal, the same bad habits and the same nickname as his wife—K-Mac.

"I remember Travis," Kylie said.

"Remember how he used to bring his son to the set whenever he could?" Shelley said.

Shelley is a storyteller with a fondness for deviating from the subject at hand and nattering on about something unrelated. Kylie refers to it as his throat-clearing process.

"Yeah, I remember the kid," Kylie said.

"Theo," Shelley said. "Sweet boy. Even when he was ten years old, he was fascinated with making movies. He's eighteen now, and he's starting at NYU Film School in September. You need more coffee?"

"No, thanks," Kylie said. "Go on with your story about Travis's pitch."

"I'm getting there," he said. "So you know how my wife laid down the law a few years ago—no more smoking cigars in the apartment."

"Yes, I knew that," Kylie said, waiting for Shelley to land the plane.

"Well, one evening after dinner, I was sitting in the park enjoying a cigar, when I spot Travis Wilkins. Just like that, he walks by, and we get to talking and I ask him what he's working on, and he says he and his son are developing an idea for a TV series. Naturally, I'm curious, so I ask him to tell me about it. He says it's still in the early stages, but here's the gist of it.

"The backstory starts a few days after Nine-Eleven. Our government is paranoid. They don't know where the next attack is coming from, so the president authorizes a special-ops team to infiltrate domestic terrorist cells and eliminate the leaders. You know, cut off the head, you kill the snake.

"A few years pass, the group is dissolved, its history is expunged, and the five assassins are put out to pasture. They have all these skills but no place to market them. So they go off on their own. In the pilot episode, it's twenty years later. They're in their sixties, making a shitload of money, and they're still at it."

"What can you tell us about the hit men?" Kylie asked.

"Travis is smart. He knows that people love characters that are bigger than life. Superman can fly. Spiderman can climb up a building. But of course, these old guys aren't superheroes, so they can't have superpowers, but he gave each of them a trademark that lets you know they're the best in the world."

"Like what?"

"Like the sniper. He was a master of the neck shot. He could hit his victim in the Adam's apple from half a mile away."

Kylie and I are trained to keep our reactions to ourselves, but this was a gut punch, and we both locked eyes. Shelley caught it. "Oh, shit. Don't tell me Warren Hellman was shot in the neck," he said.

"Were any of these hit men handy with a knife?" I asked.

"What do you think? One is good with a rifle, one with a knife, one with poison—"

"Stay with the knife expert," Kylie said. "What's his signature?"

Shelley picked up a teaspoon from the coffee station. "Most people stab like this," he said, raising his arm over his head and plunging the spoon downward. He did it again and again and again, accompanied by musical screeches, until he was sure his invisible victim was properly dispatched. "Hitchcock turned it into an art form in *Psycho*."

"And Travis's character?" Kylie said.

"Like a surgeon." Shelley jerked his head back and drew the deadly utensil across his neck from the ear to the jugular. "*Pffft*. One slice and the victim bleeds out."

One slice. The same words Dorsey-Jones had said when she examined Curtis Hellman's lifeless body on the running track.

Kylie and I didn't speak, but Shelley could read our faces. "You guys are starting to freak me out," he said. "There was nothing in the paper about how Curtis died. It just said 'stabbed.' But was it this?"

He reenacted the stabbing, capping it off with another decisive *pffft*.

In every investigation, you wait for that one instant when a door opens up and suddenly you can see a path that could lead you to an arrest. Kylie and I call it the *holy shit* moment. I looked at her. *Older hit men. Neck shot. One slice.* She looked at me, and a *holy shit* grin spread across her face.

"Shelley, we're going to need a copy of the pitch," she said.

"What are you talking about?" Shelley said. "I just told you. I was in the park having a cigar when I bumped into Travis. It wasn't a real meeting. He didn't have a hard copy of the pitch in his pocket. It was just two guys sitting on a bench talking about the business."

"What else do you remember?" I asked.

"Nothing. He was going to give me some more details, but I cut him off. I told him it wasn't my kind of show. Now I'm starting to regret it."

"And that was the last time you talked to him about it?" Kylie said.

"Yeah, that was it. Short and sweet. Over and done." He hesitated. "Except . . ."

"Except what?"

"You know me," Shelley said. "If I like someone, I try to help them out. And I like Travis, so I said, 'Look, it's not my cup of tea, but it's a good idea. It's a nice twist on the old murder-for-hire theme. You develop the show, knock on some doors, and I'll bet you find a buyer.'"

"And that's all?"

He shook his head. "No. I said, 'And if I were you, the very first door I would knock on would belong to Warren and Curtis Hellman.'"

CHAPTER 23

TRAVIS LIVED ON WEST Forty-Fifth Street just east of Eleventh Avenue, which meant we'd be crossing Manhattan at rush hour.

Kylie tossed me the car keys. "Take the tunnel. The bridge will be a parking lot."

At any other time, I would have said, "So you trust me to drive, but you're not sure I can figure out the best way to get there." But I gave her a pass. As soon as we were in the car, she was on the phone checking on Shane.

I got snippets of his progress along the way. He was in stable condition. Cheryl was at the hospital. His mother couldn't fly in from Texas, because she was recovering from hip surgery, but everyone at her church was praying for him. I also picked up something that wasn't said out loud but was abundantly clear.

Kylie was in love.

It was a little after five p.m. when I pulled up to Travis's apartment building.

"That's him. That's him," Kylie said, pointing at a man standing at the curb, two suitcases at his feet, tapping away on his cell phone. "Pull over."

I did as directed, and we got out of the car.

"Travis. Yo, Travis!" she yelled.

He lifted his head, and his face erupted with joy. "K-Mac!" he said, spreading his arms wide.

Kylie was just as happy to see him, and they sealed the reunion with a hug.

"You look fantastic," Travis said. "How is Spence?"

Kylie had kept the sudden disappearance of her husband under wraps, and even if Travis was someone she might be willing to share the news with, this wasn't the time.

"Oh, you know Spence," she said. "Crazy as ever." She pointed to the suitcases. "You skipping town?"

"Better than that," Travis said. "I'm skipping the entire hemisphere. I'm flying to Sydney. At least, that was the plan. But my Uber driver just called to say he got a flat, and now I'm trying to scrounge up another ride to Newark Airport."

"You won't get one at this hour," Kylie said. "But if you're willing to sit in the back of a cop car, we'll take you."

"Are you shitting me?" Travis said. "Don't answer that. I'd rather accept your magnanimous offer before you change your mind." He picked up both bags and then hesitated. "Wait . . . You're the poster girl for maverick cops. How many laws are we breaking here?"

"That was fiction," Kylie said. "In real life I'm a paragon of virtue. We're here on business. We came to talk to you, but since you don't have time, we can get it done while we drive to Newark."

Travis gave me a dubious look, set his bags down, and extended his hand. "Travis Wilkins," he said. "Old friend of K-Mac. Is she on the level?"

"Zach Jordan. K-Mac's silent partner," I said, shaking his hand. "She definitely pushed the envelope with that paragon-of-virtue bullshit, but as long as we don't accept any gratuities, your ride to the airport will be blessed by the department."

I chucked Kylie the car keys and picked up one of Travis's bags, and he grabbed the other.

"What's in Sydney?" Kylie said as soon as we were in the car.

"My girlfriend, Brianna, is an actress. She landed a job as a series regular on an Australian TV show. She showed her producers some of my work, they liked it, and they hired me as a staff writer for thirteen episodes. I won't be back till January."

"What about Theo?"

"Theo's eighteen. He's going off to college at the end of next month. He'll be fine. He doesn't need his old man telling him what to do or how to do it. Now can we get back to the part where you're here on business? What do you want to talk to me about?"

"A few months ago, you pitched an idea for a TV series to Shelley Trager."

"I did?"

"Shelley told us he was sitting in the park, smoking a cigar—"

"Oh, yeah, sure. Now I remember. It wasn't even a pitch. He asked me what I was up to, and the real answer was not much, but when you get an audience with Shelley, you grab it. Theo and I had just been kicking around this hit-man concept, so I threw it out there."

"How did you come up with the idea?"

"I didn't. It was all Theo's. Five guys, a black-ops team doing wet work for the government right after Nine-Eleven. Uncle Sam pulls the plug on the unit, so these dudes set up shop on their own. The idea was still half-baked when I told it to Shelley, so I wasn't surprised when he gave me a quick pass."

"Who else did you pitch it to?" I asked.

"Nobody. I told Theo about my conversation with Shelley. I also told him that I doubt if any studio is going to put up money for a series about a bunch of old farts on Medicare, and you know what he says? 'I've got two words for you, Dad. *Downton Abbey.*'"

"One more question," Kylie said, easing into rougher waters. "Do you know if Theo's idea ever worked its way to the Hellman brothers?"

"The Hellman brothers?" Travis said, putting it all together. "Oh my God. Is that what this is about? Do you think my son had anything to do with those murders?"

"Don't freak out, Papa Bear," Kylie said. "Zach and I are working the case. We're interviewing anybody and everybody who came into contact with those two. If they bought coffee at a Starbucks, we're going to question the baristas. This is not like an episode of *K-Mac* where she solves a double homicide in forty-three minutes. In real life, we spend sixteen hours a day looking under every rock. It's boring, it's tedious, and usually, it's unproductive."

"And am I under one of your rocks because I pitched Shelley an idea about a gang of geriatric hired killers?"

"No. But he told us he suggested you take it to the Hellmans. Did you pitch it to them or anyone in their organization?"

"Me? Absolutely not. I have no idea if Theo did. He's a pretty resourceful kid. Is he in any trouble if he did?"

"Travis," I said. "You're about to go to the other side of the world. If we thought your son needed you here, we would tell you not to get on the plane."

Travis's face softened. "You're not just saying that, are you?"

"My partner might," I said. "But I'm the true paragon of virtue in this relationship."

He let out an audible sigh. "Thanks."

"Now, how do we get ahold of Theo?" I said.

"He's off in Jersey shooting a little indie production, which is being funded by his biggest fan—his grandpa Claude. Let me give Theo a call and get the exact location. I'm sure he'll be psyched to talk to you. He loves crime shit."

"Well, then, we won't disappoint him," I said. "We're up to our necks in crime shit."

"I can't believe little Theo is eighteen," Kylie said. "The last time I saw him, he was what—ten?"

Travis laughed. "Then you definitely won't recognize him. *Little* Theo is now six foot two, rides around on an old Triumph Bonneville motorcycle, and is totally his own man, which is why I didn't think twice about taking a job ten thousand miles away from home. Let me show you a picture."

He tapped the photo app on his phone. "This is one of the two of us. We took it last night," he said, handing it to me.

Theo had expressive blue eyes, thick tousled brown hair, and a mischievous smile. It was a sweet picture of a good-looking young man and his proud pop. But one thing stood out. Theo was white. Travis was Black.

"Spitting image of his dad," I said, holding the photo up to Kylie so she could take a quick look as she navigated the traffic on Eleventh Avenue.

Travis laughed. "I guess you figured out that I'm not Theo's biological father."

"I'm a cop," I said. "You can't slip these things past me."

Another laugh. "His mom was pregnant when I met her. We fell in love and got married when Theo was two months old, and I've raised him like he was my own. I'm not his birth father, but I'm the only dad he's ever known."

"Do you happen to know if he told his mom anything about the story idea?"

Travis shook his head. "She died when he was six years old. It's just been me and him ever since. I didn't even start dating till Theo was fifteen. That's when I met Brianna. The two of them get along great. Last night, I told him that one day she might become his stepmother, and he said, 'What's taking you so long?'"

"He sounds like a terrific kid," I said.

"He is. Everyone at the Grove loves him."

"What's the Grove?" Kylie asked.

"Golden Grove. It's a nursing home. Theo worked there for his senior year community service project."

"Doing what?"

"Arts and crafts, playing cards with the old folks, helping them with their smartphones, but mostly he'd do the one thing they seem to need the most: just sit quietly and listen to their stories. That's how he came up with the idea for the TV show."

"What do you mean?"

"One of the residents is pretty far into dementia, and he loves to go on and on about his secret life as an assassin."

CHAPTER 24

THERE'S AN ICONIC SCENE in *Jaws* when Quint first sees the great white shark and harpoons it with a line attached to a yellow flotation barrel. Now he's confident that if he follows the barrel, it will lead him to the shark.

Kylie and I think a lot like Quint, and as soon as Travis told us that Theo's idea came from an old man who had a secret life as an assassin, we gave each other a knowing glance.

We had our yellow barrel, and we were going to follow it.

We've both seen the movie numerous times, so we know that before it ends the shark sinks Quint's boat and eats him alive, but still, a lead is a lead.

An hour after we dropped Travis at the airport, we found the film production crew parked on the shoulder of a narrow two-lane highway that wound its way through the desolate woodlands of West Milford, New Jersey.

Theo was expecting us, and as soon as Kylie got out of the car, he headed straight for her. She had told me that as a ten-year-old, he had an adorable little-boy crush on her. Eight years later, he was a physically mature and sexually aware adult, and I could see by the cartoon hearts dancing in his eyes that the crush had developed right along with the rest of him. The adorable little boy gave her an unmistakable manly hug.

"K-Mac!" he exploded. "I flipped out when my dad called. How cool is it to see you again?"

"This is my partner, Zach Jordan," Kylie said.

Apparently, Theo thought it was cool to see me as well. He gave me an enthusiastic bro handshake.

"I can't believe it. Two detectives from the NYPD Red squad, and you're here to talk to me about the Hellman murders?" he said. "I am gobsmacked."

I smiled. It's always a treat to meet a teenager who can express enthusiasm without using the word *awesome*.

"We're talking to a lot of people about a lot of things," Kylie said, trying to downplay the reason for our visit. "But first things first. What are you shooting out here in the middle of nowhere?"

"A documentary. Didn't you ever hear of this place?"

Kylie looked around. We weren't in a *place*. We were in the middle of a nine-mile stretch of barren blacktop.

"Not really," she said.

"It's legendary," Theo said, with a hint of disappointment that two cops with such impressive résumés could be so clueless. "Clinton Road is the most haunted highway in America. It's crawling with ghosts, witches, aliens, phantom trucks—all kinds of paranormal shit. Right over there is Ghost Boy Bridge. You throw a coin into the water at night, and by morning the kid who drowned there will have thrown it back on the road."

"And you believe that?"

"Doesn't matter if *I* believe it. People who live here swear it's true. They've *lived* it, and I'm getting them on film talking about their weird encounters. Speaking of weird," he said, anxious to change the subject, "it's pretty insane about the Hellmans. I mean, I'm sorry those two dudes got whacked, but how dope would it be if it had something to do with the idea I pitched them? Talk about life imitating art!"

"Slow down and back up a few steps," Kylie said. "I'm bowled over that a student filmmaker got an audience with the Hellmans. How'd you do it?"

"Connections," he said, gifting her with his most disarming teenage-boy smirk. "You know the biz."

"Mmm-hmm," she said melodically, extending him much more tolerance than any other wiseass kid would get. "But seriously, Theo, how does an unknown eighteen-year-old get to pitch to two of the most powerful producers in the industry?"

"My GF, Carly—Carly Driscoll. She's also my production manager. That's her over there next to the camera," he said, pointing at a young woman with a clipboard in her hand. "Her father is an agent. One day I told him my idea. He liked it, and a few weeks later he and his wife were at a black-tie party. They were sitting at the same table as Curtis Hellman, so Mr. Driscoll just threw it out there. Curtis was kind of lukewarm, but Mrs. Hellman said it had legs, and a few days later I was invited to pitch."

"*Mrs.* Hellman," Kylie repeated. "His wife, Brooke, liked the idea?"

"I don't know her name, but . . ." He shrugged. "I guess older women respond to my style."

The kid was shameless. Kylie pressed on.

"When did this all happen?" she asked.

"Three months ago—April first, actually. When I got the call, I thought it was an April Fools' joke, but Mr. Driscoll said it was real. He would have gone to the meeting with me, but he had to fly to London, so I went alone."

"You didn't take your dad?"

"Take him? I didn't even *tell* him. The whole thing was bizarro. I figured if anything ever came of it, I'd surprise him and say, 'Hey, Dad, you want to be the head writer on a new show the Hellmans are doing?' He would say, 'Yeah,' and I would say, 'Cool. You're hired.'"

"Where did the meeting take place?" Kylie said.

"Their office on West Fifty-Seventh Street. Twenty-third floor."

"And who did you meet with?" Kylie said.

"*Them*," he said, giving her the look we get when people think we're asking dumb questions. "I met with *Warren and Curtis.*"

"Who else was there?"

"Just the waiter. But he was in and out."

"Who?"

"The waiter. It was their private dining room. Talk about weird. They were both eating lunch, plus Warren was staring at his phone. I knew they were only seeing me as a favor to Mr. Driscoll, so I decide fuck it, I've got nothing to lose. I give them the backstory—there are five men, all trained to be lethal killers. Twenty years ago, they were working as assassins for the US government. Curtis interrupts me and says, 'Why the fuck would anyone tune in to watch a bunch of scumbags who kill people for a living?' So I look straight at him, and I say, 'That's what they said to David Chase, but he went ahead and created *The Sopranos* anyway.'"

"You got balls, kid," Kylie said.

"Well, it worked. Curtis put down his fork, Warren looked up from his phone, and I said, "I don't mean to be rude, sir, but why would you think they're scumbags? They put their lives on the line with every mission, targeting terrorist cells that were planning attacks on American soil. There's a nobility about the sacrifices they made for their country. They were patriots, unsung heroes, when the government fucked them over and pulled the plug on their unit. They're in their late forties, early fifties. How are they supposed to support their families, pay their mortgages, send their kids to college? Get a job at Home Depot? No. Killing bad guys is what they know. It's what they do best. So they go into business for themselves. I think audiences will fucking love them."

"I'm betting twenty bucks they didn't tell you to leave," Kylie said.

"Hell, no. By now they both stopped eating. I don't know what I said, but I knew I had their attention, so I started telling them about the characters."

"Theo!" It was Carly.

He waved her over and introduced us. She was cute, blond, and all business.

"Sorry, Officers," she said, "but we're ready to shoot, and we need the director on set."

"A few more minutes?" Kylie asked. "Please?"

Theo turned to Carly. The look in her eyes was unequivocal. *No more minutes.*

He snapped his head toward me. I gave him a half smile that let him know he was on his own.

"Who's up first?" he asked Carly.

"The Manchester twins," she said, not even bothering to look at her clipboard.

"Oh, man," Theo said, turning back to Kylie. "These ladies are the best—Esther and Hester Manchester. They're eighty-seven years old. Totally identical twins. Same face, same hair; they even wear the same dresses. But when they talk about all the spooky shit they've seen, they argue like crazy. You want to watch the interview? We can pick this stuff up later. Cool?"

I know my partner. She had zero interest in watching a pair of octogenarians squabble about ghoulies, ghosties, and things that go bump in the night. And she certainly didn't want to pick *this stuff* up later.

What she wanted to say was, "No, it is definitely *not* cool. We're investigating two homicides. Your geriatric twins can just sit tight till we're done." But she knew better than to get between our star witness and his girlfriend.

"You're the *director*, Theo," Kylie said sweetly.

And just like that, round one was over. Relentless detective: zero. Kick-ass production manager: one.

Carly flashed a victory smile.

I gave Theo a silent nod. *Good call, kid.*

CHAPTER 25

AT THE VERY SAME moment that Detectives Zach Jordan and Kylie MacDonald were listening to the Manchester twins bicker about whether the two apparitions they saw one All Hallows' Eve were ghosts or albinos, the man who put a bullet in Shane Talbot's chest slid his key into the top-of-the-line Schlage dead-bolt lock, turned it, and opened the door to his apartment.

"Vincent, is that you?" Priscilla called out from the kitchen.

Of course it was him. Ever since their sick, twisted fuck of a father took his last breath and went straight to hell last Christmas, it could only be him. But Priscilla always needed reassurance. Old wounds die hard.

"No, it's Johnny Depp," he sang out in his best Captain Jack Sparrow imitation. "And I'm here to ravish you."

"I think you mean '*ravage*,'" she yelled back, "but in your case, I'll tolerate bad grammar. Did you bring ice cream?"

"Does Nicolas Cage make lousy career choices?"

She laughed. She loved it when he put celebrity names in his jokes. "I'm making chicken paprikash with dumplings for dinner."

He entered the kitchen and inhaled deeply. "It smells like Mom's recipe, only without the constant ridicule and toxic criticism."

They despised their parents—wished them dead from the time they were kids. Their mother had cooperated by smoking herself to death seven years ago, but their father, despite his self-destructive lifestyle, refused to self-destruct. Priscilla had decided he needed a little push, and she recruited her brother to do the pushing.

Vincent put the ice cream in the freezer, opened the fridge, and took out a beer. It was the last one. "What the fuck, Prissy? There was a full six-pack in here when I left for work this morning."

"Father Niedenthal stopped in to see me. You know how he is— always trying to help me get back out there into the world."

"Bullshit! That old lush only comes by so he can help himself. He knows I spring for the good stuff instead of that weasel piss they have at the rectory."

He popped the top on his beer and took a long swallow.

"Sorry," she said. "Did you find anything good at work today?"

"Yeah," he snapped. "I found the keys to a brand-new Tesla, and ten thousand shares of Apple stock. It's amazing what people will toss onto the subway tracks these days."

"Look, I said I was sorry. Next time Father Niedenthal comes over, I'll hide your beer. Dinner will be ready in fifteen minutes. Can I show you something while you're waiting?"

She didn't wait for an answer. She handed him her phone. On the screen was a woman in her twenties. Her face was battered, swollen, lacerated; her skin was black, blue, brown, and yellow where the blood vessels underneath had ruptured.

"Her boyfriend did it," Priscilla said. "Her post was trending on HHNF. I messaged her to say how bad I feel for her."

"Forget it," Vincent said. "We can't help her."

"Why not? Look at this poor girl. Why can't we help her?"

He took a swig of his beer. "I fucked up, Prissy."

"What are you talking about?"

"Yesterday at the Hunts Point Market."

"You said it went well. I already crossed Redheaded Monster off my list."

"Well, you're going to have to uncross him, because it didn't go as well as I thought."

"But you said . . ."

"Damn it, Priscilla, I know what I said. But I was wrong. Which part of 'I fucked up' don't you understand?"

"Okay. So un-fuck up, Vincent. Go back and get it right this time."

"Fine."

"When?"

"I don't know. Tomorrow, the next day—I have to plan these things so I can get away. Or do you want me to just shoot him and get caught by the cops?"

"Don't be silly," she said. "Of course I don't want you to get caught."

He drained the last of his beer. "I'm going to the deli for a six-pack. Want anything?"

"Just for you to come back in a better mood."

He left the apartment, double-locked the door, and banged on the elevator button with the heel of his hand.

"Vincent, how are you?" the woman with the laundry basket said when the door opened.

"I'm good, Mrs. Frangopoulos. How are you?"

"How am I? If Mrs. Berlusconi didn't take my clothes out of the dryer while they're still damp, I'll be fine," she said, pushing the lobby button for him. "And how's Priscilla?"

"She's fine."

"I'm sure she's fine, Vincent. I meant how is her . . ." She dropped her voice to a whisper. ". . . *condition?*"

"The same."

"So she's still . . ." Again the whisper. ". . . afraid to go outside?"

"She enjoys working from home," Vincent said.

Mrs. Frangopoulos nodded knowingly. That was all the information she was going to get.

"And your father?" she asked. "How does he like Florida?"

"Loves it," Vincent said. "I spoke to him yesterday. I don't think he's ever coming back to Astoria." *Not without the help of a cadaver dog and a couple of men with shovels.*

His father was the first. The night Priscilla asked him to do it, he thought she was joking. But she wasn't. "Do it when he's passed out drunk, get rid of the body, and just tell the neighbors he moved to Florida. They won't give a shit. Nobody likes him anyway."

It was easier than he expected. And for that first month after Christmas, Prissy was the happiest he'd ever seen her. But then she found HHNF, the online forum for abused women, and it was as if she'd found her calling.

She would spend hours scouring the site, send sympathetic messages to the victims, and pick their brains for details until she finally could figure out who had to be eliminated so that these poor women could get on with their lives.

But of course, she couldn't do the eliminating. She couldn't do anything if it meant leaving the apartment. And just like that, Vincent's role in his sister's life evolved. Once, he had been her caretaker, her nursemaid, her errand boy. Now he was her vigilante by proxy.

The elevator reached the lobby, and he said goodbye to Mrs. Frangopoulos. Then he stepped outside into the clammy July night and the relative indifference of Thirty-First Avenue.

His phone chirped. It was a text from Priscilla.

> Her name is Catherine. She teaches second
> grade.

Attached was the picture of the young woman whose boyfriend had brutally beaten her. Her eyes were desperate, defeated, pleading.

Vincent sighed and texted his sister back.

> Find out what you can about the
> animal who did this. He's on our list.

CHAPTER 26

THEO TURNED OUT to be a gifted documentarian. Even Kylie, who was bummed that our mission was taking a back seat to a bunch of ghosts on a godforsaken road in New Jersey, enjoyed watching him work the Manchester sisters. Not only did he guide them so that their stories unfolded organically, but he had a knack for coaxing little details out of them that made their already engaging testimony even more fascinating.

Carly had queued up five more locals who were ready for their fifteen minutes of fame, so by the time the production wrapped, it was too dark to interview Theo on the side of the road.

"No problem," he said, still in charge. "There's a restaurant about ten minutes away. I'm starving, and they have great shepherd's pie."

The crew drove home, Theo got on his bike, and we followed him to the Grasshopper, an Irish pub on Route 23. He was right about the shepherd's pie. We waited until coffee and dessert before we got back to the business at hand.

"Your dad told us that the idea you took to the Hellmans came out of conversations you had with a man at the nursing home," I said.

"Assisted living," Theo said. "They hate it when you say 'nursing home.'"

"Sorry," I said. "What can you tell us about him?"

"His name is Martin Sheffield. Really nice guy, and supersmart. He used to be a biological researcher for one of the big drug companies. But he was diagnosed with Alzheimer's about a year ago, and the last time I looked at his chart he was at stage three."

"What exactly is that?" I asked.

"His short-term memory is going. He can tell you things he did thirty years ago, but he can't remember what he ate for breakfast. There are seven stages, and this is the point where it made sense for him to move to assisted living."

"Who made that decision?"

"He did. He knew all the signs, so he hired a lawyer to pay his bills and made arrangements with a funeral home for when he dies. I told you he was smart."

"You like him, don't you," Kylie said.

He looked at her wistfully. "I do. Some of the staff think he's kind of antisocial, but I think he's funny as hell. Not like stand-up comedian funny. More dry, kind of deadpan, like Clint Eastwood. I remember the first day I met him. He was sitting by himself in the garden, so I sat down next to him, and he said, 'You look a little young to be committed to this booby hatch.' So I said, 'You think everybody around here is crazy?' He says, 'Crazy, or boring as fuck. You don't look like you're either. What are you doing here?'

"So I said, 'I'm a volunteer.' And he goes, 'If you're looking for someone's ass to wipe, you've come to the wrong old man. Try Baumgarten in room one-fourteen.' I said, 'Ass wiping isn't my thing. I'm more into filmmaking.'

"He gives me this long, slow look. Finally, he says, 'So you're an observer of life?' I said, 'Yes sir. If you've got a story to tell, tell it to me. Maybe one day I can turn it into a movie.'

"He cracked up laughing. He says, 'I'll bet you could make a movie out of the stories I could tell you. And wouldn't that fuck with those assholes in Washington?' So, I said, 'Let's fuck with them.' And just like that, he goes, 'You're on. Let's do it.' Sure didn't feel antisocial to me.

"I take out my phone so I can get him on video, and he says, 'Put it away. They're watching. I'll just talk; you listen. Whatever you remember, you can write down when you get home. If you want to add some of your own shit, be my guest.'

"I said, 'Fair enough. And if I sell it for a zillion dollars to Netflix, we'll split it.' He waves me off. He says he doesn't need money. He doesn't have any family, so I can keep the entire zillion for myself. I said, 'Thanks. Where do you want to start?'

"He sits back in his chair and closes his eyes. I can tell he's thinking, working hard to dredge it up. Finally, he says, 'Let me tell you about Kappa Omega Delta. It's a sorority I belong to.'"

"Sorority?" Kylie said. "Did he mean fraternity?"

"He said sorority. When you work at the Grove, you learn how to talk to people who have mental health issues. You have to let their mind go where it wants to go, and then respond in a way that shows them you're interested in their story. If you start correcting them or asking questions that sound like you're fact-checking, they get defensive and shut down. You just have to listen patiently without interrupting."

Kylie nodded. Listening patiently was not her forte.

"He said there were five of them. All men. They wanted to keep their identities secret, so they gave themselves female code names. They put five letters in a hat: A, B, C, D, and E. Mr. Sheffield picked D, and he decided he was going to be Denise. The others were Alice, Barbara, Carol, and Emily. Then he said, 'You want to know what we did?' I said, 'Yes, sir.'

"And he leaned in, eyes wide open now, and he says in a real low voice, 'We killed people. All over the world. For money. Lots of money.'"

"Say the name of the sorority again," Kylie said.

"Kappa Omega Delta," Theo said.

"K, O, D," Kylie said. "Killers on demand."

CHAPTER 27

KYLIE AND I didn't hide our reactions. I don't think we could have if we had tried. We'd been panning for gold, and it felt as though we suddenly hit the mother lode. Theo had no difficulty reading the rush that surged through us.

"I guess if this were a TV show," he said, "this would be a pretty good time to cut to a commercial."

"We're not going anywhere," I said. "You had us at Alice, Barbara, Carol, Denise, and Emily."

"They sound innocent enough, don't they?" he said. "But each one is the best in the world at his killing technique. Alice is an up-close firearms genius. He can create guns out of plastic composites that look like everyday objects—cell phones, umbrellas, cigarette packs. It gets him past any security search. Barbara is the edged-weapons expert—y'know, knives and shit. He was a medic in the military—knows exactly how to slash his victims' throats so they bleed out on the spot. Carol is a world-class sniper, Denise is a poison special-ist, and Emily uses blunt objects and can stage a hit to look like an accident or suicide. Between the five of them, they knocked off about a dozen people a year. And they've been at it for twenty years."

I did the math in my head and could only hope that the Sorority

NYPD RED 7: THE MURDER SORORITY

was the toxic detritus of a degenerating brain. Because if it was real, it would be one of the most lethal clandestine death squads ever assembled.

"They called themselves the five sisters," Theo said. "And they had a strict policy. They would do the wet work, but they needed a sixth person to run the business—someone to deal with the clients, move the money to a safe spot out of the country, and make sure they got paid fair, square, and on time."

"And sister number six probably had a name that started with 'F,'" Kylie said.

"Nope," Theo said, enjoying the fact that he tripped Kylie up. "You know how all these college sororities have a house mother—some sweet old lady who lives with the girls and looks out for them? The code name for their business manager was 'Mother.'"

"What can you tell us about her . . . him . . . them—whatever the pronoun is?" Kylie asked.

"Not much. Mr. Sheffield only wanted to talk about the things they did in the field. Talking about Mother would be like making a pitch to a movie producer and telling him about your agent," Theo said. "But if you have time, I can tell you about some of their kills."

Kylie and I nodded like a pair of bobbleheads on a dashboard. We had all the time in the world.

Theo then proceeded to mesmerize us with stories he had heard from Mr. Sheffield over the course of months. Five painstakingly planned, perfectly executed murders, in five different locations around the world. In each case, the mechanics of the crime were precise, elaborate, and entirely believable.

"The Hellmans had to eat this stuff up," Kylie said when he was finished. "The genre is right in their wheelhouse, and the characters and the stories feel so authentic."

"A little too authentic," Theo said. "They knew right away that a kid who was still in high school would never come up with all those plots on his own. They flat-out asked who helped me with the idea. So I told them about Mr. Sheffield, and I promised them that he wasn't going to ask them for money."

"And how did they react?"

"Warren said, 'If we make a deal, kid, we're going to want that in writing.' I gave him one of those bullshit Hollywood head nods, like 'No *problema*. Have your people call my people.' Then Curtis jumps back in and says, 'Let's get back to the show. Suppose a person wanted to kill someone. How would he go about finding this Sorority?'"

"Good question," I said. "What's the answer?"

"How do you find a hooker? How do you find an S and M bar? How do you find anything? You gotta ask the right people. Same thing with hiring a hit man. If you want someone dead and you have the money to pay for it, the odds are you know some badass who can point you in the right direction. Curtis looks at me and says 'That's it?' And I said that's all the audience needs. They don't tune in to watch these guys get hired. They're there for the action. Same concept as *Mission Impossible*."

"What did they say?"

"I think they liked it. They said give them some time to think about it. They'll get back to me." He shrugged. "Well, I guess now they won't."

The text alert on his phone chirped. He checked it. "Carly," he said. "She doesn't like me riding around on the motorcycle this late at night. She said she won't be able to sleep till I get home. I guess I should get going."

"One last question about Mr. Sheffield," Kylie said.

"Sure."

"You said he worked in research for a drug company. But his grasp of the criminal mind is frighteningly accurate. Did you ever wonder if any of this action-adventure fiction might be true?"

"Are you kidding me?" Theo said. "I started thinking it could be true from the first day he opened up to me."

"What made you think that?"

"One of the people at the Grove is this man Gary. He's fifty-two years old and he was diagnosed with schizophrenia twenty years ago. He's on meds, and when they're working, he lives at home with his parents. But if he goes off his meds, or if he just—I don't know—snaps, Mom and Dad bring him back until the docs can restore him to some semblance of normality. When I talk to Gary, I don't need a medical degree to know he's psychotic. He's a sweet man, but he's delusional. Nothing he says is based in reality.

"Mr. Sheffield is different. Like most people with Alzheimer's, he was diagnosed later in life. And while Gary is hallucinating about things that never happened, Mr. Sheffield struggles every day to recall the things in his life that were real."

"So you think his stories are real?"

"I don't just think it. I *know* it. Like the newspaper editor in India who was shot by a sniper. That happened. I Googled it. Same thing with the music producer in Korea who was killed when he *accidentally* fell off a balcony. Every detail that Mr. Sheffield told me was just the way it was reported online."

"I think we should pay him a visit," Kylie said.

"Wait a minute. That wasn't part of the deal," Theo said. "Mr. Sheffield is an old man who read all that shit on the Internet, and then he turned it all around, and he incorporated it into his own life. A lot of people at the Grove do that. Mrs. Myerson swears she went to the moon with Neil Armstrong, but they kept it a secret because he was married. Their brains are fucked up. You can't just walk in and start grilling them like they're—"

His phone chirped again. He didn't look at it. "I've got to get out of here."

"Before you go, I want you to take a look at this," Kylie said. She opened her phone to the sketch Izaak Weathers had drawn of the suspect in Curtis Hellman's stabbing, and handed it to Theo.

As soon as he looked at it, his demeanor changed. "Where did you get this?" he said.

"Somebody drew it for me. Do you recognize him?" she said.

"What do you want him for?"

"He's just someone Zach and I would like to talk to."

"About what?"

This was a different Theo. Suddenly, he was resistant, almost adversarial.

"Look, Theo," Kylie said. "You've been incredibly cooperative—"

"And you haven't. I answered, like, a hundred questions. All I'm asking is why you want to talk to this guy. It's a two-way street, Detective MacDonald."

There's a reason why cops are so tight-lipped during an investigation. We have to be careful about giving up information that a defense attorney can claim we planted in a witness's head. But Theo was right. He expected a give-and-take relationship, and Kylie knew it was time to give.

"He's a suspect in the Hellman homicides."

Theo slumped back in his seat. "Fuck me," he muttered.

"Do you recognize him?"

Theo nodded. "I've seen him at the Grove."

"Is he a resident?"

"No. About once a month he visits Mr. Sheffield."

"Do you know his name?" Kylie asked.

"Which homicide?" Theo asked. "Warren or Curtis?"

Kylie held back a second and then gave it up. "Curtis. The stabbing on the Hudson River Greenway."

Theo shook his head, not wanting to believe what he was hearing.

"Do you know his name?" Kylie repeated softly.

"Not his real name," Theo said. "But if you want this guy for stabbing Curtis Hellman, I'll bet you any amount of money that his cover name is Barbara."

CHAPTER 28

AS SOON AS KYLIE and I were back on the road, we called Captain Cates. Even just giving her the highlights, it took us close to ten minutes to catch her up on everything that happened since we left her office that afternoon.

"*Five* assassins?" she said. "This case is exploding at every turn."

"I know," I said. "When Warren was shot, we started looking for a Son of Sam–type killer. Now it looks like Sam's part of a sorority, and he's got four sisters and a mother that we have to chase down."

"You realize what this means, don't you?" she said. "If we're dealing with a network of professional killers with a twenty-year history of murders around the world, I'm going to have to alert the feds."

"Can you stall?" Kylie said. "Zach and I just learned about this, and we haven't had time to check it out."

"I don't have to stall," Cates said. "All I have to do is talk to Liz Foster, my contact at the Joint Terrorist Task Force. She'll call the FBI. With any luck, they'll waste a day or two playing phone tag. Eventually, they'll connect, and Liz will say a couple of NYPD detectives may have a lead on some of your open cases. And you both know how much they love it when we try to play in their sandbox."

"Usually, their eyes glaze over as soon as they hear the letters *N*,

Y, P, and *D,*" Kylie said. "They think we're about as sharp as a snow globe and half as useful."

"Exactly," Cates said. "But Liz will press on, and she'll tell them that you have testimony from a teenage boy, who is reporting a bunch of stories he heard from an Alzheimer's patient in a nursing home."

"Assisted living," Kylie said.

"Whatever," Cates said. "Bottom line: they'll say thanks for calling, have a good laugh, and then they'll bury it. But our asses will be covered if anything ever comes of this. What are the next steps?"

"We're going to Golden Grove tomorrow morning," I said. "Theo recognized the sketch of our suspect in the Curtis Hellman murder as a friend of Martin Sheffield. We're hoping they keep a record of visitors, and someone can ID him."

"And last but not least," I said, "in a heroic act of futility, we're also going to interview Sheffield."

"The old man may be delusional," Kylie said, "but the crimes he talked about actually happened. It's a long shot, but we're going try to find out if he knows any details that aren't on the Internet."

"Good luck," Cates snorted. "I can't wait to tell the PC that my two best detectives are going to attempt to pry some reality out of an old man with dementia."

"Considering how much bullshit the commissioner has to wade through in his daily dealings with the mayor, the City Council, and dozens of self-serving community boards, I'm sure he'll be sympathetic to our folly," Kylie said.

Cates laughed. "Thanks, he'll appreciate that. One last question. What's the latest on Shane?"

"We haven't heard anything, so no news is good news," Kylie said. "We were going to call as soon as we finished giving you a heads-up on the Hellman investigation."

"In that case, thanks for the update," Cates said. "Tell him I asked for him." She hung up.

Kylie tapped a button on her cell phone.

"Put him on speaker," I said. "I have a vested interest."

She did, and Shane answered. "Hey, babe, how are you?"

"Don't say anything personal," Kylie said. "Zach is listening."

"Good," he said. "Hey, Zach, I need a favor."

"Name it," I said.

"Break me out of this fucking place, will you?"

"I don't know, Shane. My gunshot victims usually give Lincoln a five-star review. What's wrong with it?"

"For starters, the food is atrocious."

"Have you talked to the executive chef?"

"I'm serious, Zach. Everything they put on that tray was in-fucking-edible."

"You're right. I think they put far too much emphasis on saving lives and not enough on haute cuisine," I said. "But still, it's a small price to pay considering the fact that Dr. Lu snatched you from the jaws of death."

"I know, I know, and trust me, I thanked her. I told her she could eat at my restaurant every night till the end of time, and it's all on the house. But I'm fine now, and I'd like to go home."

"You mean you'd like to go back to work," Kylie said, jumping in.

"Oh God, I can't have both of you ganging up on me," he said. "Yes, I want to go back to work. What's wrong with that?"

"It depends," Kylie said. "What did Dr. Lu say?"

"She has me on an antibiotic drip. Some bullshit about preventing infection. She wants me to stay here at least two nights."

"And what do you want to do?" Kylie said.

"Go home."

"You keep saying home, but you mean work," Kylie said.

"Fine, work. I'm worried about the restaurant."

"Why?" Kylie said. "Your picture is all over the news. By tomorrow morning, you'll be the best-known chef in New York. You'll have even more people trying to get into your place than you did before."

"All right, full disclosure," Shane said. "It's not just work. I want to get back to you. I miss you. I want to be with you."

"Me?" she replied sweetly. "Well, then that changes everything."

"Great. Can you get me out? I know it's late, but I can catch a cab and be at your place in an hour."

"Okay, here's the plan," she said. "This morning, Zach and I posted two cops at your door to make sure that the shooter doesn't come to your room and try to finish the job. Are they still there?"

"Of course they're there. They haven't budged."

"In that case," she said, "you're fucked. You're not going anywhere, sweetheart. I'll call you tomorrow."

She hung up.

Kylie has a way with men, and I could just picture Shane Talbot lying in bed laughing his ass off.

And if he was anything like I'd been back when I was dating Kylie, he was loving every minute of it.

CHAPTER 29

"I HAD A LOUSY night's sleep," I said.

It was eight in the morning, and Kylie and I were on the Henry Hudson Parkway on our way to the Golden Grove Home for the Aged, in the Riverdale section of the Bronx.

"That's what you get for eating shepherd's pie at ten o'clock at night," she said.

"I'm serious," I said. "I couldn't stop thinking about Sheffield. When we question a murder suspect, it's always our show, our turf, our rules. But this is different. We can ask this man his name, and we might not get through to him."

"That's why we're meeting Theo," she said. "He can grease the skids for us."

"Let's hope so," I said, "because with all the pamphlets and training videos the department has on how to deal with people who are suffering from dementia, they don't have a single one that tells us how to talk to a hit man who's got Alzheimer's."

The rush-hour traffic on the southbound side was creeping, but we were headed north, so Kylie was cruising along at a comfortable fifty miles an hour.

"If it's any consolation," she said, "I had a shitty night's sleep, too."

"And you didn't eat the shepherd's pie," I said.

"No. But someone tried to kill my boyfriend, and once they find out they failed, I'm afraid they may try it again."

Oh, yeah. That. I felt stupid and was about to apologize for my insensitivity when Kylie's cell rang.

"It's Theo," she said, putting him on speaker. "What's up, kid?"

"It's Mr. Sheffield," he said, his voice cracking with emotion. "He's dead."

"Where are you?" she demanded.

"I'm at Golden Grove," he said, "I think he was murdered."

"Young man!" a female voice shouted. "How dare you!"

The car surged forward as Kylie hit the accelerator. "Who is that?" she said.

"Mrs. Millstein. She's the director. I'm in her office."

"Don't say another word," Kylie barked. "Get out of her office now and meet us in the parking lot."

"Are you there now?" Theo asked, totally shaken, all of last night's confidence and bravado gone.

"We'll be there in five minutes," Kylie said, flipping on the lights and siren. The needle on the speedometer was at seventy-five and climbing. "Get your ass to the parking lot. Now!"

Theo hung up, and Kylie let out a salvo of F-bombs. "That makes three murder victims in less than forty-eight hours," she said.

"Take it easy," I said, this time remembering that she'd spent the night thinking about how close Shane came to dying. "We have two people murdered, one old man who was suffering from a terminal disease, and a teenage boy with a vivid imagination. Let's not jump to conclusions."

"Zach, if the stories Martin Sheffield told Theo are true, then there are four professional killers out there who would want to shut him up quickly and permanently. I'm not jumping to conclusions. I'm jumping to assumptions."

"Good point," I said. "In that case, let's not jump to assumptions."

If it were any other time, she wouldn't have let me have the last word, but she was too focused on changing lanes at ninety miles an hour to argue. Three minutes later, she pulled off the parkway, ran the lights on

West 254th, turned onto Palisade Avenue, and a quarter of a mile later took a hard left into the parking lot at Golden Grove.

Theo, wearing his biker leathers, was standing next to his motorcycle. We got out of the car, and he walked straight toward Kylie. He reached out for a hug, and she wrapped her arms around him.

"I'm so sorry," she said. "I know how much he meant to you."

"Do you think it's true?" he said, stepping away from the hug. "All the stuff about the Sorority? Because if it is, then it makes sense that they'd kill him for telling me. I never should have made friends with him. He'd be alive today."

I reached out and put my hand on his shoulder. "Theo," I said, "don't do that to yourself. You did not in any way contribute to Mr. Sheffield's death. If anything, your presence in his life probably made him happier than he's been in a long time."

He nodded his head. "Thanks," he said. "But I still think somebody could have killed him. The place is wide open. Anybody could walk in."

"What about security?" I said.

"You mean Larry?" he said, pointing to a man in a blazer who was standing near a clump of bushes about thirty feet from the building with a cigarette in one hand, his phone to his ear, and his back to the main entrance.

"Guys, there is no security," Theo said. "They hire a bunch of losers for minimum wage, give them jackets with the patches on the pocket, so that if a family comes around to talk about putting Grandma in here, they see someone checking IDs. It's all part of Mrs. Millstein's bullshit to help the people who are writing the checks feel less guilty. And it works."

Kylie rubbed her hands together. "Let's see if her bullshit works on us."

Just as the three of us got to the front door, Kylie called out to the security guard. "Hey, Larry!"

He turned around, and Kylie gave him a big happy wave.

Larry smiled, returned the wave, and went back to his phone call.

"Who's the rest of the security team?" she asked Theo. "Curly and Moe?"

CHAPTER 30

"ANYTHING YOU WANT to tell us about Mrs. Millstein before we go in?" I said to Theo.

He thought for a few seconds. "I don't know," he said. "She seems nice enough, but Mr. Sheffield didn't like her—said he couldn't trust her."

"Did he say why?"

"He just said be careful. She can kill you with kindness—tell you what you want to hear, get you to trust her, and then fuck you over."

It was a good heads-up.

Mrs. Millstein had sounded pissed on the phone when Theo suggested that one of her residents had been murdered. Once he walked in with a pair of homicide detectives in tow, I figured she would go from a 7 on the anger scale to a white-hot, raging 10.

But she didn't. As soon as we ID'd ourselves, she welcomed us into her office as if we were a troubled family with a demented old granny and a fat checkbook.

Millstein was somewhere north of fifty, with a rosy smile and a pair of steel-blue probing eyes. "Coffee?" she offered, stalling for time while she sized us up from behind her desk.

"No thanks," I said. "We came here to have a chat with Mr. Sheffield, but we just learned that he passed. Can you tell us the circumstances?"

"Of course, but first let me extend my condolences to this incredible young man," she said, turning to Theo. "I know Mr. Sheffield meant a lot to you, and I hope you know how much you meant to him. He didn't have a family, but the day he met you, the quality of his life improved dramatically."

Theo murmured a soft thanks and tilted his head toward me—a subtle reminder of Sheffield's warning: she can kill you with kindness.

"So, Mrs. Millstein," I said. "When did he die?"

"Please call me Loretta," she said. "Martin enjoyed dinner with the other residents last night, said good night at about seven-thirty, and at ten I got a call from one of our staff to say that she went to his room and he was deceased.

"Why did she go to his room?" Kylie asked.

"Excellent question. It would help if you understood that we are not a nursing home. We have no doctors or nurses. If a resident falls, all we can do is call their family or an ambulance. We are designated by law as an assisted-living facility. We provide meals, clean their rooms, do their laundry, plus we have a busy activity calendar."

"I understand, *Loretta*," Kylie said, her tolerance for bullshit gone. "But why did one of your employees go to his room at that hour?"

Mrs. Millstein gave Kylie her best fuck-you smile. "As I was about to say, Mr. Sheffield also opted for our memory-care assistance package, which means that for a modest fee we assume full responsibility for administering his medications in the exact dosages and at the exact times that his physicians prescribed. The staff member who found him was bringing him his evening meds, but he apparently had died peacefully in his sleep."

"An autopsy will determine what he died of," Kylie said.

"An autopsy?" Millstein said, a half smile on her face. "He was an old man with Alzheimer's. He came here because he *knew* he was dying, and he wanted to be cared for in his final days, Detective. Mission accomplished."

"Then your work is done," Kylie said. "The medical examiner will confirm the cause of death. Until then, we're going to station a police officer outside his room to make sure that nobody enters."

"A police officer? I have a couple scheduled to tour the facility at three o'clock," Millstein said. "What am I supposed to say when they ask why a cop is standing in the hallway?"

Kylie shrugged. "I don't know. How about 'it's all part of Golden Grove's fierce commitment to safety'?"

Theo put his hand to his mouth to stifle a laugh. Kylie was playing the role of her alter ego, K-Mac the wisecracking TV cop, and the boy was loving it.

I was not amused.

"Loretta," I said, jumping in. "Mr. Sheffield's room will be in custody of the New York City Police Department. And there won't be just one cop. There'll be an investigative team, so maybe it would be best if you canceled all prospective clients until further notice. I also suggest that you keep the residents away from that section because the medical examiner will be here shortly to look at the body and take it back to the morgue."

"Too late for that, Detective," she spat out, her rosy smile gone black.

"What do you mean?"

"The funeral home removed him last night," she said. "It's very disconcerting to our residents to know there's a dead body in the next room. They came around midnight while most people were asleep. Mr. Sheffield had made prior arrangements with them."

Kylie and I exchanged a quick look. If Sheffield had been murdered, the crime scene was now contaminated. We needed to get to the body before someone started prepping it for burial.

"We'll still be posting an officer outside his room until we've gone through it," I said. "And we'll need the name and address of the funeral home."

"Of course," Millstein said. "Is there anything else?"

"Yes," Kylie said, pulling out her phone and showing Millstein the sketch Theo thought could be the hit man known as Barbara. "Do you recognize this man?"

Millstein took one look and inhaled sharply. She knew him. And she quickly figured out that if the cops wanted him, her life was about to get even more complicated.

"Yes, he's been here," she said. "He was a friend of Mr. Sheffield's."

"Do you know his name?" Kylie asked.

"No, but guests are required to sign in. I have a digital record of everyone who visited. We log it by resident, so all I have to do is pull up Mr. Sheffield's file," she said, turning to her keyboard and typing.

"Here it is. He was here three times over the past four months. Sadly, he's the only visitor Mr. Sheffield ever had."

"Do you have a photo of his driver's license?" I asked.

"No. We only require people to sign their names. It's an honor system."

I felt like screaming, *Shit, lady! Sheffield's friends were anything but honorable.*

"His last name is Berra. Like Yogi Berra," Millstein said, as if that might help.

"First name?" I asked.

"Robert."

Robert Berra. Bob Berra. Bobberra. Barbara.

Our hit man had a devilish sense of humor.

CHAPTER 31

"I TOLD YOU she was a jerk," Theo said once we were back in the parking lot.

"Don't keep me in suspense," I said. "Which one are we talking about? Millstein or K-Mac?"

The kid laughed. "Kylie really is a piece of work, isn't she? It must be so cool to work with someone like her all day," he said.

"And if by *cool* you mean exasperating, then yes," I said.

Another laugh.

Theo and I were alone. It had been Kylie's idea. "He just lost someone he cared deeply about, and his father is ten thousand miles away," she said. "He needs some quality one-on-one man time."

She was right. All I had to do was ask him how he felt, and he opened up.

"It's sad. I wish I'd met Mr. Sheffield before the dementia. I wanted to get his story on video, but he would never let me. He said, 'Let's keep it old school. Just two guys talking.' So all I have is what's up here," Theo said, tapping his head. "Plus whatever I wrote down later on."

"Kylie and I are going to want to go over those notes, but right now we have to get to the funeral home," I said. "Can you meet us at the station house around lunchtime?"

"Sure." He hesitated. "Zach . . . do you think this is real? Do you and Kylie think Mr. Sheffield was murdered?"

"Theo, we're homicide detectives. And you know what they say. When you're a hammer, everything looks like a nail." I took a card out of my wallet and handed it to him. "Here's my cell number. Anything you think of, anything you need, call me."

"Thanks." He got on his bike, and I watched him ride off. I really liked him. Travis Wilkins was a lucky man.

"What did Theo say?" Kylie asked as soon as I got in the car.

"Not much. Mostly he talked about you and how patient and understanding you are when you deal with difficult people like Mrs. Millstein."

"Well, I'm glad *somebody* gets me," she said, pulling out of the parking lot too fast.

Five minutes later, we were at Winstanley's funeral home on Riverdale Avenue. We identified ourselves to the receptionist and asked for the owner.

"Mr. Winstanley is in our gallery," she said. "I'll get him for you."

"I have a better idea," I said, not wanting Winstanley to have any time to think before we asked him our first question. "How about you take us to him?"

We followed her into a large, sterile windowless room. The floor was lined with an array of opulent caskets—gleaming oak, warm mahogany, and you-ain't-never-gettin'-outta-here steel. The lids were flipped open to reveal plush linings of silk, satin, or velvet in a range of colors from pastel pink to manly midnight blue. Gilt-framed signs in cursive fonts discreetly announced that smart shoppers could save 30 percent if you buy before you die. It was a grim testament to the fact that death is big business.

A man was standing at the far side of the room, next to a wall of ornate cremation urns. He looked up when we entered.

"Mr. Winstanley," the receptionist said. "These police officers are here to see you."

"Detectives!" Winstanley said. It was an effusive greeting, but it also felt like his way of correcting her without correcting her. She backed out of the room, and he approached us.

If we'd been casting a movie and looking for someone to play a funeral director, we wouldn't have had to look any further. He was tall and trim, with comforting eyes and a pleasant smile. His white hair was perfectly combed, his dark suit neatly pressed, and his black cap-toe oxfords shined to a high gloss.

He extended his hand. "Eldon Winstanley. I don't think we've met, and I'm pretty sure I know everyone from the Fiftieth," he said. "What precinct do you work out of?"

Kylie handed him a business card.

"NYPD Red," he said, duly impressed. "And what brings you to Riverdale?"

"Martin Sheffield."

The warm smile turned somber. "Sadly, he passed last night," Winstanley said, his voice dropping an octave.

"We're aware," Kylie said. "We'll need you to turn the body over to the medical examiner's office for an autopsy."

"An autopsy?" he said, clasping his hands in front of his chest. "I'm afraid that's impossible."

"Sir," Kylie said, "it's not only possible, but the medical examiner will be here in less than an hour with all the paperwork you'll need to release the body. It will be returned to you for burial when they're done."

"No, Detective, you don't understand. I'm not objecting to the autopsy. It's just that Mr. Sheffield's remains were cremated. I was looking for an appropriate urn when you arrived."

"When?" Kylie demanded.

"Three hours ago," Winstanley said.

"We were told you picked him up at midnight. What was the hurry?"

"There was no viewing, no service, no family, so there was no reason to store the body. I'm sorry if it sounds cold, but it's a very efficient way to run a mortuary. Every detail was prearranged by Mr. Sheffield himself. I'd be happy to provide you with all the documentation."

My cell rang. It was Theo. I flashed the caller ID to Kylie, and she gave me a satisfied smile—her way of taking credit for the male bonding experience she had effected.

"Excuse me a second," I said to Winstanley, and I took the call.

"Zach, it's Theo."

"I know. What's going on?"

"Don't get pissed, but I didn't go straight home. I decided that I needed to pay my last respects to Mr. Sheffield."

"I see," I said, doing my best to look like a bored cop fielding yet another routine call. "And where are you now?"

"I'm right outside in the parking lot of Winstanley's funeral home. And he's here, too."

"Who?"

"Oh, shit! He just got out of his car, and he's walking toward the front door."

"And who would that be?" I said casually.

"The guy from the sketch, Zach! Mr. Sheffield's friend. Barbara!"

CHAPTER 32

"THANKS FOR CALLING, Mrs. Abernathy," I said. "Why don't you wait for Detective MacDonald and me at the station."

"Mrs. Abernathy," Theo repeated. "I get it. You can't talk."

Kylie got it, too. "Mrs. Abernathy" was code. We locked eyes. She didn't know what was going on, but she was ready.

"Zach, wait," Theo blurted out. "Barbara stopped outside the front door. He's making a phone call."

A few seconds later, I heard the buzz of a vibrating cell. It was Winstanley's. My stomach dropped. Barbara was making a phone call; Winstanley was getting one. I'm a cop. I don't believe in coincidences.

"Pardon me," Winstanley said, taking the phone from his jacket pocket.

I took a good hard look at him—late sixties, keen-eyed, physically fit, mentally alert. He had fit my preconceived notion of a mortician so perfectly that I'd never stopped to consider another possibility.

Aging hit man.

He checked his caller ID. "I have to take this," he said, rewarding our patience with a deferential smile.

"This is Eldon Winstanley. How can I help you?" he said in a singsong voice that I decided had to be an alert to the person on the other end. "No, I won't be much longer. I'm just finishing up with two hardworking detectives from New York's Finest."

Well played, Winstanley. You just let Barbara know that the cops are here.

"I'll catch up with you later," Winstanley said, ending the call.

"Zach," Theo said. "Barbara changed his mind. He's walking back to his pickup truck. It's a black Toyota RAV4."

"Got it." I hung up, put my phone in my pocket, and smiled at Winstanley. "Sir, we appreciate your help," I said. Then I turned to Kylie. "It looks like we've got ourselves a ninety-two Charlie here."

Despite his extensive training, Winstanley had no idea what I'd just said. But every cop in the city knows that a 10-92C is the radio code for arrest. As soon as I said "ninety-two Charlie," Kylie flashed a smile and extended her hand. "Thank you so much for your time," she said.

Winstanley responded like a funeral director. He graciously grasped her right hand. In one swift, practiced move, she reached behind her with her left, grabbed her cuffs, and slapped one on his wrist.

But this old pro wasn't going down without a fight. And despite his age, he had plenty of fight left in him. He wheeled around, arcing his right leg toward Kylie's head. He had the skills, but the years had sapped him of some of the speed and power.

She twisted her body, and he connected with her shoulder, launching her into a velvet-covered pedestal that was displaying a mahogany casket. She hit the floor hard, and I knew I was next. I reached behind me for my ASP—a sixteen-ounce extendable steel baton that can split open a coconut in a single blow.

I brought it down hard on Winstanley's clavicle and heard the crack of bone as he went down.

"Fucking cocksuckers!" he screamed, the obsequious humble-servant facade gone as he writhed in agony, spewing venom and vowing to kill us and every member of our families. I cuffed his other wrist behind his back and dragged him across the floor.

"You okay?" I asked Kylie as she stood up.

"Shit, man," she said. "I thought Mrs. Millstein was going to be the nastiest person I had to deal with all day. This old fuck has a roundhouse kick like Jackie Chan. I'm glad I didn't run into him while he was in his prime."

I took out my cuffs and shackled Winstanley to the rail of a bronze casket.

"Theo followed us," I said. "He called to warn us that the guy from the sketch was about to come in here, but Winstanley gave him a heads-up."

Guns drawn, we ran through the funeral home and charged through the front door.

There was no sign of Barbara. No sign of his black RAV4. And no sign of Theo.

"Theo!" Kylie called out. "Theo!"

No answer.

Ordinarily, Kylie doesn't get rattled, but there was nothing ordinary about her relationship with Theo, and I could see the panic mounting in her eyes as she scanned the parking lot. "Zach, I think that psycho took Theo!"

"Nobody took him," I said. "His bike is gone."

She looked at me, calmer now, as the pieces started coming together.

"You heard what his father said," I reminded her as we double-timed it to our car. "The kid loves crime shit. And I guarantee you that right now he's on his motorcycle, chasing after our killer and loving every second of it."

CHAPTER 33

"THIS IS WHAT HAPPENS when you grow up hanging around the set of some dumb fucking cop show," Kylie said as soon as she got behind the wheel. "Call him. He's got a headset in his helmet."

I hit Theo's number and put the phone on speaker.

"Hey, partner," Theo chirped. "Where are you?"

"Don't 'hey partner' us," Kylie bellowed. "Where the hell are *you?*"

"I'm headed southbound on Riverdale about half a block behind Barbara's car."

"Are you out of your mind?" Kylie said.

"You guys didn't come out of the funeral home, so I followed him," Theo said, his tone more than a little pissy. "You're welcome."

"Theo, the man is a professional killer. Stop following him. Now!"

"Chill, bro. He has no idea I'm behind him."

"I'm not your fucking *bro*," Kylie thundered. "I'm a cop, and I just gave you a direct order. Pull over!"

"Yeah, yeah. Wait—he just crossed Two-Hundred-Fifty-Sixth Street. You should call ahead and get some cops to head him off at the pass."

Our number one priority was to stop Theo from getting himself killed. But we couldn't ignore the information he was feeding us. I grabbed my radio.

"Central, this is Red Unit. Priority message. Advise all units we have a homicide perp fleeing southbound on Riverdale Ave. in a black Toyota RAV4. He just crossed Two-Five-Six Street. Subject is white male, midsixties, armed and dangerous."

If almost any other cop had made that call, a supervisor would immediately have jumped in and quashed the request, demanding more information before sending dozens of cop cars careening through the city streets. But they know better than to interfere with Red.

"Ten-four, Red," Central responded without hesitation. "Will transmit that message across bordering divisions."

The radio came alive with responses. In seconds, cops from every corner of the Bronx would be lights, sirens, and adrenaline.

An authoritative female voice cut through the chatter. "Special Operations Division CO to Central."

Kylie and I knew her. Trina Jennings, a three-star chief—as go-by-the-book as they come.

"Clear the air, units," Central ordered. "Go ahead, Special Operations CO."

"Oh, shit!" Kylie said. "Is Jennings going to shut us down?"

Just the opposite.

"I have Aviation up and responding to assist Red," Jennings said. "I've also directed ESU truck four to stand by as needed."

"Central," I said, "thank the chief, and advise her that we need ESU to respond to Winstanley Funeral Home on Riverdale at Two-Six-One street. We have a second homicide perp handcuffed to a casket inside that location. Requesting a tactical entry."

"Red, *what* did you say that perp is cuffed to?" Central responded.

Jennings jumped in. "A casket. It's a funeral home, Central. Advise Red my guys are on the way."

I turned my attention back to Kylie, who still couldn't get Theo to pull over. She shook her head and handed me the phone.

"Theo, it's Zach," I said.

"Hey, Zach. We're coming up on Two-Hundred-and-Fifty-Third Street."

"Great. You've been a big help," I said. "We're closing in on you, and the cavalry is on the way. Now, do me a favor. Pull over and let us do our job."

"Zach, I know what you're saying, but this is too big. I just want to be there when they close in on—oh, shit!"

We heard the screech of tires. It was quickly followed by the unmistakable gut-wrenching sound of metal tearing against metal.

And then silence.

CHAPTER 34

ONE OF THE DOWNSIDES of being a control freak is dealing with the harsh realization that you can't control everything.

Kylie had never asked Theo to follow us to the funeral home, and she'd used every trick in her playbook to stop him from chasing after a world-class assassin, but that didn't keep her from blaming herself for whatever disaster had just befallen him.

"It's my fault if the damn kid gets himself killed," she yelled as she crossed over the double yellow line to pass a slow-moving car, swerving back just in time to avoid a head-on with a northbound city bus.

"That's debatable," I shouted, white-knuckling the armrest and pressing my body hard against my seat, "but it'll damn well be your fault if *I* get killed. Slow the fuck down!"

She did. A little. Half a minute later, she slammed on the brakes behind a dozen cars that had stopped because of the accident. A few drivers were already standing on the roadway, phones to their ears.

"NYPD! NYPD! Get back in your vehicles," Kylie commanded as we bolted out of the car and raced toward the wreckage.

Theo's treasured Triumph Bonneville was in the middle of the road, the front end crushed, the forks twisted up against the engine, the handlebars bent at odd angles.

NYPD RED 7: THE MURDER SORORITY 135

Theo was stretched out on the sidewalk, a woman in a tennis outfit kneeling at his side.

She held her hand up as we approached. "He's conscious. His name is Theo Wilkins, and he knows what day it is, but don't move him or try to take off his helmet until the EMTs get here and put him on a board. My name is Angela Monitto. I'm the school nurse at Riverdale Kingsbridge Academy. He rear-ended a black SUV, but the guy took off," she said, giving us as many details as she could in less than twenty seconds.

"Thank you," Kylie said as we both knelt at Theo's side.

"I'm okay," he said, sounding far from okay. "But my bike is fucked. My dad is gonna kill me."

"You'll be lucky if I don't kill you first," Kylie said. "How many times did I tell you to back off?"

"It's not my fault, Kylie. He sandbagged me. We were doing about forty. All of a sudden, he braked real hard, jammed it into reverse, and bam, I went flying."

"So then I guess your Spidey sense wasn't working when you told me he had no idea you were tailing him," Kylie said. She looked up at the nurse. "You're a medical professional, Angela. You think his super-powers just crapped out?"

By now the woman had figured out that Kylie and Theo had a history. She smiled. "It could be that or the fact that his prefrontal cortex, which is the rational part of the brain that responds to situations with good judg-ment and an awareness of long-term consequences, won't be developed until he's twenty-five."

"So you're saying he's just another teenage asshole," Kylie said.

"It's a common syndrome," Angela replied, straight-faced. "Like I said, I work in a high school. I see it every day."

By now at least a dozen cop cars and emergency units had converged on the scene. Kylie and I got out of the way so two EMTs could take Theo's vitals and determine if he was lucid.

I eyeballed a pair of uniformed cops, both of whom had twenty-year longevity pins on their chests. Without being told, they had immediately cordoned off the crash site with crime scene tape. Experienced and smart. Just what we needed. I waved them over.

"Zach Jordan and Kylie MacDonald from Red," I said. "I appreciate your securing the scene."

"Gene DeStefano, and this is my partner, Rich Maguire," the older one said. "We appreciate being appreciated. What else can we do to help?"

"The victim is a material witness in a homicide case," I said. "Could one of you follow the bus to the hospital, and the other ride in the back with him? Someone just tried to kill him, so please don't let him out of your sight. And nobody goes near him except his medical team."

They couldn't have been more receptive if I'd asked them to join me, my attractive blond partner, and the police commissioner in a sky booth at Yankee Stadium.

"We're on it, Detective," DeStefano answered.

Despite the chaos, I'd kept one ear tuned to my radio ever since we arrived at the accident. Nothing promising had come over the air.

I keyed the mike. "Central, this is Red. Anyone have eyes on that perp in the RAV4?"

One by one, the units called in.

"Five-two David, negative. Four-six Michael, negative. Aviation one, negative."

Barbara had gotten away. He was every bit the old pro that Sheffield had said he was.

"This is bad, Zach," Kylie said. "We've got to find him before . . ."

Her voice trailed off. Neither of us wanted to finish the thought.

Before he finds Theo.

CHAPTER 35

THE EMS TECH gave us the good news in three words. "Helmets save lives," he said.

"So he's going to be okay?" Kylie said.

"The docs over at Monte will CT scan him for neck and spinal damage, but from the looks of it, his brain seems to be intact."

"That's strange," Kylie said. "I was talking to him a few minutes before the crash. It wasn't working then."

The tech laughed. "Tell me about it. I've got a pair of idiot teenagers at home. Apparently, it doesn't skip a generation."

As soon as Theo was safely on his way to Montefiore Hospital, Kylie and I went back to the crash scene.

Highway units showed up to assist with traffic. CSU combed through the debris and arranged to transport Theo's bike to their garage, where they would go over every inch, looking for microscopic evidence that might help us identify Barbara's vehicle.

As soon as Kylie and I got back in the car, we called our boss.

"I'm on my way up to Riverdale," Cates said. "I took off as soon as I caught the first alert that there was a major incident involving Red. I've been monitoring the radio, but I'm sure you purposely kept some of the details off the air. Fill me in."

We took her through our morning from the time we arrived at

Golden Grove until we put Theo in the ambulance.

"I'll update the chief of Ds," she said. "I'll be at the funeral home in five."

We were there in two. In the forty-nine minutes since we peeled out of the parking lot, Winstanley's had transformed from a sedate mortuary to the vibrant mosaic of flashing red lights, plastic yellow tape, and blue uniforms that typifies every high-profile criminal investigation.

And there was no doubt about it. The radio traffic between Chief Jennings and me made this one the hottest ticket in town. Especially if you were a journalist.

TV trucks and news vans clogged the streets, and a sea of familiar faces, armed with cameras, microphones, and the First Amendment, all started screaming at Kylie and me as soon as we arrived.

We ignored them. Most of them cooled down. They're used to being brushed off in the initial stages of our tedious methodical process. But one of them was not to be denied. Megan Rollins.

A uniformed officer handed me Megan's card. She'd scrawled her outrage on the back. *"I thought we had a deal."*

She was right. She'd been a valuable source. We couldn't give her much, but we had to at least make her feel as if she was the most important wolf in the ravenous pack of reporters. We followed the cop to the side street where Megan was parked.

"We're in a hurry, Megan," I said. "So if you've got questions, ask them fast."

"No problem, Detective," she said. "You're working two crime scenes a mile apart. You have units on the ground, in the air, and this place is crawling with brass. So my first question is, why the fuck isn't my phone ringing?"

"Your disappointment is duly noted," I said. "Right now we've got sixty seconds. Make the most of them."

"Who was cuffed to a casket?"

"I can't give you a name, but he's under arrest."

"*Under arrest?* Wow, thanks. I guess the handcuffs should've been my first clue. How is he connected to the Hellmans?"

I shrugged.

"I'll take that to mean he is connected," she said. "How?"

"Right now all we can say is, we're going to take him in for questioning."

"Once again, I could have figured that out," she said. "Do you think he'll talk?"

"He will if he's smart."

"And who's the guy on the bike who wiped out during the car chase? How is he involved?"

It's a slippery slope when you cut a private deal with the media. I wanted to say no comment. But we owed Megan. I decided to split the difference.

"He's a material witness," I said.

"That's a crumb, Zach," she said. "I need meat and potatoes."

"Jordan! MacDonald!"

Kylie and I turned around. It was Cates.

"Now!" she ordered.

"It's our boss," I said to Megan. "We've got to go. I've got your card. I'll call you later."

We didn't wait for an answer. We double-timed it to Cates. "Geoghan has something," she said.

We followed her to the BearCat, a hulking armored personnel carrier that had delivered the ESU team to the funeral home. Captain Brian Geoghan was waiting for us. At forty-something years old, he still looked like the classic chisel-jawed, hard-bodied, invincible marine you see in the recruitment posters. Kylie and I knew Geoghan, and even though he was dressed in full SWAT regalia, we knew that we wouldn't hear a sound if he came up behind us.

"Kylie, Zach," he said. "Thanks for the heads-up. You said Winstanley was a tough mother, so we went in heavy. He's seventy years old, but he's got a hell of a lot of fight in him. He's on ice now, and we found this in his back pocket."

He handed me the weapon Winstanley never got a chance to use on us. I ran my fingers over the smooth leather. Then I hefted it, and I could feel the weight of the lead inside. It was old school—silent, easy to hide, and deadly: a blackjack.

"Zach," Kylie said, the familiar *holy shit* look in her eyes. "Alice is up-close firearms, Barbara is knives, Carol's the sniper, Denise was poison, and the last one uses blunt objects. Eldon Winstanley is Emily."

"Brian," I said, "this is big. What else?"

"There are three bodies downstairs in the crematorium waiting to go into the oven."

"Any white males?" Kylie asked.

"Yeah, one. Hold on." He took out a pad and checked his notes. "They brought him in from the Golden Grove nursing home last night. His name is Martin Sheffield."

CHAPTER 36

THERE WERE NO identifiable bruises on Sheffield's body, but like most homicide detectives, Kylie, Cates, and I could recognize the hemorrhaged blood vessels in his eyes, his swollen tongue, and the other signs of asphyxiation. It wouldn't take the ME more than thirty seconds to label his demise a probable homicide.

Eldon Winstanley, the man who murdered him, was upstairs in the lobby of the funeral home, hands cuffed behind his back, his ankles shackled. Ronnie Lee, an ESU paramedic, had just examined him.

"Who the hell is this old rooster?" Lee said. "He's pushing seventy, put up a hell of a fight, has a broken collarbone that has to be causing him excruciating pain. But I took his vitals, and his BP is one-ten over seventy and his pulse is fifty-six. Look at him. He's just sitting there all cool, calm, and go fuck yourself. No sign of stress."

"Let's see if I can change that," Kylie said.

She read Winstanley his rights. "You almost got away with it, Eldon," she said. "Or can I call you Emily?"

Winstanley didn't blink.

"I've got to hand it to you," she said. "You're as fierce as they come. If I hadn't managed to blindside you by snapping that cuff on your right wrist, Zach and I would probably be downstairs in your toaster oven with the dial set to two thousand degrees."

"Sixteen hundred and fifty," he said.

"It's hard to charge someone with a homicide without an autopsy," she said. "So with all due respect to your preeminent standing in the Murder-for-Hire Hall of Fame, I have to ask, why didn't you cremate Sheffield as soon as you brought him here?"

"You look like someone who appreciates irony, Detective," he said with a wry smile.

"Oh, I do. Lay it on me."

"We ran out of fuel," he said.

"Oh my God, that is practically Shakespearean," she said. "How does a crematorium run out of gas?"

He shrugged. "The propane truck broke down yesterday. He'll be here to fill up the tanks around noon."

"Well, you won't be here to sign for it, and if you're as smart as I think you are, by noon you'll be cutting a deal with the district attorney."

"It's not my nature to make deals, Detective," he said.

"Your nature, my ass!" Kylie snapped. "The government trained you, chewed you up, spit you out, and you're still living your life by *their* code? If you get caught, don't talk? Spend the rest of your life in prison? You don't work for those people anymore. You don't owe them shit. How old are you, Eldon?"

"Sixty-eight."

"You'll get twenty-five easy. Let me see, that makes you ninety-three when you get out. That sucks. You know what sucks less? Fifteen. Maybe ten. You give the DA what's in your head, you're a free man at seventy-eight. Maybe sooner if you're a model prisoner."

"I appreciate the offer, Detective," Winstanley said.

"It's the same offer we're going to make to your friend Barbara when we arrest him. And trust me, we're damn close. You're all senior citizens. First one to cut a deal with the DA is the only one who doesn't have to die behind bars."

"It's tempting, Detective MacDonald," he said. "But you have no idea what you're dealing with."

"Enlighten me."

"Sheffield talked. Told that kid about his past. They don't know what he said, but they know he talked. And he's dead."

"Who are *they*?"

"If I tell you that, I'm a dead man. And here's another bit of irony. If I tell you nothing, they won't know if I talked or not, and they're not going to take a chance, so I'm still a dead man. Don't you get it? You could reduce my sentence to two years, two months, or two days. It wouldn't matter. I'm never getting out of this alive."

Kylie looked at me and then at Cates. She was done. At least for now.

"All right, Eldon," she said. "We're going to take you to the hospital, patch you up, and give you some time to come to your senses. Let's go."

Two ESU cops helped him to his feet and escorted him from the dark, somber funeral home into the bright, vibrant world outside.

He walked haltingly, restrained by the irons around his feet and the unrelenting pain of his shattered clavicle.

The ambulance was only twenty yards from the door, but halfway there he stopped. To rest, I figured. As conditioned as he was, the last hour had to have taken a lot out of him.

He looked to his left and then to his right, slowly taking in the horde of people and equipment that had assembled just for him.

He took a deep breath, tilted his head back, and lifted his face to the sky.

Every cop, every EMS worker, every curious bystander who had gathered for the sideshow stopped what they were doing to take in the tableau of this striking silver-haired figure as he looked up to enjoy his final moments in the sun.

And then, in a booming voice, Winstanley called out, *"Honesta vita, mors honesta."*

Kylie turned to me. "What the fuck is he—"

She never got to finish. The gunshot, every bit as loud, every bit as deadly as the one that killed Warren Hellman, ripped a hole through the old man's neck, spraying the two cops at his side with blood, flesh, and bone.

Eldon Winstanley had told us he was a dead man. When he lifted his head to shout his final words to the heavens, his last contribution to his comrades in the killing trade was to make sure his executioner didn't miss.

CHAPTER 37

WINSTANLEY'S LIFE ENDED the second the bullet tore through his neck and spinal cord. But his heart, which had a mission to keep him alive, and its own independent electrical system to do the job, refused to quit.

Even as his lifeless body dropped to the ground, the valiant organ kept pumping, and blood spurted in thick red rivulets through the gaping hole in his throat, like a garden hose gone haywire.

The two cops at his side knew there was nothing they could do to save their prisoner, so they scrambled behind an ESU truck and anxiously patted themselves down to make sure none of the blood that covered their uniforms was their own.

It was a moment of madness, but it didn't last long. ESU Captain Geoghan took command immediately, first ordering the BearCat to block the front entrance to the building, then directing his team to flank out and do a perimeter search of the area where the shot had come from.

There was a small private college across the street from the funeral home. The campus was idyllic, with stately stone buildings set back three hundred yards from Riverdale Avenue, fronted by acres of thick woodland. It was as close to a country setting as you could get in a big city. It was also the perfect spot for the shooter. And if I knew anything about the man whose code name was Carol, he had planned his exit as carefully as he had executed Eldon Winstanley in front of fifty unsuspecting cops.

But Geoghan had responded within seconds of the gunshot, and our killer was on foot. He might not yet have made it out of that dense urban forest. Kylie and I jogged along the avenue until we found a quiet spot where we could monitor the northernmost end of the tree line in the hope that someone would emerge carrying a duffel bag, a set of golf clubs, or a UPS box like the one Elroy Lafontant had seen from his cell at the Tombs.

Fifteen minutes into our vigil, Cates called. "We've just been summoned downtown," she said.

"To be chewed out by our boss," I said, stating the obvious.

"No. By *his* boss."

"The *mayor*?" I said. "She's sending for us *now*, in the middle of an operation?"

"You're thinking like a cop, Jordan. When you're a politician, the first thing you do in a shitstorm is make sure there are people standing between you and the fan."

Cates was right. Cops and politicians are two different breeds. The PC would never dress down his senior people in front of the troops they command. But our elected officials can never have enough scapegoats. And so, less than an hour after Winstanley was murdered, the PC, Cates, Kylie, and I stood in Mayor Sykes's office and listened to her lay the blame for her latest political nightmare squarely on the shoulders of the New York City Police Department.

Our previous mayor, Stanley Spellman, was bombastic. Fuck up on his watch, and he would tear you a new one at the top of his lungs. Muriel Sykes was more scalpel than sledgehammer.

"I have a press conference in thirty minutes," she said, her voice calm, her anger restrained. "I plan to make a brief vacuous statement and then take questions. The first one, I am sure, will be, 'Madam Mayor, how is it possible that two prominent New Yorkers, surrounded by a battalion of cops, can be gunned down on national television in the space of forty-eight hours?'"

My entire body clenched at the words "prominent New Yorkers." Warren Hellman was a serial predator who destroyed the lives of young women, murdered a hero cop in cold blood, then used his wealth, power, and Hollywood mystique to sway a jury. Eldon Winstanley may have looked respectable on the outside, but beneath the surface, he was a cold-blooded killer who had come close to claiming my partner and me as his latest victims. He'd been gunned down by one of his own to keep him from cooperating with the police.

I didn't have to look at my partners in humiliation to know that they all were thinking along the same lines. But Colin Radcliffe stood there stone-faced, and the rest of us followed his lead.

The mayor's cell phone dinged. She picked it up from her desk. "More good news," she said, looking at the screen. "Someone on my staff just translated Winstanley's last words. *Honesta vita, mors honesta.* It's Latin for 'An honorable life. An honorable death.' That's right up there with 'I only regret that I have but one life to lose for my country.'"

She let the phone clatter to the desk and then glowered at the four of us.

"Look at you. My top cop and the rock stars of my elite unit. I don't know how this happened, but you've got two strikes. One more and *you* are out," she said, pointing at the PC.

She didn't even bother telling the rest of us where we would wind up. It didn't matter. It was somewhere between washed-up and hung out to dry. NYPD has an abundance of dead-end jobs in its elephants' burial ground for coppers non grata.

"Commissioner," she said, "it's too late to ask if this is the hill you want to die on. So let me ask a different question. Is this the team you plan to lead into battle?"

Without hesitation, Colin Radcliffe responded. "Absolutely, Madam Mayor."

"Then do it," she said. She pushed a button on her desk, and her office door opened electronically.

Minutes later, the four of us were standing on Centre Street, City Hall at our backs.

The PC looked at us. "You heard her," he said. "Do it."

Not a single word about his career hanging in the balance. Just those two words. *Do it.* A tall order, but we knew that they were backed up with the faith, trust, and conviction that we could.

We responded with an emphatic "Yes sir."

He turned and walked across the street to 1-PP.

Cates left, and Kylie and I stood there trying to decide what to do first.

My phone rang. Someone was making the decision for us.

"Detective Jordan, this is Gene DeStefano. My partner and I are here with young Theo at Montefiore."

"Everything okay?" I said.

"Everything's great," DeStefano said. "In fact, they're so good that the kid wants to check himself out of the hospital."

"Is he out of his fucking mind?"

"I'm not a medical professional, but I'm going with 'What kid his age isn't?'"

"Cuff him to the fucking bed," I said. "We'll be right there."

"Heads up. You're going to run into one mightily pissed-off reporter who can't take 'I'm sorry, ma'am, but this room is off limits' for an answer."

"Thanks," I said. I didn't have to ask her name.

CHAPTER 38

THEO HAD BEEN CHECKED into Montefiore Hospital under an alias. After the doctors cleaned up his road rash and scanned him for internal injuries, he was sequestered in a private room in the pediatric wing, with two cops guarding the door. It was all part of our effort to keep people from tracking him down.

But Megan Rollins has informants everywhere. As soon as Kylie and I got off the elevator on Theo's floor, she was waiting for us.

"Megan," I said, doing my best to look surprised. "What are you doing here?"

"Covering the story."

Kylie jumped in. "The story is at the funeral home."

"Not for me," she said. "I'm from the gravedigger school of journalism."

"Never heard of it," Kylie snapped. "Enlighten us."

"When President Kennedy was assassinated, every journalist from around the world covered his funeral. Except one. Jimmy Breslin. He interviewed Clifton Pollard, the man who was paid three dollars an hour to dig the president's grave. The column was brilliant. Sometimes, the best place to go when there's a major story breaking is where the rest of the media isn't."

Another time, another place, Kylie might have been more tolerant, but she was still raw from watching the PC get skewered. "Megan, the best place for you to go is home," she said.

"Fuck you, Detective. We had a deal. I tipped you to the fact that someone tried to kill Curtis Hellman by switching his insulin. Maybe the lead didn't pan out for you, but don't blame me because you're inept."

I held up a hand before Kylie could take it up a notch. "Megan," I said, "like I told you at the funeral home—"

"Fuck you, too, Zach," Megan snapped. "You told me nothing. You said we had a quid pro quo. But so far, all I've seen is quid pro *no*. Are you going to let me talk to the kid, or not?"

"I can't," I said.

"You can't, you won't, you're not at liberty . . . You know what I think? You haven't given me shit, because you don't *have* shit. You're up to your precious Red asses in homicides, and you haven't cracked one of them. Not only do you two suck at your job, you've gone out of your way to keep me from doing mine."

She stormed off.

Kylie shrugged. "I guess we'll be getting a call from DCPI telling us we need a refresher course in media relations?" she said. "Let's go talk to Theo."

Officers DeStefano and Maguire were parked outside Theo's room.

"How's he doing?" I asked.

"The kid is funny," DeStefano said. "He says to us, 'I'm lawyering up.' I say, 'You're not under arrest. You don't need a lawyer.' He goes, 'I need one who can get me the fuck out of here.'"

I opened Theo's door. He sat up in bed as soon as we entered.

"It's about time," he said. "Did you catch Barbara?"

"Not yet," Kylie said.

"What about Carol?"

"What are you talking about?"

He held up his phone. "Guys, it's all over the news. You arrested the old man who owns the funeral home. A sniper took him out. I told you, Denise was poison, Barbara stabs people, Carol is the shooter. Why did he kill Winstanley?"

"It looks like he was part of the Sorority," I said.

"Holy fuck!" Theo said, swinging his feet over the side of the bed. "Everyone who knows about the Sorority is getting killed. The Hellmans, Mr. Sheffield, and now the guy from the funeral home. Plus, Barbara got away. Who do you think he's coming for next? Me."

"*Now* you realize he's a trained killer?" Kylie said. "I tried to get you to back off when you were chasing him like some adolescent superhero."

"Okay, so I fucked up. But you can't leave me here. In the movies, the bad guy always shows up in the hospital wearing scrubs and kills the dumbass who can ID them. I'm that dumbass."

"For once, you and I are in violent agreement," Kylie said.

"Not funny, K-Mac. I don't care how many cops you have outside my door. If the Sorority comes after me here, I'm a dead man. Don't you get it? I know too much. That's why that reporter tried to interview me." He stood up. "It's too dicey to go back to my apartment, but I can go to Carly's house. I'll be a lot safer there."

"No, you won't," Kylie said. "If you're at risk and you stay with her, the only thing you'll be doing is putting her at risk, too."

"Well, then I need police protection."

Kylie looked at me. We both knew he was right. We could post guards outside his door, but there was no way to keep a determined hit man out of the hospital.

"We'll talk about it after you get dressed," she said.

Theo grabbed his clothes and stepped into the bathroom.

"His mother is dead, and his father is on the other side of the world," Kylie said. "I guess he can stay at my place."

"And what testosterone-charged teenage boy would turn down an offer like that?" I said. "Shane, on the other hand, might take issue with it."

"Then where?" Kylie said.

Theo threw open the bathroom door. "I'm ready to blow this joint," he said. "Where are we going?"

"My apartment," I said. "But there are ground rules."

"Like what?"

"Turn off your phone and shut down all your social media."

"Are you crazy?"

"No, I'm a cop. I'll take you to your place, you'll pack whatever you need, and once you move in with me, you don't leave unless Kylie or I are with you."

"How do I call my friends?"

"You don't. I'll buy you a burner phone. Kylie and I will have the number. She'll call your father, tell him what's going on, and give it to him."

"And *no* social media? Nothing at all? How will I know what's happening in the world?"

"You can watch CNN."

"You want me to just sit around your house with nothing to do and no contact to the outside world. That's cruel and unusual punishment, Zach."

"I know, kid," I said. "But it's a sacrifice I'm willing to make."

CHAPTER 39

"WE SHOULD SPLIT UP," Kylie said. "One of us can hitch a ride to Lincoln Hospital with the precinct guys and comfort Shane in his hour of need. The other gets to take the car and set the kid up in his new home."

"Do you have a preference?" I asked innocently.

Her eyes smoldered, and she let out a long, low, lustful growl. "I'm more of a nurse than a babysitter."

"Yeah, I know," I said. "Just don't kill the patient, Nurse MacDonald."

Fifteen minutes later, Theo and I were on the road. "Who is this Shane guy?" he asked.

He caught me by surprise. "Shane? Um . . . he's a crime victim. Someone shot him."

"And you two are looking for the shooter?"

"We were, but it was assigned to another squad."

"And yet Kylie wants to visit the poor man in his hospital bed," he said with a lecherous laugh. "The plot thickens. Tell me more."

I gave him the highlights. Kylie and Spence parted ways; Kylie met Shane; Shane got shot.

"You think Spence tried to kill Shane?" he asked.

"Jesus, Theo! No. And don't even think of suggesting it to Kylie," I said. "No more cop shit. Let's talk about something else."

"How about this. What would you do if you were locked up in a house for a year and you could only watch three films?" he said. "Which ones would you pick? You go first."

I offered up *Die Hard*, *Lethal Weapon*, and *Bullitt*. The kid came back with *Hiroshima Mon Amour*, *Rashomon*, and *The Discreet Charm of the Bourgeoisie*.

"I think we live in alternate realities," Theo said. "And for the record, all your *films*—and I use the term loosely—sounded like we're still talking cop shit."

"Give me another topic."

"Sure. How about 'greatest rock bands ever'?"

Not my category, but I dug into my nineties memory bank and gave it my best shot.

"Who the hell are Hootie and the Blowfish?" he asked.

I gave him a blank stare.

"Just fucking with you, old man," he said laughing.

I don't know when thirty-seven became old, but Theo Wilkins's zest for life was infectious, and I had to laugh along with him. Even so, I didn't let the fun cloud the fact that my mission was to keep this kid from getting killed.

"Only pack what you need," I said once we were inside his apartment.

"So, then, just clean underwear, condoms, and weed," he said, cracking himself up again.

He pulled a YETI backpack out of his closet, unzipped it, opened his dresser drawers one by one, and began randomly tossing clothes in the bag. It took him less than ninety seconds to pull together his entire getaway wardrobe.

He had his own bathroom adjacent to his bedroom. I looked inside. The wastebasket was overflowing, and the floor was strewn with towels, dirty laundry, and film magazines.

I waved my hand in front of my nose and backed away from the door. "Don't forget your beauty care essentials, Cinderella," I said.

"Way ahead of you, dude," he said, opening the top dresser drawer and pulling out a black canvas bag. "Everything I need is in here, all packed and ready to go. That way, I can't forget any—"

Something on top of his dresser caught his eye. "Aww, fuck," he said.

"What is it?"

"It's a P-38," he said, picking it up. "It belonged to Mr. Sheffield. He carried it around with him since . . . I don't know, forever."

He handed it to me. It was a short piece of metal about an inch and a half long. A hinged metal tooth folded out from the side. I knew it well. It was the can opener that was first issued to our troops during World War II.

"My uncle still has one," I said. "He was a marine. The jarheads called it a John Wayne. He got it in Nam, and I guarantee you he's still got it tucked in his pants pocket today."

I gave it back to Theo, and he plopped down heavily on the bed. "Mr. Sheffield gave this to me the last time I saw him. He said, 'hang on to it, kid. You never know when you're going to have to pop the top on a can of meat-and-potato hash.' I was going to put it on my key chain, but I never got around to it."

His eyes got watery, and he wiped them dry with his sleeve. "Sorry," he said.

"Don't be," I said, sitting next to him and putting a hand on his shoulder. "You just lost him this morning, and with all the craziness, you haven't had time to grieve. You need a few minutes alone?"

"No. Thanks. I'm good," he said, standing up. "I just have to grab two more things."

He crossed the room to a glass-topped computer desk, folded his laptop, and put it in a leather case. Then he picked up an eight-by-ten silver picture frame and brought it to where I was sitting.

"You said pack only what I need," he said. "I need this. It's the last picture of me and my mom. She died not too long after this was taken."

He handed me the frame.

"The funeral was a week before her thirtieth birthday," he said. "I was only six years old but I remember everything about it."

I could hear Theo talking, but my eyes and my brain had locked on to the photo. It took my breath away.

I finally spoke. "She was very beautiful," I said. "What was her name?"

"Sylviane. Sylviane LeBec."

"French," I said.

He smiled. "*Totalement français.* She grew up in Saint Étienne in the Auvergne-Rhône-Alpes. She came to New York as an au pair working for this couple with three kids out in Southampton. She met some guy, got pregnant, and here I stand, Theo *le bâtard*, the unexpected outcome of a glorious summer romance."

I smiled. Even in his sadness, Theo could do that to people. He was every bit the charismatic character his father had said he was.

"Are you in touch with your biological dad?" I asked. "I know you'd rather have Travis here right now, but if you have a relationship with your birth father, we could contact him, and—"

"Zach, I don't even know who the fuck he is. I'm sure if my mom had lived, she'd have told me by now, but not when I was six."

"Does Travis know?"

He shook his head slowly. "She didn't tell him, either. And not to be a dick about it, but when you talk to me about Travis, *he's* my dad. And the other guy—he's not my *birth father*. He probably doesn't even know I was born. And if he does, he doesn't give a shit. He's just a sperm donor."

"I'm sorry," I said, handing him back the picture. "It won't happen again."

He tucked the frame into the case with his laptop. "I'm ready to rock and roll," he said. "Where do you live?"

"Seventy-Seventh and Lexington."

"The fashionable Upper East Side," he said. "Lah-dee-fucking-dah."

"Trust me, kiddo, the only thing remotely fashionable about my nine hundred square feet in the sky is my girlfriend, Cheryl. We don't officially live together. We resolutely pay rent for two separate places, but we spend almost every night in one apartment or the other."

"Verrrrry interesting," he said in a thick German accent and stroking an imaginary beard. "Zounds to me like you and Cheryl haff a fear of commitment."

"She's a shrink. You can hash it out with her. I've already warned her that you're moving in with us."

He shouldered his backpack, grabbed his laptop, looked around the room, and let out a long, deep sigh. "When I woke up this morning, I pretty much felt like a normal human being. Now I've got a cutthroat contract killer after me and I'm going to the mattresses. Pretty fucking surreal, don't you think, Zach?"

He didn't wait for an answer. He left the room, and I followed him.

We were almost at the front door when I stopped. "Sorry," I said. "I've got to take a whiz before we get on the road again."

"Mmmmm." He nodded knowingly. "The aging-prostate thing. Mr. Sheffield had the same issues. I'll wait."

I retraced my steps, entered his bathroom, and shut the door. I didn't have to pee. The real reason I came back was for the single blue toothbrush hanging from a ceramic wall mount.

I ripped a page out of my notebook, took the brush from the holder, wrapped it, and tucked it in my inside breast pocket.

I waited another twenty seconds, flushed the toilet, and began washing my hands.

As I stood there, I realized that I, too, woke up this morning feeling pretty much like a normal human being. But I didn't feel normal now. Normal ceased to exist for me.

I turned off the water, stared at myself in the mirror, and whispered Theo's words to my reflection.

"Pretty fucking surreal, don't you think, Zach?"

CHAPTER 40

THEO AND I STOPPED at a bodega and loaded up on snack food, soda, cereal, and assorted microwaveable delicacies of dubious nutritional value. I also picked up a couple of burner phones. The tab ran to over two hundred bucks.

"Is the department paying for all this?" he asked.

"Oh, yeah," I said. "We have a slush fund for dumbass kids who need protective custody because they thought they were smarter than a trained killer."

He grinned. "In that case, hand me another box of those Yodels."

"I live in a one-bedroom apartment," I said once we were back in the car.

"No problem. I'm cool with crashing on your sofa. The only thing I care about is that you have a couple of serious locks on the front door."

Cheryl was waiting for us when we got home. "Hungry?" she asked after I'd introduced them.

"Zach bought me some stuff," he said.

She looked in one of the bags. "Oh, God. I mean real food. We've got a bunch of take-out menus in the kitchen. What are you in the mood for?"

I didn't catch his answer, because my phone rang. It was Rich Koprowski, one of the detectives from Red who stayed at the funeral home after Kylie and I were summoned by the mayor.

"The ME just made it official," he said. "Martin Sheffield was murdered—asphyxiated."

"Anything turn up in his room?" I asked.

"He didn't leave behind a whole lot of worldly goods," Koprowski said. "Clothes, shoes, books, and not much else. The only thing of interest was an ammo box full of photos, letters, personal papers, and military memorabilia."

"Send the photos to the facial recognition unit. Kylie and I will go through the rest of it in the morning."

"He also left handwritten instructions to notify his lawyer upon his death. His name is Forrest Nivens. I called his cell. Small problem: the paperwork is in his safe at the office, but he and his wife are on a cruise ship in the middle of the Atlantic."

"Get somebody else from the law firm to open it now," I said.

"There is no somebody else. Nivens is a one-man band. The ship docks the day after tomorrow. The first thing he has to do when he gets back to New York is track down the primary beneficiary."

"Did he give you a name?" I said. "We can save time by doing it for him."

"It won't take long. The bulk of Sheffield's estate was left to Theo Wilkins."

"You're kidding me."

"Nivens said he can't hand over the will until he files it with the probate court, but considering the circumstances, he said he'll let us read the contents, which is all we really need."

"Good job, Rich."

"There's more. Sheffield left a sealed envelope for Theo. Since it's not mentioned in the will, Nivens can legally hand it over immediately."

"Did he say what's in it?"

"He has no idea. He said Sheffield never told him and he never asked."

My call waiting beeped.

"Rich, I've got Kylie on the other line. Thanks for everything. Talk later." I took the incoming call.

"Zach, are you near a TV set?" she said.

"Yeah. I'm in my apartment. Theo is safe, sound, and about to be fed."

"I'm at the hospital with Shane. We were watching the news, and just before they cut to the commercial, the announcer says, 'When we come back, Megan Rollins will bring us her exclusive on the Hellman murders.' Where the hell did she get an exclusive?"

"I have no idea," I said. "She stormed out of the hospital pissed as hell at us. The only thing I can think of is, she went up the food chain."

"Turn on the TV and stay on the phone with me," Kylie said.

I grabbed the remote and flipped to the channel. They were mid commercial.

Cheryl and Theo came in. She had a menu in her hand. "We're ordering Greek. What's going on?" she said.

"Kylie's on the line," I said, holding up my cell. "Megan Rollins is about to go on the air with some bogus *exclusive* about our case. I have no idea what it is, but I'll bet when she's done, the weather guy comes on and warns the NYPD to brace themselves for a shitstorm."

The commercial ended, and I raised the volume on the TV as Megan's face filled the screen.

"New York City is under siege," she said. "It began two days ago when a sniper snuffed out the life of Warren Hellman only minutes after a jury of his peers found him not guilty of charges brought against him by the district attorney. Less than an hour later, his brother Curtis was brutally murdered in broad daylight as he was peacefully jogging along the Hudson River Greenway.

"Mayor Sykes and Police Commissioner Radcliffe tried to comfort an understandably frightened citizenry by assuring us that these assassinations would be assigned to—and resolved by—NYPD's elite Red Unit, ostensibly the finest of New York's Finest. Two days have passed, and now the people behind these vicious crimes have struck again and again with two more murders, the most terrifying of which I witnessed firsthand."

A video of the funeral home parking lot popped on the screen. I watched as the front door opened.

"This is Eldon Winstanley," Megan said, her tone reverent, making the white-haired man who tried to kill my partner and me seem almost saintly. "This afternoon, surrounded by more than fifty armed police officers—including the *aristocracy* of the Red Unit—he was the victim of yet another sniper's bullet."

The video froze just as Winstanley lifted his head to the sky.

"I will spare you the poor man's horrifying final moments," Megan said as the camera judiciously cut back to her. "But I will not spare you my frustration as a journalist. I have done my best to get more information from the police. I'm not asking them for critical details, which I understand should be kept under wraps. All I want from the NYPD is a progress report—something that will reassure my viewers that this investigation is in capable hands. But I have been stonewalled at every turn.

"Not only are the police refusing to give me any answers, they have made it clear that they don't even want me asking any *questions.*"

A picture of Kylie appeared on the screen behind Megan.

"Oh, fuck," Kylie breathed over the phone.

"This is NYPD Red Detective Kylie MacDonald," Megan said. "What you are about to hear is an audio clip of Detective MacDonald doing her best to stop me in my quest for the truth."

Kylie's voice came on the air. As she spoke, her words were superimposed across the screen. "Megan, the best place for you to go is home."

Megan looked thunderstruck, as if she were just hearing it for the first time. And just in case once wasn't damning enough, Kylie's voice came back again, this time on a loop.

Megan, the best place for you to go is home. Megan, the best place for you to go is home. Megan, the best place for you to go is home.

Megan pointed an accusatory finger at the camera. "I will *not* go home, Detective MacDonald. You will not suppress the First Amendment. You can try to shut me up, but you can't silence our viewers."

"I don't believe this," Kylie said in my ear.

"Ladies and gentlemen, I need your support," Megan said, leaning in. "If you've been living in fear these past two days because you have no idea where these serial assassins will strike next, I want you to reach out to the mayor and the police commissioner. Their emails and phone numbers are on the screen. Let them know that Megan Rollins has questions. And the people want answers. Thank you, be safe, and have a good night."

She stared defiantly into the camera. Her audience would see her as the resolute reporter determined to bring them the news. But I knew better. That look was meant for Kylie and me, and the message was loud and clear.

This is what you get when you fuck with Megan Rollins.

CHAPTER 41

LESS THAN THREE MINUTES after Megan went off the air, Kylie, Cates, and I got a text from the police commissioner.

> Nothing changes. You're my team. Rollins
> has a job to do, and she's doing it with a
> vengeance. Don't let her get in your face.
> And don't waste your time getting in hers.

"I guess that last part was directed at me," Kylie said.

"Don't think about it," I said. "Just focus on the first part. The PC trusts us, and he has our backs."

"So then all we have to do now is track down a couple of professional killers."

"But we have a better shot now than we did ten minutes ago," I said. "Rich called. He may have struck gold." I filled her in on my conversation with Koprowski.

"What do you think is in the envelope Sheffield left Theo?" she asked.

"I don't know, but whatever it is, it was too sensitive to leave in his room where anyone could find it, so he turned it over to his lawyer. We can't get to it for another day and a half, but I'm hoping the pictures and papers he kept in the ammo box will help us track down Barbara and Carol."

"Barbara and Carol," she repeated. "It's a little weird using their black-ops names, but I guess it's better than 'the knife guy and the sniper.'"

"How's Shane?" I asked.

"Like a caged leopard. He says he's happy to see me, but I think he'd be happier if I were an eight-burner gas range. He's running a fever, and Dr. Lu won't release him from the hospital till his temperature goes down. And even then, she said the restaurant is off limits for two weeks to give the wound time to heal."

"And he's okay with that?"

"No. He cut a deal with her. He'll stay out of the restaurant, but he's cooking dinner for the four of us the first night he's back at his apartment."

"That's a deal I can live with," I said. "But make it dinner for five. I want to keep Theo on a short leash."

"Absolutely. How's he doing?"

"I think he's still scared, but he seems happy to be here."

"I'll bet. He's got to feel good about having an armed cop around 24/7."

"I don't know. He's an eighteen-year-old with raging male hormones. I'm pretty sure Cheryl puts a bigger smile on his face than I do."

I hung up and found Theo at the dining-room table, his laptop in front of him.

"Are you and Kylie still on the case?" he asked.

"A hundred percent. Why wouldn't we be?"

"That tape of Kylie trash-talking the reporter."

"Trust me, she's done a lot worse, and we haven't been fired yet." I sat down. "It turns out you were right."

"About what?"

"Mr. Sheffield's death was ruled a homicide. Best guess is that the guy from the funeral parlor did it."

He took it in, not saying a word. Finally, he cracked a smile. "Can I call Mrs. Millstein and tell her that Mr. Sheffield did not *die peacefully* in his sleep?"

"No."

"Somebody should rub her nose in all her bullshit," he said.

"Somebody will let her know. It just won't be someone who will enjoy it as much as you would," I said. "There's one other thing. Mr. Sheffield left you an envelope with his lawyer. Do you have any idea what's in it?"

He shrugged. "No. He already gave me the P-38 can opener. He didn't have much of anything to give away. He always used to say, 'When you're on the way to the grave, it's smart to travel light.'"

"He also left a will, and you're in it."

"Are you kidding? He put me in his will?"

"More than that. You're the main beneficiary. It could amount to a lot."

"Thanks. But I'm not interested."

"What do you mean, you're not interested?"

Theo flipped his laptop shut. "I know. You're going to think I'm crazy," he said. "I'm young, I'm broke, I want to make movies, and I really loved Mr. Sheffield. But whatever money he left behind he got for killing people. It's blood money, Zach. I won't take a penny of it."

I was, to borrow a word Theo had used on me the day we met, gobsmacked. I don't think I've ever been that impressed by someone that young in my entire life.

Theo Wilkins, barely out of high school, a happy-go-lucky kid still snacking on Yodels and Mountain Dew, crazy enough to chase after a cold-blooded killer, had developed a moral compass at the age of eighteen that was straighter and truer than most people will achieve in a lifetime.

His resolve took my breath away. But then, maybe I shouldn't have been surprised. He was just like his mother.

CHAPTER 42

CHERYL AND I spent the next three hours with Theo. First we ate, and then instead of the modern-day after-dinner ritual of going our separate ways and curling up with our favorite electronic devices, we went old school. We sat around and talked.

Actually, Theo did most of the talking. Cheryl, who is so beguiling to look at that you forget she's an accomplished psychologist, primed him with her usual brand of insightful questions. Me, I'm a cop. I did a lot of listening.

By ten o'clock, Theo was sitting at the dining-room table screening the footage he'd shot on Clinton Road the day before, and Cheryl and I were in bed with the lights on and the TV off, because the last thing either of us wanted was another hyped-up news bulletin about the sniper who was terrorizing the city.

She tapped three times on the mattress, and I reached over and took her hand, knowing that it was the only physical contact we'd have for as long as we had a teenage boy living on the other side of our bedroom door.

"What's going on inside your head?" she asked.

"I've got a bunch of murders to solve. You may have read about them. It was in all the papers."

"No. You weren't thinking about work when we were talking to

Theo. You spent most of the time just staring at him and ruminating about something."

"I don't ruminate," I said. "Sometimes I cogitate. Occasionally, I muse or ponder. But I never ruminate. I'm not that deep."

She laughed, which is what I was hoping for, but she didn't let up. "And sometimes," she said, "when you don't want to deal with the question, you try to sidetrack the conversation with your rapier wit and your sexual prowess, but you're not that funny, and sex is off the table, so I repeat the question. What's going on inside your head?"

I let go of her hand, rolled onto my side, and propped myself up on one elbow. "Remember back before we were dating?" I said. "You were Dr. Robinson, I was Detective Jordan, and sometimes we'd meet for a drink after work, and you'd probe my psyche just the way you rummaged around Theo's brain tonight."

She turned and faced me. "*Probe your psyche?* You're giving me way too much credit. It was more like I knew my marriage to Fred was heading south, and I totally had the hots for you. But I also knew that you hadn't had a single serious relationship since Kylie. So I asked you a few innocent questions to see if you were emotionally available for something besides a roll in the hay."

"Not to put too fine a point on it, but you only get to call them innocent questions if we were contestants on *The Dating Game*. But when you're a department psychologist asking me how I felt about the woman who dumped me and married another guy, I'd say that borders on analysis."

"Fine," she said, sitting up and clasping her hands around her knees. "So using my professional facade as cover, I probed your psyche, lured you into my web, cast a spell over you, and here I am more than a year later, in your bed and more in love with you than I could ever have imagined. Clearly, my plan worked, but I still can't figure out what you were cogitating, musing, or pondering about when we were talking to Theo."

"I was thinking about one of those alcohol-infused therapy sessions you and I had back then. I told you a secret I never told anyone before or since."

"I hear a lot of secrets in my line of work. Remind me which one was yours."

"I told you that Kylie wasn't the first to break my heart."

"Oh, I remember that night," Cheryl said, her voice warm, almost nostalgic. "I can picture the two of us sitting in the back room of JG Melon, and you told me about the girl you met the summer before you went off to college."

"She was twenty-three—incredibly self-sufficient and worldly for her age. More of a strong young woman than a girl. I was eighteen, working a summer job in construction out in the Hamptons, and she was working for a family who lived two blocks away. We met in June. She was way out of my league, but somehow, bam!" I smacked my fist into the palm of my hand. "By the time I left for college in September, I was totally in love with her, and I thought it was mutual. She said she'd call, but she didn't. I tried her, left messages, but no response. She just disappeared. For nineteen years, I had no idea what happened to her . . . until today. She died."

"Oh, Zach," Cheryl said, sliding closer and putting her hand on my shoulder. "I am so sorry. Who told you?"

"Theo."

She stared at me, trying to put the puzzle pieces together. "How would Theo . . ."

"She was his mother," I said. "Her name was Sylviane LeBec. I saw her picture in Theo's room. There's no question. It's her."

"What an amazing coincid—" She put her hand to her mouth. "Oh, my God . . . Zach."

"I know," I said. "I did the math. He *could* be my son. I don't know if he is, but I do know that Travis, the man who raised him, isn't his birth father. Sylviane didn't tell anyone who her son's real father is."

"That would explain why she never called you."

"I don't understand," I said.

"She was a twenty-three-year-old woman. You were a kid. Why would she tell you? What would you do? Drop out of college and marry her? Dragging you into the picture would only make her life more complicated than it already was. It makes sense, Zach. A lot of women get pregnant and decide to have the baby on their own. Sylviane was lucky. She met Travis. He was older, he was stable, and from the way Theo talks about him, he's a terrific dad." She paused. "Have you told anybody else about this?"

"If you mean, have I told Kylie, definitely not. She's my partner in crime. You're my partner in life. I don't need people speculating. All I need is hard evidence, and that means a DNA test. I took one of Theo's toothbrushes, but I can't run it through the department. I'll have to find an outside service."

"I know someone," Cheryl said. "Let me do it. I'll have them send the results directly to you."

"Thanks. It's been a hell of a day, Cheryl. I think I'm going to turn in and hope for a better tomorrow."

"One more question," she said. "What will you do if he is your son?"

"Are you asking as my girlfriend or as my shrink?"

"Girlfriend."

I shook my head. "I have no idea."

"I changed my mind," she said. "I'm asking as your shrink."

"In that case, do me a favor, Doc," I said, flashing her a smile. "Stop probing my fucking psyche and turn off the lights."

CHAPTER 43

MARTIN SHEFFIELD had led the deep, dark clandestine life of a professional assassin for decades. First as a government agent, sanctioned, killing with immunity, and then moving outside the law as a private contractor. He could have taken his secrets to the grave, but as his time on earth ran out, he decided to unburden himself. He opened up to Theo. Then he left behind a box filled with history, where a smart cop like Rich Koprowski could delve into his past.

I knew that Rich would spend a good part of the night at the precinct digging through the letters, photos, and other keepsakes of Sheffield's covert existence. What I didn't know was that he wouldn't be doing it on his own.

At six a.m., Kylie texted me.

> Couldn't sleep. Went in. Working with Rich.
> Facial recognition got a hit on Alice. 3rd floor
> conference room. Bring coffee.

I got there in twenty minutes. Kylie and Rich jumped on the coffee. The conference table was cluttered with the remnants of a long night's work. Captain Cates was standing next to a wall that had been organized into five sections, each with a name at the top. Alice. Barbara.

Carol. Denise. Emily. The noms de guerre of the five mercenaries who called themselves the Sorority.

Beneath each name were pictures, printouts, and other evidence that Kylie and Rich had deemed wall-worthy.

"Kylie and I are still connecting the dots," Rich said, "but we'll show you where we are so far. I want to start with something we found in Martin Sheffield's room."

There was a photo of Sheffield in the Denise section. A handwritten letter was next to it.

Rich tapped on his laptop, and a much larger, clearly readable image of the letter appeared on the adjacent wall.

Camp David, June 4, 2004

Dear Martin,

Your service to the country following the tragic events of 9/11 has been unprecedented and unparalleled. I am humbled by your sacrifice and indebted to you for protecting the lives and liberties of countless of your fellow Americans.

I know you understand why this commendation could not be public, but that in no way should diminish my undying admiration and respect for all you have accomplished. On behalf of a grateful nation, I thank you from the bottom of my heart for your selflessness, your dedication, and your heroism.

It was signed by the president of the United States.

"There are probably four more letters just like this one," Kylie said. "It's not going to help us in the investigation. Rich and I just wanted to lead off with it, so you get a feeling of the kind of freedom these men had. They were like the real-life version of the double-oh section of MI6—licensed to kill.

"At one point, they were the good guys working for the commander-in-chief. Then they were disbanded. It was a political decision—not a reflection on their abilities to get the job done. The president could only thank them for their service in secret. We're sure they were given generous pensions in exchange for their total silence. There was only one problem that the government hadn't counted on. These men were still only in their late forties—trained killers at the top of their game. They weren't ready to give up the one thing they could do best."

"So they went into business for themselves," Cates said.

"Yes," Koprowski said. "But Theo made it clear that none of them were interested in running the business. These men were soldiers. They were trained to follow orders. They carried out missions handed down from on high. So they took on a manager."

"The one they call 'Mother,'" Cates said.

"And here she is," Koprowski said. He touched a key on the laptop, and an image flashed on the wall. It was the iconic portrait of Whistler's Mother. It made me smile, but it was also a nagging reminder of how little we knew about the Sorority's conduit to the outside world.

"She looks pretty harmless," Kylie said. "But she may be the most lethal one of them all. That's because she's the one calling the shots. Whoever put the hit out on the Hellman brothers had to go through her. When Sheffield started giving away all the Sorority's trade secrets, who do you think told Winstanley to kill him? Then when we arrested Winstanley, who do you think gave the order to eliminate him? All roads lead to Mother, and we know nothing about her—or him. Damn, these people were gender-fluid before it was cool."

"Kylie and I are both a little sleep-deprived right now," Koprowski said. "But somewhere around four a.m., that's where we netted out. These men were comrades in arms. They would never have turned on each other without being told. But once they got the order, they didn't hesitate to follow through. They understood that they couldn't allow the unit to be compromised, even if it meant killing one of their own."

"Winstanley knew that when he stepped out into the parking lot," I said. "And he accepted it. Maybe even embraced it."

"It's the way of the samurai," Koprowski said.

"Incredibly insightful," Cates said.

"There's more. We found this among Sheffield's souvenirs."

NYPD RED 7: THE MURDER SORORITY

He flashed a photo on the wall: four men on a fishing boat posing with a huge striper.

"It was taken fifteen to twenty years ago," Kylie said. "You can recognize Sheffield on the right, and that's Winstanley next to him. And the guy holding the fish looks like our sketch of Barbara."

"You get a photo ID on him?" I asked.

Koprowski shook his head. "We tried, but his hand is up in the air, and he was blocking too much of his nose and mouth for facial recognition to get a read. But this stocky fellow on the left was just staring at the camera, begging to be scanned. His real name is Leonard Cerruti. He owned an auto body shop in Passaic, New Jersey.

"Based on his passport data, Mr. Cerruti hardly ever traveled out of the country, and when he did it was always with his wife. So we reached out to US Customs and ran his photo through their database, and guess what?"

He tapped his keyboard again, and a second passport appeared on the wall. The photo was of Cerruti with a mustache, a goatee, and a different name. Koprowski popped on four more bogus passports. Cerruti's hair was silver-gray in the last one. His name was Peter Corville.

"Five fictitious identities," Koprowski said. "But they're all Lenny. He traveled far and wide over the years—Prague, Manchester, Johannesburg, Antwerp—and each date coincides with a high-profile murder during his visit. The victim is always shot and killed up close, and always in a crowded, noisy venue—a subway, a concert, a football match—and the shooter disappears before anyone is even aware there was a shooting."

"According to Theo," Kylie said, "the man they called Alice could craft a gun out of plastic, make it look like a cell phone or an eyeglass case, easily smuggle it past airport security, and trash it after each job. Rich and I are convinced that Leonard Cerruti was Alice."

"*Was* Alice?" I said. "Past tense?"

"Very past tense," Kylie said. "Two years ago, Cerruti flew to Quito as Peter Corville and spent four days there. He was on his way back to the airport when his car was run off the road and he was shot through the head multiple times. The US embassy found no next of kin, so his body was buried in a potter's field in Ecuador."

"Do you think he was killed by his own people?" Cates asked.

"No," Koprowski said. "Earlier that day, a colonel in the Ecuadorian National Police was shot and killed at a crowded church service. After Cerruti was murdered, the ENP found video evidence that put him in that same church at the time of the assassination. Our best guess is that the colonel's compadres made him as the killer and took him out before he could leave the country."

"This is first-rate police work," Cates said. "So where does that leave us?"

"Three down and three to go," Kylie said. "Barbara and Carol, who did the wet work, and one more person with a totally different set of skills, who could run the show, vet potential clients, coordinate logistics, and handle the finances."

"Any ideas who that might be?" Cates asked.

"No," Kylie said. "But about twenty minutes ago, we just got some good news from the lab. We think it's what we need to track down Barbara."

I stared at the tableau on the wall. Then I let my eyes drift over to Cates, to Rich, and finally to Kylie. She stared back at me with a fierce intensity. This was far and away the biggest, most difficult, most scrutinized investigation we had ever been a part of. I could see that she was consumed by the task ahead.

I should have felt the same way. The desire to find these killers should have filled every cell of my being. But a little piece of me was somewhere else.

I couldn't shake it from my mind. Cheryl. On her way to a laboratory. With Theo's toothbrush.

CHAPTER 44

SOMETIMES WHEN I'M DRIVING, my mind will drift off, and when I finally snap out of it, I have no idea how I managed to travel so far without running off the road.

It's called highway hypnosis. I guess there must be a conference room version of it, because by the time I shook Theo's DNA test out of my head, Kylie was in the middle of explaining something about shock absorbers, and I had no idea what she was talking about.

"Kylie, sorry," I called out. "Could you start again? Take it from the top."

"No problem," she said. "Anything wrong?"

"Nothing," I said. "I think my brain just got all twisted up with this news about Alice, and I guess I tuned out for a sec."

"Uh-huh," she said, tossing me a look that said she knew me too long and too well to buy my bullshit about Alice. "The lab called. They got a partial plate on Barbara's RAV4. It's just one number—seven—but it's a big help."

She paused and looked at me. "I was just explaining how they came up with it. You all caught up now?"

"Totally," I said. "Keep going."

"When Theo's motorcycle hit the rear bumper of the SUV, the front shock absorbers on the bike compressed, and the ass end went straight up in the air." She punched her right fist into the palm of her left hand, then tipped her right elbow toward the ceiling. "It's like doing a handstand on his front tire. The impact literally embossed the number from Barbara's license plate onto Theo's metal fender.

"Now, the world is full of black RAV4s," she said. "And hundreds of them have a seven in the plate. But how many do you think were parked in the vicinity of West Hundred-and-Second Street and Riverside Drive on the morning Curtis Hellman was stabbed?"

"And you think Barbara drove there?" Cates asked.

"We don't know. He could have taken a cab or a subway. But it makes more sense to drive. It's a lot less exposure than using public transportation."

"And if he did drive," Koprowski said, "he's too smart to expect he would find a parking space on the Upper West Side at that hour of the morning."

"Tell me about it," Cates said. "He'd wind up doing what I always do: find a parking garage and pay through the nose to leave it there for a couple of hours."

"That's the hope," Kylie said. "If he did, we figured he'd park within easy walking distance of the crime scene—maybe five or six blocks. But he's a professional. He's not going to take the easy way out. So Rich and I thought we should expand the area to ten blocks on either side."

"It's a one-mile stretch from Ninety-Second to a Hundred-and-Twelfth, and from the river to Central Park West," Koprowski said.

"That's a big chunk of real estate," Cates said. "How many garages and parking lots are we talking about?"

"Fifty-six," Kylie said. "But we've been coordinating with Cardona and Henry from the Two-Four. Their CO flew in eight more detectives from the surrounding precincts. It should go fast."

It went faster than we expected. Within two hours, we had six black RAV4s that were in and out of those garages in the time frame we'd decided on. Two of them had a seven in their license plate. Both cars were owned by men. We ran their driver's licenses.

The first man's picture popped on Koprowski's computer screen. Name: Raymond Villeneuve. Home address: West Ninety-Eighth Street, Manhattan. Age: thirty-seven.

I could almost feel the energy getting sucked out of the room.

Koprowski brought up the next picture. Name: Wesley Varga. Home address: Fitchett Avenue, Rego Park, Queens. Age: seventy-one.

And his face—his face was the spitting image of the sketch our homeless artist, Izaak Weathers, had drawn for us three nights ago at the Twenty-Fourth Precinct.

Kylie let out a booming whoop. We had found Barbara.

CHAPTER 45

THE CELEBRATION was short-lived.

It took less than a minute to find out that the address in Queens didn't exist. The name Wesley Varga was probably just as phony. Koprowski had pulled up five different passports for Alice. It stood to reason that Barbara would also have multiple identities. As for the RAV4, that was probably inside the jaws of a scrap-yard compactor within hours of the chase through Riverdale.

But one thing was real. One thing that Barbara couldn't shake. The license plate on the RAV4. It was on the car's registration, it had been entered into the computer of a parking garage six blocks from the stabbing, and with any luck, it was somewhere in the City of New York's vast database of traffic and parking violations.

Koprowski, a two-fingered typist, pecked away furiously on his keyboard.

"Got him," he said as the image of a summons appeared on his screen. "A month ago, his car was parked in front of Forty to Forty-Seven Seventy-Seventh Street in Elmhurst. Street-sweeping rules go into effect eight thirty in the morning, and he got the ticket at eight thirty-two."

"Ah, the code of the NYPD traffic agent," Kylie said. "Show no mercy."

"Two months before that, the car got an expired-meter violation at

Forty to Forty-Two Eighty-Second Street, also in Elmhurst," Koprowski said. "Hold on."

He brought up Google Maps and checked the street views on both addresses. One was in front of a bakery; the other was outside a small apartment building.

"How far apart are they?" Kylie asked.

Koprowski banged on the keys, and the map refreshed. "Three-tenths of a mile. Three minutes by car, six minutes on foot."

"You think he lives in the neighborhood?" Kylie said.

"Or works," Koprowski said. "It's pretty commercial. Remind me again—what does this one do for a living?"

"All we know is that Barbara is the edged-weapons expert," Kylie said. "Or as Theo puts it, 'y'know, knives and shit.' But we don't have a confirmed occupation."

"Wait a minute," I said. "He was a medic in the military. Theo said he knows exactly how to slash his victims' throats so that they bleed out on the spot."

"Doctor!" Kylie said.

"Surgeon!" Koprowski said, right on her heels.

"Elmhurst Hospital!" I said, tapping the screen just below the two markers where Barbara got the summonses.

"Great minds . . ." Kylie said. "I'll get the car keys."

"I'll call the local squad and find out who's in charge of hospital security," Koprowski said.

It was an easy twenty-minute ride over the Ed Koch Bridge into Queens. We were halfway there when Kylie sandbagged me.

"What's going on with you?" she said.

"Me?" I said. "Nothing."

"Zach, you totally spaced out when I was explaining how the lab came up with a partial plate number on Barbara's car. And don't expect me to believe that crap about your brain being caught up with all the details about Alice. What's really going on?"

There was no way I was going to tell Kylie about my relationship with Theo's mother. Not yet. Maybe not ever. "All right. You want to know that truth?" I said, my mind racing to come up with a better lie. "Cheryl and I had a fight last night."

"About what?"

"Our living arrangements," I said, grabbing a totally plausible explanation out of thin air. "I think she should give up her apartment and move in with me permanently. She's dragging her heels."

Kylie laughed. "Jordan, you are such a bad liar. If that were really what was bothering you, you'd have dumped it on me as soon as we got in the car. If you don't want to tell me what's going on, fine. But don't expect me to believe your—"

My cell rang. It was Koprowski. I put him on speaker.

"I talked to a friend of mine at the One-Ten," he said. "The head of security at Elmhurst Hospital is Clayton Rayborn. Do you know him?"

We both responded with a quick no.

"Deputy Inspector Rayborn was the CO at the One-Ten," Koprowski said. "He retired two years ago and stepped into the top spot at Elmhurst. I called him, told him what's going on, and he's expecting you."

"Thanks," I said.

"One more thing," Koprowski said. "Rayborn was well-liked. The word is, he doesn't act like a boss, and when the shit hits the fan, he doesn't hesitate to jump in the trenches with the troops."

"Good to know," Kylie said. "Because if it turns out that the man who murdered Curtis Hellman works at Elmhurst Hospital, DI Rayborn is going to need a very big shovel."

CHAPTER 46

CLAYTON RAYBORN was waiting for us in his office. As soon as we entered, he stood up and came around his desk. He was in his mid-fifties, about six-two, solidly built, wearing a tan suit, white shirt, and gray tie that worked well against his chestnut skin.

"Inspector," I said.

"Thank you for that," he said, "but civilians don't have rank. Call me Clay."

He shook our hands and closed his office door. "The fewer people that know about this, the better."

He might be a civilian, but he thought like a cop.

"Detective Koprowski filled me in," he said. "Wesley Varga, former medic, wanted killer, and based on his parking violations, it's possible he works here at Elmhurst."

We sat down, and he swiveled his computer screen so Kylie and I could see it.

"He's not in our database," Rayborn said. "I went through the names of past and present employees going back five years. I came up with sixteen people named Vargas with an *S*. Nine of them male, none of them Wesley, and no one in the system named Varga. But he could still be here under a different name. Do you have his picture?"

Kylie handed him a copy of Varga's driver's license. "His code name is Barbara."

"Jeez," Rayborn said. "Barbara's a little long in the tooth, isn't he? But then again, so are most of my favorite rock bands."

He turned to his computer. "Every single person, from the head of the hospital down to the candy striper who volunteers once a week at the gift shop, is issued a badge with their photo on it. If your man is in here, we'll find him."

"How many employees do you have?" I asked.

"About forty-two hundred, give or take."

"Wow," I said. "I never would have guessed."

"I know. But we have five hundred and fifty-seven beds, and more than six hundred thousand people come through our doors every year. It takes a small army, but don't worry, I can narrow it down fast," he said, putting his fingers on the keyboard. "We can start with medical professionals—doctors, nurses, therapists, techs. That will eliminate about seventy percent."

"Can you just pull up white males over fifty?" Kylie asked.

"In the old days, I would have had to say no," he said. "But now it's all about diversity. Human Resources keeps track of how many women, how many people of color, and as you well know, we no longer live in a world with only two genders. Bottom line: all I have to do is enter the criteria, and I can slice and dice our entire workforce six ways to Sunday."

"Slice away," Kylie said.

Within seconds, Rayborn pared down the pool of possibles to 114. We scrolled through their pictures one at a time. *Click. Click. Click.*

About fifty clicks into the process, Rayborn took his hand off the mouse, and the three of us stared at the man who killed Curtis Hellman.

"Barbara," Kylie said softly.

"His real name—or at least the one he's using here—is Barnett Drucker," Rayborn said. "He's a nurse. Jesus, he's been on our staff for seven and a half years."

"What time does he come in to work?" Kylie asked.

A few strokes on the keyboard, and a new screen popped up. "He swiped in at seven fifty-four this morning," Rayborn said. "He signed out the bloodmobile at nine fifteen."

"What does that mean?"

"We have a forty-five-foot mobile blood unit. A couple of times a month, we staff it with nurses and volunteers and go out into the community. It's all part of our outreach program for blood donations."

"Where do they set up?"

"Anywhere and everywhere. We usually partner with corporations, colleges, churches—any organization that can help us generate volume. Then we turn it into an event—y'know, give a pint, get a T-shirt or a gift card. That kind of thing."

"And where's the bloodmobile now?"

"I don't know, but Bonnie Green, our director of nursing, will," he said. He dialed his phone and put it on speaker.

A woman answered. "Clay," she said. "To what do I owe the pleasure?"

"I was just wondering where the bloodmobile is today. I've got a friend who wants to give you a pint. He's AB-negative."

"Oh, my goodness, Clay. That's my favorite flavor. We never have enough AB-neg. Hold on a sec."

Rayborn sat there in silence, probably thinking about the shitstorm that would upend his life when the hospital found out it had a murderer on staff.

Nurse Green came back on the phone. "The bloodmobile is at Citi Field today. We're doing a promotion with the Mets. Give a pint; get a free ticket to one of their home games. Give two pints, and you have the option of not going to the game and having to sit through the agony of watching them lose."

Rayborn responded with a laugh. "You're a Yankees fan, aren't you?"

"Diehard."

"Thanks. Talk to you soon."

He hung up. "Citi Field," he said. "It's going to be packed with families. We've got to call the whole event off—get that bloodmobile back to the hospital."

"Sir," Kylie said, "Barbara is a professional. He knows we're looking for him. If you do something out of the ordinary like that, he'll know we're onto him."

Rayborn was also a professional. He nodded. He knew Kylie was right. "Then I at least have to give the CEO of the hospital a heads-up."

"Please . . . inspector," Kylie said. "You can't—"

"Damn it, MacDonald, don't tell me what I can or can't do. I am not a cop. I have a responsibility to my bosses. Or do you want them to read about it in tomorrow's papers—*Hospital blood drive turns into Citi Field bloodbath?*"

"Clay," I said, "you may not be a cop, but I am, and I guarantee you that if you tell your bosses, one of them will pick up the phone and fire this man on the spot, thinking whatever he does now is not the hospital's responsibility. Not only will they blow our chances to catch him, but Barbara will know he's a cornered rat, and he'll do anything to get away. And that means taking hostages."

"Jesus," Rayborn said. "God forbid."

"Give us a few hours to call in the Violent Felony Squad," I said. "You know them, sir. They're smart; they're cunning; they can surround him and take him down before he even knows we're there. Kylie and I will call you as soon as we have cuffs on him. You have our word."

"You make a lot of sense, Detective, but I'll be damned if I'm going to sit here in my office waiting for the phone to ring. I'm going with you."

"Clay, please," I said. "You're a civilian."

"Maybe so, but I've been to dozens of these blood drives. I know exactly how everything is set up. I know where all the players are. I know the entire operation inside that bloodmobile and out. I'm not just a civilian. I'm an asset."

Kylie and I exchanged a quick look. Rayborn was right. He could help us in the field. Maybe just as important, we'd be able to keep tabs on him just in case he had a change of heart and decided to call his boss.

"All right," I said. "You can come with us and be our eyes. But you are not a cop, and you have absolutely nothing to do with the action."

"Trust me, Zach," he said. "I'm not tagging along so I can do your job. I'm going so I can save mine."

CHAPTER 47

LESS THAN AN HOUR after Barbara's face popped up on the Elmhurst Hospital employee database, the operation to take him down was in full swing.

"I forgot how much I missed doing this shit," Clayton Rayborn said as the three of us pulled into one of the visitor parking lots at Citi Field.

I'd been reluctant to bring him along, but he swore he'd be an asset, and he kept his word. The entire team—eighteen of us in all—had a tactical meeting at Arthur Ashe Stadium, about a mile from Citi Field. Sergeant Ed McSpirit of the Violent Felony Squad was running the show, and he hung on every word as Rayborn took us through the blood donation process.

As he spoke, it was clear that at almost every step, the nurses would be too close to the civilians for the team to move in on him. And then Rayborn gave us what we needed.

"There's only room for three donors at a time in the bloodmobile. This event is going to draw a big crowd, so the Mets are going to set up a tent with a dozen donation stations. The bloodmobile will be off to the side, plugged into a light pole so that we can power the refrigerators, but it will be off limits to the public. The only ones in and out will be the nurses carrying in the bags of blood."

"Hold on," McSpirit said. "You're saying that the subject will separate from everyone else and walk to the bloodmobile alone?"

"Absolutely," Rayborn said.

"How long will he be in there?"

"A minute or two. Just long enough to put the blood in the fridge and log it into the computer."

"That's all the time we need to move in on him," McSpirit said. "Shabel, Dupré, and Bock, when I give you the green light, you get in position. As soon as he steps out of that mobile unit, take him down. The rest of the team and I will keep an eye on the crowd. He may have an accomplice with him. Plus, we're all wearing plain clothes. We want to make sure people know we're the good guys."

The tactical meeting took less than fifteen minutes. The game plan McSpirit laid out was smart, simple, solid.

Detectives Louie Ziffer and Sarah Herman would be our eyes and ears. Decked out in Mets gear and wired so they could broadcast on a closed channel, Louie would pose as a donor, and Sarah would be his girlfriend. They'd get close enough to the subject to confirm that he was there, report on his movements, and then get out of the way when McSpirit and his team went in for the capture.

The rest of us would be nowhere near the action. Tommy Barnwood from the Hostage Negotiation Team had been called in just in case things went south and Barbara grabbed a bystander. Captain Cates would be in her car, giving the commissioner a play-by-play as the operation went down. Rayborn, Kylie, and I were relegated to watching the action from a distance. She wasn't happy about it, but she kept quiet until we took up our position at Citi Field.

"I hate sitting on the sidelines and missing out on all the fun," she said.

"And I hate getting blood all over my Paul Stuart suit," I said. "This is what Violent Felony does, and they're better at it than we are. Besides, didn't you have enough fun yesterday when Winstanley drop-kicked your ass across the room?"

She responded with her middle finger.

The blood drive was taking place near the main gate. A grove of trees separated us from them. It was the perfect cover: dense enough to keep us out of sight, but with plenty of gaps to let us watch it all from a thousand feet away.

I picked up my binoculars and scanned the area. It was late morning, but at least a hundred people were milling about—some to give blood, others who just showed up to enjoy the circus-like atmosphere. Music, peanuts, popcorn, a souvenir stand, and, of course, the team mascot, Mr. Met—a man in a Mets uniform with a large baseball for a head.

Our radio came on. It was Louie Ziffer. "Leader, this is Team Alpha. We just parked our car, and we're headed for the registration table."

"We're in position," McSpirit radioed back.

"You mind if I take a look?" Rayborn said.

"Be my guest," I said, handing him the binoculars.

Sarah Herman's job was to wander around while her boyfriend was signing up to donate blood.

"I have a positive ID on our subject," she said over the radio. "There are four nurses—two female, two male. Ours is the one in the dark purple scrubs. Right now he's with a donor, center row, third table from my right. She's wearing blue shorts and an orange Mets T-shirt."

"Got him," McSpirit said. "And that's a positive ID on the male nurse in the dark purple scrubs."

"No question," Herman said. "He looks old enough to be the other nurse's grandfather."

"Team Alpha, you're clear," McSpirit said. "We'll take it from here."

That was the signal for Louie to zero in on one of the questions on the intake form. Have you gotten a tattoo in the last three months? If you answer yes, you're rejected immediately. It's the law in New York.

"Excuse me," I heard him say to the woman who was signing him up. "Why are you asking about my tats? I'm giving blood, not skin."

I never heard her answer. The radio was drowned out by the sound of Clayton Rayborn bellowing.

"Shit, shit, shit, shit! Shut down the operation. Call it off. Now!"

Kylie turned in her seat. "What the fuck, Clayton? This is going down. You can't change your mind here."

He handed her the binoculars. "Look at the guy with the white hair, khaki pants, plaid shirt. He's got two kids with him."

She took the binoculars and dropped them on the front seat. "What about him?" she said.

"He's my boss!"

"I thought you were the boss."

"I'm head of Security. That's Mason Asher, the president of the fucking hospital. He's a big Mets fan. That's him with his two grandsons. They can't get caught up in the middle of this. Radio McSpirit. Abort the mission while we still can."

He pulled out his phone.

"Clayton," Kylie said, leaning over the seat so that her head and shoulders violated his space. "Put that fucking phone away, or I swear to God, I will arrest you for obstruction and drag you back to the precinct you used to run. In cuffs."

CHAPTER 48

AT HIS CORE, Rayborn was still a cop. He knew that Kylie's ultimatum was not an idle threat, and he made a quick decision. Back off or suffer the consequences. He slid his phone into his pocket and slumped down in his seat.

"I'm sorry," he said.

"It's understandable," I said, my voice calm, my demeanor relaxed—my usual counterpoint to Kylie's in-your-face style. "Seeing all these civilians is unnerving, but you of all people know how skilled Violent Felony is. If you're storming a fortress in full battle gear, you call ESU, but if you have to surgically remove a threat like Barnett Drucker or Wesley Varga or whatever Barbara's real name is, there's nobody better than Ed McSpirit and his team. They'll get it done. I know they will."

He nodded, accepting what I'd said, although I doubt that he believed it. I couldn't blame him. I had lied. Or at best, I'd overpromised. Barbara had been killing for decades and was still going strong at age seventy-one. I *hoped* McSpirit and his squad would get it done, but the truth was, I didn't know shit. None of us did.

I picked up my binoculars and trained them on the tent. There was a donor at every one of the donation stations, and the four nurses kept busy moving from one to another.

I scanned the crowd. Shabel, Dupré, Bock, and McSpirit were

slowly drifting toward their assigned spots closer to the bloodmobile. The rest of the team was also moving into position. Louie Ziffer,
who had seemingly bounced back from his disappointment of being
turned down as a donor, was now soaking up the party atmosphere
with Sarah Herman. The two of them snapped pictures, checked out
the souvenir stands, and updated us with a running commentary of
all the activity under the tent.

About five minutes into the wait, Sarah's voice came on the radio.
"Nurse on her way to the bloodmobile."

One of the two female nurses walked across the parking lot and
entered the mobile unit. When she came back out, Sarah reported.
"Total time inside: a hundred and fourteen seconds."

A few minutes later, the second female nurse made the same trip.
Ninety-seven seconds.

More than enough time for our guys to get in position.

Five minutes passed, and Sarah came back with the call we were
waiting for. "Subject just wrapped up a collection. He's marking the
bag. This could be it."

Louie cut in; his voice urgent. "Golf cart approaching from the plaza.
It's some sort of official Mets vehicle. Not sure what they're doing here.
This wasn't in the script."

Both Kylie and I zeroed in on the cart as it pulled up between the
tent and the bloodmobile. Two men stepped out, both dressed identically
in khaki pants, blue shirt with patches on the sleeve and breast pocket.

"Mets security guards," Louie said. "They don't seem to be on a
mission. It looks like they're just checking things out."

The binoculars were powerful enough to give me an up-close view
of the guards. Sports arena security is an easy transition for retired cops
whose careers are behind them and who are looking for a fun part-time
gig. These two men were both in their early fifties, and I figured they
came from any of the hundreds of police forces in the tri-state area.

The driver seemed to be enjoying himself. He strolled around chatting up the fans. And then somebody caught his eye. He yelled something
I couldn't hear.

NYPD RED 7: THE MURDER SORORITY

"Shit," Louie said. "The security guy knows McSpirit. He's waving at him. Calling out his name."

I swung the glasses to look at McSpirit. He didn't flinch. Instead, he gave the man a dead-cold stare.

The guard had to be an ex-cop, because as soon as he caught the look, he knew McSpirit was on a job. He called to his partner and the two of them hustled back to their cart and rode off.

"Subject is walking toward the bloodmobile," Sarah announced.

Kylie keyed the radio. "Did he see or hear the guard call out McSpirit?"

"Can't say. Subject was marking the blood bag. He didn't look up."

Kylie put the radio down and turned to me. "Of course he didn't look up. He's too fucking smart to look up."

I took a quick glance at Rayborn. His hands were over his face, no doubt imagining the worst.

Barbara opened the bloodmobile door, stepped inside, and closed it behind him. One by one, McSpirit's team moved into their prede-termined positions. Brian Bock had his Taser at the ready. As soon as the fifty thousand volts dropped Barbara to the ground, the entire team would dogpile on him.

"He's been in there sixty seconds," Sarah announced.

Louie cut in. "The other male nurse is on his way to the bloodmobile."

"Intercept him," McSpirit ordered.

I watched as Louie ran over to the man, his mic still on. "Excuse me, Nurse. My girlfriend is feeling a little woozy. Can you help me?"

"Sure," the nurse said. "Where is she?"

Sarah had picked up on the cue and immediately sat on the ground. Louie and the nurse knelt down beside her.

"Ninety seconds," Sarah said, counting the count.

And then a diesel engine roared to life. It was the bloodmobile. A shower of sparks erupted as it lurched forward, ripping the electrical connection from the light pole.

The entire team was blindsided. Bock lunged at the door, tried to open it, but the forty-five-foot bus was moving too fast.

People scattered as Barbara plowed into a souvenir stand, then swerved to take out one of the tent poles, then a second. The heavy canvas tent came down hard on the blood donors and medical staff below.

"I told you to call it off!" Rayborn screamed at Kylie. "I told you!"

Kylie didn't say a word. She pushed a button, and the electronic door locks opened with a *thunk*. Rayborn bolted from the car.

I buckled my seat belt and turned to look at Kylie as she stepped down hard on the gas. She was in the zone now, her eyes filled with determination, her focus razor sharp, and for the first time since she found out we'd be sitting in a parking lot watching the action from a thousand feet away, a smug, self-satisfied smile spread across her face.

"You look like you're actually enjoying this," I shouted at Kylie over the wail of the siren as she made a hard left onto Northern Boulevard.

She yelled back, "If by 'enjoying,' you mean is it more fun than sitting out a takedown while some ex-cop whines like a little boy who pissed his pants, then yes. Abso-fucking-lutely!"

We were closing in on him fast. By the time he turned onto Astoria Boulevard we were practically on his bumper.

I turned up the radio. It was a nonstop barrage of calls about the fugitive bloodmobile. Not only had every cop in the borough of Queens been alerted, but units were being brought in from Aviation, Harbor, and the Port Authority police.

"Sounds like McSpirit called in the entire cavalry," I said.

"Don't care," she said. "All I know is that we're at the front of the pack, and he can't outrun us."

"He's driving a fucking bloodmobile," I said. "He knows he can't outrun us. His only shot is to create havoc so he can escape in the confusion."

As soon as I said the words, the big green overhead sign rushed up at us: LAGUARDIA AIRPORT, NEXT RIGHT.

The bus barely braked as it made a wide right, hopped the median, clipped two cars and a motorcycle, and barreled up Eighty-Second Street. We were right behind him. McSpirit, his team, and a dozen screaming cop cars were on our tail.

The cacophony helped clear a path, but seconds later he fishtailed onto Marine Terminal Road and sideswiped a taxi that was too slow getting out of the way.

"Fucking lunatic!" Kylie yelled as soon as he ran the red light at Runway Drive. "You know where he's going, don't you?"

I knew. But before I could answer, the big bus crashed through a guardrail and a chain-link fence and onto the grassy runway safety area. Port Authority police and Emergency Service vehicles had lined the length of the fence. One was close enough to open fire. Bullets peppered the side, but the bloodmobile was unstoppable as it lumbered onto the taxiway and headed for Terminal A.

"He's going for the planes," I said.

There were three occupied jetways at the terminal. All Barbara had to do was ram one of them, and all hell would break loose. As impossible as it seemed, he could escape in the madness.

"I'm a better shot," Kylie yelled, "but I'm driving. You got this?"

I already had my gun out. "Fucking A, I got it!"

She peeled out from behind the bloodmobile and pulled up alongside. By now my window was down and I was kneeling on the front seat, with both hands gripping my gun.

I had sixteen rounds, and I put eight of them into the front tire. The rubber shredded in an instant, the rim dug into the taxiway, and as the vehicle slowed, I fired the remaining rounds into the driver's-side window.

The bloodmobile spun out of control, skittered onto the apron, flipped onto its side, and slid into a cluster of baggage carts.

Kylie and I jumped out of our car. I threw a fresh magazine into my gun, racking the slide as we ran to the front of the overturned bloodmobile.

Barbara was lying halfway out the windshield, bleeding profusely, his body riddled with bullets and glass shards.

Kylie looked at me. "Nice work, partner. Four down. One to go."

CHAPTER 49

THE AFTERMATH of the incident that one newspaper would dub BLOODY HELL ON WHEELS looked a lot like the final scene of *Die Hard*. Twisted wreckage, emergency vehicles, flashing lights, a dead villain, the media clamoring to get as close to the chaos as possible.

In the movie, Bruce Willis, the cop who prevented a fictional monumental disaster, hops in the back of a limo with his wife while the soundtrack kicks in with an upbeat version of "Let It Snow."

But in real life, Kylie MacDonald and Zach Jordan, the cops who prevented an *actual* monumental disaster, were about to be interrogated by Internal Affairs Bureau.

I knew I'd get the brunt of it. I'd killed a man. It didn't matter that he was about to drive a twelve-ton bus into a plane full of people and there was no other way to stop him. IAB would be on a mission to figure out what I'd done wrong and nail me for it. Every split-second decision I made would be analyzed for months. I've gone through it before. It sucks big-time.

The wheels on the bloodmobile had barely stopped spinning when Kylie gave me the heads-up. "The vultures are circling."

A black Ford Excursion pulled up. The door opened and Marko Horvat, deputy commissioner of Internal Affairs, stepped out. The head vulture had come for its pound of flesh.

"You should be flattered," Kylie said. "He almost never shows up at a crime scene."

Horvat was a large man who looked as though he ate well—and often. I doubt if he'd seen the inside of a gym since high school. One of his minions pointed at Kylie and me and gifted us with a full-frontal scowl.

"He looks a tad peevish, wouldn't you say?" Kylie whispered.

"Don't make me laugh," I said. "I'm in enough trouble as it is."

Horvat tried to stride my way, but his thighs were so thick, it was more of a waddle.

"Well, there's your problem right there," Kylie said. "The poor man is chafed. A little corn starch would turn that frown upside down."

I put my hand over my mouth to stifle the smile, and as Horvat advanced, I braced myself for the harangue.

"Commissioner Horvat," a voice called out.

It was Captain Cates.

"What?" he barked, slowing down but still coming my way.

"A word. In private, sir."

"Make it fast."

Horvat gestured to his minion to follow him because he knew how easily a private moment with a female cop could be twisted.

The conversation lasted less than thirty seconds. It ended abruptly with Horvat making a quick about-face and stride-waddling back to his car.

Kylie leaned in and whispered, "I think she just neutered the fucker."

"Jordan, MacDonald," Cates called out. "Let's go."

We followed her to a mobile command center vehicle that was parked on the apron about fifty feet from the mangled bloodmobile. She opened the door, and the three of us stepped up into it.

"You guys okay?" It was Horvat's boss, the only person who could have sent him packing: the PC himself.

"We're good," I said. "Thank you."

"No. Thank *you*," he said. "That plane was ready to take off for Phoenix with two hundred and twelve souls on board. If he had rammed the fuel tank . . ."

He shook off the thought. "Look, you're squared away with IAB."

"Thank you, sir," I said.

"For now," he added. "You're still going to have to answer questions, but it won't be a witch hunt."

"Much appreciated, sir," I said.

"I spoke to Mayor Sykes. She called Brooke Hellman and gave her the news. According to the mayor, Ms. Hellman would like to personally thank the officers who got the job done."

"Does she know it's us?" Kylie asked.

"The mayor made sure she knew it was the two of you who took out the man who killed her husband. I guarantee you that your next meeting with Ms. Hellman will be a lot more congenial than the last one."

We thanked him again.

"I also spoke to Mason Asher, the head of the hospital. There were a few minor injuries when the tent came crashing down on people, but nothing serious."

"How about Rayborn?" Kylie asked. "He was convinced he was going to be fired."

"He was right. Management is always looking for a scapegoat when the shit hits the fan, and Rayborn was at the top of Asher's hit list." He paused. "However, I reminded Mr. Asher that Rayborn didn't hire Drucker. The hospital did. And as soon as Rayborn found out that the man was a dangerous killer, he worked in concert with NYPD so that the final shootout was in a public space, not the corridors of Elmhurst Hospital."

"So Rayborn is now a hero," Kylie said.

The PC shrugged. "I know I'm stretching the truth here, but that's the way the hospital will spin it, and a man who gave thirty-seven years to this department will get to keep his retirement job. Now, where are you on the man who killed Warren Hellman?"

"Closing in," Kylie said, stretching the truth herself. "The lives of the five hit men in the Sorority are intertwined. Martin Sheffield, the old man in assisted living, led us to the funeral director, Eldon Winstanley. Winstanley led us to Nurse Barnett Drucker."

"Like dominoes," the PC said.

"Yes sir," Kylie said. "And now we're going after the next domino—the man they call Carol."

"Good. Keep me posted."

We thanked him yet again, and the two of us stepped out of the command center.

Three of Horvat's men were still at the bloodmobile taking pictures, sifting for evidence, probing for anything that would prove I should be drummed out of the department for shooting the poor old white-haired nurse whose lifeless body was still hanging out of the windshield.

One by one, they looked up and glared as Kylie and I walked across the apron to our car.

The vultures were still circling. But they could tell by the kiss-my-ass grins on our faces that they would go hungry today.

CHAPTER 50

AS SOON AS WE got back to the car, both of our phones chirped with a text. It was from Steve Edlund at the Four-One.

> Major progress on the Shane Talbot shooting.
> Call me.

Within seconds, we had Edlund on FaceTime.

"You guys are all over the airwaves," he said, a grin on his face. "Congratulations on taking another killer off the streets."

"Thanks," Kylie said. "What's your big news?"

"We just got ballistics on the bullet Dr. Lu removed from Shane. The same gun was used in two recent homicides."

Neither of us said a word, but he could read our reaction. The man who shot Shane had now been upgraded to a serial killer. This was a game changer.

"It gets better," Edlund said. "The two previous vics are Greg Upton, the radio talk-show guy who was shot at a bookstore signing back in April, and Troy Silvers, an Upper East Side dentist who was gunned down on a tennis court in Central Park."

"Holy shit," Kylie said. "Those are both our cases."

"I know. That's why I'm calling you. The same gun was used in all three shootings. There's no doubt about it. Ballistics said it was a perfect match. We can't be certain it's the same shooter, but the MO is identical. Lone gunman. White male, mid- to late thirties. Public place. One bullet to the chest."

"Does Captain Graham know this yet?"

"He's the one who told me to call you. Whoever shot Shane is probably the same killer you and Zach have been looking for. You've got a learning curve. Graham said we'd be crazy to run separate investigations."

"You know he told me to keep my distance because of my connection to Shane."

"Yeah, but that's out the window. Now he'd like you to team up with me and McDaniel and work this case together. You game?"

"Am I game to hunt down the scumbag who shot my boyfriend? Hell, yeah."

"Great. There's one more weird wrinkle. According to ballistics, the same gun was used in a botched bodega robbery. The perp's name is X. L. Gaston, but he's not a suspect in the homicides, because he was already behind bars."

"Getting himself locked up is X. L.'s superpower," I said. "He was a half-assed chain snatcher who decided he was ready to move up in the world and try his hand at armed robbery. So he walks into a bodega, points a gun at the clerk, but his hand is shaking like a willow in a windstorm. The clerk grabs the gun, it goes off, shoots the clerk in the foot, and X. L. races out the door empty-handed."

"I've got his case open right here," Edlund said, looking at his computer screen. "He was picked up less than two hours later."

"It wasn't exactly a citywide manhunt," Kylie said. "The bodega was only three blocks from X. L.'s mother's apartment. The patrol guys immediately recognized him from the surveillance video, so they parked outside Mom's place and waited. X. L. showed up, and they arrested him. But he didn't have the gun."

"Yeah, but he knows what happened to it," Edlund said.

"Right. When Zach and I caught the Upton homicide, ballistics connected the murder weapon to the same gun that shot the clerk. So we reached out to X. L. We told him that his gun had been used recently. He wasn't a suspect, and if he told us what he did with the gun after the bodega job, we could help him out with the DA."

"He should have grabbed the deal," Edlund said. "But I see that he clammed up, wouldn't cooperate. Why the hell not?"

"He hadn't gone to trial yet for shooting the clerk," I said. "We think his lawyer told him if he gave us the whereabouts of the gun, it would hurt his case."

"He should have gotten a better lawyer," Edlund said. "I've got an update. X. L. had his day in court, and he went down in flames. It took the jury less than half an hour. He's now doing ten in Green Haven."

"Green Haven," Kylie repeated, a smile spreading across her face. "X. L. is kind of the fragile type. Not at all cut out for maximum security. I'll bet he's sorry he didn't take our offer when he had the chance."

"He still knows what happened to that gun," Edlund said. "This might be a good time for you guys to give him a second chance."

"We can't reduce his sentence," I said. "But I'm sure he'd feel much happier showering in Otisville."

"I know you guys are swamped," Edlund said. "How soon can you find the time to do it?"

"You're in luck," I said. "A team from our squad is on the way to court as we speak. They're applying for a warrant to search the residence of the perp we just took down. So we're on a lull between mass murderers. Kylie and I know the deputy warden at Green Haven. It's less than ninety minutes away. We can pay X. L. a visit right now."

"That's a home run," Edlund said. "I'll be waiting by the phone."

As soon as he hung up, Kylie pumped a fist in the air and let out a whoop. "First Barbara, and now this. Our day just keeps getting better and better."

It wasn't exactly a Hollywood ending, but I could almost hear the upbeat music as we drove out of the airport.

CHAPTER 51

TWO HOURS LATER, Kylie and I were sitting in an attorney-client consultation room at the Green Haven Correctional Facility in Stormville, New York. A guard led X. L. Gaston in, sat him in a chair, shackled him to the cuff bar on the table, and left the room.

X. L. looked around, clueless why he was there. His face was bruised and swollen; his eyes were red and filled with terror.

"Hello, X. L.," Kylie said. "It looks like prison agrees with you. And you still have nine years and three hundred and forty-nine days left to enjoy it."

"Whatever it is, I swear I didn't do it," he whined.

"That's what you said the last time. 'I didn't do it.' And yet the jury seemed to think otherwise."

"Last time" was a clue, and he stared at us, trying to remember where he had encountered us before. It had been only three months since we sat down with him and offered him a deal, but the blows to his head had taken their toll on his brain.

"Do you remember us?" I asked.

"Cops," he said.

"Yeah, cops. I'm Detective Jordan, and this is my partner, Detective MacDonald. We visited you at the Tombs back in April, when you were awaiting trial. We offered to go to bat for you with the DA if you came clean about what happened to the gun you used to shoot the bodega clerk."

That sparked his memory. "Oh, yeah," he said, a smile of recognition spreading across his face. It was the same smile he'd given us when he turned down our offer. Only now there were fewer teeth.

"I shoulda took the deal," he said, "but my lawyer was a fucking moron. He told me if I copped to the gun, it would hurt my chances in court. That's what they call ineffective assistance of counsel. I know my rights. I'm appealing the verdict."

"X. L.," Kylie said, "it took the jury less than thirty minutes to lock you up for ten years. You can't chalk that up to bad lawyering. Even if you do appeal, you'll be lucky to get a hearing before your ten years are up."

"Is that why you're here?" he said. "To tell me that I'm fucked?"

"No. That gun has been used in a couple of homicides since you last saw it. We're looking for it. If you help us track it down, we may be able to help you find more pleasant accommodations."

His eyes filled with hope. "You mean you could get me transferred outta here?"

"I'm told that Otisville is lovely this time of year," Kylie said.

"Otisville?" he said. "Are you shitting me? My cousin Rios is there. Nobody fucks with Rios. Could you fix it so we're cellies?"

"We know the warden personally. I can't promise he'll put you in the same cell, but I'm sure he can find you a nice safe place with a view of the laundry facility. Compared to this hellhole, it'll be like the Riviera."

"I'll take it. I'll take it. What do you want to know? I'll tell you anything."

"You put a 9mm slug into the clerk's foot when you tried to hold up the bodega," I said.

"Yeah, yeah. It was a 9mm Lorcin. Piece-of-shit gun. That's why it went off in the bodega. I never even pulled the trigger."

"Of course you didn't," I said. "Maybe you can sue the manufacturer while you're appealing the verdict. Let's get back to why we're here. The piece-of-shit gun wasn't on you when the cops picked you up a couple of hours after the robbery. Who'd you give it to?"

"Nobody. I tossed it."

"Bullshit," Kylie said. "You don't strike me as the kind of person who throws away a gun, even if it was a piece of shit. You'd give it to a friend. Or you'd sell it."

"Yeah," X. L. said. "And then the guy you sell it to sticks up a liquor store, gets caught, tells the cops how he came by the gun, and I wind up getting charged with his crime. No thanks. How stupid do you think I am?"

Kylie ignored the question. "Okay. You tossed it," she said. "Where?"

"As soon as I ran out of the bodega, I ran to the subway. I got on the six train—the local, going downtown. My heart's pounding. I wait a couple of stops, and then I go between cars, and I chuck it into the tunnel about halfway between One-Sixteenth and One-Twenty-Fifth. I figure that's a pretty safe bet. No homeless guy who needs to take a shit is going to go back that far."

"And that's your story?" Kylie said. "You threw the gun onto the subway tracks."

"Yeah. That's what I done. Why would I lie to you? You guys are my only shot to get outta here."

"No can do, X. L.," Kylie said. "The deal was you have to help us find the gun."

"So I told you where I tossed it. Just go and look. It's probably still there."

"It's not there, X. L.," I said. "We told you. Someone is using it to kill people."

He smacked his head and laughed. "Oh, yeah. My brain's a little scrambled. These guys in here are psychos. One of them beat the shit out of me. When I asked him why, he said, 'because I can.' That wouldn't happen to me if I had Rios around."

"You're right," I said. "It wouldn't. And if you let us know how to find the gun, you'll be on the first bus out of here to Otisville." I called for the guard.

"No, wait. I'm telling you the truth. I swear on my mother's life. I got rid of the gun in the subway tunnel. Please, you gotta help me get away from these animals."

The guard dragged him off ranting, begging, crying. I had no sympathy. At his core, X. L. Gaston was a low-life long-term criminal, and I doubted he'd be any different when he got out in ten years.

We called Steve Edlund from the car and gave him the bad news. The gun was a dead end.

"Do you believe him?" Edlund asked.

"He swore on his mother's life."

Edlund laughed. "If God actually took that shit seriously, there'd be a pile of dead moms all over the city. So then, I guess we're back to square one."

"Maybe not," Kylie said. "Shane has had a few days to calm down after the shooting. He's being released from the hospital tomorrow. He'll be home; he'll start cooking; he'll start feeling like his old self again. Now that I'm allowed to work the case, I'll see if I can get him to remember a few things that the trauma suppressed."

"Go for it," Edlund said.

"I'll do my best," Kylie responded. "At the very least, I'll get a great dinner out of it."

CHAPTER 52

VINCENT DOWNED THE LAST of his beer and set the glass on the scarred walnut bar top that had been a refuge for the locals for forty-seven years. Within seconds, a callused hand whisked the empty away and replaced it with a full one, the glass cool, wet, and sparkling clean, the head sitting on top of the amber brew, mushrooming about an inch over the rim.

"On the house," Smitty said. "But you gotta do me a favor."

"Name it," Vincent said, lifting the beer.

"Smile, will ya? You're giving happy hour a bad name. Customers are starting to complain."

Vincent did more than smile. He laughed out loud. That was why this became his go-to watering hole. Smitty could crack up a church full of grieving widows.

"So what is it?" Smitty asked.

"What is what?"

"Come on, Vincent. What's my mantra, my core credo, the unshakable doctrine that guides my life and that I willingly share with every sad sack who drags his ass into my saloon?"

Vincent, still grinning, shook his head.

"Say it, Vincent, or I'll take the beer back."

Vincent let out a weary sigh. "If it's got tits or wheels, it's gonna give you problems."

"Now you're talking," Smitty said. "And since I know you ain't got a car, that eliminates the wheels option, which leaves us with what? Women."

Vincent nodded, enjoying the performance.

"And since you've been parking your ass on that stool since five years before you were legal, I know you well enough to count the women in your life on three fingers. How am I doing so far?"

"You're batting a thousand," Vincent said. "But I'm an easy read. We can't all have four ex-wives like you."

"Three ex-wives. The dead one don't count. Now, where was I?"

"You narrowed down my problems to three women."

"Right. The one is your sister." Smitty held up one finger on his right hand. "Priscilla drives you crazy all the time. And when she does, you come in here all worked up, ready to pounce, like a rat trapped in a corner.

"Or," Smitty said, raising a finger on his left hand. "It could be your girlfriend. When Valerie pushes your buttons, you're a whole different kind of angry. More pissed at yourself than at the rest of the world. Like she pressed that old familiar 'you're not good enough' hot button that was installed, lo these many moons ago, by candidate number three— your dear departed mother."

"Jesus, Smitty," Vincent said.

"Hey, tell me it ain't true, and I'll never say it again. But come on, Vincent—your mom? I seen her do it all the time. She was always taking people down a peg, and you and your sister got the worst of it. Why do you think I let you drink here when you were only sixteen? Why do you think Priscilla don't come out of the house and deal with the world? It's a shame how your mother treated you kids. But she's gone. Don't let her live rent-free inside your head."

He took a dry towel and rubbed the ancient wooden bar top hard enough to coax a hint of the old luster out of it. "I'm sorry, kid," he said, looking up at Vincent. "I have this bad habit of thinking everyone comes here for the gospel according to Ernie Smith. It's just that I know you got a great girlfriend who loves the shit out of you, and she's got two kids who treat you like the dad they always dreamed about, and you have a damn fantastic life ahead of you. And then you come in tonight, and you're not pissed off, like when Priscilla is driving you batshit, and you're not looking all pussy-whipped like Valerie called you out on something, so I was trying to guess what the fuck was wrong with you, and I came up with the ghost of Ingrid Ackerman."

"It's not my mother," Vincent said. "It's Valerie. She wants to get married."

"That's fucking fantastic! What are you sitting here drowning your sorrows for? You'd be crazy not to marry her."

"I know. I wanna. I love her. And her kids—my God, I'd throw myself in front of a bus for them."

"So what's the problem?

"Valerie is from the Dominican Republic. Her roots are there. Her whole family is there. She wants to marry me, but only if the four of us move there."

"So go! The DR is beautiful. It's summer all year long. You been with the MTA twenty years. Take an early retirement and go make a life for yourself. What the fuck is in Astoria that would keep . . ." Smitty stopped. "Oh, right. Priscilla don't want you to go."

"I haven't told Priscilla," Vincent said.

"Yeah, but she ain't blind. How long have you and Valerie been together? A couple of years? Priscilla had to know this was bound to happen. Maybe she didn't expect you to move out of the country, but she had to know that one day you'd move out of the apartment."

"That's the thing that's been eating at me, Smitty. I never told Priscilla about Valerie. She doesn't even know Valerie exists."

"Oh, Jesus," Smitty said. "Your own sister has no idea you have a life?"

"Right. I couldn't tell her. She . . . she depends on me too much."

"How old is she?" the bartender demanded.

"I'm thirty-eight, so she's thirty-six."

"You've gotta get on with your life, kid. And if she's thirty-fucking-six, she's got to start living her life on her own. She's gotta shop for her own groceries, do her own laundry, buy her own fucking magazines at the newsstand . . ." He groped for another example.

But Vincent was already ahead of him. *Kill her own victims.*

"You have to tell her, Vincent," Smitty said. "I know it won't be easy for her. But she's your sister. She'll come around. She'll be happy for you."

"You're right. She's my sister," Vincent said. "I'm gonna tell her."

Smitty picked up a bottle of Jameson and poured them each a jigger. "Can we drink to that?"

Vincent picked up the shot glass. "Sure."

There was a large brass bell behind the bar. It got rung every night at last call, every time someone left a surprisingly hefty tip, and on the rare occasion that someone wanted to buy a round for the entire house. Smitty put his hand on the cord. "Can *everybody* drink to that?" he said.

"Are you nuts?" Vincent said. "This place is packed."

"Well, damn it, son, it wouldn't be a very magnanimous gesture if the fucking joint was empty. Now, is this gonna be just another forgettable night at your local pub, or do you want to commemorate the moment? Life is short, kid. Make up your mind."

Vincent, caught up in Smitty's joy, didn't hesitate. "Hell, yes! Ring it!"

Smitty yanked vigorously on the cord, and the clapper struck the soundbow—once, twice, again, again, and again. The clang of the bell resonated through the old tavern until everyone stopped what they were doing, and all eyes were smiling on the bearer of good tidings.

"Ladies and gentlemen," Smitty bellowed, "it is my great pleasure to announce that despite his advancing age, his thinning hair, and his expanding waistline, our good friend Vincent Ackerman is at long last engaged to be wed."

Cheers from the crowd.

"Sadly, he will be leaving the charm and allure of Astoria for the sun, the surf, and the total dearth of snow of some tropical island in the Caribbean."

The room responded with a chorus of catcalls and boos.

"So whether you're happy to see him get hitched, or glad to see him leave town, let's celebrate. The next round is on me."

The room erupted. At least a dozen people rushed the bar, hands extended to congratulate Vincent.

Jesus, he thought, downing the Jameson and slamming the glass on the ancient slab of walnut. *I'm about to hurt my poor sister worse than anyone has ever hurt her in her entire life, and they're all happy for me.*

CHAPTER 53

I WOKE UP the next morning with Cheryl's head on my shoulder and her body nestled against mine. I rolled onto my side and let my fingertips graze her cheeks, her lips, her neck. Then my hand drifted gently over the curve of her breast, slid slowly down to her hip, inched its way to her thigh, and lingered there, feeling the heat of her skin, waiting for the familiar moan of anticipation.

"I don't know," she whispered. "Theo is up."

"So am I," I whispered back.

She looked at me, her dark coffee-brown eyes filled with mock doubt. "*¿Es verdad?*" she asked, breathing out the words, the seductive Spanish making me even harder.

She pressed her hand to my chest, working her way across my rib cage, down to my stomach, and finally . . . "*¡Dios mio!* You're a man of your word."

I put my lips to her ear. "Can I take that as a yes?"

"Theo's in the kitchen. Can we do this quietly?"

"Like a pair of randy church mice."

She kissed me. "And you don't think you're setting a bad example for someone who could be your son?"

"The jury is still out," I said, my hips undulating in response to her touch. "But even if he is, at his age he'd be proud of his old man."

I moved my hand, and she responded with a gasp. Her legs parted, and she let out a long, throaty moan, the universal language for *don't stop now.*

I didn't.

It was quiet. It was gentle. It was glorious.

And if Theo heard anything, he didn't let on. When I came out of the bedroom, he was sitting at the kitchen table, AirPods in his ears, MacBook at his fingertips, the sugary remnants of a teenage boy's idea of a healthy breakfast still in front of him.

He's not a morning person, but today was different. Today, Theo was meeting with Martin Sheffield's lawyer, hearing the details of his will, and, most importantly, taking possession of the sealed envelope Sheffield had left behind. With luck, something in that envelope would lead us to the man who killed Warren Hellman, Eldon Winstanley, and God knows how many others.

Theo's head was moving to the rhythm of whatever he was listening to. I leaned over and popped out one of his earbuds. "You all ready for your big day?" I said.

"Psyched."

"You working on your movie?"

"Nah, I'm just reading some bullshit on the Internet," he said. "It's all about these so-called hero cops who chased after a deranged killer in a bloodmobile and brought him to justice."

I grinned. "And that's bullshit?"

"Yeah, man. There's not a single word about the cool young film-maker who clued the cops in to the five hit men, took them to Golden Grove, tipped them off when Barbara was about to ambush them at the funeral parlor, then wrecked his bike and almost got himself killed trying to do their job."

"That totally sucks for you," I said. "Those cops hogged all the glory and didn't let the news media pick up on your connection to the case."

"Exactly."

"They're probably thinking Carol is still out there, and he can shoot the nut sack off a fruit fly in a hailstorm, and you're a hell of a lot safer if your name isn't in the news."

"I guess they want me to keep a low profile," Theo said.

"More like no profile," I said. "They want you invisible until anyone and everyone who could possibly want to kill you because you know too much about the Sorority is locked up or dead. Until further notice, you don't exist."

"That is so fucking cool," Theo said.

"Don't take this personally, kiddo," I said, "but not many people would think that the possibility of a trained assassin with a .50-caliber rifle coming after them is all that fucking cool."

"Yeah, but I don't think like other people. Life is full of great stories, and if you have the opportunity to be in the middle of one, shut up and make the most of it."

"That's a hell of a philosophy," I said.

"I think I probably get it from my mother."

I smiled. I knew he got it from his mother.

CHAPTER 54

I'M SURE MARTIN SHEFFIELD was as methodical about choosing a lawyer as he had been about planning his murders.

Forrest Nivens was a perfect choice. After spending three decades at a top corporate law firm in Manhattan, he packed it in at the age of fifty-five. Instead of retiring to the golf course or a life of leisure, Nivens took a different path.

He rented a small office on the second floor, over a barber shop on Sutphin Boulevard in Jamaica, Queens, and opened a one-man law practice. He gave up handling nine-figure M-and-A deals to resolve insurance claims, custody disputes, employment discrimination, and other legal issues faced by the low-income people in his community. And for those who couldn't even afford his modest fees, no problem. They could pay him with homemade baked goods or by shoveling his driveway in the winter.

Reading his reviews online, Kylie and I could see he was exactly what Sheffield was looking for: a solo practitioner with decades of experience, who was honest, reliable, and above all, someone he could trust.

Nivens welcomed us into his office, and Kylie and I identified ourselves.

"And this is Theo Wilkins," I said.

He shook Theo's hand. "It's a joy to finally meet you, young man, even on such a joyless occasion," Nivens said. "Martin spoke so highly of you."

Theo accepted the compliment with an aw-shucks nod.

Nivens turned to Kylie and me. "I was devastated to hear about his death. The fact that it was a homicide rocked me to the core. He was such a sweet man. And he was in declining health."

"He told you about his condition?" I asked.

"From the get-go. He said he was in the early stages of Alzheimer's and he wanted to get his affairs in order while he was still capable of making critical decisions. I hope you find whoever did this."

"We can't give you the details," I said. "But I can tell you that the killer was someone from his past, and he was apprehended."

"Thank you for sharing that. It's comforting to know that Martin will get justice."

"How long had you known him?" Kylie asked.

"Let's see . . . this is July," Nivens said. "I remember he walked in one snowy afternoon in January. So about six months."

"Walked in?" Kylie said. "No appointment?"

"This is a storefront law firm. People rarely schedule appointments. They just show up. If I'm busy, they wait." He smiled. "Same basic business model as the barbershop downstairs," he added with a wink.

"So you knew nothing about him. He was just a run-of-the-mill walk-in."

Nivens chuckled. He tried to shake it off, but instead it blossomed into a hearty laugh. "I'm sorry," he said. "It was a walk-in, but it was hardly run-of-the-mill. Jamaica is predominantly Black and Hispanic. I don't get many white clients coming in off the street. And in twelve years, I've never had anyone of *any* race, religion, or creed stroll through the door and ask me to draw up a will for an eight-million-dollar estate."

Theo put his hands to his cheeks. "Eight . . . eight million?" he said. "*Dollars?*"

"That's a round number," Nivens said. "I'm not only the attorney of record; he asked me to be the executor as well, so I still have to file the will with the probate court. And since the money is spread out over multiple accounts—many of them abroad—there's a lot of paperwork involved, but eight million is a pretty close estimate."

"Minus your fees," Kylie said.

"No, Detective," Nivens said. "Martin paid all my fees up front. Everything in those accounts will go to Theo."

"What if I don't want the money?" Theo asked.

"Martin warned me you might say that," Nivens said. "And that's your prerogative. But Martin had no heirs, and he didn't name any secondary beneficiaries, so let me give you my best advice. Honor his wishes and accept the bequest. Once it's in your name, you don't have to keep it. You can give it away or donate it to a worthy cause."

"What happens if he waives the inheritance?" Kylie asked.

"It will wind up in the coffers of the state of New York. Every penny."

Theo grimaced. "Well, that sucks."

Nivens smiled and rested a hand on Theo's shoulder. "Only if you give it to them, son."

Theo returned the smile. "I'll take it."

"Excellent. There's one more thing," Nivens said. "Last month, Martin called and asked if I could pay him a visit on a Tuesday at two thirty—right after his yoga session. Apparently, stretching and meditation helped the fog lift. I got to his room, and he gave me this blank stare. Finally, he said, 'Who the fuck are you?' And then he yelled, 'Gotcha!' and cracked up laughing—still his old irascible self. We talked for about ten minutes, and he started to fade. He said, 'I may not know you the next time I see you, so let me thank you while I still can. Please give this to Theo after I'm gone.'" He took a padded envelope from his desk.

Theo tore it open and pulled out a handwritten note. He read it out loud.

"Dear Theo, thank you for helping me get the most of my final days. You're a great listener, and the time we spent together made me realize that the missions I carried out for our government, and my subsequent career as a private contractor, are a story worth telling. And you're the only one I trust to do it. I hope this helps. Your partner in crime, Martin."

Theo reached back into the envelope, pulled something out, and stared at it. He tried to speak, but he couldn't. Tears streaming down his cheeks, he handed me the final gift from Martin Sheffield.

It was a flash drive. A tiny message was taped to it.

It said, THIS IS NOT A CAN OPENER.

CHAPTER 55

WE DROVE to the precinct in total silence. Theo needed space, and we gave it to him.

Cates was waiting for us in the third-floor conference room. I plugged the flash drive into a laptop, and the icon popped on the screen. I clicked on it to view the contents. Only two files. A video four minutes and twenty-five seconds long, and a second, shorter video, only two minutes and fifty-two seconds. It didn't bode well. I'd been hoping for more. Volumes more.

I hit play.

The image of Martin Sheffield's room at the Golden Grove appeared on the screen. A small writing desk was in the foreground.

"Okay, we're rolling," Sheffield said as he entered the frame and sat down behind the desk. He was wearing an olive drab T-shirt with the letters "SFMF" stenciled on it. I hit the pause button.

"Do you know what that stands for?" I asked.

Theo smiled. "Yeah. He was a marine. It stands for SEMPER FI, MOTHERFUCKER. He wore it a lot."

I hit play.

Sheffield looked straight at the camera and started talking. "Hey, Theo. Look at me, making a fucking movie. I don't know what I'm doing, but it beats sitting in the dayroom watching TV with the rest of the drooling zombies."

There was a yellow pad on the desk. He picked it up and studied it. "Can't do this without a cheat sheet. That's the thing about dementia. It creeps up on you. In the beginning, it was the little things. I chalked it up to brain farts. But then there would be gaps of time I couldn't account for. I started leaving Post-It notes all over the damn place. Reminders on my phone. I knew it was only going to get worse, so I checked into this rat trap so I wouldn't leave the oven on and burn the house down.

"And then you came along and said you could tell my story. Those talks we had every day—man, I lived for them. And I never told you this, but when you weren't here, I started documenting everything on paper. Back then I was in what they call 'mild decline,' so as soon as I woke up in the morning, I'd write shit down. Funny thing—I couldn't remember what I had for dinner the night before, but I could summon up every vivid detail about killing the head of a cybersecurity firm in Dubai a dozen years ago.

"I cranked out almost a hundred pages, and I mailed them to an old cohort of mine and told him to send it to you once I'm gone. It may take a while before you get it, because he'll forward it through four or five people around the world, so nothing comes back to him."

He checked his yellow pad. "I think I should tell you a little about Mother," he said. "I know I haven't told you much about her, but if you're going to do this movie, you should know that without Mother, there would be no Sorority."

Theo shot Kylie and me a look. Mother's critical role was news to him.

Sheffield went on. "Twenty years ago, when they pulled the plug on our unit, I didn't know how I was going to cobble together a living. Uncle Sam paid us off, but there was no lump sum. All we got were monthly checks. Chump change when you think about what we did for our country. Fuck you very much for your service, marine. Plus, we had to sign a contract. If any one of us opened our mouth, all of us would wind up in federal prison. They assigned us a JAG lawyer out of Quantico to handle the paperwork. I can still remember the first thing that lawyer said when the six of us were all behind closed doors: 'You fellas could make a shit-load of money doing this on your own.' That was the golden goose that made us millionaires. That JAG lawyer became Mother.

"Mother put the organization together. First thing she did was help us create new identities. We were civilians now, so she set us all up with low-visibility jobs. Me at the pharmaceutical company, Emily in the funeral home, but Carol was so damn good at what he did that he turned his humdrum job into a world-class career.

"That kind of notoriety isn't exactly an asset for someone in our line of work, but Mother turned it to our advantage. She realized that with his credentials, Carol could travel anywhere in the world. And with all those equipment cases, he could have smuggled a howitzer into Buckingham Palace."

He stopped to check his notes. "Vancouver," he said, reading from the pad. "What the fuck happened in Vancouver?"

His face went blank. I could see the fear in his eyes as he felt his mind slip away. And the desperation as he realized he couldn't retrieve it. He stood up sharply, flipping the desk over.

"Give me a fucking minute," he bellowed as he walked off camera. The video ended abruptly.

I looked over at Theo. His arms were folded tightly across his chest. "How you doing?" I said.

He shrugged.

"You okay to sit through the next one?"

"Yeah," he said. "I've seen him lose it before. It's just not how I want to remember him."

"He said at the end of the first one to give him a minute," I said. "But according to the metadata, he shot this next one six days later."

I hit play. The desk was back in position, but this time Sheffield entered the frame wearing a long-sleeved plaid shirt that was badly in need of ironing.

He sat down, his face showing the strain of the task ahead. But I could feel the determination. "I went back over what I already shot, and I was going to tell you about Vancouver. I got more notes this time."

He picked up his yellow pad. "One day, Mother called me and said I got a contract from a biker gang in Canada—the Lords of Agony. The target was the gang's former president. The cops in Vancouver nailed him on drug-trafficking charges. He was looking at twenty-five years, so they offered him a deal. Give up everything he knew—not just the suppliers and the stash houses, but the cops, the judges, and the politicians on the payroll—and in return he would get immunity and a new identity. No prison time."

He looked up from the pad. "Theo, that is one big fucking lifeboat they floated to this guy. So you can imagine how much dirt he had. His testimony would have put away more than a hundred of them."

He went back to his script. "The Vancouver PD was stashing this dude in a five-star hotel—I can't remember the name. I got a job washing dishes in the kitchen for two weeks beforehand. I found out what room he was in right away. All I had to do was wait for a room-service order and poison everything before it went up. It didn't matter if a few cops died, as long as he did. I'd be gone before anyone knew what happened.

"A week went by, and the fuckers never ordered. They had all their food sent in from the outside. Two days before the trial, Mother sent Carol up to Vancouver. He checked into the hotel across the street. A day goes by, and Carol still can't get a clear shot. The clock is ticking, so what does he do? He goes up to the roof and takes out the fucking biker dude with a grenade launcher to the bedroom. It blew a fifteen-foot-wide hole in the side of the building, which is not exactly his signature shot, but it's gonna look great in the movie."

Sheffield clapped his hands together, enjoying the story as if he were hearing it for the first time. "Quick as a wink, Carol disassembles the grenade launcher and packs it up. But instead of getting his ass out of there, he pulls out his camera, takes a bunch of pictures of the mess he made, and sells a bunch of them to AP. Cool shit, right? Couldn't have done it without Mother."

I hit pause. "Carol is a photographer," I said. "He has credentials and equipment cases big enough to hide a howitzer."

"Or a .50-caliber BMG," Kylie said.

"Now we know why there were only four of them in the picture on the fishing boat," I said. "Carol was behind the camera."

"Excellent," Cates said. "As soon as we're done here, I'll call DCPI and have them reach out to whoever handles press for Vancouver PD."

"There's less than a minute left," I said, hitting PLAY.

"I've got one last thing," Sheffield said, looking at the yellow pad. "Let's talk about the eight-million-dollar elephant in the room. Mother handles all the business arrangements. Whatever I earn goes to her. She gives me whatever I need, which isn't a hell of a lot. The rest she invests. Until I had my lawyer check my bank accounts, I had no idea she'd socked away eight million dollars for me.

"I didn't come by that money in a noble way, Theo. But it's my legacy, and I'm leaving it to you because I trust you to do the right thing with it. It's not going to buy me redemption, but I can tell you this: I'll be the happiest son of a bitch burning in hell knowing you're up here doing a whole world of good for a whole lot of people. Go get 'em, kiddo."

The video ended.

I looked over at Theo. He was smiling now. But tears were streaming down his face.

CHAPTER 56

WITHIN MINUTES, the manhunt for Carol was underway.

Cates called her friend Captain De León at DCPI, told him about the Lords of Agony trial in Vancouver, and the murder of the key witness, and asked for a list of every American journalist who applied for a Canadian press pass to cover it. As soon as she said it was connected to the Hellman murders, the request, which would normally have taken days, skyrocketed to the top.

"Give me an hour," De León said. "I'm going to loop in the deputy commissioner."

Ten minutes later, Cates's phone rang. It was Vera Parnell, the deputy commissioner herself.

The top brass almost never get involved in the day-to-day, but Parnell's office was spitting distance from the PC's, so she'd be as invested in finding Warren Hellman's killer as he was. With her permission, Cates put the call on speaker.

"I reached out personally to my counterpart at Vancouver PD," Parnell said. "It happened six years ago. The hotel was the Tourmaline, and VPD lost two cops in that explosion, so this is personal for them. They'll email you a list of every American reporter who covered the trial. And of course, I promised them a quid pro quo."

"Yes, ma'am," Cates said. "I'll keep them up to speed going forward."

"Thank you, Captain," Parnell said, and hung up.

"Bosses talking to bosses," Kylie said. "It sure gets shit done fast."

My phone rang. It was Rich Koprowski, who was heading up the team searching Barbara's apartment.

"What have you got so far?" I asked.

"Bubkes," he said. "No electronics, no computer, no TV—he probably got his news off his phone. He's got one drawer full of medical scrubs, all dark purple, and another with T-shirts and jeans, all black. The bathroom has one toothbrush, one razor, one towel; the kitchen has one place mat, some coffee, sugar, and a collection of take-out menus, plastic utensils, and packets of salt, pepper, ketchup, and soy sauce. The guy was a total loner.

"He has a collection of books, mostly history. We're cataloging them and going through each one, page by page. The place is sparse, but we're still looking, still canvassing the neighbors. Was there anything of value on that flash drive Sheffield left for the kid?"

We gave him the details of the videos.

"That JAG lawyer is a solid lead, but he or she won't be easy to track down," Koprowski said.

"I know it's the military," I said, "but we've done it before. Everything is in a database somewhere. The trick is finding the right person to give us access."

"That's regular military, Zach. These guys were black-op marines, and high level at that. Their records won't be in any electronic database."

"You mean they just disappear?" Kylie said.

"No. This is America. We never completely expunge someone's military history. The hard copies are buried somewhere deep in the bowels of a vast seven-acre complex in St. Louis. I spent an eternity out there one week."

"We don't have that kind of time."

"There may be another way," he said. "It's a stretch, but since you're both busy chasing Carol, I could give it a shot."

"Yes. And we're hanging up before you change your mind," Kylie said.

"I'll be back this afternoon," Koprowski said. "First thing I want to do is take a look at the videos on that flash drive."

As soon as I hung up, Cates motioned me over.

"Yes, boss," I said.

"Theo," she said. "He's a good kid, but he can't sit around in the middle of a police investigation. Take him down to the front desk and ask Sergeant McGrath to have a couple of uniforms drive him back to your apartment. And make sure they stay with him till you get home. He's still a potential target."

"Yes, ma'am," I said.

By the time I got back from putting Theo in a squad car, Kylie was all smiles. "Good news," she said. "Shane is being released from the hospital. He has Dr. Lu's blessing to cook for us tonight as long as he lets someone else do the shopping."

"And he's okay with that?"

"More than okay. He reminded her that the last time he went to the market, he got shot. He says he may never go shopping again."

Fifteen minutes later, Cates got the email we'd been waiting for. The Canadians had compiled a list of twenty-nine different US entities that applied for press passes to the trial—mostly the West Coast papers, the wire services, and cable news. A total of eighty-seven passes were issued, most of them to reporters and TV crews. Only six to photographers, four of them men.

We searched the web. Three of the men had published photos of the aftermath of the explosion. Two covered the chaos from the ground. One had a spectacular shot taken while the flames were still erupting, the debris swirling, the black smoke pouring out of the victim's bedroom.

"It looks like it was taken from a high floor or the roof of the building across the street," Cates said. "Same angle as the grenade launcher."

The photographer's name was Wayman Tate.

"Sheffield said Carol was a world-class photographer," Kylie said. "But I never heard of him."

"Have you heard of *any* world-class photographers?" I said.

"Point well taken," Kylie said. "Google the fucker."

Google had heard of him. We checked his website, his Wikipedia page, and his social media. In addition to his award-winning body of work, he taught photography at major universities in the United States and Europe. He was sixty-eight years old, and before becoming a photojournalist, he had served honorably in the marines. Wayman Tate fit the profile perfectly. With one exception.

Our eyewitness said the shooter was about Kylie's height—five-seven. Crime Scene scanned a surveillance video of him standing next to the UPS truck and determined that he was a half inch on either side of five-seven.

Wayman Tate was six feet four.

"He's not our shooter," Cates said.

"Yes ma'am," Kylie said. "But according to Sheffield—"

"Martin Sheffield had Alzheimer's," Cates said. "He's a totally unreliable witness. I can't go to the DA with anything that includes the phrase 'according to Sheffield.'"

"Why not?"

"*Why not?* Kylie, didn't you just watch a video of the man totally losing his shit when his mind failed him?"

"No. I watched a video of a man who had a lifetime full of secrets in his head. He was desperately trying to get them out, and granted, some of them came out wrong. By the same token, he led us to Drucker and Winstanley, and that's not exactly *unreliable*. It's almost like Martin Sheffield was ladling soup from a tureen and poured some of it onto a flat dinner plate instead of into a bowl."

Cates responded with a puzzled look. "Your point?"

"Even though his brain was misfiring, the stuff he spilled was still soup."

Cates nodded almost imperceptibly, letting the words resonate.

"Look, boss," Kylie said, "I know our top priority is to find the man who shot Warren Hellman. And I agree it's not Wayman Tate. But everything else about him jives with Sheffield's description of the man we know as Carol, and I'm convinced he's part of the Sorority. I'd like your permission to put him under surveillance and see where he leads us."

"No," Cates said. "You're right that Tate is a person of interest. But if he's the professional hit man you say he is and we put a tail on him, he'll make us in two minutes, and we'll never get a second chance. At this stage, I think our best bet is to go up on his phone."

"You think a judge will sign a warrant for a tap?" Kylie said.

"Tate is a viable suspect in an international terror attack in which two police officers and a state's witness were killed. Add to that the fact that he's been linked to the incident at LaGuardia. I'll call Selma Kaplan at the DA's office. I think between the two of us we can convince a judge that phone surveillance is in order."

Kylie shot her thumb up. "Thanks, Cap."

"I'd just like one thing from you in return," Cates said.

"Name it."

"Don't ever use that dumbass soup metaphor on me again."

CHAPTER 57

"DINNER WAS AWESOME," Theo said.

"Five stars," Cheryl chimed in.

"You're even better now than before you were shot," I said.

We were in Shane's apartment, and we all turned to Kylie to get her take on the twelve-course meal he had laid out for us to feast on.

"Hell hath no fury," she said.

"I've had better reviews," Shane said. "But if that's what you think."

"Oh, come on," Kylie said. "You know I love your cooking. I was thinking about what the gunman said to you just before he pulled the trigger."

"I thought you were ordered *not* to think about my case," Shane said.

"Didn't I tell you?" Kylie said, the picture of innocence. "Those orders were rescinded. It turns out Zach and I were already looking for the perp. He shot two other guys before he shot you."

"Insanity," Shane said. "Maybe the three of us should start a club."

Kylie slowly shook her head. "You can't."

"Good God," Shane said, and poured himself some more wine. "We've got to stop this guy. I'm meeting with a police sketch artist in the morning."

"And I'm going with you. But right now I keep thinking about those four words and wondering if the shooter said the same thing to his other victims. So I Googled it. I thought it was Shakespeare, but it's from a seventeenth-century tragedy called *The Mourning Bride*, written by William Congreve. The exact quote is, 'Heav'n has no rage, like love to hatred turn'd, Nor hell a fury, like a woman scorn'd.'"

"Thanks," Shane said. "You just helped it make even less sense."

"It makes *perfect* sense. It means if you reject a woman, she's gonna come down on your ass. Hard."

"May I remind you that it wasn't a woman who shot me?"

"But a woman could have hired him," Kylie said. "Work with me here. Think about the women you dated. Who did you piss off?"

Shane looked at me. It was a cry for help. I responded with a shrug that I hoped read as *I wish I could help you, bro, but I can't. Just humor her.*

"Kylie, I appreciate what you're trying to do," he said, "but the other cops danced around the same subject. I couldn't come up with a single woman scorn'd."

"Okay, let me phrase it this way," she said. "Am I the other woman?"

He gave her a blank stare. "What are you talking about?"

"You and I have been together for what, six weeks? Is there a woman somewhere, like maybe back in Texas, who thought you two were going to live happily ever after, found out you're sleeping with me, and decided that the best way to end it would be to put a bullet through your heart?"

Shane's face lit up. "Ohhhhhh, you mean Monica."

"Who's Monica?" Kylie said.

"Oh, man . . . me and Monica, we'd been together for seven years. She cried her sweet blue eyes out when I packed up and moved to New York."

"Well, then she could be the one who hired someone to shoot you."

Shane shook his head. "Mmmmm, I kinda doubt it. Monica's a kick-ass mountain girl. She'd've put the bullet through *your* heart and brung over some beef jerky and a case of Rolling Rock to celebrate."

That got a big laugh from Cheryl, Theo, and me. Kylie didn't appreciate the humor.

"Fuck you, Shane Talbot. I'm trying to help here."

NYPD RED 7: THE MURDER SORORITY 229

"And I'm trying to tell you that there is no other woman! I love you, goddamn it!"

The room went silent.

Shane looked down. "Sorry," he said. "I'm still on drugs."

Kylie softened. "Wait, so now you're taking that back?"

"Just the 'goddamn it' part," he said. "I stand by the rest of my statement."

Cheryl tapped a spoon on her wineglass. "Excuse me, would you two mind if a professional jumps in here?"

"Be my guest," Kylie said. "I've had better luck getting confessions out of mass murderers."

"I hate to rewrite a classic," Cheryl said, "but one of the things I learned in shrink school is that hell hath no fury like a woman who *thinks* she's scorned. Did you ever see the movie *Misery*?"

Kylie and I both nodded yes.

"I watched it four or five times," Theo said. "Kathy Bates won a Best Actress Oscar and a Golden Globe for playing Annie Wilkes."

"Never saw it," Shane said. "Can I sit out the rest of the game?"

"Sorry, cuz, but there's no game without you," Cheryl said. "Here's the short version: Paul Sheldon is a novelist. Annie Wilkes is his biggest fan. But when he kills off her favorite character Misery Chastain in his new book, she hobbles him with a sledgehammer, and lashes him to a bed until he writes a new book bringing Misery back to life."

"How could I miss a love story like that?" Shane said. "What's your point?"

"Maybe you did something that felt innocuous to you, but it lit the fury in some woman, and she's taking it to the nth degree. So let's rephrase the question. Have you ruffled any feathers lately—I mean, besides Kylie's?"

"Let's see, last week I overcooked some woman's asparagus."

Cheryl didn't give up. "Go a little harsher."

"Well, there was this one time when it was raining, and I saw some old lady about to get in a cab, so I punched her lights out. But in my defense, I was in a hurry. And like I said, it was raining."

Theo cracked up. Kylie shot Cheryl one of those "men are impossible" looks.

"Try again," Cheryl said. "Try to land somewhere in the middle between Boy Scout and serial killer."

Shane sipped his wine and finally gave the question some serious thought. "Well, I don't know if this is anything, but I fired my accountant."

"A woman?"

"Yeah. Natalie. Natalie Brinsmaid. One day, I walked into my office and she was going through my emails. She said she was looking for some purchase order, but that was bullshit. Then I caught her stealing—nothing valuable, just personal stuff."

"Like what?"

"When I got my first real job, my mom bought me a chef's knife—a Wüsthof. She had it engraved '*Chef Shane*,' and I've taken it to every restaurant I ever worked in. One day it went missing. Luckily, I have security cameras in the kitchen. I guess Natalie didn't know they were there, because I watched her cop it, plain as day. She just grabbed it and put it in her purse.

"I called her on it, and she swore she didn't take it. Showed me her purse. Nothing. So I went to her locker, cut the lock, and opened it. There was the knife, along with one of my chef's jackets that also had my name monogrammed on it, and a headband. I buy them by the dozen, so I didn't know it was missing."

"Was your name on it?" Cheryl asked.

"No. Just a lot of dried-up sweat, which made it even creepier."

"Did you ask her why she took them?"

"Nope. I just canned her on the spot."

"Look her up on social media," Cheryl said.

A few minutes later, we were looking at Natalie Brinsmaid's Facebook page. We scrolled down to the date Shane said he fired her.

"I was terminated today by the most ungrateful man I ever worked for," the post read. She went on to trash the man, never mentioning him by name, but with blatant references like "new restaurant on Bank

Street" and "redheaded celebrity chef," anyone with a search engine could zero in on Shane in seconds.

He seethed as we read the post. But it was the closing sentence that put him over the top. *He used me to build his empire, and then he kicked me to the curb.*

He exploded. "Fiction! Pure fucking fiction!"

"Scroll down," I said to Theo, who was sitting at the keyboard.

"Haven't you read enough?" Shane spat out.

"Natalie Brinsmaid didn't shoot you," I said. "But she might have incited others. I want to know how people reacted to this post."

Natalie didn't have that many followers, so there were only thirty-two likes and eight comments. Theo scrolled through them.

"Whoa!" he said when he got to the fifth one. "Check this one out."

It was short. Posted by a middle-aged white woman. *You go gril, this shuld beon hhnf.*

"Check what out?" Shane said. "It's illiterate."

"Not totally," Theo said. "People type fast and hit send. They don't spell-check. The first part says, 'You go, girl.'"

"Yeah. I figured out that *gril* is *girl*. Then it says, 'This should be on' something, but *hhnf* is a typo I can't figure out."

"Hold on," Kylie said, tapping on her phone. "I think she means *hanf.*"

"What the fuck is hanf?" Shane said.

"I never heard of it, but according to the Cambridge Dictionary it's a drug made from Indian hemp."

"So the person who made the comment is telling Brinsmaid to smoke weed to help her get through her toxic ordeal of working for me?" Shane said.

"I don't know," Kylie said. "It doesn't make sense."

"Makes sense to me," Theo said. "Think of the word with all upper-case letters. HHNF. 'This should be on HHNF.'"

"Great. What's HHNF?" Shane said.

"I'm not a detective," Theo said. "But my best guess is Hell Hath No Fury."

CHAPTER 58

"NICELY DONE, THEO," Kylie said. "I totally missed that one."

"Smart kid," Shane said. "Maybe you guys should consider recruiting him."

I didn't say a word. I just stood there grinning like my third-grader brought home a perfect report card.

Cheryl caught the grin. I couldn't tell if she approved or disapproved. She just looked at me with that classic, cold nonjudgmental stare that shrinks use to drive their patients crazy.

Theo ignored us all. He was busy typing into the search bar. A page of possibilities popped up. He clicked on the top one, eyeballed it quickly, and said, "This is kind of cool."

"Jesus, kid," Shane said. "Somebody tried to put a bullet through my left ventricle. I was hoping for more than *kind of cool.*"

Theo didn't miss a beat. "Okay, how about this? Watson," he said in a thick British accent, "the game is afoot.'"

"What have you got?" Kylie asked, still not in the mood for male humor.

"It's some guy's blog," Theo said. "I don't know who he is. It doesn't matter. There's a zillion bloggers out there posting shit all the time that nobody ever looks at."

I leaned in. "Don't get mad, get even," I said reading the headline.

I squinted at the rest of the page. "Maybe he could get more people to read this crap if he used a bigger font."

"Or maybe he's catering to a generation that's not yet ready for reading glasses," Theo said. "Sit down, old man. I got this."

Cheryl's perfect deadpan face cracked wide open. She was enjoying Theo as much as I was.

"Is the neighbor's dog shitting on your lawn?" Theo said, effortlessly slipping into an authoritative narrator's voice. "Is some asshole from your office stealing your yogurt out of the fridge in the coffee room? Did the flight attendant make you check your carry-on bag because there's no room left in the overhead compartment? Hey, we all have issues. And for those of us who want to dump our First World problems on the rest of the universe, we can vent on Twitter or Facebook or Reddit. But those are PG-thirteen compared to the anything-goes, no-holds-barred freedom of the dark web.

"The shadowy underbelly of the Internet is not only a destination for people looking to buy guns, drugs, or child pornography, but a breeding ground for those who want to incite, even recruit, others to help a jilted lover or a pissed-off neighbor get even with the sons of bitches what done 'em wrong. Jilted love—did you catch that, Shane?"

"I didn't jilt anybody!" Shane said. "I'm the injured party here."

"Okay, okay, then this is for you," Theo said, returning to the blog. "The three sites at the top of the get-rid-of-your-grudge heap are tit4tat, revenj, and hhnf, which the informed know stands for Hell Hath No Fury, and which caters, as the name implies, to women scorned."

Theo sat back. "There's more, but I think we got what we were looking for."

"Great job," I said.

"Yeah, thanks," Shane said. "Now what?"

"Hey, I'm not running the investigation," Theo said, "but the first thing I would do is go down to the snake pit and see what other nasty shit Natalie is saying about you."

"Can you do that?" Shane said. "On *my* computer?"

The kid grinned. "Could you cook dinner on *my* hot plate?"

Cheryl shot me a look. Clearly, my third-grader with the perfect report card was a lot more complex than I'd reckoned.

Shane grabbed another bottle of wine, and the four of us adjourned to the living room. Twenty minutes later, Theo called us back in.

"This is the HHNF site," he said. "Natalie Brinsmaid isn't on here—at least, not by name. But look at this post from CPA1040."

We read it. It was everything she'd said on Facebook, only ramped up to make Shane sound like a heartless monster, and Natalie like his innocent, tormented victim. It was meant to fuel the flames of hatred and incite retaliation. The responses were even more toxic than the original post.

"Shut it down," Kylie said after we'd read the first handful. "We'll have TARU go through them all first thing in the morning."

Theo tapped on the keyboard, and the computer went dark.

So did Shane. He lowered his head and stared into his wineglass. "What a fucking cesspool. The sick thing is, they all believe her. I wonder how many more of them want to kill me?"

"Don't think like that," Kylie said. "She put that post up a month ago. Almost all the comments went up in the first twenty-four hours. A lot of people read these, get off on joining the chorus, and then move on. Only one of them acted on it. He's done it twice before, but this time Zach and I are going to nail him."

"Why is this time any different?"

"Because this time we're going to come down hard on the sicko who got him going. Natalie Brinsmaid, woman scorn'd."

CHAPTER 59

THE NEXT MORNING, KYLIE, Shane, Theo, and I drove to One Police Plaza in Lower Manhattan. It's an austere thirteen-story brick-and-steel box that was designed for function over fashion. And while it may be architecturally uninspired, for cop junkies like Theo, it's sexy as all get-out.

I got a rush knowing I was there to watch him get his first look at the nerve center of the largest police department in the country.

"Monumental," he said. "Iconic."

A fitting reaction, I thought. So much better than the predictable teenage "cool" and "awesome."

We went through security and walked to the elevator bank.

Shane was nervous. He was there to describe the man who shot him to a police sketch artist, and he was afraid that after four days, his memory wouldn't retain enough detail.

"You'll be fine," Kylie said. "The artist will show you a bunch of eyes, ears, noses, and lips, so it's not just about what you remember. It's what you recognize."

An elevator arrived, and a uniformed cop with a German shepherd stepped out. The patch on his left pocket said, "Emergency Service Canine." The patch on the right pocket had his name, Lowery, and his badge number.

Theo lit up, thrilled to see a working police dog up close and personal.

And then it got really personal. The dog started barking and sat down in front of Theo, blocking him. Lowery gave a verbal command in German, and the dog stopped. The handler turned to us. "She's trained for firearms."

"There's a lot of cops around here carrying guns," Kylie said. "She's going to be busy."

"Detective MacDonald," he said, reading her name off the ID card clipped to Kylie's lapel. "She's trained to sniff out spent gunpowder. Did you guys just come from the range?"

"No, and she doesn't seem interested in us. She's focused on him," Kylie said, gesturing toward Theo. "And he's a civilian."

"Did you toss him?" Lowery asked, his voice all business.

"He went through security," Kylie said.

"Yes. Metal detectors," Lowery said. "But they're looking for guns. Jinx is looking for gunpowder."

I jumped in. "Zach Jordan, Red Unit. Give me a minute here, Lowery," I said. I motioned Shane to step back, and then I turned to Theo. "What do you have on you?"

He was dumbstruck. "Nothing."

"Jinx doesn't react to nothing," Lowery said. "Son, have you fired a weapon in the past few days?"

"No, sir."

"Take off your hoodie and toss it on the floor about ten feet in that direction."

Theo did as instructed, and Lowery released the dog. She went straight for the hoodie.

"*Hier! Sitz!*" he ordered.

Jinx returned to her handler's side and sat waiting for the next command.

I put on a pair of latex gloves and picked up the hoodie. It had a kangaroo pocket large enough for two hands with openings on both sides. I reached in and eased my way toward the center until I felt something. I pulled it out. It was a business card. The name on the front was Megan Rollins.

I held it and walked toward the dog. Lowery had to restrain her from going after it.

"Jinx is a five-year-old pro," he said. "That card has got gun powder residue on it. I guarantee you."

"Got it," I said. I turned to Theo. "You have an explanation?"

"I don't know," he said, panic rising in his voice. "Maybe the fireworks."

"What fireworks?"

"A couple of weeks ago I went to Chinatown with some friends, and we bought some firecrackers and a few other things that maybe aren't totally legal."

"For the record," Kylie said, "*not totally legal* means totally illegal."

"Come on, Kylie. You know what I mean. The legal ones are lame—sparklers and snappers and crap. We weren't exactly stockpiling weapons of mass destruction. All we did was buy a bunch of skyrockets and Roman candles and shit—that kind of thing. I stuck some in my pocket and shot them off on the Fourth of July."

"The dog is trained for explosives," Lowery said, "but that was a week and a half ago. I don't think she'd have picked up the scent after that long, but you can run it over to the lab. They'll tell you what it is."

"Thanks," I said. "And thank Jinx for us."

"*So ist brav,*" he said to the dog. She responded with a single bark, and the two of them walked off.

"When did Megan Rollins give you her card?" I asked Theo.

"When I was in the hospital. Do you remember she came to my room?"

"Did she hand it to you directly, or did she first give it to the cops outside your room?"

"She gave it straight to me. She asked one of the cops if she could, and he said okay. Then they told her to leave."

"Does anybody want to explain to me what's going on?" Shane asked.

"We will as soon as we figure it out ourselves," Kylie said. "But first let's get you upstairs."

The sketch artist was waiting for us. He had no issue with having Theo hang out and watch the process. We waited five minutes until they settled in, and then we took the elevator down to the lobby.

"How the hell does Megan Rollins's business card have GSR on it?" I said.

"We know that the shooter in the UPS uniform left gunpowder residue all over the parapet of the building across from the Tombs when he shot Warren Hellman," Kylie said. "I wouldn't put it past Megan to sneak up to the roof and tamper with the evidence."

"Couldn't happen," I said. "Crime Scene sealed that rooftop off as soon as we called it in."

Kylie shrugged. "Fine. You got a theory?"

"Yeah, I do," I said. "I think Megan Rollins got gunpowder on her hand the same way everybody does. She fired a gun."

CHAPTER 60

"YOU THINK MEGAN fired a gun?" Kylie said as we headed toward the car. "When? Where? Why?"

"Great questions," I said. "I wish I had answers."

The NYPD Forensics Laboratory is in Jamaica, Queens. Kylie got on the FDR Drive toward the Queens Midtown Tunnel, and I called Cates to tell her about the gunshot residue on Megan's business card.

"Megan Rollins?" she said. "The one who will bang any cop who can give her insider information? The same one who trashed Red on the air, then egged on the public so they swamped the mayor's office with emails and phone calls because we were supposedly denying her First Amendment rights?"

"That's the one, Cap. Kylie and I are taking her card to the lab. I'm sure they'll get right on it as soon as I tell them it's a priority."

Cates laughed. That's because almost every cop who submits evidence to be analyzed thinks their case is the biggest thing to come down the pike since the Son of Sam killings. Everything that comes through the door is a priority. Which means nothing is a priority.

Unless you have juice.

"I'll call Inspector Woolsey," Cates said.

Woolsey is the CO at the lab. All Cates had to do was let him know that the thirteenth floor at 1PP was waiting on the results of this one, and it would go to the front of the line.

I thanked her and hung up.

"I have a thought," Kylie said.

"Lay it on me," I said.

She did, and I wanted to smack myself in the head for not thinking of it first.

By the time we got to the lab, Cates had worked her magic. They were expecting us. We met with Ananda Singh, their senior criminalist, and gave her the background.

"I'll get right on it," she said. "I'll call you in about two hours."

As soon as we got back in the car, Kylie called Shane. "How's it going?" she asked.

"I'd rather be dicing onions, but Theo is having a blast. Did you talk to Natalie yet?"

"We're on our way to her apartment now," Kylie said. "Any message you'd like me to pass on to her?"

Shane laughed. "Yeah, send my best, and tell her to let me know if she needs a letter of recommendation for her next job, which, if I had a vote, would be cranking out license plates for the State of New York."

I opened the file we had pulled together on Natalie Brinsmaid and took one last look. There wasn't much. She was thirty-five, born and raised in Forest Hills, and went to Queens College, where she got her CPA degree. Her parents had retired to Florida, and her two married sisters lived in Connecticut. Natalie didn't have a rap sheet, but her social media pages were rife with vitriol, which is not a criminal offense. In fact, her posts were careful not to slander, but she was a serial shamer, and her targets were always men.

She lived alone on Queens Boulevard in one of the many cookie-cutter red-brick apartment complexes that sprang up in the borough after World War II. There was a hydrant in front of the building, and Kylie pulled up to it.

The doorman came scurrying out. "Where you leave your car is none of my business," he said, making it his business, "but the parking police around here are ruthless."

Kylie flipped the visor down, exposing a sign that said, "NYPD Official Business," which almost always gets a laugh from the traffic agent who is writing the ticket. I showed him my ID.

"I guess you can park wherever you want," he said. "What can I do for you, Detectives?"

"We're here to see Natalie Brinsmaid," I said. "Apartment five-C. Do you know if she's in?"

"Oh, she's in. The question is, is she ever coming out?"

"Meaning what?"

"Meaning usually, she comes and goes, I see her, we chat, but these past four or five days she's been barricaded up in her apartment. The first day, I rang up to see if she's sick, but she said no. End of conversation. Haven't heard from her since."

"You said you and she chat," Kylie said.

He held up his hand. "I should amend that. She talks. I listen."

"What does she talk about?"

"You know those people who love to advertise their misery? That's her. It's like tuning into a soap opera. *Natalie's Daily Drama.* My wife is a hairdresser. She gets that from her customers all day. My one brother owns a bar. He gets it all night. I tell them both I'll put Natalie up against their biggest bellyachers and I'll win hands down."

"We're going up to her apartment," Kylie said. "Do not ring up and let her know we're coming."

His face broke into a big, wide smile. "Not to worry, Detective. My other brother is a cop." He winked. "This ain't my first rodeo."

CHAPTER 61

KYLIE AND I TOOK the elevator up to the fourth floor.

"Do you smell that?" Kylie asked as soon as we got to Natalie's apartment door. "Pine-Sol."

I rang the doorbell. Once. Twice. Then I pounded on it. Hard.

Finally, the meek response from the other side. "Who is it?"

"Police," Kylie said.

"You must have the wrong apartment. I didn't call the police."

"Natalie, we're here to talk about Shane Talbot. Please let us in."

"Do I have to?" she pleaded.

"We all want to get to the bottom of this, don't we, Natalie?" Kylie said. "Now, please open the door so we can talk."

One lock clicked loudly. Then a second. The door opened just wide enough to allow Kylie and me to enter the apartment single file. The foyer was spotless, the mahogany console table was polished to a high gloss, and the mirror above it gleamed. The smell of lemon oil and ammonia blended with the Pine-Sol disinfectant. Natalie had been cleaning up a storm. A symbolic gesture that may have helped to ease her mind, but it did nothing to undo the damage she'd done.

She was tall, angular, and gaunt. Her hair was a vapid shade of brown cut just above the shoulders. It was so iconic that even I could recognize it—the Rachel haircut that Jennifer Aniston had sported on the hit TV series *Friends*. Someone must have told Natalie how good it looked on her back in the nineties, and she stuck with it ever since.

"Terrible news about Shane," she said, her hands trembling. "I saw it in the paper."

"You *saw* it in the paper," Kylie repeated, her eyes brimming with disgust.

Natalie's lips started quivering. "Do you mind if I sit down?" she said. "I haven't eaten much lately. I'm a little shaky."

We went into the living room, which was every bit as immaculate as the foyer—not a single throw pillow or knickknack out of place. Natalie lowered herself onto the sofa.

"I had nothing to do with it," she volunteered unprompted. "I swear."

"Are you trying to convince yourself that you're innocent?" Kylie said. "Because if you're trying to convince us, we're not buying it. Try again."

She started to whimper. "He fired me."

"Which was very generous of him," Kylie said. "You stole from him. He could have pressed charges. He let you off easy."

"I guess you're right," she said, the tears coming on fast. "I never looked at it that way. I was angry, so I vented. Everybody does it. It's not a crime."

"It's not a crime to vent the truth," Kylie said. "But what I read made him sound like a monster. You stole, and then you rewrote the script so that you became the victim. You wanted people—total strangers— to take your side. You were hoping somebody would pay him back for the wrongs he supposedly did to you. And now you're saying you had nothing to do with it?"

Natalie couldn't speak. She picked up a pillow, put it to her face, and sobbed into it, her body heaving. Kylie let her go for a solid minute, then sat down on the sofa and put a hand on her shoulder.

"Natalie, it's okay. We know you didn't pull the trigger. We need your help finding out who did."

It took another minute for her to regain her composure. She put the pillow down on her lap. "I don't know how to find her," she said.

Her? We were looking for a man. But we weren't about to give away how little we knew.

"Start with her name," I said.

"I don't know her real name. Online, she goes by BeenThere2. After I posted on HHNF, she started sending me private messages. I never gave her Shane's name. I just talked about my boss. I guess she figured it out."

"You guess?" Kylie said. "Your Facebook page shows you all happy about working at this cool new restaurant, with pictures of the exterior and the menu. How hard would it be for her to figure out who your boss was?"

"I didn't think of that. I just wanted to vent. At first, it felt good to be supported, but then . . . then she took it to the next level."

The dam burst again, and Natalie buried her face back in the pillow. If she was hoping for any genuine compassion from either of us, she was sorely mistaken. Kylie leaned over toward me and whispered through gritted teeth, "Fucking screwball."

It took another two minutes for Natalie to cry it out.

"Show us the messages BeenThere2 sent to you," Kylie said.

"They're in my laptop. I'll get it."

"I'll go with you," Kylie said, and followed her into the bedroom.

They came back, and Natalie opened her computer to the HHNF page we'd seen last night, but now we could read the direct messages. There were dozens, often coming minutes apart. Even without analyzing them carefully, it was easy to see how seamlessly BeenThere2 went from being a sympathetic observer to a champion of women's rights, to an avenger ready to punish the offender on Natalie's behalf.

"We're taking your laptop," Kylie said. "And we want a list of all your social media accounts, along with your usernames and passwords."

Natalie nodded her head in instant agreement.

"And if you want to stay out of jail, do not access your social media from any device, whether it's yours or anyone else's."

"I promise," Natalie said.

We stood up and headed toward the door. "Any questions?" Kylie asked.

"Just one," Natalie said. "How is Shane?"

"Shane was lucky," Kylie said. "He survived. Which is more than I can say for the others."

"There were others?" Natalie said, choking on the words. "And they're . . . they're . . ."

"Dead," Kylie said, spitting out the word.

Natalie clenched her eyes tight.

"Open your fucking eyes!" Kylie said.

Natalie went wide-eyed.

"And keep them open," Kylie told her. "You brought these evil people into your life, and they did evil things on your behalf. Our job now is to stop them from doing this to anyone else."

"Thank you."

Kylie opened the front door. "So keep your mouth shut, and as soon as we leave, lock this behind us. We'll talk to the doorman on the way out, but don't open it for anyone you don't know."

We left, and Natalie shut the door. Just as the elevator arrived, she swung it open again. "Detectives!" she said, her voice a loud whisper.

"What?" Kylie snapped.

"Tell Shane I'm sorry," Natalie mewled through fresh tears.

Kylie turned away and stepped into the elevator. "Yeah," she muttered. "That ought to make him feel better."

CHAPTER 62

AN HOUR LATER WE were back at 1PP, this time sitting at a console while Detective Noah Hirschfeld hunched over the keyboard of Natalie Brinsmaid's laptop.

Before he was a cop, Noah was a victim. When he was eight years old, he was dragged into a van, taken to a basement apartment in Long Island City, and sexually abused for three days until he surprised his assailant by jamming a rusty screwdriver through the man's larynx.

Twenty-five years and 250 pounds later, Noah was working for the Special Victims Unit, luring pedophiles online by posing as an underage boy or girl.

Hirschfeld finished typing and swiveled in his chair. "Ask me if I feel sorry for this Natalie chick," he said.

"I'm going to take a wild guess and say you don't have a single ounce of compassion for her," I said.

"Spot-on, bro. She's like Madame Defarge in *A Tale of Two Cities*— evil to the core, secretly knitting the names of her victims and letting others do the dirty work for her."

"Noah, has anyone ever told you that you're more literate than ninety-nine percent of the cops in this department?" I said.

"I hear the *ninety-nine percent* a lot. But it's always *fatter than*. As for my literary prowess, thanks for noticing, but I should point out that

Charles Dickens is required reading for most high school sophomores. If you really want to get me going, buy me a pitcher of beer, give me a couple of hours, and I'll take you through Gabriel García Márquez's *One Hundred Years of Solitude*, one generation at a time."

He looked back at the computer. "Here's my take on this BeenThere2 character who's been messaging Natalie. White, female, mid-thirties, physically and sexually abused by a drunken father. Daddy is out of the picture now, probably with a little help from his loving daughter, and now she's trolling the dark side, looking to rescue other women from a similar fate. I'd categorize her as a stay-at-home serial killer. She has someone else—a male, maybe a relative or a friend she trusts—shoot her victims. I just composed a message that *Natalie*—a.k.a. yours truly—is going to send to her."

"Let's hear it," I said.

"Dear BeenThere2, just a quick note to say I met a woman online whose story is as devastating as ours. You inspired me to help her. I only hope I can be as good at this as you are."

"That sucks, Noah," Kylie said.

Hirschfeld knows Kylie well. "Okay, to hell with my twelve-year career working sex crimes. I'm sure you have a better way of putting it. Let's hear it."

Kylie cleared her throat. "Dear Fuckface, you're going to regret the day you put a hit out on Kylie MacDonald's boyfriend, because she's going to nail your raggedy ass and put you in prison with a bunch of horny psycho bitches who will make your father look like a paragon of parenthood."

Hirschfeld laughed out loud. "Once a street cop, always a street cop, eh, MacDonald?"

"You know what they say, Noah. Hell hath no fury."

"I feel your pain, but trust me, I'm a professional. *Natalie* is going to send my version of the message to BeenThere2, along with this picture."

He clicked his mouse, and the screen was filled with the bloodied, brutalized face of a woman in her twenties.

"Is that real or Photoshop?" I asked.

"If a detective first grade has to ask, then I've done my job," Hirschfeld said. "If you don't like her, I've got at least a hundred more. My photo file looks like Freddy Krueger's wallet."

"And do you think BeenThere2 will reach out to Natalie and offer to help?"

"Doesn't matter. There's a Trojan horse embedded in the file. As soon as she clicks on the picture, I'm inside her computer."

"Send it," Kylie said.

Hirschfeld poised a finger over the return key. "I just have to triple-check," he said. "Tell me one more time that you have a warrant for this."

"We do," Kylie said. "Judge Hahn signed it in less than two minutes."

Hirschfeld poked the key, and the gratifying whoosh of data hurtling through cyberspace confirmed that the deed was done.

"Now we wait," Kylie said.

"Not long, I'd bet," Hirschfeld said. "Based on her almost-immediate responses to Natalie's messages, our perp is never far from her electronic link to the outside world."

As if on cue, his desktop beeped.

"We're in," he said. "We are now the masters of her domain. Why don't you guys hustle over to the coffee room for a couple of minutes and let me look around?"

"Do you want anything from the vending machine?" Kylie asked.

He swiveled his massive body around. "Do I look like I'd want anything from the vending machine?"

We gave him fifteen minutes and returned with an assortment of snacks and drinks.

"Did you find anything?" Kylie asked.

Noah popped the top on a can of Coke. "Did Hamlet kill Polonius and drive Ophelia mad with grief?"

He opened a pack of Day-Glo cheese-and-peanut-butter crackers and made two of them disappear in a flash.

"Her name is Priscilla Ackerman. She lives in an apartment on Thirty-First Avenue in Astoria. I'll get you the details, but here's the good news. She's got HHNF message chains about your two prior victims, the dentist and the radio talk-show host, plus two more that are either operations in the works, or murders that we haven't yet connected to this case."

"Anything on the accomplice?" I asked.

"The bread crumbs lead to an older brother, Vincent, but right now that's only an educated guess."

"Does she have any photos of the brother?"

"More than I have of my kids."

"Can you do us a favor, please? Shane is upstairs working with a sketch artist as we speak. Can you pull a picture of the brother, put it in a photo array, and see if Shane picks him out as the shooter?"

"Sure thing."

"Even if we don't get a hit, do we at least have enough to bring in the sister?" Kylie asked.

"Not really. She's written a lot of incriminating shit, but a second-year law student would know enough to say that all her rantings are flights of fancy—one unhappy woman's imagination doing push-ups."

He polished off the rest of the crackers and opened a bag of potato chips. "Priscilla is your perp. I have no doubt. But I also have no proof. If you go to the DA now, you'd get shut down in a heartbeat," he said. "It's not my place to tell you two rock stars how to do your job, but if I were you, I wouldn't go near her yet. If she knows she's on your radar, she and brother Vincent will start covering their tracks. We need more on her. I've got a couple of hundred more gigs to wade through. While I'm doing that, you guys might want to have a face-to-face with someone who doesn't seem to be a big fan of Ms. Ackerman."

"And who would that be?" Kylie asked.

"Alvin Jeong. He's a tenant in her building. Called the cops on her three times in the past year. The first time was for vandalizing his property, but there was no proof it was her. The second time, he claimed she yelled racial slurs at him, so he accused her of a hate crime, but that didn't fly either. Finally, she tossed a flowerpot out of her window, which almost hit him on the head and killed him. That got a detective to pay her a visit, but nothing came of it. I think if a couple of sympathetic cops went to see Jeong, he might have some dirt on her, and he wouldn't tip her off that you're planning to nail her raggedy ass and put her in prison with a bunch of horny psycho bitches."

"You've immortalized my words," Kylie said. "I'm flattered."

"I also quote Shakespeare and Louis C.K. My repertoire has no boundaries."

"And you got all that intel in fifteen minutes?" Kylie said.

"Ten. But I didn't want to interrupt your trip to the vending machine."

"Do you have a phone number for Mr. Jeong?"

"It's *Doctor* Jeong. Hold on." He tapped on his keyboard, and Kylie's phone beeped. "And now you have his entire file. Does that help?"

"Does that help?" she said, giving him her best killer smile. "Did Norman Bates have mommy issues?"

CHAPTER 63

DR. ALVIN JEONG turned out to be a veterinarian. His practice was on Steinway Street, three blocks from his apartment. Kylie and I walked in unannounced, and in less than a minute we were escorted inside, leaving the owners of an overweight beagle and a hyperactive Yorkie wondering how two petless latecomers got bumped to the head of the line.

Dr. Jeong was sitting behind his desk, waiting for us in his office. I carry two different business cards. The one that says *homicide* tends to intimidate people. I gave him the more benign version that simply says *NYPD*.

"Detectives," he said, wasting no time. "I cannot for the life of me imagine what this is about. What's going on?"

"There's been an increase in racially motivated crimes in the area," I said, "and the department is taking a closer look at a number of grievances that were filed in the past. We know you've called with complaints about one of your neighbors, and we'd appreciate it if you could take us through some of the issues one more time."

Jeong was in his mid-forties, relaxed, confident without being cocky. "If you're talking about Priscilla Ackerman, there's only one issue. She's a racist."

"I'm sure you know that in and of itself, racism isn't a criminal act," I said. "A bias-motivated crime occurs when a perpetrator targets a victim because of their race or religion."

"I was born in Newark, New Jersey. I grew up with a target on my back, so I know what a hate crime is. In the grand scheme of things, she's just another ignorant person who gets her jollies shoving Chinese menus under my door."

"We all get those unwanted menus, sir," Kylie said.

"Mine come streaked with human excrement. Also, *someone*—I can't prove it's her—smeared duck sauce on my doorknob and left me a fortune cookie with a strip of paper that said 'Go back to China, slant eyes.'"

"Subtle," Kylie said.

"And factually incorrect. I'm Korean, not that that would make a difference to a bigot. I called the cops twice, and it didn't go anywhere, so I stopped calling. But when that flowerpot came whizzing by my ear, I gave it one more shot. I have a wife and a two-year-old. I couldn't ignore it. The detective was polite, but I had no proof that it was anything more than an accident. So I gave up."

"I'm sorry if you quit trying to do the right thing because of the department's response," I said. "That's why we're here. Tell us what you can about Ms. Ackerman."

"She's agoraphobic. I've never seen her come out of the house. I guess she doesn't have to. She doesn't work. She's on disability, so the city pays her rent."

"How do you know that?"

"She brags about it. Takes pride in the fact that taxpayers like me are footing the bill for her three-bedroom apartment."

"Three bedrooms? Why does she need that much space?"

"They started out as a family of four. The mother died before I moved in, but her legend lives on. Evil incarnate. The father was no better. Nasty. Heavy drinker. Some nights, he'd come home so shit-faced, he couldn't open the door, and the daughter wouldn't let him in. So he'd sleep in the hallway. If he needed a bathroom, he'd ring for the elevator, piss in it, and go back to sleep. I don't blame her for fucking him over."

"How so?"

"He moved to Florida about six months ago. But his union pension checks still come to the apartment building. The super brings the mail up and leaves it outside her door. I doubt if the old man ever sees the money, because I know for a fact that the brother cashes them over at Smitty's, the local bar."

"What can you tell us about the brother?"

"Vincent. He's the only decent one of the lot. I nod to him in the elevator, and I see him at Smitty's. He's quiet, but people seem to like him. The other night, Smitty bought a round for the entire house to help him celebrate."

"What's the occasion?"

"He's getting married and moving out of the country."

"Out of the *country*?" Kylie said. "Where?"

"Wow, you ask a lot more questions than the other detective," Jeong said. "I appreciate how thorough you are, but I think I've given you all I've got on Priscilla. I really should get back to my patients."

"No problem," Kylie said, "but just to finish up where we left off, you said the brother is moving out of the country. Do you know where?"

"Somewhere in the Caribbean. I wish he would take his sister with him, but I think she's what he's running away from. Her and that horrible job of his."

"What horrible job?" Kylie snapped.

Jeong tried to maintain a genial attitude, but I could see that his patience was wearing thin. He was done. But Kylie wouldn't let him go.

"Vincent works for the MTA," he said. "He's a trackwalker for the subway system."

A trackwalker for the subway system. A big fat yellow barrel bobbed up out of the water, and I could almost hear the dadum . . . dadum . . . dadum, dadum, dadum shark theme from *Jaws*.

Jeong stood up and came around his desk.

"Thanks for your time, Dr. Jeong," I said, shaking his hand. "Just to be clear, when you say *trackwalker* . . ."

"I know, it even sounds awful, doesn't it?" he said. "Basically, he walks miles of subway tracks all day every day, looking for anything that might need repair and picking up shit people throw on the tracks. You know, like newspapers, coffee cups, soda cans . . ."

Handguns, I thought. I looked at Kylie, knowing she was thinking the same thing.

CHAPTER 64

"A TRACKWALKER," Kylie said as soon as we got back to the car. "It looks like we owe X. L. Gaston an apology and an all-expense-paid trip to Otisville. He said he tossed the gun out of a moving subway, and now we know who found it."

"And what he's been doing with it since then," I added.

"Noah Hirschfield called me while I was chatting with Dr. Jeong," Kylie said, "but I didn't pick it up."

"And by *chatting with*, you mean *browbeating*," I said.

"Po-tay-to, po-tah-to, Zach. All I know is, I pumped Jeong long enough to get him to tell us that the brother of the woman who befriended the accountant who posted all those lies about my boyfriend is a trackwalker."

"Your dogged police work pays off again," I said. "Let's get Noah on the phone and give him the good news."

We called. Noah had some good news of his own. "Shane picked out Vincent Ackerman as the man who shot him. I gave him a photo array of six white males, late thirties to mid-forties, and he jumped on Ackerman in a heartbeat. No question. Add to that the fact that his sister had an online relationship with the woman Shane fired, and I think the DA has more than enough to prosecute the two of them."

"Thanks for your help, Noah," Kylie said. "We'll keep you posted."

We hung up, called Shane and Theo, let them know that we were closing in on the shooter, and arranged to get them both home safely. Then we called Edlund and McDaniel at the Four-One and gave them an update.

"Sounds like we have enough for a collar," McDaniel said.

"We'd like to get them both together," I said, "which means we have to wait until Vincent is home. Can you check with the MTA, get his work schedule, and even if we have to wait till Smitty's closes, we'll get a warrant and arrest them around two o'clock tomorrow morning."

"We're on it," Edlund said.

Kylie and I were both starved. We drove back to the precinct, parked the car, and walked around the corner to Gerri's Diner.

As soon as we walked in, the owner, Gerri Gomperts, stepped out from behind the counter and pounced.

"How's Shane doing?" she said.

"He's out of the hospital and on the mend," Kylie said. "Thanks for asking."

"I would have asked sooner," Gerri said, "but you haven't been here for close to a week. I thought you liked this joint."

"We do," Kylie said. "Mediocre food, rude service—it's the total New York experience."

"Oh my God," Gerri said. "My marketing team had been looking for a new slogan. That's perfect. I'm going to write it down and have them repaint the sign on the window. As long as you're here, would you like to try today's special? It's calamari fra diavolo over linguine. It got two stars on Yelp, although it's possible that the second star was a fly."

"Hard to resist," Kylie said, "but I'll stick with the tried-and-true. Tuna and tomato on whole-wheat toast."

"Grilled cheese and bacon," I said.

"You're in luck," Gerri said. "They both come with a side order of gossip. Grab a seat. I'll be back in a couple."

That's one of the other reasons so many cops eat at Gerri's. She has a gift for knowing everybody's business, and if you're lucky enough to be in her inner circle, she's quick to share it with you.

She came back with our food and sat down in the booth with us.

"Your favorite girl reporter has been in here a couple of times this week," she said. "Once with Buchanan, the community affairs officer, and once with Lieutenant Delmonico, the good-looking special-ops guy."

"And?" I said.

"She was pumping them for leads on the Hellman shooting. I didn't hear what was in it for them, but I think we all know how Megan Rollins takes care of her sources. I kept coming back to refill the coffee cups so I could pick up on what they were saying, and neither of those guys gave up a thing."

"Thanks, Gerri," Kylie said. "That's a big help. Anything else?"

"Yeah," she said, getting out of the booth. "She's a lousy tipper."

"It's not hard to figure out why Andy Buchanan didn't tell her anything," Kylie said once Gerri was out of earshot. "He's got nothing to give. He's not in the loop. And I know Mickey Delmonico. He's too good a cop to leak anything to the press, but he let her take him to lunch hoping he'd get laid anyway."

We ate, thanked Gerri again, and went back to the office. Steve Edlund called just as we settled in.

"I spoke to Vincent Ackerman's boss at the MTA. He didn't come in to work today."

"You think he's on the run?" Kylie asked.

"According to the boss, he just took a couple of vacation days. It's been on his schedule for over a month. It's his girlfriend's birthday, and they're going off on some romantic getaway, whereabouts unknown. But just to be on the safe side, we called Homeland and put his passport in the system. He's not getting out of the country. He'll be back the day after tomorrow, but we can pick his sister up now."

"Too risky," I said. "If he calls her and she doesn't answer the phone, he'll know we're onto him, and he really will be in the wind. But if you can ping his phone, we can grab him first. We know she's not going anywhere. Call the DA and get a warrant so we can track him. If we can't find him, we'll just have to stick with the plan. We know he's not going to leave Priscilla alone for too long. We can wait another thirty-six hours."

"We're on it," Edlund said.

"Shit," Kylie said. "I was looking forward to having the Ackermans in custody before Shane woke up in the morning."

"And celebrating with some kind of . . . what should I call it—victory dance?"

"The thought crossed my mind," she said.

"Life is full of little disappointments. Your happiness will have to wait another day."

My phone rang. It was the lab.

"Detective Jordan, this is Ananda Singh. I have the results of the analysis you asked for."

"It's been a long day, Ananda, and it's not even close to being over," I said. "I hope you're calling with good news."

"It's not good news, Zach," she said. "It's great news. The items you brought in this morning were very probative. I can't be a hundred percent certain, but I think you've zeroed in on the person who killed Warren Hellman."

CHAPTER 65

THERE'S AN OLD MAXIM: "Success has many fathers, but failure is an orphan." Nowhere do those words ring truer than in the New York City Police Department.

As soon as Kylie and I got the details of the forensic analysis, we reported the news to Captain Cates. She immediately called Chief of Detectives Harlan Doyle, and within minutes the smell of success wafted through the rarefied air of One Police Plaza. Red was closing in on the department's most wanted criminal, and everybody with brass on their lapels or politics on their agenda wanted to be part of the action.

Ninety minutes after Ananda Singh called, Kylie and I were downtown in the chief of Ds' private sanctuary. The room had an old-timey New York feel. The walls were lined with pictures of all those venerable commanders who ruled the roost before Doyle, and every chair around the massive oak table was filled with the aristocracy of the department, all dreaming of the victory party, where the mayor praised the police commissioner and they could cautiously raise a glass because his job—and, in turn, theirs—was secure until the next crisis.

Kylie and I were assigned to boil down Singh's tech-heavy thirty-minute monograph on gun powder residue to an easy-peasy executive summary for twenty men and women who are laser focused on results and not particularly interested in details.

Case in point: Singh reminded us that professionals like the person who shot Warren Hellman wouldn't be caught dead buying a box of ammo at Walmart. "They pride themselves in making their own ammunition," she told us. "They craft their bullets to perform to their exact specifications, and this guy has his own personal recipe. He creates a primer with an extremely low flash point, adds his own special blend of high-flash pistol powder—much finer granules than the BBs you'd find in a standard cartridge—then adds military-grade rifle powder."

Singh went on, but if we repeated her report verbatim, either our audience would fall asleep or the chief of Ds would say get to the fucking point.

So we skipped the science and got to the fucking point. "The killer who took out Warren Hellman made his own bullets," Kylie said.

"How do you know that?" the chief of Ds asked.

"We found gunshot residue on the roof where the shot came from. The criminalist who analyzed it had never seen anything like it before. It's our killer's own signature formula."

Head nods.

"The second item we had the lab analyze was a business card that the reporter Megan Rollins gave to our witness Theo Wilkins approximately two hours after the Winstanley shooting at the funeral home. There was GSR and a patent thumbprint on the card. The GSR was an exact match to the residue we obtained from the roof."

Kylie paused, then dropped the bombshell. "And the print belonged to Megan Rollins."

Even a roomful of veteran cops can be blindsided, and their reaction was a mix of shock, disbelief, and not-appropriate-for-the-average-workplace language.

I could see the hint of a smile on Kylie's face.

But, of course, there's always someone at the table who can't wait to build themselves up by knocking us down. Today, Detective Rudy Jenson, a lifelong house mouse who never walked a dark street in his entire career, stepped up to the plate.

He was standing in the back of the room—more of a party crasher than an invited guest. "So you're saying," he sneered, looking around the table to make sure all eyes were on him, "that Rollins was able to sneak up to the rooftop, finger-fuck the gunshot residue, and completely contaminate your evidence."

Eyes rolled.

"No, Detective," Kylie said. "We wouldn't be wasting everyone's time with a tampering charge. The two shootings were sixty hours apart, and the GSR on that business card was too fresh to be residue from the first shooting. In fact, the criminalist said it was exactly what she'd expect to find from someone who had handled the firearm used in the Winstanley shooting that afternoon."

Silence.

"Rudy," the chief of Ds said.

"Yes, sir."

A single flick of the thumb, and Jenson left the room.

The chief of Ds turned back to Kylie. "It's no secret that Rollins has a giant hard-on for this department, especially for Red. Are you *absolutely sure* those are her prints in that GSR? Also, she's a reporter. How do we even have her prints on file?"

"Sir, Rollins has a habit of crossing press lines at crime scenes. She'd been given countless warnings and ignored them all. Two years ago, she crossed the line at the Giambalvo mob hit. Some chief was finally fed up with her entitlement bullshit, and she was arrested for obstructing. She was brought in and fingerprinted. That's definitely her thumbprint on the card."

"So the two shootings are linked," Doyle said. "Identical signature cartridges."

"Yes sir," I said. "We're still analyzing bullet fragments, and we suspect the findings will prove that the same gun was used in both homicides."

The chief of Ds turned to his deputy commissioner for legal matters. "Theresa, do we have enough to charge Rollins?"

The answer was immediate and unequivocal. "No, sir."

Doyle folded his arms across his chest and settled back. "The floor is yours, MacDonald," he said, hoping for more.

There was. It had been Kylie's idea, but she wouldn't take credit for it. At least, not in this room. She wouldn't taunt me with her investigative prowess until we were alone.

"Thank you, sir," Kylie said. "About thirty minutes before the Winstanley shooting, Rollins gave an identical business card to a uniformed officer. He, in turn, handed it to Detective Jordan. We submitted that for examination as well. The lab determined that Rollins's thumbprint was on it, along with those of the two cops who handled it, but there was no gunshot residue present."

The chief unfolded his arms and leaned forward. "You have clear-cut proof that she handed you one business card before the shooting, and there was no trace of gunpowder. But the card she gave to your witness two hours *after* the shooting had her print in GSR?"

"Yes, sir!"

Several audible wows. Zero stupid questions.

Doyle looked back at his legal counsel. "Theresa?"

"Chief, I'm trying to come to grips with the concept that the cheery reporter on the six o'clock news could be a killer, but the evidence is damning. However, we don't have her with the gun in her hand. She could still lawyer her way out of a charge. This is stellar police work, but we need more."

"Jordan? MacDonald?" Doyle said. "Can you get us what we need?"

"Yes sir," Kylie said with 100 percent certainty.

I wasn't nearly as positive, but in for a penny . . . "Absolutely, sir," I said. "And we won't let up till we do."

CHAPTER 66

CAPTAIN CATES ASKED if she could ride back to the precinct with us, and since rank has its privileges, she sat in front and I crammed my body into the back seat.

"Explain something to me, Cap," Kylie said as we headed uptown. "How did an idiot like Rudy Jenson wind up in that room, but not Rich Koprowski?"

"Don't ask me how Jenson has managed to stay around all these years," Cates said. "He's like a mistake that nobody wants to own up to. As for Rich, he would have been there, but he's busy trying to track down that JAG lawyer Sheffield talked about in the video. And speaking of lawyers, the commissioner of legal hit the nail right on the head."

"That we need more evidence before we can charge Rollins?"

"Well, that, yes," Cates said, "but Theresa said out loud what I was thinking. I can't picture Megan Rollins, with her perfect hair, makeup, and made-for-television smile, on a rooftop in a UPS uniform, pulling the trigger on a .50-cal and scattering Warren Hellman's trachea all over Centre Street."

"I can picture her," Kylie said. "In fact, if you look at the surveillance videos, the person getting into that UPS truck was right at Megan's height. I know it doesn't prove anything, but it doesn't eliminate her. Also, Megan was her predictable overbearing self at the funeral home right before Winstanley was shot. And yet, she was nowhere to be seen on the day the Hellman jury announced a verdict in the most publicized trial in this city in years."

"Circumstantial," Cates said. "The ADA would wave you out of her office."

"How about Megan's thumbprint etched in gunpowder on her business card?" Kylie said. "Fingerprints don't lie."

"But they don't always hold up in court," Cates responded. "Which brings us back to the chief of Ds' burning question. Can we get what we need to charge her?"

"No problem," Kylie said, as cocksure now as she was when the chief asked us.

"How?" Cates said. "I'm all ears."

So was I.

"Simple," Kylie said, taking the ramp to the FDR Drive at the posted speed limit like a law-abiding citizen instead of her usual NASCAR driver racing for the checkered flag. "We give Megan what she wants."

"And what would that be?" Cates said.

"She's been fanning the freedom-of-the-press flames and pressuring the PC and the mayor to find out what we know about the murders that she may well have committed. So let's give it to her. Plant information that Red is closing in on some photographer who took out a material witness at a trial in Canada. No names, minimal details. Then we see what she does with it. We're up on Wayman Tate's phone. If she calls him, we've got her."

"It's a good thought, but it won't work," Cates said. "She won't buy it. She doesn't trust cops, and she especially doesn't trust you and Zach."

"I agree. Which means she's got to hear it from someone she *does* trust," Kylie said.

"Like who?" Cates said.

"Theo."

"Hell, no!" I snapped.

"I agree with Zach," Cates said.

"Hear me out, Cap," Kylie said. "Don't we ask sex crime victims to contact their abuser, and then we monitor the phone call? I've seen it work several times where women call their attacker, engage him in a dialogue, and get him to make an admission."

"Hold on," I said. "It's one thing to enlist an adult victim to call the guy who date-raped her. But you're talking about asking a boy to go one-on-one with a professional assassin."

"Theo is not a boy," Kylie said. "He's over eighteen, incredibly smart, deceptively charming, and he's the only person on the planet that Megan *wants* to talk to. She knows he has information, and I'm willing to bet she'll jump at the chance to get it out of him. Zach, I'm not suggesting he meet her for lunch at Gerri's Diner. I'm talking about one phone call that we supervise. Theo plants the seed, and we take it from there."

"Kylie has a point," Cates said. "Megan gave Theo her card. All he has to do is reach out to her and let her think she's pumping the information out of him. It could work, because as cautious as Megan Rollins is, she's not going to think of Theo as a threat. She'll see him as a kid."

A kid, I thought. *Very possibly mine.*

CHAPTER 67

BY THE TIME KYLIE and I laid out the scenario for the phone call, it was five thirty.

"Megan goes on the air at six," I said. "And most nights, she stays at the studio till after the eleven o'clock broadcast."

"We'll do it tomorrow," Kylie said. "But we won't prep Theo till the last minute. The kid is a master of overthink."

The next morning, we were back at Gerri's Diner, touching base with Edlund and McDaniel.

"We're still not picking up a signal from Vincent Ackerman's cell," McDaniel said. "It could mean he knows we're onto him, but it's more likely that his girlfriend is tired of having to share him with his sister and she told him to turn off his phone or their romantic little getaway won't be as romantic as he planned."

"I think you're right," I said. "The poor bastard just wants to get laid."

Edlund lifted his coffee cup. "To Vincent's last hurrah."

The four of us drank, and Gerri appeared out of nowhere with a coffeepot. "What's the occasion?" she said, pouring refills.

"A friend of ours is moving upstate," Kylie said. "We're planning his going-away party."

At eleven a.m., Kylie and I drove to my apartment. "One thing," I said as she pulled into an illegal space. "I know you've already decided that Megan Rollins is our shooter, and you're hell-bent on bringing her down."

"That's our job, isn't it?"

"Yeah, but she eviscerated you on the six o'clock news, so I think you may have a bit of a personal vendetta going."

"Get to the point, Zach."

"Theo has become a pawn in all this shit, Kylie. Don't sacrifice that pawn to get to the queen."

"Are you fucking kidding me?" Kylie snapped. "After all you and I have been through together, why the hell would you even question my—"

"Theo may be my son," I said.

Kylie is never at a loss for words. But this was a gut punch, and she just sat there stunned into silence.

"I had a summer romance with his mother nineteen years ago. I did the math. It's not only possible; it's likely."

"Jesus, Zach. Does he know?"

"Cheryl knows. And now you. That's as far as it goes until I get the DNA results back from the lab."

She closed her eyes and rubbed her forehead, trying to wrap her mind around it. "It's starting to make sense now," she said, opening her eyes. "I saw how you took to this kid, how . . . how you kind of, I don't know, hovered over him. I know it's our job to protect him, but you were like . . ."

"Paternal?" I said. She smiled. "Paternal-*ish*. I'm having trouble picturing you as a dad."

"You and me both," I said. "Now, let's go upstairs and trick the kid who might be my son into helping us bring down a murderer."

"There's a thought you don't often see when you're shopping for Father's Day cards," she said.

Two cops were with Theo when we got upstairs. We had told him they were there to keep him safe, but that was only partly true. Theo was a loose cannon, and having a babysitter was the only way we could keep tabs on him.

"Did you collar Vincent Ackerman?" he asked as soon as the cops left.

"You know too much," Kylie said.

"I was with Shane when he identified the guy from the photo you sent. Nice police work. Did you bring him in?"

"Not yet," I said, "but we caught a break in the Hellman case, and we could use your help flushing out the perp. You game?"

"Are you kidding? You want me to help you catch the guy who killed Warren Hellman?"

"I didn't say *catch*. Kylie and I do the catching, but we could use your help smoking him out."

"Hell, yeah. You see this shit on TV all the time. Once again, life imitates art. Tell me what you need. I'll come up with the scene."

"Not so fast, Tarantino," Kylie said. "The script has already been written. All you have to do is play it out. You know that reporter who gave you her business card? We want you to give her a call."

"I thought you told me you *didn't* want me to call her."

"We didn't want her to interview you on camera and plaster your face all over TV. This is different. We want you to call and tell her you went to the precinct to pick up your laptop, and you overheard Zach and me talking about the man who shot Hellman. You didn't get a lot of details—just that he was a photographer, he shot some guy in Canada, and based on the things Mr. Sheffield told you, you think he's the hit man who went by the name of Carol."

"Is any of that true?"

"All of it is. And if you give it to someone like Rollins, she'll have it on the air as soon as possible, and that will drive Carol out of his hiding place."

"Why can't *you* tell her? Why me?" Theo asked.

"Because she doesn't trust us. She'll listen to you, and she'll believe you."

"Don't you think she's gonna wonder why I'm suddenly helping her out?"

"Just tell her you know she's connected to people in the film industry. You figure if you do her a solid, you're hoping that what goes around comes around."

"So I tell her about this photographer, and then what?"

"She's going to ask if she can meet with you and interview you," I said. "Say yes, but not now. Until the cops catch this killer, you're keeping a low profile."

"Sounds easy. Let's do a dry run."

Theo was a quick study. Ten minutes later, he had his spiel ready. He dialed Megan's number. She picked up on the first ring. "I don't recognize this number," she said. "Who is this?"

"Theo Wilkins. I'm calling from a burner phone."

"Theo! How *are* you?" Megan gushed. She didn't wait for an answer. "I've been *dying* to talk to you."

"I know you wanted to interview me, but—"

"Interview you? You mean about chasing that maniac on your bike? Sweetie, that was a thousand deadlines ago. Old news. Now I've got something completely different and way more interesting."

Theo turned to me. Megan was off script, and he didn't know how to respond. I twirled my hand in the air and mouthed the words "Keep her talking."

He took a deep breath. "'Way more interesting' sounds, um . . . way more interesting. What did you want to talk to me about?"

"After I left you in the hospital, I called a few of my friends at NYPD. It didn't take long to find out that the guy who was driving the pickup you crashed into was a suspect in Curtis Hellman's killing. So I called his widow, Brooke. She knew nothing about the man you were chasing, but when I gave her your name, she knew you. She told me all about the TV pitch you made to the brothers. Theo, I love it. It's got *megahit* written all over it."

Theo's face lit up. "You think?"

"Sweetie, I don't just think. I know. That's why I called Kirby Diehl."

"Kirby . . . Kirby Diehl?" Theo stammered. "The producer?"

"The *A-list* producer who now *loves* your idea. Meet me at my apartment for a drink, and we can talk about it."

Theo looked at me. I waved my arms back and forth like a referee calling "no basket."

"Your apartment?" Theo said, losing his swagger. "I . . . I . . . I don't know if that's such a good idea."

"Oh, Christ, Theo. Did the cops tell you to beware of the black widow who wants to lure you into her web? Fine. I'll meet you in a crowded public space. The front steps of the Metropolitan Museum of Art on Fifth Avenue. One hour."

"I . . . I, um . . ."

"For God's sake, kid, don't be such a wuss. Grow a pair. Yes or no? Three seconds."

Theo froze. I was still signaling no, but he was no longer looking at me.

"Two!" Megan decreed.

"Kirby Diehl," Theo said, mesmerized by the possibilities.

"Opportunity of a lifetime," Megan said, digging the hook in deeper. "One! Yes or no?"

The word exploded from Theo's mouth. "Yes!"

"I'll see you in an hour," Megan said, and hung up.

CHAPTER 68

THEO PUMPED A FIST into the air. "Boo-yah!" he screamed victoriously.

"What the hell are you so happy about?" I threw back at him.

"Did you hear what she said? Kirby fucking Diehl is interested in my hit-man concept. Do you even know who he is?"

"Yeah, I know! Now ask me how many fucks I give. We're trying to catch a murderer here. When did this manhunt suddenly become about your career?"

"Jeez, Zach, lighten up. You said Megan wanted to interview me. But you were wrong. You asked me to plant some information. How was I supposed to do that if she thinks I'm old news? Then she brought up the whole Kirby Diehl thing, and I saw an opportunity."

"For who?"

"Okay, I admit I almost shat my pants when she said my idea has *megahit* written all over it, but I also knew that if I could get her talking about my show, I could work in all that photographer stuff about Carol."

"I specifically told you not to meet with her."

"No, you didn't. You said don't meet with her *now*. Tell her I'm keeping a low profile. You thought I could get it done over the phone, but that wasn't going to happen. Now it will. Plus, I get to pitch my show to the best producer in the TV business. Sounds like a win-win to me."

"You're not meeting with her!"

"Why not? I thought she's on our side. Plus, she called me a wuss. You want her to think she's right?"

"Zach." It was Kylie. "Let's take it outside. Theo, give us a few minutes."

Kylie and I left the apartment and went to the stairwell. "Go ahead," I said. "Say your piece."

"We lied to the kid," Kylie said. "We didn't tell him Megan is a probable killer. We told him she was the perfect conduit to get to the real suspect."

"So we fucked up. We'll get her another way."

"Bullshit. If Theo doesn't show up at the museum in one hour, Megan will know we set up that phone call, which means she'll know we're onto her, and if she's the world-class assassin we think she is, she will have her go-bag in the trunk of her car, and she'll disappear in a New York minute."

"That sucks for us, but at least we won't be putting Theo's life at risk."

"Don't kid yourself, partner. Megan said she talked to Brooke Hellman, which means she knows that Sheffield told Theo the Sorority's deepest, darkest secrets. She can live with the fact that he's shared it with us, but she'll do anything to keep him from sharing it in court. Did you forget how far they went to keep that Canadian biker from testifying? Until we put Megan, Carol, and Mother behind bars, Theo's life will *always* be at risk."

She was right. Our mission was still the same. Only now it was complicated by the presence of an eighteen-year-old stranger who just might be the most important person in my life.

I checked my watch. We had fifty-six minutes left to pull the operation together. I called Ed McSpirit at the Violent Felony Squad and filled him in. Forty-five minutes later, his team, all in street clothes, was in place. Two on rooftops, and the rest on the ground, mingling with tourists, locals, and the hundreds of day-trippers who arrived by the busload.

The museum takes up four city blocks, from Eightieth Street to Eighty-Fourth along Fifth Avenue. In the center is a three-tiered staircase, more than 150 feet wide at street level. It was peppered with people lounging, reading, sketching, soaking up the sun, and because I had done a stint with Narcotics, I knew that somewhere in the midst of all those art lovers and people watchers, someone was probably copping drugs.

And, of course, there was a slew of vendors to make sure they didn't go hungry. At least twenty food carts were lined along the avenue cooking up a storm, and the smells of souvlaki, pork stir-fry, lamb vindaloo, and potato knishes filled the air.

Fifty-nine minutes from the time Megan set up the meeting, one of our spotters radioed that she was walking west on Eighty-Second Street.

Theo was still six blocks away in the back of one of the department's yellow cabs. As soon as I knew that Megan was on the ground and not lining him up in the crosshairs of her .50-cal, I signaled the driver. "Deliver the package."

Megan crossed Fifth Avenue and arrived at the museum steps just as the taxi pulled up to the main entrance and Theo bounded out.

She waved and called his name. He waved back, and they came together. He extended a hand, but she ignored it and gave him a quick hug. Not very subtle, but I could see by the grin on his face that it was effective.

"How are you?" she said. Her voice came in loud and clear. We'd wired Theo so that we could hear him, but we couldn't risk giving him an earpiece so we could talk to him. A pro like Megan would have made it in seconds.

"You must be so upset about your bike," she said. "Is the insurance going to cover it so you can buy a new one?"

Theo fielded the question, and then Megan started to talk about her first bike, a Harley-Davidson Street Glide.

"What the fuck?" Kylie said. "What's with the small talk? We know she's here to pump him for information. Why doesn't she start pumping?"

"I know," I said. "He's eighteen. It's not like he needs any foreplay."

"I don't like this, Zach. Something's not right here. What is she up to?"

Theo also knew that he wasn't there to talk about motorcycles, so he changed the subject. "I really appreciate you talking to Mr. Diehl on my behalf," he said. "Thanks."

His statement didn't require an effusive response. A simple "you're welcome" would have been enough. But instead, Megan threw her arms in the air. "Are you kidding?" she said, wrapping them around his neck and pulling him close.

That's when we heard the shot. My eyes had been on Theo, so I couldn't tell where it came from, but I knew the bullet didn't hit him.

"The food cart!" Kylie yelled.

The hot-food vendors all use propane to cook. The shooter was a pro. He knew that a bullet, even an incendiary round, wouldn't blow up a twenty-gallon propane tank, so he'd aimed at the hose that connected the tank to the grill, and cut it clean through. The hose began bucking and thrashing as the gas spewed out.

I knew it would only be a matter of seconds before the fuel reached the open flame on the burners. The vendor knew it, too. I'd never seen him before, but I knew one thing about him: He was a veteran. The strip of concrete in front of the museum steps is so coveted that the city issues licenses for that space only to men and women who have served their country.

His military training saved lives. He didn't try to extinguish the flames on his stove. There wasn't enough time. Instead, he yelled, "Bomb! Run! Bomb! Run! Run! Run!"

The crowd, already in a panic after the gunshot, ran.

The explosion was deafening. The cart burst into flames, shooting plumes of fire in all directions. Dozens of people were thrown to the ground, rocked by the concussion or brought down by flaming debris. Thick clouds of smoke filled the air, and then a city bus, one of those sixty-foot-long monsters with the accordion center, desperately trying to maneuver past the chaos, crossed in front of Kylie and me and blocked our vision.

I grabbed my radio. "Central, this is Red Unit. Priority."

No response. I tried again. And again. But the airwaves were jammed. There had to be hundreds of 911 calls coming from the people who had been outside the museum. Hundreds more coming from people in the nearby apartment buildings, inside the buses and cars on Fifth Avenue, and those in the museum who were probably now on lockdown.

Communication was cut off. I needed an army of cops, but I couldn't get through to the dispatcher at Central.

I switched to the closed channel we'd designated for the operation. "This is Red Leader. Talk to me. What have we got, guys?"

"Zach, it's Sarah Herman. I was at the top of the museum steps, eyes on traffic. A blue Chrysler was in the bus lane and slowed to a stop on Eighty-Second even though the light was green. I didn't see the gun, but I saw the muzzle flash. I could tell by the angle that Theo wasn't the target. I started racing toward him when the explosion happened. One of the bystanders running in the other direction bowled me over, and by the time I got up, the Chrysler had pulled up half a block and stopped in front of the fountain on the south side of the steps. Megan had her hands on Theo's neck, shoved him in the back seat, and jumped in behind him. I tried to get to them, but it was bedlam, and the car took off before I could get to it."

I keyed the radio. "Anyone have eyes on the subject?"

"Zach, it's Louie Ziffer. I'm on the roof of One-Thousand-One Fifth, directly across the street from the museum steps. I had eyes on the kid. Megan wrapped her arms around him just before the gunshot. I lost them in the smoke screen for about twenty seconds; then I saw them get in the car. The driver cut through the park at Seventy-Ninth Street, and I lost him. We had three mobile units in position, but as soon as that explosion detonated, a lot of drivers abandoned their cars and ran for their lives. The entire area around the blast zone came to a complete deadlock. No amount of lights and sirens could get our guys rolling. I kept trying to get through to Central but—"

"I know," I said. "It's a clusterfuck. Keep trying to call it in and give them a description of the vehicle."

I looked up, and Kylie was at my side.

"We had her!" she said. "We knew Megan was the shooter, but we had no idea she was onto us. She gamed us, Zach. We had her, and she played us big-time."

I didn't know if we ever really *had* her. But I didn't want to debate the point. All I could think about was the fact that Megan Rollins was a cold-blooded killer. And right now she had Theo.

CHAPTER 69

SIXTY-THREE PEOPLE were taken to the hospital with cuts, bruises, burns, or broken bones. More than a hundred others were treated on the scene. But thanks to the quick action of a combat-trained marine, nobody had been killed.

Within minutes of the explosion, the entire city was on high alert. Fifth Avenue was on lockdown from Seventy-Second Street to Ninetieth. Park and Madison Avenues were closed except for emergency vehicles. The PC, the mayor, the governor, and the media were all asking questions.

I had only one.

Where was Theo?

Sarah Herman from our field team located his phone and the wire we had taped to his body. They'd been thrown from the car window onto the roadway of the Seventy-Ninth Street Transverse.

Kylie called his father in Australia. I don't know what she said or if she was even capable of explaining how she and I had gone from "Don't worry, Travis, we'll keep an eye on your son" to "We were trying to take down a pair of international assassins, so we enlisted your teenage kid to take part in a dangerous police action, and . . . um, well, they abducted him."

"Travis is on his way back to New York," Kylie said after she hung up. "It's the middle of the night in Sydney, so it'll be another six hours before he can get on a plane, and another twenty-four in the air."

Under ordinary circumstances, I wouldn't be able to imagine what those next thirty hours would be like for the man. But these circumstances were far from ordinary. This time, the terror was just as real for me.

Theo was my son.

There was no question about it. The DNA results were in my email when I got back to my desk. Cheryl had the lab send the report directly to me.

"You have to know before anyone else," she said. "You can tell me if and when you're ready. But you have to live with it first."

After what I had done to put my son's life at risk, I didn't know if living with it was possible.

My phone rang. It was Rich Koprowski. I picked up.

"Zach, put me on speaker. Kylie needs to hear this."

I tapped the icon. "Okay, you've got us both. Where are you?"

"The ninth circle of hell, also known as the National Personnel Records Center in St. Louis. It's where our government stores the data on every single person who served in our armed forces since Washington crossed the Delaware. Okay, maybe I'm exaggerating, and when I say *stores the records*, I'm flat-out lying. It's easy to find pay stubs for your grandfather who fought on Iwo Jima in 1945, but finding the JAG who swept the post–Nine-Eleven black ops under the rug takes a little more time."

Kylie and I didn't even know that Rich was in St. Louis. Cates must have authorized it. But right now we had only one question.

"The JAG," Kylie said. "Did you find him?"

"Her," Koprowski said. "She was a young lawyer who enlisted in the navy right after law school."

"Do you have her name and where we can find her now?" I said.

"Oh, I think you know where to find her," he said. "Her name is Sonia Blakely."

"Sonia Blakely?" Kylie said. "Rich, are you telling us that the same woman who helped Warren Hellman beat a murder charge was running the hit men who killed both brothers as soon as the verdict came down?"

"I know it doesn't add up. But—and this was buried deep in the bowels of the military archives—when these five hit men were killing for the government, they needed a smart lawyer to cut red tape, build their cover stories, and hide their tracks. Blakely got the assignment."

"And according to Sheffield, that JAG lawyer became Mother," I said. "He called her 'the golden goose that made us millionaires.' Can you prove that she was still in contact with any of them after they left the military?"

"You bet I can," he said. "Before I called you, I called Selma Kaplan at the DA's office and got her to do some digging for us. It turns out Blakely is not only attorney of record to the heavy hitters of Hollywood, she also represented humble funeral director Eldon Winstanley in Bronx Criminal Court when he was collared for a DWI. And remember Leonard Cerutti—Alice—the one who was killed by the military in Ecuador? A few years earlier, Lenny was down in Miami and got himself into a bar fight. He shattered a guy's jaw with a beer mug and then sent him flying through a plate-glass window. The cops charged him with felony assault. The next morning, Blakely flew down to Florida, put up twenty grand bail money out of her own pocket, and the case was dismissed two days later because she made financial restitution to the victim. So, yeah, I think it's safe to say that Sonia Blakely had a deep and meaningful relationship with two known assassins long after their time in the military."

"This is gold, Rich," Kylie said. "When did Blakely leave the navy?"

"The letter to Martin Sheffield from the president of the United States was dated June 4, 2004. Sheffield, Cerutti, Drucker, Tate, and Winstanley were given an honorable discharge on that date. Three weeks later, Blakely followed them out the door. She had planned to make the navy her career, but she suddenly changed her mind and didn't re-up."

"Can't blame her," Kylie said. "She could make a hell of a lot more money running the Sorority."

"Plus, she still had plenty of time to build up her legal practice. Selma gave me a roster of her clients. Some of them make the Hellmans look like choirboys. She helped a lot of scumbags clean up their dirty laundry, and I'll bet murder for hire was just one of the services she could provide."

"And she did it all under the protection of attorney-client privilege," Kylie said.

"Yeah, but she'll throw every one of those clients under the bus if you cut her a deal," Rich said. "Selma can't wait for you to bring her in. She's got a lot a questions for Ms. Blakely."

So did I. The first one was, *Where the fuck is my son?*

CHAPTER 70

SONIA BLAKELY'S OFFICE was downtown. But we knew if we showed up and she wasn't there, her assistant would text her before we were out the door.

"We have her cell," Kylie said. "Ping it."

We did. She was at Forlini's, a family-owned Italian restaurant on Baxter Street that was so old-school, it had become Instagram trendy. At lunchtime, it would be packed with judges, prosecutors, defense attorneys, bail bondsmen, and of course, criminals.

Blakely was at a booth with three men, enjoying her last meal as a free woman.

Kylie and I approached the table. She looked up, recognized us immediately, and forced a smile.

Kylie smiled back. "Hell-l-l-lo-o-o-o, Mother," she said, stretching the two words out into a very un–New York languid drawl, letting them hang in the air—bad tidings dripping with honey.

Blakely let the fork drop from her hand, and Kylie snapped the cuffs on her.

"What the fuck do you think you're doing?" she bellowed.

Kylie yanked her out of her seat and toward the front door.

Blakely was apoplectic. "Are you out of your fucking *minds*? I'll have you fired. Then I'll sue your asses, and I won't let up until I've taken your homes, your cars, and every penny you have in the bank."

People looked up from their *paglia e fieno* or their veal chop valdostana. Most of them shrugged and went back to their lunches. They had spent their lives in the criminal justice system. They'd seen it before.

We perp-walked Blakely out of the restaurant. Kylie remained stone-faced, but I knew that inside she was doing cartwheels. She would gladly have paraded Blakely through the crowded streets, past the county courthouse, Foley Square, and the rest of Lower Manhattan, where friends and enemies alike knew that her reputation was legend.

But there was no time to revel in the collar. We put her in the car, still ranting, and within minutes we led her into the building at One Saint Andrews Plaza.

Her wrath turned to fear. "What are we doing here?" she insisted. "You have no right to take me here."

"Here" was the US Attorney's Office for the Southern District of New York. As soon as we walked her through the door, Blakely realized that she would no longer be dealing with the city, the county, or the state. We had kicked up the charges to the most punishing court in the land: the federal government. And as every lawyer knows, when you end up fed, you end up dead.

Blakely is combative by nature. She thinks she's at her best when she's arguing her case. But we hadn't said a word to her since we took her from the restaurant, and I could see that our silence had her unnerved. She was trembling as we took her upstairs to the fourth-floor conference room.

The welcoming committee was already there: Selma Kaplan from the Manhattan DA's office, two FBI agents who had been called in because Blakely's crimes crossed state and international lines, and Edward Owen, an assistant US Attorney.

Sonia knew him. "Ed, I don't know what's going on," she said, "but tell these morons who I am and get these fucking cuffs off me."

"You're a prisoner, Sonia," Owen said. "The cuffs stay on."

Not the response she'd expected, but she fought back. "This is outrageous. I want to speak to my lawyer. How can you allow them to interrogate me without reading me my rights?"

"You have no rights," Owen replied. "You get no lawyer. *Dickerson v. United States* reaffirmed that the Miranda rule is out the window if these officers have determined someone is at immediate risk of death or serious injury."

The last ounce of bravado drained from her face. She didn't ask whose life was at risk. She knew.

Owen gestured to a chair, and Blakely sank into it. Then he nodded to me and Kylie. I gave my partner the honors.

Kylie moved closer to the chair and looked down at Blakely. "Where are Megan Rollins and Wayman Tate?" she demanded.

"I don't know," Blakely said. It was a lame response. A stall while she ran her options through her head.

"They kidnapped a teenage boy," Kylie said. "If anything happens to him, you're looking at the death penalty. Now, where are Megan Rollins and Wayman Tate?"

Blakely turned to Owen. "I want a deal," she said.

"I'm listening," he said.

"Total immunity."

"No," he said, his voice cold and uncaring, making his response all the more menacing. "I could have you tried, convicted, and on death row in three weeks. Here's my best offer. You'll do time in a federal prison, and if you stay healthy, you won't be leaving in a box. How old are you?"

"Forty-nine," she said, her lower lip quivering. "I'll be fifty in September."

"If you give us what we need, and if no harm comes to that hostage, you can get out of prison by your seventieth birthday. Don't bother doing the math. It's twenty years, and it's a gift."

Before she could negotiate, Owen looked at his watch. "I have a meeting in two minutes," he said. "My generous offer expires as soon as I walk out the door."

I remember seeing a documentary where an old lioness was surrounded by a clan of twenty hyenas, and the camera moved in on the pitiful look of defeat in her eyes when she realized she couldn't survive the ordeal. Sonia's eyes welled up with tears and that same mournful look of resignation. The queen of the jungle knew that her reign was over.

"Thank you," she said, her voice barely above a whisper. "I accept the deal."

Owen responded with a look that was part contempt, part pity, and he walked out of the room.

"Where are Megan Rollins and Wayman Tate?" Kylie said for the third time.

"I don't know where they are right this minute," Blakely said, "but I have a plane on the way to get them out of the country."

"Details," Kylie said.

"It's a Gulfstream G650. Pickup is at Monmouth Executive Airport in New Jersey. Eighteen hundred hours."

"Where are they going?"

"Bogotá, Colombia."

"Who will be on the plane?"

"Just the two pilots. They've worked for us for years. I pay them enough so they don't ask questions. They'll land, pick up the passengers, and take off."

"What about Theo Wilkins?" I asked.

"He's with them. Sheffield told him a lot. They'll interrogate him in flight."

"And what happens to him when he gets to Colombia?"

"I don't know," she said, turning away from me.

I grabbed her chin and turned her face toward mine so she could see the rage in my eyes. "Don't . . . you . . . fucking . . . lie to me," I said, spitting out the words. "What happens to the boy after they've beat everything out of him?"

She began sobbing, lowering her head to her chest.

I dropped to my knees and screamed in her ear. "ANSWER THE FUCK-ING QUESTION! Where are they taking Theo when he gets to Colombia?"

She looked up. "I'm sorry," she said, whimpering, gasping for air. "I'm really, really sorry. They're flying over the Atlantic Ocean. He's never going to get to Colombia."

CHAPTER 71

SONIA BLAKELY KNEW her craft. The airport in rural central New Jersey was the perfect choice for getting two wanted killers and a hostage out of the country. No tower, no air traffic control, no flight delays, and a 7,300-foot runway. Just touch down, load up, and take off.

It was a balmy July evening, ideal for flying. No wind, ceiling and visibility unlimited, and the sun wouldn't set till after eight p.m. The sleek Gulfstream landed exactly at six, and I could almost picture Megan and Carol checking their watches, thinking they would be out of US airspace in minutes.

Megan and Carol. The relationship baffled us. We'd learned a lot about Carol. Wayman Tate was a sixty-eight-year-old marine-trained sniper who had served his country with honor and then, along with four other men from his generation and his military background, spent the next two decades disproving the time-worn adage that crime doesn't pay.

Martin Sheffield's ramblings about the Sorority had sounded more like fantasy than fact when Theo first told us about it, but little by little, every inconceivable piece turned out to be true. It all added up.

With one exception. Megan Rollins. How did this high-profile millennial news reporter become part of this clandestine band of baby boomer assassins? Sheffield never mentioned her. It could be that he forgot about her. But Megan was only thirty-four years old. More likely, he never knew she was part of the team.

If we'd been able to spend more time with Sonia Blakely, we'd have interrogated her until we got what we needed to connect the dots. But as soon as she told us the Sorority's plans for Theo, everything else that Blakely knew could wait. Kylie and I bolted from the AUSA's Office and headed for Jersey.

The G650 taxied to the end of the runway and turned around to get ready for takeoff, and the cabin door opened.

Megan, Tate, and Theo were nowhere to be seen.

But as soon as the Airstair was lowered, the three of them emerged from the tree line alongside the runway and walked toward the plane.

Theo was in the lead, with Megan right behind him, and Tate taking up the rear. Theo's wrists were zip-tied, and when he got to the base of the stairs, he placed both hands on the right handrail and took a step up. Megan followed him, her right hand holding on tightly to his belt. Tate stood on the tarmac, pistol at the ready, making sure that no one came up behind them.

One by one, Theo gingerly sidestepped his way up the stairs. As soon as his upper body came through the door, I grabbed him by the collar and hauled him into the plane. Megan, still clutching his belt, was propelled inside the cabin with him.

I karate-chopped her hand, and as soon as she let go of Theo, I shielded his body with mine.

The look in her eyes was a mix of shock, panic, and total bewilderment. How could I have possibly gotten on her rescue plane?

"Police! Don't move!" Kylie yelled from the opposite side of the door.

Megan's instincts kicked in. She lunged at Kylie. Big mistake. She may have been a world-class long-distance shooter, but she had all the hand-to-hand skills of a TV anchorwoman. Kylie unleashed a right hook. I heard bone crunch as Megan flew backward, skittered down the stairs, and hit the tarmac headfirst.

Tate, who'd had his back to the cabin door, wheeled around, gun in hand. He fired at Kylie, who was standing at the top of the stairs. The bullet went wide. One of the deadliest snipers in the world had missed.

He never got a second chance. A volley of gunfire rang out from the cops and FBI agents who had taken positions inside the terminal and in the parking lot two hundred feet away.

Kylie, gun drawn, ran down the stairs to where Megan was sprawled on her back, not moving.

"She's out cold," Kylie yelled up to me, and as our backup team came running toward the aircraft, I turned and looked at Theo.

"You okay?" I said.

"I'll be a lot better if you can get me out of these freaking cuffs," he said.

"Hold on," I said. "I've got a knife."

"No, Zach, wait. Do me a favor. Reach under the waistband of my jeans. Left side. I've got a can opener." A wide grin spread across his face. It'll be a better ending for the movie."

Tears welled up in my eyes. I wanted to wrap my arms around him and tell him I loved him more than I'd ever loved anyone in my life.

But I didn't say a word. I pulled back the waistband and found Martin Sheffield's trusty little P-38 that he'd carried since Vietnam. I folded out the metal tooth and slowly gnawed away at the plastic zip tie until it finally snapped.

Theo rubbed his wrists.

"How do you feel?" I asked.

"Gobsmacked," he said, pulling out his favorite twenty-dollar word. "How the fuck did you and Kylie get on this airplane?"

"We found Mother. She's Sonia Blakely, the Hellman brothers' lawyer."

His mouth opened, but he couldn't find the words.

"Once we had her, we cut a deal," I said. "As soon as she told us about the plane, we had her call the pilot and tell him to pick up two passengers at Teterboro. Kylie and I came onboard, arrested them, brought in a crew from NYPD Aviation, and the rest, as they say, will soon be television and/or motion picture history."

"Cool," he said, reverting to teen-speak.

"That's exactly what I'm hoping the police commissioner and the mayor say."

"Zach! Zach!"

It was Kylie. I went to the cabin door. Megan was still flat on her back on the tarmac.

"She's okay. She's coming to."

Megan sat up slowly, realized she was in handcuffs, and let two cops help her to her feet.

She squared off with Kylie, face-to-face, hate in her eyes.

Kylie returned the gaze with a smile. "Hey, Megan," she said. "Looks like you and I are going to be on the eleven o'clock news together."

Megan turned around, and for the first time, she saw her partner in crime lying on the ground a few feet away, his body riddled with bullet holes.

Her shoulders hunched up. She dropped to her knees and let out a wail that filled the air with pain, agony, and inconsolable grief. A single heart-wrenching word that told us all we needed to know to solve the final piece of the puzzle.

"Daaaaaddyyyyy."

CHAPTER 72

I CALLED CHERYL and told her that Theo was safe and sound and that despite his claim that as a material witness he was essential to the ongoing investigation, he was getting a police escort back to our apartment.

"Don't worry," she said. "If he tries to leave, I'll cuff him to the armoire. Love you."

"Love you more," I said. Not a word about the DNA results. I wasn't ready.

Kylie called Shane and then texted the good news to Travis Wilkins, who was somewhere between Sydney and New York.

An FBI paramedic checked Megan for signs of concussion and declared her good to go. Kylie and I had no jurisdiction in New Jersey, so a federal agent put her under arrest and drove the three of us back to the city. It took almost two hours, and none of us said a word.

Once we got inside the precinct, Kylie broke the silence by reading Megan her rights.

Megan declined an attorney. "I have a feeling my lawyer has her own legal problems to deal with. Sonia's the only one who knew where we'd be. She was the only one who could have managed to get you on the plane. Nicely done, by the way. If I'd been on the air tonight, I'd have given you glowing reviews."

"I'm sorry for the loss of your father," I said.

"It's okay. He's not sorry," she said. "I'm sure that as soon as he saw the two of you on that plane, he figured out there had to be a small army on the ground. But he was too old to be dragged off to prison. I guarantee you that when he pulled his gun, he'd already made the decision to go out the way he always wanted. Semper fi. Oorah! Blaze of glory, and all that shit."

She took a deep breath and let it come out as a sigh. "I can accept his death. My only regret is that my father was an incredible photographer, but all he'll be remembered for is this."

"We didn't know he was your father," I said.

"Nobody did," she said. "We kept it under the radar."

"What was it like growing up being his secret daughter?"

"It could have been disastrous, but he made it thrilling. I felt like the most special kid in the world. I was only seven when he told me his job was to stop bad people from doing bad things. Sometimes, those people might get mad at him, so he had to keep me and my mom a secret, so that the bad guys didn't get mad at us, too. By the time I was twelve, I started to figure out the real story, but even then I didn't know he was a hit man. I thought he was with the CIA, and I was excited to be part of all that cloak-and-dagger stuff."

"When did you find out the truth?"

"I was on a break during my senior year in college. We flew off to Montana on a hunting trip. I didn't know it at the time, but Sonia had sent him out there on a job, and I guess this was his version of Take Your Daughter to Work Day."

She closed her eyes for a few seconds and traveled back in time. "Black bear, wolves, Big Sky Country—I can't begin to tell you how excited I was. The first night we were there, the two of us were sitting around the campfire. It was a little chilly, so I got as close to the fire as I could handle and wrapped myself in a blanket.

"'Meg, you're too close,' he said. 'Move away. Now.' I was about to tell him that I knew what I was doing, when a sudden gust of wind blew sparks and burning embers right at me. The blanket was acrylic and caught fire immediately. My father didn't hesitate. He threw me to the ground, beating at the flames with his bare hands and ripping the blanket off me. By the time the fire was out, I had some first-degree burns on my shoulders, but his hands were pretty bad.

"The next morning, he told me everything. His work for the government. The Sorority. The five men with female code names. Everything. He told me he came to Montana because he was hired to kill a man who had a history of abusing children. I said, 'Dad, I'm twenty-one. This man is a demon, a serial pedophile. I'm glad you're going to kill him.' He held up his hands, which were wrapped in bandages, and said, 'Sweetheart, today I couldn't kill a squirrel from ten feet away.' He told me he was going to have to call Mother and have her send someone else to take over the assignment. I asked if that meant he wasn't going to get paid for the job. He didn't answer, but I knew that meant no. And I knew it was a lot of money. So I said, 'Don't worry, Dad. I'll do it.'"

"What did he say?"

"Nothing. He just sat there mulling it over. He knew I had the chops. He gave me my first shooting lesson when I was five years old. After that, we'd go to the gun range all the time, like some kids go to miniature golf courses, and I looked forward to hunting season even more than I did to Christmas. I wasn't as good as he was, but I was a damn close second.

"I told him I could use the money for grad school, and then I told him that his hands would heal in about a month, and if he let me finish the job, no one would ever know that he couldn't. It would be another one of our little secrets. Finally, he said, 'Okay. But just this once.'

"Two days later, I put a bullet through the perv's neck from a hundred yards out. I felt fantastic. It was like sex. I was ready to do it again. But we had a deal. One and done. I retired. Until Sonia asked him to take out Warren Hellman."

She shook her head as she transitioned from one of her happiest memories to the event that led up to her father lying in a pool of blood on the tarmac.

"Can you tell us what happened?" I said.

"It was a big job. The payout was a million dollars. But he knew he couldn't handle it. A month earlier, he'd been diagnosed with Meniere's disease. It's a disorder of the inner ear that can lead to vertigo and hearing loss. The symptoms can come and go, but he couldn't take a chance on lining up a shot from that rooftop and getting dizzy before he could pull the trigger. So he went to Sonia and told her I could make the shot. She knew me, of course, but she never knew that I pinch-hit for him thirteen years ago in Montana. He promised her I could get it done. And I did."

"Did your father ask you to shoot Winstanley?"

"No. That was Sonia. Barbara called her and told her you'd arrested Emily at the funeral home. It was one thing for Sonia to get Winstanley out of a drunk-driving charge, but we knew you had him for killing Sheffield. Sonia called me. She said Emily's time at the Sorority was over. The only thing we could do was give him an honorable death. And once again, I did.

"Three murders," she said. "I know that sounds heinous, but think about it. One was a pedophile, another was a cop killer, and . . . well, I like to think of Eldon Winstanley as an assisted suicide."

"What about Theo Wilkins?" Kylie said.

"Damage control. We would have turned him loose once we got to Colombia," she said.

Kylie and I made eye contact. That's not the way Sonia Blakely told it.

"Look, it's been a long day and I'm exhausted," Megan said. "Do you mind getting me processed so I can get some sleep."

"Sure," I said. "One last question. Actually, it's a two-parter. Who put up the million to kill Warren Hellman? And who put up the money to kill his brother Curtis?"

She told us. And as mind-boggling as her stories about her father had been, this was an even bigger shocker.

Megan Rollins would get some sleep after we processed her, but we wouldn't. Kylie and I were going to have to pay a late-night visit to Curtis's grieving widow, Brooke Hellman.

CHAPTER 73

THE LAST TIME we arrived at Brooke Hellman's penthouse on Riverside Drive, she opened the door, took one look, and said, "Oh, Christ. You two again?" This time we were greeted like conquering heroes.

"Kylie! Zach!" she gushed, using our given names for the first time. "Come in, come in. Would you like something to drink?"

We politely declined, but clearly, bygones were now bygones. We'd gone from the doghouse to "Are you sure? I just opened a lovely Chardonnay."

We followed her to the living room, and the three of us got comfortable.

"I told the mayor how grateful I was that you caught the man who killed Curtis," she said, "but this latest arrest has me in shock. Megan Rollins? How is that possible? She was such a role model for women."

"There was a lot more to Megan than meets the eye," Kylie said.

"And you're sure she shot Warren?"

"She admitted it," I said. "And now that we have her confession, our forensics team will reexamine the UPS truck that the killer used. We're confident they'll find her DNA."

"Shocking," Brooke said. "But why did you arrest Sonia Blakely? There's nothing on the news that explains it. I hope it's all a misunderstanding, because I'm counting on Sonia to run the business."

NYPD RED 7: THE MURDER SORORITY

"Sonia was already running a business of her own," I said.

"I'm not sure I understand."

"I believe you're familiar with the organization known as the Sorority," I said.

"Yes, of course. I first heard about it from Sean Driscoll. It was a proposal his daughter's boyfriend came up with. A gang of hit men who were still going strong well into their seventies. I encouraged Curtis to look into it. He and Warren met with the writer, and they were seriously considering optioning the idea. I thought it was a delightful concept."

"It was more than a concept," Kylie said. "It was a reality."

I watched as a wave of clarity washed over her. "The man who killed Curtis," she said. "His picture was all over the news. I was surprised at how old he was, but I never made the connection."

"He was one of five. All in and around seventy years old. Sonia knew them since their military days."

"And you arrested her because she was their attorney?"

"No, ma'am," I said. "She ran their operation."

Brooke inhaled sharply and put a hand to her chest.

"Sonia Blakely was their legal liaison when they were in the military," I said. "When they left, she joined them in civilian life and managed every aspect of their business. She was the interlocutor—the middleman between the clients and the killers."

"You're telling me that someone sat down with her and hired her to have my husband—a man who trusted her and worked side by side with her for almost twenty years—gutted like a pig?"

"Not quite. There was no sit-down. Sonia never met face-to-face with any of her clients. The Sorority worked in complete anonymity. There was no way a buyer could ever point a finger at them."

"Then how did people contact them in the first place?"

"They had a website," Kylie said.

Brooke gawked at us the same way we had stared at Megan when she told us.

"A website," she repeated.

"Yes, ma'am. KappaOmegaDelta.com."

"That's . . . that's insanity. You can't advertise murder to the public. Why didn't the cops shut them down?"

"The site is on the dark web," I said. "It doesn't say anything about murder. It says, 'Welcome to Kappa Omega Delta. Effective. Discreet. Global. A $250,000 deposit is required to open an account.' And then it gives wiring instructions for a bank in Singapore."

"That's preposterous," she said. "It sounds like one of those Internet scams, only dumber. Nobody would send ten cents to something like that."

"That's why it worked," I said. "People who were told how to contact the Sorority knew it was legitimate, and sent the money. Anyone else who might stumble on it—cops included—wouldn't give it a second thought."

"And Sonia brokered the deal?" she said. "She snuffed out the life of a man who did so much for her, for a lousy quarter of a million dollars?"

"The total price was a million dollars," Kylie said. "The two-hundred-and-fifty thousand was just a down payment."

Brooke leaned forward. "How . . . how do you know that?"

"Megan told us. She also told us who paid for the hit," I said. "That's why we're here. She'll tell the press first chance she gets. We thought you would want to know before it goes public."

"Curtis had his share of business rivalries," Brooke said. "But you don't murder your competition. Outside of work, he was a good man. Warm, congenial, generous. He had friends. Lots of them. I have spent every waking hour of this past week trying to come up with the name of a single person who would have done this to him, and I couldn't. So yes, I think I might sleep easier at night if you told me who paid to have him killed."

"It was Warren," I said.

CHAPTER 74

BROOKE FROZE. She was, to borrow Theo's go-to descriptor, gobsmacked.

"Warren?" she finally stammered. "They were brothers. They went through the usual sibling bullshit, but they were friends."

"And business partners," Kylie reminded her. "According to Megan, Warren was desperate to get out of the partnership."

"So he had his brother killed?" she said. "Because of the fucking settlements?"

"What settlements?" Kylie asked as if we were hearing about them for the first time. But, of course, we knew all about them. On the day the Hellmans were murdered, Megan had given us all the sordid details of Warren's sexcapades and how he had shelled out fifty million of the company's money to silence the victims.

But Megan's version of the story was designed to convince us that Brooke was the mastermind behind the two killings. Now it was time to hear Brooke's side of the story.

"Warren was a serial womanizer," she said. "The classic Hollywood producer stereotype. 'You want to be in my show? Suck my dick.' He did it for years, and then it finally started to catch up to him. One woman sued, and he settled out of court. Then another. So he wrote another check and bought her silence. Then the word got out, and it snowballed. He paid a fortune to stay out of jail. Not his money, the company's. Half of that belonged to Curtis, and there were more lawsuits pending. Then came the murder charge. He was accused of killing a decorated police officer. A lot of people didn't wait for the trial. They decided he was guilty, and began boycotting our television shows.

"Curtis decided to bail and open his own company, but Warren couldn't afford to buy him out. They fought, but then in January Curtis wound up in the hospital in a diabetic coma. It was three days of hell. I thought he was going to die. But he pulled out if it, and I told him to forget all about the business and focus on his health."

"Do you know how your husband wound up in a coma?" Kylie asked.

She shrugged. "He was under stress. He didn't sleep well. He got careless. It wasn't the first time he mismanaged a dose. I was furious at him for not paying more attention, and—typical Curtis—he said, 'Hey, shit happens.'"

"It wasn't an accident," Kylie said. "The FBI has been interviewing Sonia for the past eight hours. Our team and theirs have been keeping each other posted with key discoveries. Warren paid Curtis's driver twenty-five thousand to switch the insulin vials. The man's been arrested and he confessed."

"Oh my God," Brooke said. "Warren sat with me at Curtis's bedside when he was in a coma. He held his brother's hand. We prayed together."

"I doubt if he was praying," I said. "More likely, he was thinking about how to get it right the next time. And then a few months later, Theo Wilkins pitched the Murder Sorority, and Warren had his answer. He contacted his friends in the mob, and they pointed him to the Kappa Omega Delta website. He wired his two-hundred-and-fifty-thousand-dollar deposit, and then paid the other seven hundred and fifty thousand after Curtis was killed."

"Wait," Brooke said. "How is that possible? Warren was dead before they killed Curtis."

"That's the brilliance of Sonia Blakely. Warren's bank was authorized to release the seven-fifty that evening at six o'clock. If Curtis hadn't

NYPD RED 7: THE MURDER SORORITY

been killed by two p.m., all Warren had to do was put a stop on the payment. Eight hours after he was dead, Warren paid in full for his brother's murder."

Brooke's hands were trembling. We'd given her a lot to process. And we weren't done.

"I always assumed that one person had them both murdered," she said.

"So did we," I said, omitting the part that she was our number one suspect.

"But if Warren had Curtis killed, who paid to kill Warren?" she said. "Do you know? Because I'd like to send them a thank-you card when they get to prison."

"You can't," I said. "It was Curtis."

"Impossible! If Megan Rollins told you that, she's lying. Curtis had blowouts with Warren all the time, but he would never want to see him harmed."

"Brooke," Kylie said, "I think that all changed when Curtis found out that Warren had tried to kill him. About a month after his insulin overdose, the FDA suspected that the insulin had been tampered with. They asked for Curtis's help in the investigation, but he refused."

"He knew?" Brooke said. "He never said a word to me."

"He never said a word to anyone, but I could imagine he lost a lot of sleep thinking Warren might try it again. And then both brothers learned about the Sorority. They both saw it as the answer to their problems."

"Curtis paid a million dollars to have Warren killed?"

"The FBI has access to Sonia's banking information. They've already verified the transaction."

"I don't understand. Sonia didn't only represent Curtis and Warren. She was on the inside. They let her invest in projects that they knew would pay off. She made a fortune. Why would she end all that for two million dollars?"

"Because it put her a heartbeat away from owning the company," Kylie said.

"I'm afraid you're going to have to check your facts, Detective," Brooke said. "Hellman Productions is a private company. Curtis and Warren were the only two shareholders. If either of them died, the company would go to the surviving brother. Warren had no heirs, but Curtis's will is crystal clear. In the event of his death, everything he owns goes to me. And now that I own the company outright, if I die, it goes to my sister Pat in Denver."

"No, it won't," I said. "The DA's Office has waded through all twenty-three pages of the company's shareholder agreement, which Sonia had revised two months ago. You're correct—you now own the company. But there's a paragraph buried on page sixteen that says in the event of your death, the company and all its assets go to Sonia."

"Curtis would never sign that!"

"But he did," Kylie said. "So did Warren. They trusted Sonia. She slid contracts across their desks all the time. I doubt if they ever did anything more than flip to the last page and sign. I know you don't want to hear this, but Sonia Blakely had a team of assassins at her disposal. She had them kill Warren, she had them kill Curtis . . ."

Kylie stopped short. It was a sentence she didn't have to finish.

"And I was next," Brooke said.

Kylie put her hand on Brooke's shoulder. "Yes. But now you're safe."

And with that, the tower of strength that had gone from coat-check girl to successful investor, to film company executive, crumbled.

She fell into Kylie's arms and wept.

"Thank you," she said when she finally regained her composure. "I apologize for treating you so badly in the past. Thank you for coming. I'm sorry to have kept you so long. I'm sure you have a million other things to do."

"Not tonight," Kylie said. "It's been a long day. Zach and I are ready to clock out and get a drink." She flashed a warm smile. "Is that Chardonnay still an option?"

Brooke brightened. Of course it was. And she'd been right about the wine.

It was lovely.

CHAPTER 75

"THE MAYOR CALLED a press conference for ten thirty," Cates told us the next morning.

"Oh, good," Kylie said. "I can't wait to hear how she took down an entire army of criminals and saved Gotham from the clutches of evil."

Cates cracked up. "It's not an order, but it would be smart politics if you were in the audience applauding her leadership."

We would have gone, but something better came up. Steve Edlund called. "Vincent Ackerman just turned his phone back on."

"Where is he?"

"His apartment. McDaniel and I are on the way."

"We're right behind you," I said.

We were crossing the Ed Koch Bridge when I got the call. "Detective Jordan, this is Alvin Jeong, Priscilla and Vincent Ackerman's neighbor. They're at it again. And it's much louder than usual."

"What are you hearing?"

"She's screaming, 'You can't leave me! If you go, I'll kill myself!' It sounds like he's trying to calm her down, but she's—oh, shit, I hear glass breaking. She's throwing things. She's never been this bad before. I think you better send somebody."

"We're on the way. Lock your door and don't leave your apartment."

Kylie radioed for backup, and I called Edlund. "It sounds

like Vincent told Priscilla he's getting married, and she's taking it badly."

We were there three minutes later. A man was standing outside the building, waving at us. "I'm the super. Dr. Jeong called me. Is there anything I can do?"

"Ackerman! Do you have a key?"

"Apartment four-B," he said, pulling a key off his ring.

Edlund and McDaniel rolled up behind us.

"Take the fire escape," Kylie said as we strapped on our vests. "We've got the stairs."

As soon as the four of us were in position, I pounded on the apartment door.

"Go away," a female voice yelled.

"Priscilla, it's the police. We're here for Vincent."

"Are you here to arrest him?"

"We have questions for him. He's coming with us to the precinct."

"He's not. He can't. He can't go anywhere. I need him here. He's staying with me."

"You can come with us," I said.

"I can't leave the house. Ask anybody. I'm on disability."

"Vincent," I said, changing tactics. "Are you okay?"

"I'm fine," he said, his voice tight with desperation. He sounded whipped, trapped—a man at the end of his rope. "Give me a minute, will ya?"

And then silence.

I radioed Edlund. "Can you see anything?"

"They're in the living room," he said. "She's on the sofa facing the front door. He's in an armchair looking at her. They're talking."

"Not loud enough for us to hear," I said. I waited another thirty seconds and pounded on the door again. "Vincent, don't make matters any worse. Open the door."

"Zach," Edlund said. "Vincent got out of the chair. He's walking toward the door."

"Don't . . . you . . . fucking . . . go *anywhere*," Priscilla wailed.

"Gun! Gun!" Edlund said in a sharp whisper. "She's up. She pulled a gun on him."

"Go ahead, Prissy," Vincent yelled. "Shoot me. Put one right through my fucking heart. It don't matter. I don't have a life anyway."

"*I'm* your life!" came the instant response. "I cook for you. I keep the apartment clean. I make you laugh. I protect you from neighbors who want to know our business. I'm the one who made Dad go away! You think your precious girlfriend is going to do that for you?"

"Youuuuu fuckinnnnng cuuuuunt!" Vincent screamed, turning it into a war cry. And then the crash of furniture splintering, glass shattering, and Priscilla shrieking.

Kylie and I looked at each other. It was now or never, and we both knew it.

"Go!" she said.

We already had the key in the lock. We turned it and swung the door open. Priscilla and Vincent were on the floor almost twenty feet away, thrashing, the gun nowhere in sight, their hands shielded by their bodies.

"Police! Don't move! Police, don't move!" I ordered as we rushed at them, guns drawn.

But they didn't stop. They either didn't hear me or didn't care. It was just the two of them, a brother and sister in a life-or-death struggle that had been building for years and had finally come to a flash point.

And then the gun went off. A single muffled explosion, and the thrashing stopped. Priscilla was on the bottom of the heap. Her head jerked, her lungs grabbed for air once, twice, three times, and she let out a final breath.

Vincent rolled to his side, and the gun clattered to the floor.

Edlund and McDaniel, who had come through the window, cuffed him, searched him, and pulled him to his feet.

"I'm thirty-eight years old," he said. "I did everything to make her happy all her life, and after all I did for her, she'd rather kill me than see me go off and find some happiness of my own. I don't get it. I don't understand."

I looked at Kylie. We understood. We'd learned it from a fellow named William Congreve.

Heav'n has no rage, like love to hatred turn'd, Nor hell a fury, like a woman scorn'd.

CHAPTER 76

BY THE TIME I got to the office the next morning, Kylie had left copies of the *Times,* the *News,* and the *Post* on my desk. "Just in case you don't keep a diary," she said, "everything we did this past week is front-page news."

"I know," I said. "I have a friend at Fox. He said this is like a managing editor's wet dream. It's Christmas in July for the media. And not just in New York. It's gone viral around the world."

For me, it was just another reminder that the public's appetite for the latest dirt on boldfaced names is insatiable. Whatever Megan, Sonia, the Hellmans, and Wayman Tate may have accomplished in their lives, they would forever be remembered for every mortal sin, heinous crime, and minor peccadillo they ever perpetrated.

And then, in the middle of it all, there was Theo, an eighteen-year-old nobody who was about to become somebody. But on his own terms.

Never mind that every newspaper, magazine, radio station, and TV network wanted to interview him, Theo stayed out of sight. His steadfast refusal to meet the press or even make a statement only enhanced his mystique. In no time, #WhoIsTheoWilkins was trending on Twitter.

The two of us sat down for a cup of coffee and a can of Red Bull that morning before I left for work.

"I'm not talking to anybody until I talk to my father," he said.

"Good call," I said. "After work, Cheryl and I will drive you to the airport to pick him up. Then the plan is to meet Kylie and Shane over at his place for a victory dinner. Unless you and your father would rather have some private time together."

"Heck no," he said. "I think my dad is going to want to spend some quality time with the two cops who kept me from getting on the plane to South America."

"We're also the same two cops who handed you over to a murderer at the museum," I said.

"We can downplay that part," he said. "Besides, my dad knows Kylie from the old days, and I think you and he will totally hit it off. You have a lot in common."

"I'm sure we do," I said.

The rest of the day, Kylie and I got caught up juggling meetings and phone calls with the PC, three deputy commissioners, the chief constable of the Vancouver Police Department, even Mayor Sykes herself. But the one that mattered the most was the unexpected visit we got just before we left the office.

Evan Belmont, Jonas's son, showed up.

"My father was my idol," he said. "Ever since I was a kid, I wanted to be a cop just like him. I'm sure if he were alive, there'd still be a lot of things he'd have wanted to teach me. I just want to thank the two of you for picking up where he left off. This morning I went to his grave and told him how sorry I was for the way you were treated when you came to my house just to do your jobs. Now I'm here to apologize to you."

Kylie and I thanked him, shook his hand, and promised to get together soon. He walked toward the door, shoulders slumped, the burden not yet lifted.

"Evan," I said, catching up to him.

He turned. "What?"

I put my hand on his arm. "Your old man would be proud of you," I said.

We all have our emotional breaking points, and Evan reached his.

"He'd be just as proud of you, bro," he said, no longer able to hold back the tears. "I don't know if he ever told you, but he loved you like a son."

That's when I hit my own breaking point. After everything that had happened since that indelible moment when I came upon Jonas Belmont's lifeless body on the rug of Warren Hellman's town house, I lost it.

He and I stood there, arms wrapped around each other. Two tough cops. Crying.

An hour later, Cheryl and I were in the car on our way to pick up Theo. I stopped at a red light on Park Avenue.

"The DNA report came back," I said. "Theo is my son."

The news came out of left field, but she didn't blink. She responded like a professional. "How do you feel about that?"

"How do I *feel* about it? I don't know. How do I *deal* with it? I know even less. For now, you're the only one I can tell. I told Kylie I took the paternity test, so at some point I'm going to have to tell her the results."

"And Theo?"

"The kid's been through hell. I'm his *birth* father. He's about to reconnect with his real father. Maybe I'll tell him someday, but now's not the right time."

"Thank you for sharing with me," she said.

Theo was waiting for us in front of my apartment building.

"So how did your day go?" Cheryl asked as soon as he got into the car.

"Fantastic," he said. "I made a decision not to get sucked into watching the news on TV, so I took the subway out to Brooklyn Botanic Garden. My mom used to take me there. When she died, I stopped going. First because I didn't want to go there without her, and by the time I was eight or nine, I was like, flowers are lame compared to video games."

"Wild guess," Cheryl said. "They weren't lame today, were they?"

"No. I sat in the water garden for about an hour, trying to let go of all the shit that happened this past week and move on with my life."

"Did it help?" Cheryl asked.

"A lot. I started to think about the eight million dollars that Mr. Sheffield left me. I wasn't going to take it at first, but Mr. Nivens, the lawyer, told me if I don't, it'll just go to the state. He said take it and give it away, so that's what I'm going to do. I decided to open a foundation."

"Theo, that's wonderful," Cheryl said. "Have you thought about your mission?"

"That was the easy part," he said. "There are a lot of kids like me who want to become filmmakers, but they can't afford it. Mr. Nivens agreed to help me set it up to work with film schools like NYU, USC, and Howard to give out scholarships and grants. He said he thought it would mean a lot to Mr. Sheffield that every dime of his eight million dollars is going to help young people fund their dreams and change their lives."

Cheryl rested a hand on my arm, and I could feel the lump growing in my throat.

"I decided to name it after my mom," Theo said. "The Sylviane LeBec Wilkins Foundation for the Cinematic Arts. I can't wait to tell my dad about it."

I wanted to hug him. I wanted to tell him how proud I was of him. But I couldn't speak. I couldn't even turn to look at him. Because for the second time in a couple of hours, tears were streaming down this tough cop's face. And I realized that I hadn't felt this good in a long, long time.

SOME WELL-DESERVED THANK-YOUS, A CONFESSION, AND AN INVITATION

I have to admit it. Writing crime fiction is fun. I love digging into the dark recesses of my brain and discovering what twisted thoughts lurk therein. Some may say I'm not a healthy man. To them I respond, killing people in print is cathartic, it's legal, and I have a shrink who's been exploring my tortured soul for forty years, and he promises me that I'm starting to exhibit signs of mental health.

"So, then, can I stop coming here?" I ask him.

"No," he says.

"Please," I whine. "I mean, I already put your four kids through college. I thought you'd let me go when the last one finished grad school."

"Not yet," he says. "My wife and I want to remodel the kitchen. Also, you have to take it slowly. If you get too stable, you'll be out of a job."

And so, on my doctor's advice, I will continue to explore the shadowy corners of my psyche and conjure up criminals whose heinous acts stretch the limits of your imagination.

But my cops and my attention to the details of law enforcement will be obsessively authentic. And for that I need help. Which brings me to my first thank-you: Danny Corcoran.

If that name sounds familiar, it may be because he's the fictional hero in my previous book, *Snowstorm in August*. But there's a real Danny Corcoran—a decorated veteran of NYPD who spent five years as an undercover narcotics cop, was a 911 responder working at Ground Zero, saved countless lives as a member of the department's elite hostage negotiation team, and wrapped up his twenty-four years of service as a first grade detective at the Manhattan North Homicide Squad.

I met Danny six years ago, and my books—and my life—have been better ever since. He's my partner in crime, who (ironically) keeps me honest. His insider knowledge of cops, the criminal justice system, the politics at 1PP, and the streets of New York—be they mean or posh—goes deep. I get a lot of feedback from people in law enforcement who love the fact that my crime fiction has the ring of truth. I can't take the credit. That's Danny.

I also want to thank another expert who took time off from his busy days helping people stay healthy. Dr. Neal Smoller is my neighborhood pharmacist and the owner of the Village Apothecary in Woodstock, New York. But he's always willing to humor my homicidal tendencies to show me how someone might use a life-saving drug to kill a friend or relative.

Thanks also to the usual cast of characters on my speed dial, who are always ready to answer questions about the law (my brother Joseph Karp), fashion (my daughter, Sarah Karp Charles), aviation (my pilot buddy, Dan Fennessy), and just about anything else (Bob Beatty).

Thank you to my long-time support team, Mel Berger, Bill Harrison, Maddee James, and Riley Mack. Thanks to Josh Stanton and everyone at Blackstone Publishing, and most especially to Michael Carr, whose editorial chops and wicked sense of humor made this a better book, and to Kathryn English, who is as gifted at working with writers as she is at design.

Finally, my undying gratitude to my wife—the woman they call Saint Emily—to my family, and to Sean, Ed, Tommy, and Dennis, who fill my life with love, courage, hope, and laughter every other Tuesday night.

Oh, about that invitation. Every now and then I do a pop-up Zoom call with some of my readers. If you want to get on the invitation list, send an email with the subject "Zoom Me" to marshall@karpkills.com. I promise it won't be boring.

Thank you for supporting my life of crime.

JAMES PATTERSON,
DAVID BALDACCI,
MICHAEL CONNELLY,
DONALD E. WESTLAKE...
JUST TO NAME A FEW.

y novels have been praised by some of the bestselling authors in the world,
d I am always in awe when I see their blurbs on one of my books.

1 happy to say there were a lot of quotable reviews and compliments for
owstorm in August, the first book in my newest series featuring Captain
anny Corcoran (NYPD, Ret.) and the Baltic Avenue Group.

t if I have to single out the one quote that made me feel the best, it was this:

"Best first chapter ever."
—SEAN FITZPATRICK

u may not recognize Mr. Fitzpatrick's name. He's not a famous author. He's
reader, so for me, his opinion goes a long way. He posted those four glowing
>rds on my Facebook page. And since hardly anyone goes to my Facebook
.ge (including me), I wanted to share his comment with you.

.lso wanted to share that first chapter of *Snowstorm in August*. Because even
you don't 100 percent agree with Mr. Fitzpatrick that it's the best first
apter ever, I'm hoping you'll be intrigued enough to find out what happens
chapter 2 and beyond.

Thank you for supporting my life of crime.

Marshall

CHAPTER 1

Aurelia gladstone twisted her silver hair up in a loose bun and pinned it in place. She smiled. The granny look, which she had been sporting for decades, was suddenly in. Women sixty, even seventy, years younger than she were dying their hair gray.

"I'm ninety-two years old," she had said to Maddee at dinner last night, "and all of a sudden, I'm trending!"

"Just your hair, Miz G. Just your hair," her housekeeper had snapped back. "But that dusty rose lipstick you insist on wearing screams World War II."

"Jerry loved it," the old lady responded. "The lipstick, not the war."

That ended the discussion. Whenever Aurelia played the dead-husband card, Maddee immediately backed off.

But maybe she was right, Aurelia thought. She leaned forward and stared at her pale-pink lips in the vanity mirror. Okay, so it was a tad ghostly, but . . .

That's when she caught the first glimpse.

Impossible, she thought, turning around in her chair. She stood up and walked slowly toward her bedroom window ten stories above 5th Avenue.

And there it was, swirling in powdery funnels, leaving a white blanket on the cars below and the green trees that stretched across her beloved Central Park.

Snow.

In August.

"Maddee," she called nervously. No answer.

"Maddee!" she said again, raising her voice a notch and putting some urgency into it.

No use, Aurelia thought. Maddee was in the laundry room with the dryer spinning and those damned earbuds attached to her head. *There's no way she'll hear me.*

Or believe me.

It didn't snow in August. Hadn't in the ninety-two years since Aurelia arrived on the planet, and while she hadn't paid a hell of a lot of attention to all that global-warming business, she didn't think that glaciers melting in Antarctica translated to snow falling over New York City in the middle of summer.

But there it was. Snow. Not dust or soot or any of the usual crap you might see eddying around the yellow-gray skies of New York. This was the white, flaky stuff that everybody was hoping would arrive on December 25, and here it was four months ahead of schedule.

For a second she thought about calling her nephew, but she dismissed it immediately. Giles, with his pandering phone calls and his obsequious "How's my favorite auntie?" compliments, was the last person she should be calling. He and his odious little wife Kimberly were waiting for her to die.

Barring that, he'd be happy to tuck her away in a nursing home—correction: *assisted living facility*. Fuck him. She was old, but she didn't need any damn assistance living, thank you very much. She had Maddee and Mr. Philips, the building super, and four very lovely doormen, and a kitchen drawer piled high with menus, which let her order whatever kind of food she was in the mood for, whenever she wanted.

Call Giles and tell him I think it's snowing in August, and the son of a bitch would have me committed.

"Maddee!" she demanded as loudly as her rheumy voice could go.

"For God's sake, Miz. G., I can hear ya. No need to carry on."

Aurelia turned around. Her short, squat, sharp-tongued housekeeper of thirty-seven years was standing in the doorway.

"Sorry, Maddee," she said. "I thought you were in the laundry room."

"I was. And now I'm on my way to the kitchen to fix us some lunch. I can make a nice tuna salad, or I could call down to the diner, and . . ."

"Lunch can wait. First, come over here and look out the window."

"What's going on?"

"It's snowing."

"Ha!" the housekeeper bellowed. "What's *really* going on?"

"You tell me," Aurelia said, stepping aside so Maddee could get close to the window.

"Holy Mary, Mother of God. It's like a winter wonderland out there," she said.

The two women looked down at the cars, their wipers on high. A bike messenger peddling furiously and weaving in and out of traffic skidded on the slippery streets and plowed into a woman with a baby carriage who had been trying to cross against the light. People were pouring out of the park. Those who had managed to get to the east side of 5th Avenue were ducking under awnings.

"It's supposed to hit ninety degrees today," Maddee said. "What the heck is going on?"

"I don't know," Aurelia said. "Turn on the Weather Channel. They'll know."

They didn't. Not yet. But half a mile to the west, Officer Brian Saunders of Central Park's Twenty-Second Precinct was about to find out.

He had pulled his three-wheeled scooter up to the Loeb Boathouse and jumped out of the cab when he spotted a jogger caught by the sudden storm drop to the ground. As he approached the man, a second jogger went down and, seconds after that, a cyclist. Someone at the café outside the boathouse yelled for help. A child lay facedown on the cobblestone path. Two more people were sprawled on the no-longer-green lawn.

Saunders realized what was happening. He didn't understand, but his job wasn't to figure it out. It was to call it in.

He ran back to the scooter, his uniform dusted with flecks of white, climbed inside the cab, and grabbed his radio.

"Central, this is Two-Two Precinct scooter. I need ESU forthwith. I have a hazmat condition outside the Loeb Boathouse. At least eight people down, maybe more."

"Unit, we are receiving numerous calls about a freak snowstorm falling in the park," the dispatcher replied. "Can you confirm if—"

Saunders cut her off. "Central, be advised that it's definitely coming down hard, but it's not snow that is falling in the park. It's . . ."

He took a breath, only barely believing what he was about to report.

"It's cocaine."

ABOUT THE AUTHOR

MARSHALL KARP is an international #1 bestselling author, TV and screenwriter, and playwright. Working with James Patterson, Marshall cocreated and cowrote the NYPD Red series. After six bestsellers, Marshall will carry the series forward on his own, beginning with *NYPD Red 7: The Murder Sorority*. Marshall is also the author of *Snowstorm in August*, as well as the critically acclaimed Lomax and Biggs novels, featuring LAPD Detectives Mike Lomax and Terry Biggs. For over twenty years he has worked closely with the international charity Vitamin Angels, providing tens of millions of mothers and children around the globe with lifesaving vitamins and nutrients. More at www.KarpKills.com